PRAISE FOR

The MIRACLES *of* PRATO

"With painterly language and writerly skill the authors of *The Miracles of Prato* draw the reader into the lush, sensory web of Italian Renaissance color and forbidden love. An age-old story of the triumph of the human heart over rules, money, and propriety is set against a backdrop of artistic passion, overwhelming talent, and stunning beauty. This is an enchanting story and it will carry the reader away."

—Judith Koll Healey, author of *The Canterbury Papers*

"Like Fra Filippo's paintings, this love story, set in one of the most intriguing historical periods, is suffused with clear, warm color and fine attention to detail."

—Debra Dean, author of *The Madonnas of Leningrad*

"This novel based on the life of Fra Filippo Lippi will be lapped up by fans of historical romance."   —*Publishers Weekly*

"*The Miracles of Prato* is a time machine, taking the reader back to the height of the Italian Renaissance, revealing a world of childlike innocence and illicit passion, harsh injustice and saintly miracles, and wafting around it all like rare perfume, the creation of art for the glory of God."

—Eleanor Herman, author of *Mistress of the Vatican*

"In this richly imagined novel, Laurie Albanese and Laura Morowitz weave fact and fiction into a luminous tapestry. Inspired by the true story of the artist Fra Filippo Lippi and the woman whose beauty inspired his most famous works, *The Miracles of Prato* is a captivating story of artistic vision, dark betrayal, and forbidden yearnings."

—Christina Baker Kline, author of *The Way Life Should Be*

"A richly detailed and thoroughly engrossing story told with equal measures of ardor, tenderness, and compassion, *The Miracles of Prato* offers a poignant portrayal of the heartbreak of two people caught in the Church's grip during the Italian Renaissance."

—Judith Lindbergh, author of *The Thrall's Tale*

"Richly textured Renaissance romance. . . . The authors have fashioned an irresistibly passionate novel steeped in art, history, and the miracles wrought by love." —*Booklist*

"The story easily could veer into the melodramatic—or perhaps the soap-operatic. Albanese and Morowitz by and large avoid that. They manage an even more difficult feat: They make Lucrezia a genuinely sympathetic character, rather than solely a victim or a cipher. That's tricky to manage with a central character who is passive, who propels the story more by what happens to her than by what she does. . . . The secondary characters are many and well-written. . . . The authors are surest when they write about Lippi making his art."

—Philadelphia Inquirer

Daniel Epstein

About the Authors

Laurie Albanese is the author of the novel *Lynelle by the Sea* and the memoir *Blue Suburbia*, which was named a Book Sense Book of the Year and an *Entertainment Weekly* Editor's Choice selection. Please visit her website at www.laurielicoalbanese.com.

Her best friend and coauthor, Laura Morowitz, is an associate professor of art history and coauthor of *Consuming the Past: The Medieval Revival in Fin-de-siècle France*.

They both live in New Jersey with their families.

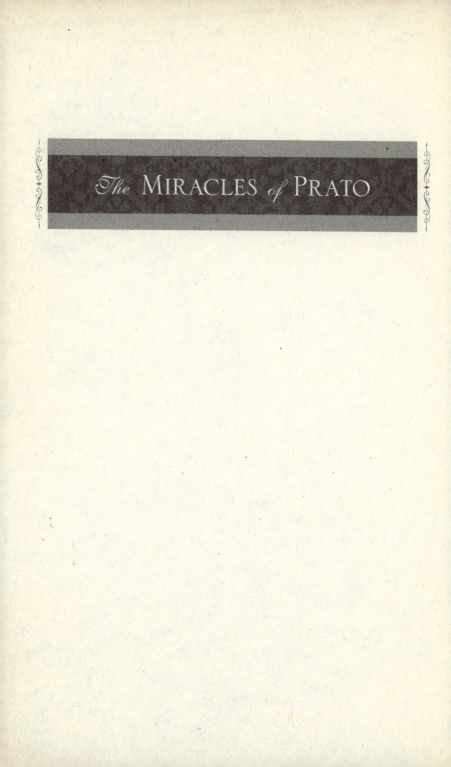

The Miracles of Prato

Laurie Albanese & Laura Morowitz

The MIRACLES of PRATO

HARPER

NEW YORK · LONDON · TORONTO · SYDNEY

A hardcover edition of this book was published in 2009 by William Morrow, an imprint of HarperCollins Publishers.

HarperCollins books may be purchased for educational, business, or sales promotional use. For information please write: Special Markets Department, HarperCollins Publishers, 10 East 53rd Street, New York, NY 10022.

FIRST HARPER PAPERBACK PUBLISHED 2010.

Designed by Susan Yang

The Library of Congress has catalogued the hardcover edition as follows:

Lico Albanese, Laurie, 1959–
    The miracles of Prato : a novel / Laurie Albanese and Laura Morowitz.
    —1st ed.
        p. cm.
    ISBN 978-0-06-155834-4
        1. Lippi, Filippo, ca. 1406–1469—Fiction. 2. Monks—Fiction. 3. Nuns—Fiction. 4. Italy—History—1268–1492—Fiction. I. Morowitz, Laura. II. Title.

PS3562.I324M57 2009
813'.54—dc22   2008019437

ISBN 978-0-06-155835-1 (pbk.)

10 11 12 13 14 OV/RRD 10 9 8 7 6 5 4 3 2 1

To our own miracles

Melissa, John, Isabelle, Olivia, and Anais

with endless love and gratitude

Love, and do what you will.
(*Dilige, et quod vis fac.*)

Grant me chastity and continence, but not yet.
(*Da mihi castitatem et continentiam, sed noli modo.*)

—SAINT AUGUSTINE, BISHOP OF HIPPO

Rendering of Time in the Fifteenth Century

-~-~- The Liturgical Hours -~-~-

In monastic life, the day was divided by the cycles of prayer:

- Lauds (at dawn)
- Prime (first hour after daylight—about 6 A.M.)
- Terce (third hour after daylight—about 8 A.M.)
- Sext (sixth hour after daylight—about 11 A.M.)
- Nones (ninth hour after daylight—about 2 P.M.)
- Vespers (twilight)
- Compline (last cycle of prayers before bed)
- Matins (night prayers—between 2 and 4 A.M.)

-~-~- The Liturgical Calendar -~-~-

The year was divided into liturgical seasons:

- Advent (four Sundays before Christmas through Christmas Eve)
- Christmastide (Christmas Eve to January 13)
- Time After Epiphany (January 13 to nine Sundays before Easter)
- Septuagesima (nine Sundays before Easter to the Tuesday before Ash Wednesday)
- Lent (forty-day period from Ash Wednesday to Palm Sunday)
- Holy Week (Palm Sunday to Easter Sunday)
- Easter Season (Easter Sunday through the octave of Pentecost)
- Time After Pentecost (second Monday after Easter through the Saturday before Advent)

The Miracles of Prato

Prologue

The Convent Santa Margherita

Prato, Italy
The Feast Day of Saint Augustine, the Year of Our Lord 1457

There's always blood: that's what the midwife is thinking. Blood when the virgins are opened, blood on the bed linens, blood to forge the vows. Again and again young women open of their own will or against their will, and when the men are done, the women come to the convent to finish what's been started.

The old midwife holds a rag soaked with a tincture of birthwort to the mother's cleft bleeding place and watches it fill crimson and maroon-black. She frowns as she looks for clots in the darkened blood. The birth has been long and difficult, lasting from the cycle of Nones prayers through Matins. It's now past the twelfth hour and still the poultice of chamomile and verbena has barely stemmed the bleeding. A quarter moon tints the eastern sky over the small city of Prato. The new mother on the ticking bed moans and calls for her child. Her eyes are sunken, her face twisted in anguish.

The midwife pushes back the edge of her wimple and looks across the candlelit chamber of the *infermeria* to where a novitiate stands pale and shaken, holding the swaddling infant in her arms. The smell of the chamber is not unlike the smell of a barnyard after a slaughter. The air is smoky and thick with the tinny scent of blood.

The old woman moves toward the novitiate and studies the infant's skin color to judge his health. She watches his chest rising and falling as he takes his first breaths among the Augustinian nuns. On the bed, the mother groans.

The young attendant blanches. The novitiate has seen no more than eleven winters; her thin body is not yet ripe for the taking. Yet it was she who held the legs of the mother as the midwife eased the infant's shoulders into this world. It was she who assisted through the hours of wailing, she who fed the mother a stew of fennel to keep up her strength. Her shock is the midwife's intention.

"There's always blood," the old nun says. "This is what comes from carnal knowledge."

The novitiate avoids the midwife's eyes. She holds the baby aloft, against the backdrop of the airless chamber with its dusty limestone walls. The mother calls out. The midwife takes a plain blanket, faded from so many cleanings with a wire whisk, and covers the mother's shivering body. At the sight of the midwife leaning over her with a white wimple like an angel's halo, the young mother turns her head weakly. Her gaze falls on the large wooden tub, which holds the water used to rinse the baby. The water, too, is tinged with blood.

"Let me hold him," she says. She reaches a pale hand toward the midwife's own. "*Per piacere*, give him to me."

The midwife holds a thimble of calendula and nettle tea to the mother's lips.

"Drink," she says, and the mother obediently purses her lips and swallows the bitter herbs. Before the tea has passed her throat, she's crying out again.

"Bring him to me," the mother begs, her hand clawing the empty air. "Please, let me hold my baby."

The novitiate dares not utter a word. But the child lets out a lusty cry, as if to answer his mother.

In the cupboard by the door is a letter from the prior general of the Augustinian Order, Ludovico Pietro di Saviano, sealed with his ring in a pool of wax the color of blood. The old nun, tired from her duties as midwife, picks up the parchment and reads it again. Her gray eyes are keen and she sees the prior general's words even in the shadows. Her gaze moves to the heavy wooden crucifix mounted on the wall above the bed. The woman knows it isn't her place to question the prior general's instructions. She's merely a servant of the Lord and as a woman she is the lowliest of all His servants. Yet she mutters a prayer under her breath before moving across the small room and making the sign of the cross on the infant's forehead. She holds a reddish twig of avens and waves it across the child's temples, baptizing him for the uncertain journey ahead as she murmurs the words she's spoken many times, over each new child ushered into the world by her hand.

"Ego te baptizo in nomine Patris et Filii, et Spiritus Sancti."

The novitiate's face glows as she hears the words that bind the child to Christ. The novitiate rubs the infant's arms, bends his knees and elbows, strokes his small fingers. The child opens his mouth and mews, a kitten's tongue. The novitiate flushes. With a deep sigh, the midwife tucks the twig into the child's blankets to keep him safe from evil, and instructs the novitiate to bundle the newborn for a journey. The young assistant doesn't utter a word, but her face asks its own questions and the midwife's nod, her whispered *"Andiamo!"* spur the girl to action. Her hands are deft as she wraps a second blanket around the child tightly.

"Be sure his head is warm," the midwife whispers. "He may be traveling far."

"*Bambino mio,*" the mother calls out. There's new urgency in her voice.

The midwife ignores the mother's cries. She takes the child from the novitiate, opens the infirmary door, and passes the infant to the Augustinian sister who waits outside, under the moon. Swiftly, the nun carries the child through the chapter house garden, her feet making no sound on the dusty ground. She doesn't allow herself to look at the infant. In the convent courtyard she passes the child into the arms of a man in a brown traveling cloak. His hood obscures his face. The baby's feet kick softly against the swaddling cloth as the man hurries to a waiting mule cart. The man slaps the mule, and they pass onto the road. The convent gates close behind them with a heavy thud.

The midwife's work is almost finished. She dismisses the novitiate quietly, with only a slight hint of praise for the girl's hard work. Squaring her shoulders, the midwife holds a bundled stick of dried rosemary and sage, lights it in the candlewick, and blows out the flame. A thick plume of smoke issues from the smudging stick. She paces the edge of the room, pausing over the prostrate mother to waft the smoking herbs above her body. When the smoke has clouded the chamber, she sets the smudging stick in a tin plate and begins cleaning the infirmary. Silently she gathers and drops the bloodied bed sheeting into a basket. She drags the full wooden tub across the limestone floor to the doorway, where it will be carried away at first light and used to water the herbs in the garden pots. She ignores the soft weeping of the young woman on the bed as she picks up the knife, the bowl with the afterbirth, and the crude iron forceps which were not needed. She carries all of this in the folds of her generous apron, holding the corners of it like a basket. Finally the midwife blows out the candle, and the shadows in the room are plunged into the flat planes of an ordinary night.

"Where's my child?" The young woman's rasping voice cuts the air. "What have you done with him?"

The old nun's heart isn't hard, but she's become adept at putting off the mothers. This one must be managed as the others have been managed.

"I've followed the prior general's orders. The child has been baptized. He'll be well cared for."

"No, no, no," the young woman wails. Her pleas can be heard in the halls of the convent dormitory where the nuns lie in their cots, listening. "*Bambino mio.* My baby."

"Please. It's not in our power to question the prior general." The midwife's tone is gentle for the first time this long night. "God's will must be done."

"The prior general." The mother shrieks his name and moves as if to rise. Her hair, which has been caught up in a net, comes loose and shimmers like pale moonlight. She sobs. "*Dio mio*, don't let the prior general do this to me. Please, I beg of you, Sister."

The old midwife has seen a new mother's tears before, and long ago pledged never to let their salty bitterness sway her.

"We've delivered of you a healthy son, but we won't speak of it again. This will be best. You'll see," the midwife says as she leaves the room and shuts the door on the young woman's pitiful sobs.

Alone in her narrow cell, the midwife lights her candle, removes her wimple, and lets her gray braids unravel to her waist. With weary fingers she unplaits the hair and massages her scalp. She opens a small pot of lavender oil culled from the herb garden she tends each day, and rubs a few drops briskly between her palms. The woman kneads her stiff hands. She strokes the scented oil across her forehead, along the length of her hair, across the back of her neck. Her skin tingles with this small pleasure.

The cell is snug, in accordance with the Augustinian Rule, and the scent of lavender fills it easily. The tiny room accommodates only a narrow cot, a crude wooden writing table, and a weathered Book of Hours. This has been her home now for almost fifty years. Long ago, the woman couldn't bear to come here until she stumbled into the room, exhausted and ready for sleep. Now the old nun is relieved to be alone.

"Dear Lord," she prays as she moves slowly to the writing table. "Is this Your will? Is this what's best for all? *Sanctus Christus.* Blessed be."

She thinks of the young mother's sunken eyes, the lovely face racked with pain and fear. This isn't the first unwed woman whom the midwife has tended in birth. But this is the first time the nun has felt so close to another's sin of conception.

Putting the candle on the table, she takes up a piece of parchment and sits on the heavy stool. She dips her quill into a pot of ink, colored with dye yielded from her garden, and begins her letter to Prior General Ludvico di Saviano. Carefully, her quill tip scratches across the parchment in a slow rhythm as she recounts the events that have taken place at the Convent Santa Margherita.

Early this morning, on the Feast Day of Our Blessed Saint Augustine, a male child has been born of my hand. The birth was difficult, but the mother is young and strong and her body will heal. In accordance with your instructions, the mother has not been permitted to hold the child or to give him a Christian name. He has been baptized and sent to a wet nurse who will see to his care. No record has been made of his birth.

At this, she touches her head and then her sternum, making the sign of the cross. She continues to write.

*The cord and placenta have been buried near the pear tree outside the mon-
astery wall. There was no caul, but there is a red birthmark on the child's
buttock. The mark is roughly the shape of a cross.*

This is a fact, the nun tells herself. The birthmark can't be omitted.

*The infant is a pure soul, and I trust he will be sent to a home where true
Christian parents may claim and raise him as their own. I have done this at
your will.*

When she is satisfied with what is dispatched in her careful penmanship, she folds the parchment and seals it with the wax from her
candle. Into this wax she presses her thumb, the only seal a nun is
permitted to use.

Every word the midwife writes to the prior general is true but for one:
in the mind and heart of his mother, the child does have a name.

"Dear Lord," the new mother speaks into the sage-smoked darkness. "Protect my son until we're together again. Mother Mary, by the
power of the Holy Belt, I beg your forgiveness."

Then she says the child's name aloud and waits. But there is no
thunder from the Lord, no hand of the Virgin to soothe her. She
hears no denial, no acknowledgment, no anger. If not for the smell of
blood in the room and the torn place between her legs, it would be as
if the child had never been born.

Chapter One

Lucrezia and Spinetta Buti arrived at the Convent Santa Margherita in early July, on Monday of the fourth week after Pentecost. They came in a simple carriage drawn by two fine horses that gave pause to all who saw them along the dusty road from Florence. Farmers who labored in the olive groves drew off their caps as they passed, and shepherd boys tending their flocks in the golden hills outside of Sesto Fiorentino waved, hoping a pale hand might toss coins, sweets, or small colored beads from the carriage.

Gleaming in the midmorning sun, the horses trotted through Prato's main gates and whinnied as they slowed outside the convent. Prioress Bartolommea, sitting in her small study, squinted up over her account books.

"Who are we expecting?" she asked Sister Camilla. "Is it the procurator?"

"The procurator is still in Montepulciano, at the new convent under his ministration," the secretary answered.

"Then is it the prior general?" Mother Bartolommea asked as the gates were opened and the carriage rolled into the courtyard.

"If it is, Madre, he's not come at an appointed time," said Sister Camilla, who stood and peered out the window. "Nor has he come in his usual carriage."

The women crossed themselves and glanced toward heaven. Un-

announced visits from Prior General Saviano, head of the Augustinian Order, were distressing: he rarely stayed less than four nights, ate
heartily, and consumed more than his share of wine without replenishing the nuns' meager supply.

"Perhaps it's someone to see Fra Filippo," said Sister Camilla.

"Perhaps," the prioress said faintly. She patted the younger woman's hand as she thought of Fra Filippo Lippi, the famed painter and
monk. Despite her distaste for the Carmelite brother's gruff voice
and salacious reputation, the prioress brightened whenever he crossed
her mind. Fra Filippo's acclaim for painting the most beautiful Madonnas in the Italian states was growing, and the prioress hoped his
presence in Prato, along with his recent assignment as chaplain to her
nunnery's small collection of souls, might yet bring some glory to
Santa Margherita.

In his workshop near the Piazza della Pieve, Fra Filippo Lippi
was also aware of the fine horses that trotted through the
streets of Prato. As they reached the church square, the monk put
down his brush and hurried to the window. Sunlight fell on his features, revealing a strong mouth, heavy brow, wide Roman cheekbones,
and deep blue eyes. The passing carriage was modest, and the monk
saw quickly that it didn't belong to the Carmelite Order, nor did it
bear banners displaying the Medici crest of six golden *palle*. Whoever
it carried, the passengers were not coming to his *bottega* to demand
past-due work or debts owed, and the painter was greatly relieved.

The horses turned the corner onto Via Santa Margherita and
Fra Filippo went back into his cluttered *bottega*. Well into his fourth
decade, the monk moved easily among the pots and containers of
paint and tempera that filled the shelves and speckled the floor with

color. With his mind on his work, the man barely noticed the wooden panels stacked against the walls and filled with images of angels and saints and patrons in various stages of living, praying, or dying as they awaited the life that came from his hand.

Running a thick palm across his tonsured scalp, the monk stood before his easel and stared at the panel he'd been laboring over for days. The painting was a commission from Ottavio de' Valenti, Prato's wealthiest citizen, and Fra Filippo forced himself to focus on this small portrait of the Madonna and Child.

"A Madonna. *Una bella Madonna con bambino*," Signor Ottavio had requested, pressing ten gold florins into Fra Filippo's palm to seal the commission. "For my blessed Teresa, now *in attesa*. God willing, she'll bring me a son at last."

The monk's Virgin sat on a wondrous throne painstakingly rendered with tiny jeweled detailing. Her robe was a sumptuous blue of the finest lapis lazuli, carefully ornamented in gold leaf and red madder. The cherubic Christ child was in her arms, looking up into the Virgin's face.

But there was no face. There was only a light sketch in red crayon on a flesh-colored oval, awaiting the painter's brush.

Slowly, the Buti sisters stepped from their carriage. The local boys who tended the convent's barnyard animals stopped to watch, and the nuns within sight of the courtyard peered from under their wimples.

Spinetta, the younger of the two, came first. She was pale in her brown traveling cloak, but her cheeks still had their fullness, and wisps of blond hair framed her face. She kept her gaze on the ground as she moved aside to let her sister descend.

All eyes were on Lucrezia as her boot stepped from the carriage, followed by the hem of her bold magenta *cotta*, a gloved hand, a narrow waist, and a braided blond head wrapped in a *reta* of gold netting. In her twentieth year, Lucrezia Buti was beautiful, with an eye trained for finery in the home of her father. Her features were placid and delicate: a high, smooth forehead, wide-set eyes, full lips. She stood by her sister, and raised her chin to look at the dusty courtyard.

Lucrezia took in the goats and boys, the limestone cloister walls, the fragrant bay laurels that stood beside the prioress's study, the quiet solemnity of the convent yard. She saw the tight face of an old nun staring from a narrow window, shadowed by a younger, gape-mouthed nun with a large nose and thick, furrowed brows.

"Mother of God," Lucrezia murmured. She brought a small linen satchel of dried flowers to her nostrils, remembering how her fingers had deftly sewn the crushed petals into the clasp of fabric on her last night at home. "Mother Mary, give me strength."

At the study window, Sister Camilla took in Lucrezia's beauty, the sisters' silk gowns trimmed in impractical velvet brocade, and in a glance she knew they'd been whisked to the convent with little under-standing of what lay ahead.

"It must be the young novitiates sent from Florence by Monsignor Donacello," she said to the prioress. "They've arrived a day early."

A moment later, the secretary was striding toward the carriage, raising dust around the hem of her black robe.

"Welcome to the Convent Santa Margherita," she said evenly.

Lucrezia presented a sealed parchment to Sister Camilla, and waited as she carried the note inside.

The letter, from the Monsignor Antonio Donacello of Florence,

contained a brief summary of the young women's diminished circumstances due to the untimely death of their father, Lorenzo Buti. It promised that alms would be given to the convent in gratitude for the sisters'
safekeeping. And it extolled the virtues of their character and piety.

"They are the daughters of a silk merchant, recently taken by
God," the prioress said, peering at the note. "The youngest of five
girls and a single brother. Apparently there has been some dispute as
to the nature of their father's mercantile dealings."

The two nuns again looked out the window of the study, which
was housed in a building of pale stucco, the words *Sanctus Augustus*
carved above the door.

Oblivious to the women's gaze, Spinetta pressed her palms into
her quartz prayer beads and moved her lips. Lucrezia lifted a hand to
her face and inhaled the chamomile fragrance of her sachet.

"She has the face of an angel," Sister Camilla said.

"But it will do her no good here," Mother Bartolommea replied.

❦

Fra Filippo selected a thin-handled brush from a jumble on
his worktable. He dipped it into the fresh tempera and raised
the bristles to the blank oval, preparing to make a mark that would
define the Madonna's cheek.

"I don't see it," Fra Filippo mumbled to himself as his hand
stopped. "I don't see the Madonna I've promised."

Fra Filippo knew he needed only to follow the lines he'd drawn
in order to have a Madonna that would please his patron, Ottavio
de' Valenti. But the monk was never satisfied by simply filling in the
lines he'd sketched onto a panel. His Virgin had to be beautiful and
tragic; a Mary full of grace yet already seeing beyond the joy of her
son's birth, to His sad end.

"Matteo!" The painter's voice echoed through the open rooms of his *bottega,* and Fra Filippo remembered that again that very morning he'd dismissed yet another young assistant—the stupid oaf had left the gesso brushes unwashed, and they lay stiff and useless on the ground. The monk kicked the brushes across the floor, and grabbed up a heavy jug of wine.

Fra Filippo had accepted the commission from de' Valenti knowing that he would need to work swiftly. He rarely turned down work, and never refused a wealthy man who might protect him from the vagaries of an artist's life. Being a monk was no insurance against the perils of his own passions, as Fra Filippo well knew. Although Cosimo de' Medici had recently called him the greatest living painter in all of the Italian states, Fra Filippo was heavily in debt, often short of money, and always behind in his work. His growing reputation as a brilliant painter brought him ever-increasing commissions, but hadn't altered the monk's tendency to procrastinate, or to make trouble for himself.

Many had heard tales of his great bravado, the power of his appetites, and the roar of his pride. But few understood the hours Fra Filippo spent warding off doubt whenever he feared his talents would elude him. And as he often did at such moments, Fra Filippo felt overwhelmed by all that God and man asked of him.

"Why do you ask me to paint what I don't see, Lord?" the painter asked aloud, letting his brush fall to his side. "If this is your will, then show me a face worthy of the Virgin."

***

*L*ucrezia and Spinetta followed Sister Camilla past the convent's small barn, stinking pigsty, and herd of braying goats. Ignoring the sweat that ran down her back, Lucrezia stepped carefully along a crooked stone pathway, past a fountain in the cloister garden that seemed to mock her with its cool, bubbling water.

"When you enter the convent you surrender all worldly goods and vanities," Sister Camilla said, her voice floating to them through the thick morning air. "Everything for a life of prayer and work is provided by the Lord, and the healing herbs from Sister Pureza's garden help us to maintain a healthy balance of our humors."

Lucrezia gazed at a stooped nun who was looking at them across a stone wall. The woman held a basket filled with yellow flowers in her arms and watched as they entered a low stucco building. When Lucrezia looked back over her shoulder, the old nun's bright eyes were still on them.

"You'll wear these robes," Sister Camilla said after she'd led the sisters to their cells, barely large enough for a narrow cot and small washbasin, and handed each a black garment. Her eyes passed over their ornate dresses. "Someone will come for your clothes."

The secretary looked at the young women's long hair, and swatted at a fly that buzzed near her cheek.

"The convent has abandoned the custom of shaving our novitiates' heads," Sister Camilla said. "The prioress believes hair is not a vanity but a necessity provided by the Lord to keep us warm in the cold winter months."

She left without another word.

Alone in the airless cell, Lucrezia sat on her cot and wept. Until this moment she hadn't believed that God would let her fate come to this. But neither pleas, prayers, nor tears had kept her from being carried inside the convent walls and locked behind its heavy gates.

Wearily she began to undress, laying each piece of clothing on top of her fragrant sachet. Before she finished there was a knock on the door and the thin wooden plank was pushed open by the old woman she'd seen in the garden.

"I am Sister Pureza," the woman said. "You must finish dressing. *Vieni.*"

Over the old woman's shoulder, Lucrezia could see another nun knocking on her sister's door and issuing the same brief instructions. Spinetta came to the doorway wearing her black robe, and thrust her favorite gown into the waiting nun's arms.

"Everything, please," said the other nun. "Your *mantello*, and also the traveling bag. It will be sold for your dowry, of course."

Sister Pureza gazed at the novitiate in front of her.

"*Andiamo*, Lucrezia. I know it is warm, but there is much to be done." Sister Pureza smiled kindly, revealing even more wrinkles in her old face, and nodded at the robe with her chin.

"Yes, Sister," Lucrezia said. "Forgive me."

She turned her back to the old woman and removed her silken *gamurra*, her boots, and the linen stockings soaked with perspiration. She stood in her thin undergarments, the *panni di gamba* she'd stitched by hand.

From the doorway, Sister Pureza watched. Like Lucrezia, the old nun had also been the beautiful daughter of a merchant who lived in a fine palazzo. She'd traveled to Rome to see Pope Martin V's coronation, and tasted fine wines from her uncles' cellars. But her beauty had led her to shame and finally to the gates of the convent where, in time, she'd surrendered her baptismal name and taken the name Sister Pureza Magdalena.

At the sight of the novitiate standing in her chemise and bloomers, her thin back heaving with emotion, the old nun let out a small sigh.

"My father," Lucrezia said softly.

Turning, she dropped to her knees and fingered the *panni di gamba* at the place where she'd secreted her silver medallion of Saint John the Baptist, patron saint of Florence, into its hem. *"Mio padre."*

Sister Pureza put a palm on Lucrezia's head. Dirt from the herb garden was crusted in her nailbeds, and a few granules fell onto the girl's hair. She looked down and saw the fine lines of Lucrezia's collarbones, the outline of her breasts below the damp silk.

"Please." Lucrezia touched the chemise where she'd made her most delicate stitches. "This silk was a last gift from my father. I'm not ready to say good-bye."

"Oh, child," Sister Pureza intoned softly. The old nun knew luxuries would fade slowly from the girl's life until the memory of them was but a dream. She glanced at Lucrezia's *panni di gamba* and nodded, once. A look passed between the young woman and the old one.

"It's time," Sister Pureza said, breaking her gaze. "Come."

In black robe and tunic, Lucrezia knelt in the sanctuary of the small stone church. The room smelled of moss, the air thick and fertile. Sister Pureza dipped her fingers into a bowl of holy water, and touched Lucrezia's forehead.

"In the name of the Father, the Son, and the Holy Spirit," she said. "Are you prepared to renounce everything to the Sacred Order of Santa Margherita of the Augustinians, in the name of Christ and the Most Holy Virgin?"

Sister Pureza waited patiently for Lucrezia to remember the phrase the monsignor had taught her.

"I ask for the Mercy of God and the Son and for the habit of the Augustinian Order, that I might prepare myself to become a worthy bride of Christ."

A white wimple was placed on Lucrezia's head, a stiff scapular marked with the blue line of a novitiate draped across her shoulders to secure the headpiece. Lucrezia didn't shut her eyes, as was the custom of most of the new novitiates. Instead, she watched the woman's hands, surprised by the smell of lavender on her skin.

"*Dominus Christus,*" Sister Pureza said, tracing the sign of the cross on Lucrezia's forehead. "Now you will live by our Rule. You are in the service of the Lord. All will be ordained to you. Praise the Lord."

Chapter Two

Dropping her feet onto the cool stone floor, Lucrezia bent to the basin and splashed water onto her face. The bell was calling her to worship, but beyond the convent walls the city of Prato was dark and silent. She squeezed a few drops from a fresh lemon and rinsed the film from her teeth, fumbled for her robe, and pulled it over her silk undergarment. Then she braided and wrapped her hair and put on her wimple.

Lucrezia found Spinetta waiting in the dark hallway, and hugged her. Hushed footsteps and the light of a single candle approached as a small line of nuns moved silently toward them. The sisters followed the others into the underground passage that led to the chapel sacristy. Before entering the church Spinetta paused to pull a circle of pink quartz beads from her pocket. The prayer beads had been a gift from her mother on the occasion of her confirmation, and they were Spinetta's most prized possession.

"I couldn't bear to part with them yesterday," Spinetta whispered, pressing the carved crucifix to her lips.

Knowing what comfort even the smallest token from home could provide, Lucrezia quickly snatched up the beads.

"Don't give them up," she said, slipping them into her tunic where they slid safely into the folds of her *panni di gamba*. "I'll keep them for you."

In the church, illuminated by flickering candlelight, Lucrezia and Spinetta took their places on the rough floor beside young Sister Bernadetta, and bowed their heads.

Facing one another in two rows, on their knees, the sixteen women of Convent Santa Margherita welcomed the dawn with the chanting of Lauds, followed by a reading from the Gospels which the prioress spoke in a hushed voice. When they'd finished, and filed out of the church, a thin red line broke on the horizon and a rooster crowed.

At a long table in the refectory, set with wooden plates and cups of water tinged with wine, each nun took a honey-colored bun still warm from the oven. Surprised by the ferocity of her appetite, Lucrezia forced herself to eat slowly as she gazed around the room. The nuns looked as she'd feared, with dull features, loose chins, and moles sprouting hairs. Only a few had a light in their eyes; the others were gray and worn.

"Chapter three." The prioress stood and began to read from her worn leather book. "The Rule of Saint Augustine."

As her voice droned through the refectory, Lucrezia snuck a sideways glance at her sister. Spinetta appeared content, but then, she'd always known that she would someday live a monastic life.

"Develop your soul and your mind, Spinetta," their mother had said gently, year after year. "You are from God, and you are for God."

Even as a child, Spinetta had bowed to her fate. But Lucrezia had seen her three older sisters marry in splendor and believed she, too, would someday be the mistress of her own home. She'd been promised to a master weaver whose father expected to join his fortune to the silk business of Signor Lorenzo Buti, and since the age of fifteen she'd watched her father's activities closely, preparing to some-day share all she knew with her future husband. At her father's side Lucrezia had learned the artisans' methods of cultivating herbs and blending dyes; she'd seen the finished yards of *picciolato* covered with tiny flowers. She'd learned what was required to make the highest-quality silk, and how a disreputable merchant might try to bring second-quality silk to market with a false seal. In a city known for splendid costume and dress, Lucrezia Buti had understood the precious beauty of silk, and had set her future on its bounty.

Then her father died suddenly, and the troubles began. Representatives of the Arte della Seta, the powerful silk guild, falsely claimed that Buti's wares were below standard, and weeks of arguing and sifting through Lorenzo Buti's private account books had not satisfied the inspectors. In the end everything was seized, the silks and materials carted from the shop, the record books thrown in the back of a rough cart and taken away.

In black widow's clothing, Signora Buti had spoken alone to Lucrezia the following day.

"Everything your father promised for you is gone," she'd said, a tray of cakes sitting untouched in front of them.

"But father saw to my dowry. Surely Antonio will offer me a brother's protection."

"*Figlia mia cara,*" her mother said. "My dear daughter, there is nothing left. You must go to Prato with Spinetta." Her mother blinked away tears. "You must go to the Convent Santa Margherita."

A week later Lucrezia had entered the convent, and left everything behind. Now she missed her mother's smile, and her shrewd father who'd always smelled of leather and mulberry. She missed the cool glide of silk against her skin, and the brisk feel of her golden hair being brushed by Beatrice, the maid. She missed the air of excitement and the drumbeats of the young boys on *festa* days, when the streets of Florence were crowded with people in the grips of merriment. She missed the easy joy she'd believed would always be hers.

A tiny pinch from Spinetta drew Lucrezia back to the present. She straightened, said the final *amen* with the others, and made the sign of the cross. As the nuns filed out of the refectory, Sister Pureza came up alongside Lucrezia, and greeted her kindly.

"Dear Sister Lucrezia," the old nun said. "It's my duty to tend the herb garden and the infirmary, and I am in need of someone to assist me. My bones grow old, and I don't have the stamina I once had. Each novitiate is put under the instruction of an elder here at Santa Margherita, and I think perhaps you might be suited to this work."

Lucrezia was taller than Sister Pureza. As she looked down into the woman's old face, she saw it was full of soft wisdom.

"Sister Camilla cares for our small library and sees to the convent's correspondence," the nun said. "Her duties require an educated mind, and she's also asked for someone to assist her. You may feel more drawn to this task. Yet I see that your sister is delicate, while you have the upright carriage of one who might be able to take on greater physical demands."

Lucrezia answered slowly.

"I was often by my father's side in the silk shop," she said. "From the time I was very small I spent my mornings in the garden, looking over the plants with my father. But of course, you won't be growing herbs for silk dyes here. Perhaps it's best if my sister is given the chance to take in the air as much as possible."

Sister Pureza smiled.

"Here at Santa Margherita we have the honor of providing herbs to a master painter for his pigments," she said. "This new duty has taxed my reserves, and if you have such knowledge then perhaps it's the Lord's will that brought you to me."

"So my sister is correct." Lucrezia felt a faint stir of pleasure. "There is a painter in Prato."

"Yes, my child. Fra Filippo Lippi is here with us, working on a series of frescoes in *la pieve*," said Sister Pureza. "He's recently begun serving as our chaplain at Santa Margherita."

Sister Pureza gave a small laugh at Lucrezia's confused expression.

"Fra Filippo is a painter as well as a monk, in a most benevolent bestowing of gifts by Our Father," said the old woman. "He lives in a small house on the edge of the piazza, where he's been granted special permission to live *in seculum* so that he may maintain an artist's workshop and be closer to the church where he labors."

Taking Lucrezia by the elbow, Sister Pureza turned toward a door at the back of the church.

"Even here, in such modest surroundings, you'll find great beauty," she said as they stepped into a narrow chapel.

Lucrezia stood in darkness until the old woman pulled back a wooden shutter. A shaft of sunlight illuminated the chapel's smooth wooden beams, and Lucrezia found herself facing a small altar. Behind the altar was a beautiful painting framed by two narrow panels.

"The Coronation of the Virgin," Sister Pureza said, her voice soft as she lit two candles. "The altarpiece was a gift to the convent from Fra Filippo."

Lucrezia stepped closer to study the tumult of angels crowding around a bearded Christ as he placed a shimmering gold crown on a demure young Virgin.

"I've never seen a painting so fine, except in the great cathedrals of Florence," Lucrezia said. "Is this the work of our chaplain?"

"It is." Sister Pureza was pleased at Lucrezia's delight, and pushed away thoughts of the unpleasant rumors she'd heard about Fra Filippo's coarser instincts. "I'm told he's known throughout Naples and Milan, as well as in Florence."

Lucrezia leaned forward to have a better look at the Blessed Virgin's robe and the sweet-faced angels who hovered around her in Heaven, playing harps and trumpets. She had never seen such iridescent silks, with colors that seemed to change with each movement of her eyes. Indeed, the fluid figures in the painting were charged with a graceful, dancelike energy. She could almost hear the notes of the tiny violins and horns, the chorus of joyous angels.

"Here is Saint Catherine." The old nun directed Lucrezia's gaze to a side panel adorned with a woman holding a book and looking toward the heavens. "She, too, preserved her virginity in honor of the Lord."

Seeing the saint's radiant face, Lucrezia was reminded of all that was expected of her.

"There's more, my dear," Sister Pureza said. "Perhaps you're aware that the Virgin's Holy Belt is kept in the Church of Santo Stefano, where it helps shield us from evils that abound in the world."

Lucrezia nodded. She'd known the legend of the *Sacra Cintola* of the Blessed Madonna since she was a small girl, and once had fashioned her own sash of green silk, tied it about her waist on the feast day of the Sacred Belt, and pranced about in the garden pretending she was the Holy Mother. This drama had greatly amused her father.

"You'll find many small miracles in Prato," Sister Pureza said gently. "Surely the Lord has put something here that will please you."

⸙

Fra Filippo was late as usual. His mind was on the unfinished Madonna and Child for Ottavio de' Valenti, and he barely saw the cobbled street in front of him as he hurried along Via Santa Margherita toward the convent. The painter hated to leave his workshop to attend his clerical duties, but the post as chaplain was one he could ill afford to lose. Only last week he'd received a missive from Prior General Saviano reminding him of debts owed for his meager sustenance, not to mention the price demanded by a neighbor who claimed Fra Filippo's rooster had entered his henhouse and spoiled two days' worth of eggs with his banter.

The prior general had written in his terse penmanship:

Fra Filippo Lippi,
It is of utmost import that you faithfully fulfill and retain the post of chaplain at Convent Santa Margherita while you complete the frescoes in Santo Stefano, for this small stipend will cover the many debts charged to the Order in your name during Lent and Easter last. I urge you to attend your duties with great vigilance, and cease to succumb to the vanity that supposes your artistic talents supersede your obligation to the Order, which is the first duty for every ordained brother in Christ.

Pausing at the heavy gate, Fra Filippo took the key from his belt and entered the convent feeling parched and irritated. Not only was he late, but he'd left his breviary in the chapel and had to retrieve it before he could begin the day's reading.

To his surprise, the small chapel door stood open, and someone was kneeling at the altar. The unfamiliar figure wore the blue stripe of the novitiate on her scapular, and as he drew closer the monk saw that she was gazing at the altarpiece he'd painted.

At the sound of his step in the doorway, Lucrezia turned. Expecting to see Sister Pureza, she was startled to see a monk's white robes. His figure was large, his silhouette blocking the single shaft of light from the window.

"Excuse me," Fra Filippo said.

The candles on the mantel illuminated Lucrezia's face, and the monk was taken by the young woman's beauty. Even her swollen eyes and reddened nose didn't distract from the perfection of her features, which she hid as he stepped forward and took his prayer book from the altar.

Searching for something to say, Fra Filippo straightened. He lingered a moment longer, inhaling a distinct whiff of chamomile before the bell summoning the nuns began to ring.

Breviary tucked under his arm, the monk joined the nuns in the chapter house garden, near the well. Taking his place at the head of the small gathering, Fra Filippo saw the novitiate from the chapel slip into the group beside a second, unfamiliar young woman. The nuns bowed their heads and the bell, rung by Sister Camilla, ceased.

"Greetings from Our Lord and Savior, Jesus Christ," Fra Filippo said, looking over his breviary. "Today, we have a reading from Psalm 66: 'Make a joyful noise unto God, all the earth. Sing forth the Glory of His name . . .'"

As the nuns joined him in chanting the midmorning psalms, Fra Filippo allowed his eyes to wander over the group. As usual, Sisters Bernadetta and Antonia swayed in rhythm, Sister Isotta whispered her words in a lisp, and Sister Pureza held her hands clasped high in front of her face. The unfamiliar novitiates kept their heads bowed, but when the cycle of intonation ended, the two lifted their chins and

Fra Filippo saw that both were fair, with faces that had been protected from the wind and sun. The smaller one, whom he'd seen in the chapel, was even more beautiful than the candlelight had revealed.

"Chaplain, God has blessed our convent with two new arrivals," Mother Bartolommea announced after the others had filed out of the garden. "Allow me to introduce Sister Lucrezia and Sister Spinetta, sent to us from Florence."

Flanked by Sisters Pureza and Camilla, the novitiates offered a humble greeting with their heads bowed. Lucrezia let her gaze flicker across the monk's feet in thick sandals, the flecks of green and gold paint splattered along the hem of his robe.

"*Benvenute*," Fra Filippo said. "Welcome."

He reached a hand toward the young women and put a palm on Lucrezia's bent head, another on Spinetta's, and invoked a quick prayer. As he removed his palms, the scent of chamomile rose into the air.

"We're blessed to have you with us, Sister Spinetta and Sister Lucrezia." The monk noted the sisters' soft hands, so different from the callused palms of the others, and willed Lucrezia to meet his gaze. "I'm sure the good sisters of Santa Margherita will educate you in the many manners of devotion to the Lord," he said.

The sisters nodded.

"I have seen—" Lucrezia broke the silence, then stammered as she saw the robes around her stop their gentle swaying. She did not look up. "I have seen your magnificent work in the chapel, Fratello."

Sister Pureza put a gentle hand on the novitiate's shoulder.

"Our young sister has admired your *Coronation* only this morning," Sister Pureza said. "It allowed her to contemplate the rich gifts God has given us here at Santa Margherita."

Tongue-tied by a rare flash of modesty, Fra Filippo merely nodded.

"May God bless your stay here," he said finally. "I will be honored to attend to your spiritual needs."

As he prepared to step away, Lucrezia raised her eyes and Fra Filippo saw they were a startling blue, a lapis lazuli as wonderful as the sky over the Bisenzio Valley.

She smiled at him almost imperceptibly.

"Thank you, Fratello," she murmured.

Her lips moved and the monk's mind flew into the world of *fantasia* where his paintings began, and he heard the voice of his intuition urging him to memorize each detail of her face.

Morning prayers flowed into the hour of Sext, and Fra Filippo lingered at the convent. He offered himself to the service of the prioress, and let his eyes linger on Lucrezia whenever he dared. After the midday meal, when he could think of no other excuse to remain, the monk walked quickly back to his workshop with her face still burning in his mind. He'd almost reached the piazza when he heard the unwelcome greetings of Gemignano Inghirami, provost and head of the confraternity of the Church of Santo Stefano. The provost rarely left the shadowy halls of his church, and Fra Filippo had no doubt the cleric had come solely to see him.

"So there you are, Fratello." The provost's voice grated the air.

Arranging his features carefully, Fra Filippo smiled.

"*Buongiorno,* and God's blessings to you." The monk threw out his arms in greeting as Inghirami dragged his red robe across the dusty path.

The provost was a thin man with a rangy, beaklike nose and a sharp gaze. He gave Fra Filippo a weak smile and stepped back from his embrace.

"I've just come from the church," Inghirami said coolly. "It appears there's been no progress on the frescoes since you laid down the underpainting in sinopia. Nor are there any lines on the *intonaco*, where the scenes of Saint John are to be." The provost laughed unpleasantly. "Unless they are visible only to the chosen few."

As provost and rector of Santo Stefano, Inghirami was the most powerful church figure in the city. Along with his clerical duties he was charged with guarding the *Sacra Cintola*, the Sacred Belt of the Blessed Virgin, which was said to possess the power of miracles. The relic was visited yearly by hundreds of pilgrims whose generous alms enriched the church's coffers and allowed the confraternity of Santo Stefano to commission costly works and adornments, of which Fra Filippo's fresco series for the church's *cappella maggiore* was the grandest.

"I've been eager to show you my progress," said the monk, putting an arm around him and turning him toward the piazza.

"Progress?" Inghirami muttered. "I haven't seen anything."

"Then you haven't looked carefully, Padre, begging your pardon."

Fra Filippo had been paid five hundred gold florins for the fresco cycle, and would receive many hundreds more when it was completed. But instead of finishing the work in three years, as he'd agreed, the painter had accepted yet another commission to design a stained-glass window for the church's main chapel. He'd acquired several more commissions from the Medici family, and there was still de' Valenti's Madonna to deliver before the woman's birth pains began.

"Let us look together," the monk said. "And I can explain my progress."

Keeping a firm grip on Inghirami's thin shoulders, Fra Filippo led him quickly across the Piazza della Pieve. On this warm summer day the city's central plaza was filled with housemaids and messengers from the grand palazzi in the Santa Trinità quarter, stout merchants' wives who hurried to and from the market, and monks whose sandals scuffed slowly across the square.

The air inside the *pieve* of Santo Stefano was scented with incense and candles, and markedly cooler than on the streets. The two men made their way down the nave, under the high Corinthian columns, and stopped to genuflect before climbing the *alberese* staircase, passing behind the altar, and stepping into the grand chapel of the church, the *cappella maggiore*.

The chapel was dominated by a maze of rough scaffolding and a large open window at the rear, and buzzed with apprentice painters and two stained-glass artisans from the Florentine studio of Fra Lorenzo da Pelago. The visiting artisans stood at a large worktable studying Fra Filippo's design for the window that would replace the one Inghirami had ordered removed.

"You see, it will be as you wished." Fra Filippo kept up a constant dialogue with Inghirami even as he greeted the young men and surveyed the elaborate window sketch. "The lunette window will celebrate the Madonna's *cintola* and by extension, of course, commend your honor in keeping the Holy Belt safe these many years."

Inghirami scowled and nodded as the painter described in detail the colorful glass arrangement that would depict the scene of the belt being passed from the Virgin to Saint Thomas.

"The window will take many years," Fra Filippo said with a loud bravado. "But my fresco series is already well under way."

Keeping his hand on Inghirami's shoulder, he turned his attention to the cycle of six frescoes which would fill the high walls of the grand chapel. The series was to illustrate the lives of Saint John the Baptist and Saint Stephen, to whom the church was dedicated, beginning at the top of the walls with scenes from their births, and ending at the bottom, with a scene from the end of each saint's life.

Using a rich palette of green and gold, daring perspective, and animated expressions that brought his figures to life, Fra Filippo intended to make these frescoes his greatest achievement to date. But after three years, only the scene of Saint John taking leave of his parents contained any finished *giornata,* the work that marked the rhythm of the fresco painter's life. Everything else remained largely in the painter's mind.

"See here, among this patch of *arriccio?*" The painter directed the provost's gaze to the middle tier, which was covered with a layer of preparatory plaster. It was clearly uneven, and needed to be smoothed. "Here is where I'll place the scene of Saint Stephen's disputation in the synagogue. You can see where the drape of the saint's robe might fall to the floor."

The monk waved a hand, and in his mind's eye saw Saint Stephen's black and red robe, and his bald head covered by a rich silk *berretto.*

"The synagogue steps will be here." Fra Filippo scanned the wall until he found a blemish in the preparation, roughly the size of a man's head. "And here is where you will stand: in the synagogue, worthy of your presence. I've prayed deeply on this matter, but didn't want to proceed until I had your consent."

"Myself?" The provost's mouth fell open. "In the fresco?"

It wasn't uncommon for a painter to include a patron in his work. But it surprised Inghirami that he would be commemorated in the frescoes, because the commission had been given to the painter by the provost's predecessor and not by Inghirami himself.

"If it honors you, blessed provost," Fra Filippo said, bowing slightly. "Of course you'll want to study the arrangement, and prayerfully contemplate it." The monk gestured toward the wall. "Naturally, I won't proceed until I've heard from you further."

Inghirami squinted, and took in the painter's strong profile. In the records, the painter had been given a dignified name: *Frate Dipintore*, Brother Painter. The great Medici and all who claimed to know such things said the angels and saints created by Fra Filippo were more alive than those of Fra Giovanni the Dominican, his figures weightier than those of Piero della Francesca. Inghirami couldn't see the difference between one painting and the next, one hungry artist or another. But he trusted what was said in Florence and Rome.

"So be it," the provost said with a toss of his chin. "I will consider what you have proposed."

Leaving Inghirami staring at the nearly empty wall, the monk hurried out, shaking with silent laughter.

Finally alone in his workshop, Fra Filippo sank onto a stool and put his face to his hands. The monk knew beauty when he saw it, and he'd seen it in Lucrezia Buti as certain, as vivid, as the wounds in Christ's flesh. God had heard his prayers, and sent him the most exquisite face he'd ever seen. A face caught in the moment between childish innocence and womanly beauty. A face about to blossom and break open with love, joy, and sadness.

Lifting his head, the painter took up a piece of red crayon and a soft sheet of parchment, and drew the simple lines of the novitiate's countenance. He drew a graceful line for her cheek, another for the jaw that anchored the face, then the long neck.

Fra Filippo Lippi was a butcher's son: he knew the shape of the skull, the span of the limbs, the size of the delicate bones of the hands. For years he'd watched his father quarter calves, cows, lambs, and sheep. He knew that first there was bone, then ligament, sinew, muscle, veins, and flesh. And he knew that after all of this there was life, and beauty.

Fra Filippo drew Lucrezia's lips, her shoulders, and her arms below her robes. He drew the ribs, the delicate clavicle, and the backbone that snaked and bent the length of torso from neck to buttocks. He saw each limb and muscle and understood how one connected to the other, how all sprang from the same center. Other painters drew faces; Fra Filippo created men and women with the breath of life.

The day faded and the painter's hand grew more certain. Images and sounds from childhood came to him as he worked. The painter saw himself as a small boy in tattered breeches, kneeling in his father's dank butcher shop sucking on a piece of smoked beef. He saw his mother's face sighing over him as she held out a crust of bread, leaning to kiss him good night in their thatched shack near the Ponte Vecchio. He heard the Arno River passing, the neighbors' cries, his father's shouts, the cold thud of a stripped sheep carcass as it fell into the river.

He remembered the months after his parents' deaths, when he'd wandered the streets of Florence with his brother, hungry and frightened. The monks of Santa Maria del Carmine had taken them in, giving the boys food, shelter, and the education young Filippo had sorely resisted. In time they'd given Filippo what he loved best: the feel of a brush in his fingers; the chalky smell of gesso; the chance to watch the master painter Masaccio creating frescoes of Saint Peter's life in the Brancacci Chapel.

These gifts were great, but they'd come at a price. In order to have an artist's life he'd taken monks' vows of poverty and chastity, and been ordained as a priest. Fra Filippo lived alone, and owned only the small residence that adjoined his workshop. The *bottega* where he worked was rented, and even his white robes belonged to the Carmelites. As a member of the Order he was held to a high standard, and punished when he strayed. An impetuous man, he'd been jailed, whipped, and endured stinging shame for acts of lust, greed, and temptation. He believed this was the price God exacted for his talents. When the work transported him to a place of fantasy and intuition, or the Medici lauded him with praise and riches, it seemed a fair fee. But on days when he didn't feel the spirit move in him, and nights when Fra Filippo wished for a woman in his bed, it seemed he'd given up too much.

Sketches in hand, Fra Filippo lit two oil lamps and stood before the small *Madonna and Child* for Ottavio de' Valenti. He'd gone through an entire red crayon, half a softened silverpoint, a dozen pieces of parchment. On the blank oval of the Virgin's face the painter could now see the novitiate's eyes, he could feel her soft cheeks. Already he knew the precise amount of madder he would need to capture her lips' rosy tint.

Shadows fell across the workshop as Fra Filippo moved to the wooden block that served as a table for his knives, scrapers, bowls, and crumpled rags. Carefully, he ground green oxide for pigment, and poured the last of the egg yolks into his pestle. He made a fresh batch of green *verdaccio*, and a small bit of ochre tempera. Then he dragged a stool over to the easel and studied his work. He looked from the sketch of Lucrezia's face to the oval and gently began transferring the drawing onto the panel.

Chapter Three

"We haven't had enough rain," Sister Pureza said in a low voice. "The marjoram and lemons must have plenty of water or they won't survive."

Lucrezia nodded, although it was dark in the night stair and she couldn't be sure if Sister Pureza was addressing her, or talking to herself.

"We'll need the marjoram," Sister Pureza went on. "And birthwort, too. The child is coming at de' Valenti's palazzo, and Signora Teresa is well past the age of five and twenty."

Following the old nun up into the church, Lucrezia found her place between plump Sister Bernadetta and Spinetta, and knelt. It was Saturday, the Buti sisters' fifth morning at Santa Margherita, and they were gathering for confession in preparation for Mass and Holy Communion in honor of the Feast Day of Saint Lawrence. It was still dark, but the air was already thick and warm.

"Surely the rain will come soon," Lucrezia said under her breath.

"Hush." Spinetta opened her eyelids only a sliver. Her voice softened at the sight of her sister's face. "Remember, Lucrezia, there's no speaking between confession and the time of communion."

Again, Lucrezia envied the ease with which her sister had taken to the cloistered life, the way the words and rhythms of the prayers unfurled easily from her tongue.

Closing her eyes, Lucrezia thought back to the plush kneeler in the Church of Santa Maria del Carmine, where her mother had taken her to visit the Brancacci Chapel and make a final confession before entering the convent. There, Lucrezia's eyes had lingered on Masaccio's great frescoes—the illustrated stories of Saint Peter's life, Adam and Eve's anguished faces as they were expelled from the Garden—and she'd begged the monsignor to save her from the cloistered life.

"I don't want to give my life to the church," she'd said. "I beg you to intercede on my behalf."

"Your life already belongs to God," the monsignor had said firmly. "It is only by His mercy and generosity that we speak these words. Your fate is in the hands of the Lord, and there it will be well."

Now, in the small church of Santa Margherita, Lucrezia entered the airless confessional, knelt on a rough wooden slab, and faced the dark cloth that hung between her and the chaplain.

"Yes, my child?" Fra Filippo Lippi waited impatiently. He'd worked late into the night, furiously revising his sketches for the provost of Santo Stefano, who'd confounded his plans to include him in a scene by demanding a sketch to present to the *Comune di Prato* for approval.

"Chaplain, I am very troubled," Lucrezia said.

Her voice caught Fra Filippo's attention. All morning he'd listened to the weary prattle of nuns confessing to the small transgression of an extra bun at breakfast, or a flash of jealous vanity. Of course he recognized their voices, knowing it was always plump Sister Bernadetta who sinned with her hand in the larder, and thin Sister Simona who was pained by her own lack of compassion for the weaker among them. Only the prioress occasionally surprised him with her desire for greater recognition for the small convent, petitioning men far beyond her reach and harboring anger when her requests for greater resources or an invitation to the councils of the highest convents were ignored.

"Since coming to the convent I've been filled with despair," Lucrezia said with far more passion than she'd intended. "I wake each morning feeling bitter and old. And angry."

The monk leaned closer to the cloth that hung between them. He looked to the floor, and saw the tip of a clean boot. The young woman's voice broke, but not before Fra Filippo recognized Lucrezia's voice.

"Everything has been so sudden and unexpected," Lucrezia struggled to keep her words steady. "First, my father died. Then the shop was emptied to settle his debts, and before I knew it my dowry was gone."

"Go on," he said. He wanted to pull aside the curtain and look into the face that filled his studio, the eyes that looked out at him from the vellum, the sad smile that now graced the panel of his *Madonna and Child*.

"I never wanted to be a nun." Lucrezia paused. "I expected to have the life of a Florentine *signora*."

Fra Filippo had heard many novitiates lament their internment, and it always brought him back to his own reluctant initiation into the Order: the surrender of all property, the vow of celibacy, the constant vigilance against temptation.

"Reluctance isn't a sin," he said at last. His voice was deep, and it soothed Lucrezia.

"In words I've renounced everything," she said carefully. "But in my heart I still want so much. I desire and I yearn, and my thoughts are neither humble nor pure."

For a moment the friar didn't respond.

"Go on, my sister. Speak of this desire, this yearning."

"It's a sin, I know, but I miss the beautiful silks in my father's shop, I miss the garden I saw from my bedroom window. Fratello, I wanted a wedding pall of fine *seta leale*. I wanted my children to rest in an embroidered blanket sewn by my hand. I can't be pious or gracious when I've lost so much."

She paused, expecting the chaplain's rebuke.

"Go on," he said.

"I miss my world." Lucrezia was driven to speak what she'd choked down for days. "I want my pearl baptism bracelet. I want the blue pitcher in my mother's house. I want my mother. I want my father."

She went on, her voice breaking.

"Why does God ask me for devotion and sacrifice without showing me the way?"

This question struck a chord in the monk's heart. Hadn't he asked nearly the same question just hours before he'd first seen her face?

"I'm only a conduit to the Lord's ear," he said thoughtfully. "But I believe God understands those who long for beauty.

"It's no sin to want these things," he said carefully. "Even here, in the monastic life, we have beauty and art and pleasure."

Something in the chaplain's voice had changed. Lucrezia leaned forward.

"God made the world so beautiful." Fra Filippo closed his eyes, imagining the curtain between them might lift and allow him to look at her face.

"There's no shame in finding the world beautiful, and celebrating that beauty." He searched for the right words. "The holiest men have known this world is a *speculum majus,* a mirror of the Lord's kingdom. The beauty we find here and the beauty we make here pleases God, for it makes our world closer to His."

Lucrezia waited.

"God has a plan for each of us, my child. I don't pretend to know His plan, but I know we must trust in Him and pray that He sees fit to show us the beauty that we're part of creating. Trust the Lord. He sees everything, and knows everything."

Fra Filippo paused, but Lucrezia was silent.

"Remember, Saint Paul said that in surrender, there is holiness," he said. "Here, among the sisters of Santa Margherita, you will have a good life."

Still, she said nothing. The monk heard Spinetta cough as she waited on the cold stones for her turn in the confessional.

"For your penance, you must say twenty Hail Marys."

"Yes, Fratello."

"Say them when the sun is high and the garden surrounds you. And while you pray, you must look for the Lord's radiance in His world."

She waited while the chaplain offered his final blessing.

"Through the ministry of the Church, may God give you pardon and peace, and I absolve you from your sins in the name of the Father, and the Son, and the Holy Spirit."

Brushing past Spinetta, Lucrezia found her way to the garden. The humidity had lifted and the sun was bright but not scorching. The green hills were visible over the garden wall as she knelt on the straw scattered below a clump of hollyhocks.

"*Ave Maria, gratia plena.*"

Forgetting the required silence, Lucrezia began her act of contrition in a whisper. She tipped her face to the sky.

"Blessed is the fruit of thy womb, Jesus," she prayed, thinking of her own womb, which would remain barren forever. "Holy Mary, Mother of God, pray for us sinners."

When Lucrezia finished her penance she stood and stretched.

As if she'd been watching for some time, Sister Pureza stepped silently from the thick garden foliage. She handed the young woman a sharp blade and an iron trowel, indicating for Lucrezia to follow her to a chaste tree shrub, where the old woman demonstrated how to harvest the dark berries and fragrant flowers. Later, the berries would be pounded with nettle to make a tincture for the relief of weakness and pain in the limbs, and the flowers dried for sachets.

"You came to us with a chamomile sachet," Sister Pureza said, watching the girl's hands work. Lucrezia looked up, surprised. "I found it among your clothing, and I kept it."

Lucrezia felt the silver medallion, secret and warm inside the hem of her undergarment, and nodded.

"It belongs to the convent now," said Sister Pureza, who felt it was more important to reach Lucrezia in her sadness than it was to observe the Rule of Silence before communion. "But this doesn't mean you can't enjoy what you've made with your own hand. It's in the *infermeria*, where you may find sanctuary whenever you need it."

Lucrezia fell into a comfortable motion, cutting the chaste berry branches at their divide, dropping the petals into a burlap sack and the berries into the deep basket. Soon her fingers were working on their own, and Lucrezia let her mind wander to the chaplain's words. Was it truly not a sin to long for pleasure and beauty even here in the convent? By preserving her chamomile sachet, and reminding her of it at this moment, hadn't Sister Pureza just said as much, also?

In the week since her arrival, Lucrezia had been going through the days in rote motion. She'd knelt with the others, prayed when they prayed, followed Sister Bernadetta as the nuns moved from church to refectory to work. At night she'd tumbled onto her hard cot nearly asleep, and stumbled from dreams before dawn.

Now, in the heat of the garden, in the silence of the long day before the Holy Eucharist, something began to stir in Lucrezia's heart.

She felt it like a timid flower poking through the hard ground. And when Sister Pureza, who'd begun dragging clay pots into the shade, looked across the garden and saw the trouble easing from Lucrezia's face, she prayed the girl had found the surrender that would make the veil easier for her to bear.

Chapter Four

The Feast of Saint Lawrence, the Year of Our Lord 1456

Far from the serenity of the convent garden, behind the rusticated walls of the Palazzo Medici in the heart of Florence, the day was neither silent nor placid. All of Italy was embattled in a tug of wills among the great states of Milan, Venice, Naples, the Republic of Florence, and the papal city of Rome. Only that morning, a messenger had arrived from Naples with a letter from King Alfonso, addressed to Cosimo de' Medici. In the letter, the monarch had asked the Florentine power to affirm his allegiance to the court of Napoli. It was in the greatest interest of Florence that this alliance be forged, so that the Republic could stand together with Naples and Milan against Pope Callistus III and the leaders of Venice. The pope was ailing, but the alliance would be struck and the joint resources of Rome and Venice would be formidable. Florence needed to assert herself swiftly.

In his chamber, stout Cosimo de' Medici sat in the high-backed chair behind his mahogany desk and issued loud orders to his emissary, Ser Francesco Cantansanti.

"Tell Lippi I want to see immediate progress." Cosimo banged on the table for emphasis. "Tell him in no uncertain terms."

Cosimo de' Medici was head of the great banking family and the de facto ruler of Florence. His father, Giovanni di Bicci, had secured his fortune in the new mercantile world of Florence, and been named *gonfaliere* of the state. For three decades the Medici had been ascending in power through cunning and monetary influence, and Cosimo had extended the family's influence beyond his father's dreams. Now he wanted his son Giovanni to journey to Naples to secure their position with King Alfonso. Giovanni would carry a spectacular altarpiece completed by Fra Filippo Lippi, and the king's acceptance of this painting would affirm the alliance between Firenze and Napoli.

"We've already given the painter thirty florin, and you've spent my lire liberally on lapis and gold," Cosimo said. "This work must be the best the monk has ever produced. It must be the finest work Alfonso has ever seen."

The banker had entrusted the commission to his son, but Giovanni was young and unsure of how to wield his power, while Cosimo was a forceful man. A shaft of sunlight glimmered on the thick gold ring that encased Cosimo's fat pinky, and he made it known in a glance that he expected Ser Francesco to exercise the power and will of the Medici family in this instance as certainly as he'd done in the past.

"Pope Callistus will not budge in Rome's allegiance to Venice and the Doge," Cosimo said. "Milan is already allied with Naples. We must secure our position alongside them. And we will not go without the painting."

He motioned for his secretary to bring the sketch of the triptych that Fra Filippo had sent with the contract from May of 1456, securing their agreement. Cosimo spread the documents open on the dark table.

"We must get to Naples before the Sforza of Milan can advance a position against us, as I know they will try to do," Cosimo said. "We were promised the painting in one year's time. Now it's almost summer's end and Lippi's sent us nothing more."

No one understood better than Cosimo the power of the pen—

and the paintbrush—to sway public opinion. He had secured his influence over the Republic of Florence by turning it into the greatest city since the Roman emperors walked the earth. Poetry, philosophy, science, humanism, and the arts flourished under his leadership: Brunelleschi had completed the glorious dome above the cathedral of Florence, while Ghiberti's bronze doors gave the church baptistry the finest portal in the land. Michelozzo's palaces ornamented Florence's streets, and Ghirlandaio's spectacular frescoes graced the walls of the Medici Palace. Both Fra Giovanni and Fra Filippo had become great artists under his patronage.

The banker truly lived by his motto—*Operare non meno l'ingegno che la forza:* Exercise intellect as much as force—and the wealthier he became, the more he lavished on Florence. The allegiance with Alfonso of Naples was the linchpin that would secure the Medicis' future against the dual threat of Rome and Venice. But King Alfonso the Magnanimous was not an easy man to impress.

"Remind him that we could have had Fra Giovanni," Cosimo said, referring to the Dominican monk whom he had paid richly to complete a famed series of frescoes at the San Marco monastery. "The saintly painter would have been very happy to have another thousand florins for this commission."

Cosimo looked at the parchment before him, where Fra Filippo Lippi had sketched his plans for the triptych. The artist was irascible, and one always had to chase after him. But his work was filled with the brooding beauties and scruffy lads that ran the streets of Florence, and he used the perspective and style encoded in the new artistic treatises of the age to turn out works that were alive with earthly passions. For the King of Naples, Cosimo had commissioned a scene depicting the adoration of the Christ child in a manner newly conceived and filled with the progressive spirit of the age: a beautiful

Madonna, kneeling in a grassy wood, gazing at her sleeping infant. This was to be a work filled with all the mysticism of the Incarnation; a triptych that showed the hand of God written in leaves and stones and streams. Only this would be a gift fit for King Alfonso.

"I've entrusted this to you," the great Cosimo cautioned his emissary. "What did you accomplish three months ago in Prato when you delivered the contract? Didn't you make it clear to him then that our honor rests on his work?"

"Of course, Your Excellency. The monk is truly grateful to be in your good graces." Ser Francesco Cantansanti spoke with the greatest deference. "Believe me, sir, the painter hasn't forgotten the many occasions you've used your influence to protect him from the ecclesiastics."

Both men well recalled the sight of Fra Filippo, his usually generous frame thin with anguish, bowed in disgrace before the courts of the Archiepiscopal Curia in Rome the year before.

"Your will shall be done, Your Excellency," Cantansanti vowed. "By God's good graces I will return with evidence that the panels are well under way."

Cosimo nodded and dismissed the emissary with a wave of his hand.

Outside the chamber, Cantansanti shook his head. He understood Cosimo's impatience and would do his bidding with the painter. But he had to admit that he admired Fra Filippo's talent and irrepressible spirit. His ingenuity made him one of the most sought-after artists in Florence and, like it or not, Ser Francesco had to stay on the painter's heels.

Chapter Five

Fra Filippo Lippi sat beneath the window in his *bottega* and studied the nearly finished *Madonna and Child* for Ottavio de' Valenti. The likeness was breathtaking. He knew he should disguise the resemblance to Sister Lucrezia, but the Virgin's expression was flawless, her features exquisite. Even her high brow, as suited a woman of great intelligence, couldn't be altered, for this would change the face that illuminated all the Virgin knew, and all she understood. He needed only some madder for the Virgin's lips and the jewels on her crown, perhaps the smallest bit of lapis lazuli to enhance the blue of her eyes. In all else, this Madonna was perfect.

Hanging his worn leather pouch from his corded belt, Fra Filippo set out for the convent. Heading toward Via Santa Margherita, he passed an old prostitute who lived with her twisted arm in a sling, shunned now by all but the meanest men. As the friar said a silent prayer for the aged peddler of sin, he wondered at the fates that led some women to God, and others to Satan.

⚜

I've seen this in my father's garden," Lucrezia said to Sister Pureza, holding soft dill needles in the flat of her hand. "And this," she said, fingering the sharp rosemary spikes. "This I know from Beatrice's bread."

Lucrezia held a sprig of rosemary to her nose. The air was filled with the scent of crushed herbs. The heat had broken, and it was very soothing to be in the garden.

"Rosemary is used in the infirmary as well as in the kitchen." Sister Pureza bent slowly and snapped a sprig from the healthy bush. "It clears the head of all weakness and aches, and may be rubbed vigorously on the hands and feet to chase away pain. But married women must always take care, for too much of it can rid the womb of its blessed contents."

As the old woman examined the herb bush, Lucrezia studied her with quiet envy. In her time at the convent, Lucrezia's bleeding had not come as expected, and she wondered, not for the first time, if the Virgin in her wisdom had chosen to spare her from the monthly curse so that she might sooner become a placid older woman, like Sister Pureza.

Except during prayer and mealtime, or when someone needed her attention in the infirmary, Sister Pureza could always be found in the herb garden, tending the plants that served the body, the spirit, and the mind. Always, as now, she appeared to be fully absorbed in her task.

"Many herbs have more than one use," Sister Pureza said. "It's our duty to find the purpose God intends for each plant, in each instance, and then serve His will."

The garden was nearing the full bloom of late summer. The quince trees were heavy with young fruit, and the lavender spikes were just breaking into purple blossom. The stone birdbath was filled with small sparrows, sunflowers poked merry faces over the garden wall, and colorful hummingbirds hovered in the air collecting the last of the hollyhock nectar. There was a city of more than four thousand souls beyond the convent gates, but here they enjoyed the quiet solitude of a country garden, and the fragrant air took Lucrezia back to the carefree summers she'd spent at the family's small farmhouse above the hills of Lucca. Her life then had been filled with simple joys: planting pole beans and red peppers, packing fresh fruit preserves in terra-cotta jars, and climbing in the small *vigneto* with its clusters of deep purple grapes.

"Buckthorn is used primarily by the artisans, to obtain a deep green," Sister Pureza said as she showed Lucrezia how to take each branch gently in hand and find the place where it was nubbed. She trimmed carefully, shaping the unruly bush into a plump mound. Then she gave Lucrezia another set of iron shears, and the two worked side by side until Sister Simona appeared at the garden hedge, pale and silent in the bright sun.

"I'll attend to our Sister Simona, while you keep at your work," Sister Pureza said.

Lucrezia looked on as Sister Simona raised her arm to show a pustule of lumps on her skin.

"You aren't fevered," the old nun said to the thin one, putting a hand to her brow. "Perhaps it's something in the lye or ash from the washroom. I'm sure I have a poultice that will soothe this."

She ushered Sister Simona into the cool infirmary, leaving Lucrezia alone in the garden.

⚜

The friar swung open the low gate of the herb garden, and the back of a nun's black robe caught his eye. Only when he saw the delicate hand pruning the boxwood leaves did he realize it was Lucrezia.

She turned at the sound of the latch.

"*Benedicte*, Sister Lucrezia. Do I disturb you on this fine morning?"

Although she'd been working for hours, Lucrezia looked as fresh as dawn as she knelt beside the bush. Beside her was a basket filled with leaves.

"*Buongiorno,* Brother Filippo, and God's grace to you." Lucrezia ducked her head respectfully, and stood. Even at a distance, she could feel the energy that radiated from him. "I'm afraid Sister Pureza is tending an ailment."

"Who is ill?"

"It's nothing serious, only a rash on Sister Simona's skin. Would you like to wait?"

Lucrezia glanced toward the bench along the garden wall.

"I'm sure I can locate what I need," Fra Filippo said. He was a bold man but found himself subdued in the presence of this young woman. "And I'll have to ask Sister Pureza for what I need from the apothecary, for she's very jealous of her careful storage system."

Lucrezia looked up at Fra Filippo, avoiding his face but eyeing his white robe and the leather pouch that resembled the one her father's master dyer had carried. She remembered the delight his *Coronation* had offered her that first morning at the convent, and cringed at the intimacy of her tearful confession only days ago. Already the monk knew much about her, and she felt an urge to hurry him out of the garden.

"Maybe I can help you, Fratello," she said softly. "What have you come for this morning?"

Fra Filippo paused and smiled. Yes, he believed his painting caught the likeness of the novitiate very well. He looked quickly at her eyes, pleased to note they were as he'd remembered, with many shades of blue and even a hint of green sparkling in the sunlight.

"Lavender," he said. "And woad. I'll need the woad today, as it takes some time to ferment."

"Yes, it does," Lucrezia answered, flushing brightly at the mention of the fermenting process.

Fra Filippo saw she was biting her lip.

"I think you may know something about woad, Sister Lucrezia, although I can't imagine how or why."

It was true. Lucrezia knew that urine was needed to ferment the woad to its fine blue hue, and remembered her father's workers drinking their fill of beer and wine when the supply of woad arrived each year. She'd been told that the alcohol they expelled with their frothy golden urine provided just the right bath in which to soak the woad so it released its deep blue dye.

"My father," Lucrezia said uneasily. "He used woad to dye the blue silks in his shop."

Of course Fra Filippo remembered that Lucrezia's father had been a silk merchant. In fact, he remembered everything about Sister Lucrezia.

"Ah, yes," said Fra Filippo. "And are you familiar with other herbs, as well?"

"Yes, Fratello." Lucrezia nodded. "My father taught me what he could about dyes. He knew a great deal."

"Yellow," he said, curious to learn what else she knew. "I also need something for yellow."

"Back home we used saffron." The reply came to Lucrezia easily, for her father often had tested her knowledge in a game that went much like this one. "But I know it's very costly. The weld will yield a good yellow, too. I can gather some for you. Or better still," she said quickly, for in spite of herself, she was pleased to be showing off her knowledge. "Some *margherita*."

Both turned their eyes to the rich clusters of golden *margherita* that grew in the southern corner of the garden, and their gazes met. *Margherita*. Santa Margherita. Although he'd never seen it, Fra Filippo was suddenly sure that Lucrezia's hair was the exact color of *margherita*.

"Dandelion is abundant in the meadow, and if you soak it for as long as you can the magenta will be almost as deep as your *cinabrese*," Lucrezia said. Her discomfort faded, and words spilled off her tongue almost as easily as they had at home as she pointed to various leaves and plants.

Listening to her lovely voice, Fra Filippo was struck with a desire to fold back her wimple and then to paint her exactly as she was at this moment, a beautiful virgin in a garden *clausura*.

"Boxwood makes a fine green, Fratello, and we've been trimming it just today. Perhaps you'd like to take some of the leaves?" Lucrezia looked up and saw that the monk's attention had wandered. "But I've gone on too long, Brother Filippo, forgive me, I was carried away with myself. Let me get you what you came for." She bent clumsily to reach for a branch of lavender.

"No," Fra Filippo said a bit too quickly. "*Per piacere*. Go on. Your learning is impressive."

"Truly?" She responded earnestly. "I remember what you told me, Fratello, that the world is a *speculum majus*, a mirror of the Lord's kingdom. It eases me to think of this when I work, and when I pray I remind myself that everything is a mirror of God's miracles."

Lucrezia opened her palms in a small gesture meant to include the garden, the sky, the chaste berry, and even the heavy shears she'd been using to prune the bushes. For the first time since their meeting, Lucrezia smiled a real smile and met Fra Filippo's blue eyes.

"Fra Filippo." She spoke his name too quietly for the painter to hear. Then, adding volume to her voice, she said, "I'm very honored to help you in my humble way."

Fra Filippo saw her smile in relief and in shadow, and was imagining how he would capture it when the bell began to ring, calling the nuns to prayers.

"Already!" he cried, looking up at the sun's position in the sky and turning away. "I'll have to return after the prayers. I haven't yet gathered any supplies."

As he rushed from the garden, Sister Pureza emerged from the infirmary and stood beside Lucrezia.

"Fra Filippo must have a great many needs today," the nun said quietly.

"Yes, he was waiting for you." Lucrezia resisted the urge to glance at her face. "He said you guard the herbs carefully."

"Indeed." The older nun turned her eyes upon Lucrezia, and the young woman saw they were veiled. "I guard this garden and everything in it with great care. A gardener must be sure her plantings are not trampled or harmed by a careless hand."

The bell was still pealing. Sister Pureza took the shears from Lucrezia, and placed them carefully in the basket of boxwood trimmings.

"*Andiamo,*" the old woman said, turning to lead the way out of the garden. "It's time."

Chapter Six

Tuesday of the Tenth Week After Pentecost, the Year of Our Lord 1456

A glance at the fine steed tied just beyond his window confirmed Fra Filippo's fears: Ser Francesco Cantansanti had arrived.

Casting a hurried glance around his workshop, the painter considered making some order of the chaos. But the emissary had come to see his progress on the altarpiece for King Alfonso of Naples, and no empty showing of methodical workmanship would make up for his procrastination now.

"Ser Francesco." Fra Filippo flung open his door and greeted the emissary with a smile. "You've come for the *festa!*"

"Brother Lippi." Cantansanti nodded. He cut an elegant figure in his *farsetto* and the bright *calze*, silk stockings. *"Buongiorno."*

Unlatching his cape, Ser Francesco stepped into the *bottega*. He smiled slightly, remembering the year the great Cosimo had ordered Fra Filippo locked into his country workshop so he would finish a commission instead of roaming the streets at the devil's hour in search of prostitutes.

"The altarpiece?" he asked Fra Filippo without delay. "What is your progress? Cosimo wishes to set a date for Naples."

"Yes, yes, there's plenty of time to discuss these matters. First, my friend, can we share a glass of wine?"

The monk held out his jug, but the emissary shook his head. Fra Filippo took a swig and wiped his mouth with the back of his hand.

"Well, what of it?" Cantansanti looked around the cluttered workshop. "They're awaiting news of your progress in Florence. Where is it?"

There was no use stalling. Fra Filippo knew from the past that gamesmanship would only anger the emissary.

"It's not quite ready to be seen."

"Not quite ready?" Cantansanti raised his voice. "Why not? Do you think the Medici will wait forever?"

"The wings have been started." To his own surprise, Fra Filippo sounded calm. He could see Ser Francesco scanning the room, looking for signs of the altarpiece. "Please, let me show them to you."

The painter pulled the draped linens off two rectangular panels, each half as high as a man.

"Look," he said. "I've done as Giovanni and Cosimo instructed. Saint Michael's golden hair and silver armor shine like a Greek warrior's."

"*Bella.*" The emissary pursed his lips as he studied the carefully executed painting of Saint Michael, and the portrait of kindly Saint Anthony Abbot. "*Molto bene.* And the Blessed Mother? Surely you've transferred the sketch onto poplar by now?"

"Not yet," the monk admitted. "But the sketches for the central panel have been expanded, and the *disegno* is finished."

"*Per l'amore di Dio,* Filippo, stop stalling. I don't wish to bring an ill report back to Florence."

He stared at the monk. Outside, the sun had burned through the morning haze, and the men heard the horse braying.

"I'm staying at the home of Ottavio de' Valenti until the *Festa della Cintola.* I'll be keeping a close watch on you."

As Cantansanti walked slowly back through the *bottega* he paused in front of de' Valenti's *Madonna and Child.*

"This is splendid," he said, leaning closer to look at the lines of the face, the clear blue eyes. "The Madonna is exceptional—you must do the same for the Medici, Fratello. Remember who your greatest patrons are!"

Fra Filippo sank onto a stool, the bottom of his cassock creating a pool of white as he lifted the jug of wine to his lips and emptied it.

He felt the terrible weight of his obligations pressing down on him, and the painter recognized the feeling: it was exactly this burden that had plagued him the year before, when he'd been overwhelmed with commissions and in debt to his assistant for the grand sum of one thousand lire.

With no way of paying Giovanni di Francesco de Cervelliera, Fra Filippo had issued a false payment receipt, and the indignant assistant had brought charges against him. Soldiers of the court of the Archiepiscopal Curia had come for the monk that Monday morning in May as he was getting ready to put the details on a small *Nativity*. Two men seized him by the arms and dragged him before Antonino the Good, Bishop of Florence, where the painter was pronounced guilty almost before he could protest, and sentenced to a punishment of thirty lashes.

Stunned, he'd been carried directly into the jail and stripped of his robe. The monk's pleas for mercy fell on deaf ears, and the lash cut into his back cruelly. Afterward he was thrown into a cell, where he composed elaborate altarpiece designs in his head and dreamed of his mother's face, picturing her as the Virgin of his altarpieces, the Madonna of his private heaven, to keep himself from despair. On the fourth day of his imprisonment, Fra Filippo was awakened from a troubled sleep by a jailer who thrust before him a scroll containing the signature and wax seal of Cosimo de' Medici.

"Get up," the jailer said. "You're leaving."

Fra Filippo was eternally indebted to Cosimo. The powerful patron had saved his skin and paid his debts. He'd arranged for the painter to return to his work on the Prato frescoes, and helped in his appointment as chaplain of Santa Margherita.

Now, Cosimo and his son, Giovanni, wanted results. They wanted what Fra Filippo had promised: a glorious and newly imagined composition of the Madonna worshiping her babe in nature, in the forest, as no one had ever painted Mother and Child before. The idea was there, the sketches made. But the fulfillment of this vision required inspiration, and a work for the king of Naples demanded unsurpassed majesty to secure the future of Florence.

Fra Filippo felt his stomach churn, and wished for a soothing infusion from the herb garden of Santa Margherita. Shaken, he turned his face toward the window and caught a view of the small panel with the Madonna's face, her blue eyes.

"Lucrezia," he whispered.

The painter envisioned Lucrezia's face on the altarpiece. He saw her ivory skin, her golden hair set under a delicate *benda*. He saw the Virgin kneeling in the woods, sunlight dappling the ground where the Child lay.

The picture came alive in his head, so that he could almost hear the finches in the trees, smell the citrus and eucalyptus in the thick groves surrounding the virgin Lucrezia. Of course, Lucrezia was the answer to his prayers. If she could grace the central panel of his triptych for the Medici, the painter knew he could complete it with all the glory worthy of a king.

But as Fra Filippo meditated on the scene, it seemed to dissolve into an abyss.

To paint the Virgin in the forest, as he imagined her, Fra Filippo would need to gaze upon Lucrezia's face in full daylight. He would need her to sit for him as a model sat for a master, in his studio, where his paints and pigments and the heavy wooden panels were at his disposal during the high morning sun. He would need the impossible, for truly this would be not only difficult but improper. Unless he could make a plea to the prioress, and offer her something formidable in return for her consent, a novitiate would never be permitted to visit him here in his *bottega*.

Prioress Bartolommea de' Bovacchiesi was having a hard week. The rain wasn't plentiful, late summer sun was baking the ground, and she feared the convent's vegetable garden wouldn't yield a bountiful harvest. She'd received notice from Florence that Prior General Saviano would be spending eight nights in their hostel before and after the *Festa della Sacra Cintola*, and preparations had to be made. In addition, Sister Simona had broken out in a rash of strange pustules and been replaced in the kitchen by Sister Bernadetta, who had neither the skill nor the patience for turning out perfect rolls or rich black bread.

Dipping her stylus in a pot of ink, the prioress looked out the small window of her study and saw a large white mass moving toward her building.

"*Benedicte*, Mother," Fra Filippo said softly as he pushed open the door. "I pray I'm not disturbing you."

Mother Bartolommea took in the artist at a glance. His jaw had a trace of graying stubble, his corded belt sat crooked above his waist. Although it was midmorning, he looked as if he'd just dressed, and in haste.

"No, Brother Filippo, of course you may enter."

Unlike the novitiates, the prioress made it a point to meet the gaze of the men who stepped onto the grounds of Santa Margherita.

"*Per piacere*, do begin," she said with a hint of impatience.

"Thank you, Madre." Fra Filippo lowered himself slowly onto a narrow chair, his large frame overflowing the seat. "I've come to ask your concordance in a rather unusual request."

Prioress Bartolommea's dark eyebrows lifted, her wimple moving slightly with the motion.

"Of course I don't ask this on my own behalf, but in the name of His Excellency, Cosimo de' Medici, may the good Lord Jesus Christ bless and honor him."

The prioress nodded.

"As you are aware, the Medici have entrusted me with the commission for an altarpiece that is intended for King Alfonso of Naples." Fra Filippo paused so that the significance of these names might be impressed upon the prioress. "The fashion of the day is to work directly from life. It's said that soon all the best painters will require a model to sit for them. Only with the beauty of God's children right before our eyes, can one truly capture life."

Guardedly, Fra Filippo watched the expression on the prioress's features turn to surprise. He continued.

"In his own painting of the Blessed Virgin, Saint Luke shows her as a young woman with a sweet countenance. So I would have it be for my painting, Prioress. Clearly, if one is already fair of face, the task is that much easier, for the painter need not deviate much from the work of God."

Anticipating rejection, the painter quickened his speech.

"I humbly ask your permission, therefore, to copy the face of the novitiate Sister Lucrezia. She is young and fair and would be a fitting model for the Madonna. You are aware, of course, that my work must be done in my *bottega*, where I have my paints and tools at my disposal. It's the same for all the great masters who've paved the way before me. I believe it would please Cosimo—"

"What?" The prioress's eyes widened.

"I beg your indulgence, Mother. I wish only to create the most powerful work for the glory of Florence. With a model before me, my work would surely go quickly. My workshop—"

"*Per l'amore di Dio!*" Prioress Bartolomeo sputtered. "Would you have me violate the sacred rules of the *claustrum*, the very rules of modesty and sanctity laid down by Saint Augustine himself?"

The prioress's voice grew louder. "Fra Filippo, here at Santa Margherita we do not answer to Cosimo de' Medici, or to the King of Naples. We have only one master, Jesus Christ, Lord and King. I'll not have love of earthly riches destroy the good name of this convent!"

Fra Filippo pressed on. He'd seen her ire many times before, and the stout woman didn't intimidate him.

"I've clearly upset you, but in God's name, please believe I hope only to bring a greater glory upon Prato and upon this convent, of which I am a humble servant," he said. "I may be able to offer you a substantial repayment, and as with the prayers and words I recite here, my aim is to glorify God through my painting. Perhaps I have been misunderstood."

"It seems you are often misunderstood, Fra Filippo." The prioress spoke so quickly, she barely registered the monk's mention of substantial payment. "As in the courts of Bishop Antonino."

At her stinging remark, Fra Filippo rose from the chair. Immediately, the prioress became acutely aware of his imposing size and recalled the force of his anger.

"I've spoken out of turn, Chaplain. I apologize." She resisted the urge to speak hastily. "My worry over your request has loosened my tongue. Today, in these wretched times, a novitiate can ill afford any stain connected to her name."

"You needn't worry, Madre," Fra Filippo responded stiffly. "You've made yourself perfectly clear."

***

Reaching the grand palazzo of Ottavio de' Valenti, where Ser Francesco Cantansanti was staying, the painter stopped to catch his breath. The building's beautiful orange and blue tiles glowed in the dusky light and Fra Filippo admired their rich glaze as he lifted the brass knocker and waited for a servant to open the door.

"You've come with good news, my friend?" The merchant wore a costly black tunic trimmed in silk, and his arms were outstretched as he strode down the grand staircase.

"*Si, si,* your painting is completed," the monk said assuredly. "The final touches of *cinabrese* are drying now."

"Fabulous, maestro." The thick-haired merchant clasped a bejeweled hand over the painter's own. "I know my wife's spirits will be lifted when she sees your exquisite work. Please, I was just about to take my midday meal. Won't you join us?"

Fra Filippo was gratified to see Ser Francesco Cantansanti at the table in de' Valenti's inner courtyard, surrounded by potted lemon trees, flowers, and a bubbling fountain. The monk greeted Ser Francesco with the necessary bows, which the emissary accepted with an arched eyebrow.

"Only a day has passed," Ser Francesco said. "Surely you haven't finished the altarpiece already?"

"No, but I've found my inspiration, Your Emissary," the monk said. "You will have a masterpiece fit for a king."

The large table was laden with roasted fowl, fresh fruits, artichokes, cheeses, and bowls of thick bread soup. The monk joined the men as they ate, drank wine far richer than any Fra Filippo could secure for himself, and spoke of business in Florence and Rome.

"All the world waits to see who will take the place of Pope Callistus III, now that the depths of his illness have become apparent," de' Valenti said, eyeing Cantansanti. He poured more wine for the emissary.

"In Florence, the Medici family is grooming Enea Silvio Piccolomini, Bishop of Siena, for the seat," Cantansanti said easily, raising the wine to his lips. "They're expecting Piccolomini's detractors will propose the Archbishop of Rouen, but d'Estouteville is a weak candidate."

Fra Filippo listened closely to the discussion of papal politics. Whoever held the power in Rome also held the church's ample purse strings. It was well known that the sitting pope, Callistus III, had no great interest in art. But a pope with the Medici's backing would surely favor the family's beloved painters, and Fra Filippo counted himself among them.

"And you, Brother Filippo, what do you hear from the Carmelites?" Cantansanti looked across the table in a pleasant manner, and Fra Filippo answered in a way that could offend no one.

"I hear nothing but the prattle of the prioress, I'm afraid," he responded, tucking his belt up under his full belly as he spoke. "I hear only the worries of the nuns, which are the petty concerns and small jealousies of women everywhere. Vanity follows them into the convent, my friends, never believe otherwise."

The men chuckled.

"Of course, I also hear the daily groans of the provost," Fra Filippo said, rolling his eyes. He knew Inghirami irritated de' Valenti, and that Cantansanti had little admiration for the skulking man, either. "He's forever complaining that the parishioners aren't generous enough, my work on the frescoes not quick enough, and of course his preparations for the Festival of the Holy Belt are more demanding than ever before."

"The man is a genuine pox," de' Valenti exclaimed, and the men at the table laughed heartily.

Sensing the mood was right, Fra Filippo seized this moment to bring his business to Ser Francesco. He spoke quickly of the altarpiece for King Alfonso, describing in detail his vision for the Madonna kneeling in the forest, and the face that would complete that vision.

"Yes." Cantansanti nodded thoughtfully as the painter spoke. "Yes, this is what must be delivered to the King of Naples."

Emboldened, the monk described the face of a woman now living in the Convent Santa Margherita whose beauty surpassed even the finest paintings ever done.

"So there you have it, friends," Fra Filippo said when he was finished. "A pure young woman cloistered in Santa Margherita. Is there anything more fitting for the representation of the Madonna? Only a few things stand between us and this glory for His Excellency, Cosimo de' Medici, may the Lord Jesus Christ grant him strength and continued good health."

"There are many things of value in the city of Prato," Cantansanti said, raising his glass to Fra Filippo. "I'm certain we'll convince the prioress to do what's best for all."

*S*ister Camilla, sipping a cup of thin broth after Nones two days later, was sure she'd misheard the prioress. It couldn't be right. Perhaps the steam from the hot soup had garbled her words.

"Beg pardon, Mother, but I didn't hear you."

"I said," Mother Bartolommea repeated. "The novitiate Lucrezia will sit for Fra Filippo's altarpiece, an important work of great consequence which has been commissioned by the Medici. Under normal circumstances I would never allow it." She leaned closer to Sister Camilla. "But since he's a man of the Church, our very own chaplain, it's not the compromise it might seem at first. After all, his workshop is nearly, by extension, a part of our convent."

As Sister Camilla stared silently, the prioress continued in a whisper.

"For our trouble and generosity we'll have the *Sacra Cintola* here, at the convent, under my secret protection. Think of it!" she exclaimed. "With the Holy Belt in our possession, imagine what favors might be bestowed upon us from the Blessed Mother."

The prioress looked at Sister Camilla, waiting for her response. She leaned forward, and repeated herself.

"I said, Sister Camilla, that we shall have the Holy Belt, sacred relic of the Virgin Mary, here in our convent. Of course, it will be solely in my possession and no one will know but the two of us."

Sister Camilla put down her cup and stared at the prioress. She assumed the good mother was making some kind of joke.

"I'm only telling you in case something should happen," the prioress said. "But with the belt here, what harm could possibly come to us?"

Sister Camilla wasn't sure how to respond. She was sought out for her quiet wisdom, and wasn't one to make rash remarks.

"There's more." The prioress puffed out her chest. "I've also arranged for a beautiful new altarpiece to be commissioned for Santa

Margherita. The painting will depict the Madonna at the moment when she passes the *Sacra Cintola* to Saint Thomas. I shall be included in this painting as a patron kneeling before the Holy Virgin."

The prioress let out her breath, her figure seeming to shrink as she exhaled.

"I shouldn't be so boastful," she muttered, straightening her wimple. "It's against our Rule."

Despite her disclaimer, the prioress was deeply flattered by the notion of appearing for all of eternity in one of Fra Filippo Lippi's paintings. Like the famed Medici, the powerful Milanese Sforza family, and the lauded saints whose likenesses graced the churches of the land, Prioress Bartolommea de' Bovacchiesi's face would be painted and preserved for posterity, her special intimacy with the realm of the blessed on display for all to see and her entry into heaven virtually assured by this single indulgence.

"I'm sure you've thought this over with great deliberation and consulted the heavens for guidance," Sister Camilla said gingerly. "Lucrezia is under the guidance of good Sister Pureza, who will see to it that she doesn't neglect her duties or her obligations as novitiate."

"Indeed, Sister Camilla, I've done well, don't you agree?" The prioress nodded in great satisfaction. "Lucrezia will go to the painter's workshop only on Tuesdays and Thursdays after Sext, returning before Vespers. She'll be accompanied by a chaperone and will always bring a book of prayer and the Rule of the Order to study and meditate upon during her sitting. I've thought this all out carefully. The words of Saint Augustine will help the novitiate remain in the cloister in mind and spirit, if not in body."

Sister Camilla nodded.

"How long will this take?" the secretary asked weakly.

"We'll have the blessed relic here only until the Festival of the

Holy Belt. You see, in a way, the treasure of the Holy Mother is put in our protection as a matter of exchange. The belt here, and Sister Lucrezia at the painter's *bottega*. Nothing at all can befall us," she said again.

"Yes," Sister Camilla said, again lifting her cup. "Nothing at all can befall us."

"I've decided that *you* will be the girl's chaperone, Sister Camilla."

Sister Camilla furrowed her brows and sputtered, but the prioress held up her hand demurely.

"There's no need to thank me, Sister, truly," Mother Bartolommea said, lowering her eyes and achieving what she felt was the proper tone of modesty, at last.

Chapter Seven

A uniformed Medici messenger entered the convent courtyard on Tuesday as the sisters were finishing Sext prayers. Prioress Bartolommea quickly closed her prayer book and rushed outside. The messenger bowed, his silver sword glinting in the sun.

"Good afternoon, Prioress. I have been sent on the orders of Ser Francesco Cantansanti, emissary to the great Cosimo de' Medici."

"Yes," the prioress responded somberly. "We've been awaiting your arrival."

Feeling the stable boy's gaze, Mother Bartolommea turned and gave him a sharp look. He quickly resumed brushing a horse's tail.

"Perhaps you have something to deliver to me?" she asked with extreme delicacy.

The messenger withdrew a velvet pouch from his pocket, and handed it to her.

"I beg your patience while the sisters ready themselves for the journey," she said, slipping the pouch under her sleeve before turning to signal Sister Pureza.

At the sign from her superior, Sister Pureza helped the novitiates make their final preparations for the day outside the convent wall. Leading Lucrezia and Spinetta to the vestry, she gave each a coarse black *mantello* with a hood that covered their heads. Into Lucrezia's hands Sister Pureza thrust a worn breviary and a copy of the Rule of the Order, written in plain black script. Spinetta received a roll of blank parchment, upon which she would copy the Rule with ink from the stores in Fra Filippo's *bottega*.

"You must always be on guard when you are outside our walls," Sister Pureza said sternly to Lucrezia. She had expressed her objection to the outing, but had been unable to stop it. "Honor is our duty above all else. If you have a face the painter wishes to copy, then that face has come from God and should be used only to glorify God. Vanity is a great weakness, Sister Lucrezia. It's the devil's mask. Do not take it up."

As Prioress Bartolommea watched the stooped nun approaching the messenger, framed on either side by the willowy Buti sisters, she tried not to think she had made a terrible compromise. The *Sacra Cintola* was in her possession now, and this more than made up for the sacrifice of the convent. Soon a new altarpiece with her distinct pro-file would grace the main chapel of the Church of Santa Margherita and, hopefully, the metal chest in which she kept coins of silver and gold would again feel heavy in her hand. Surely the Holy Belt had the power to do this much.

As they stepped outside the convent gates, Lucrezia felt a breeze from the Bisenzio River. Her boots hit the rough cobbled stones and she nearly laughed at the familiar sound of tapping heels. She took a great gulp of air and lifted her chin. Above the city walls she saw the lush hills of Tuscany.

The messenger walked two paces in front of them, leading the way. Spinetta put her arm through Lucrezia's. Below her hood, Spinetta's eyes were bright, too.

"How good it feels!" Lucrezia whispered.

The sun beat down on their dark cloaks, but the heat didn't dampen the sisters' spirits.

"How strange that *I* should be chaperoning *you*," Spinetta said, thinking of the many years her older sisters had kept watch over her. "But I am so very glad of it!"

Lucrezia smiled at Spinetta, whose piety had become quite weighty these past weeks.

"Thank goodness I wasn't sent with dour Sister Camilla," Lucrezia said, and the two burst into laughter.

"Did you see her this morning?" Spinetta asked. "When Mother Bartolommea said Sister Camilla had to stay and help in the kitchen because Sister Simona and Sister Bernadetta both have the rash now, I thought she would burst."

"She would have been such a terrible bore to have along. I'm so happy that it's you, instead."

Walking slowly along Via Santa Margarita, the novitiates looked shyly at the women passing in workday clothes. One was bent under the weight of two heavy water buckets, another hurried by with a hog's head wrapped in brown paper held between her heavy arms.

"Look, it's Paolo, the boy who tends our goats," Lucrezia said, pointing to a young *ragazzo* who smiled when he saw them.

"Paolo, *buongiorno, garzone*," she called. The boy's feet were bare. With only a moment's hesitation, Lucrezia tossed him the parcel of thick rye bread and nuts that Sister Maria had wrapped in a cloth for their midday lunch.

A low moan came from a dark doorway on the right, and the sisters turned to see a ragged woman, one arm in a sling, the other held out for alms. The sisters paused, and their faces clouded.

"*Venite, Sorelle*," the messenger said, gently prodding them.

The sisters quickened their step, but their mood had grown somber.

"The prioress said I'm to sit for the chaplain in service to all of Florence," Lucrezia said in a low voice, bending her head toward her sister's. "But she was very careful in warning me not to let him draw too near, even in the course of his work."

"I've heard the prioress and Sister Camilla speak of the painter," Spinetta said carefully. "They say he's had much trouble with the Bishop of Florence, and that he's been known to consort with women of an indelicate nature."

Lucrezia hesitated, thinking of the power she felt in the monk's presence.

"But he is greatly admired," she said. "Perhaps the prioress is jealous because the chaplain lives outside of the cloister, where he has the attention and patronage of the great Cosimo de' Medici."

"Maybe," Spinetta agreed. She knew the prioress did worry about the convent's finances, and attached great importance to the alms that came to them as a result of the painter's position there. She told her sister so.

"And you?" Lucrezia didn't look at her sister directly. "What do you think of our chaplain?"

"I think he's fine," she pronounced. "When he comes through the front gates, it seems a breath of life is coming into Santa Margherita."

"Yes," Lucrezia said. "To create such beauty as Brother Filippo does must please the Lord, right, Spinetta?" She held her breath. "And it's honorable for me to help the painter if I can, isn't it?"

"You're only doing what's asked of you," Spinetta answered.

They rounded the corner and the tall bell tower, the prized campanile of the Church of Santo Stefano, came into view. Horses trotted briskly toward the piazza, merchant carts rumbled, and women called out to their children. Under Lucrezia's placid exterior, she felt a great excitement. In truth, she couldn't wait to see the monk.

."Look there." Spinetta pointed to the green and white bell tower visible over the rooftops. "That must be the *pieve*, Santo Stefano."

Only steps away from the Piazza della Pieve, the messenger turned up a small walkway that led to a simple stucco building with a thatched roof.

"We're here," Lucrezia whispered. She saw the monk peering over the edge of a tall window. He spotted the sisters, smiled, and hurried to the front door as the messenger knocked.

"Welcome," Fra Filippo said as the novitiates lowered their heads and their escort bowed. "I hope your walk was pleasant."

Lucrezia felt suddenly shy. She wished she were wearing a fine *cotta* and *fazzoletto* instead of the glum black robe and white wimple. She was surprised when Spinetta, always so demure, spoke first.

"Oh, Fra Filippo, we enjoyed our stroll, truly," Spinetta exclaimed. "The fresh air, the new sights. What a blessed fortune on such a lovely day, praise the Lord!"

Fra Filippo laughed.

"I do hope you'll feel that way after visiting my workshop," he said. "I'm afraid we must work indoors, and you might find it terribly dull."

"Not at all." Spinetta smiled boldly, her fine white teeth in a neat row. "I've been sent with the task of copying the Rule of the Order onto a parchment." She took the book from her sister, and lowered her eyes. "And I am to ask you for a pot of ink."

Usually such requests from the prioress vexed him, for he didn't like to part with his supplies. But on this day, nothing seemed too great to ask.

"Of course," Fra Filippo agreed.

The four stood in awkward silence. From the road came the sounds of wheelbarrows and the clinking metal of horse harnesses hitched to posts along the row of simple shops.

"Fratello," said the messenger. "I've been instructed to see the blessed sisters safely into your workshop, and will return before Vespers to bring them back to the convent."

"*Si. Scusi!*" The monk blinked as though awakened from a dream. "Please, Sisters." He motioned for the sisters to step over the threshold. "Please, come inside."

The novitiates followed the monk into the small antechamber, where a low wooden desk stood beneath a tiny window.

"You may sit here, Sister Spinetta, where it's pleasant," he said, whisking away a pile of dirty linens he'd collected for the kitchen girl to wash. "The light is quite good here, and will be for many hours."

Fra Filippo placed a pot of ink and some freshly washed quills on the table. On the other side of the table he put an earthen jug with water, and a small plate of cheese.

"I'm sorry it's not a richer offering," Fra Filippo said.

"It's very thoughtful, Fratello," Spinetta said.

Lucrezia stood silently to the side with her cloak still on her shoulders. She felt weak from the heat.

"*Allora!*" Fra Filippo said, as if he'd read her mind. "The day grows warmer. Please, take off your cloaks. Then, if it pleases you, I can show you around my workshop."

The painter had put away the many sketches of Lucrezia, and turned de' Valenti's *Madonna and Child* to face the wall. The *bottega* floor was swept, the wooden tabletops wiped clean, and the cobwebs were gone. The monk had hung a curtain around one corner of the room to hide a small pile of clutter.

"Of course I'm in the midst of many projects," Fra Filippo said. "The frescoes at Santo Stefano are only partially completed, and I've much to do on them still."

Fra Filippo fell into the familiar language of his artistry, and his confidence returned. He'd been a master of his craft for many years, and was comfortable in his studio no matter who might be his guest.

"Here are the sketches for the life of Saint Stephen, which will be on the north wall of the chapel." He showed them the carefully measured birthing chamber where the saint's mother would lie under a fine velvet blanket, and the synagogue steps where the saint would be confronted by angry rabbis.

Seeing the hidden staircases and complex architecture in his designs, Lucrezia spoke for the first time since their arrival.

"It looks very difficult, Fra Filippo," she said. "So many lines and walls, rooms inside of rooms."

"Ah, yes." The monk was pleased that she perceived, so quickly, what was important to his work. For a generation, painters had understood perspective thanks to the works of Brunelleschi and Alberti, but Fra Filippo strove to go beyond what had already been achieved. He pointed to the place where the fresco would turn the corner in the chapel. "See, here, the figures will appear as if they're stepping out of the painting and into the room."

Fra Filippo's enthusiasm for his work was contagious. As the sisters grew comfortable, Lucrezia felt her body begin to relax.

"It's necessary to secure many commissions at once, for I must keep all of my patrons happy or they'll find other painters to do their work. But of course, the altarpiece commissioned by the Medici takes precedence above all others. Their emissary has graciously arranged for your visit here so I might paint your likeness in full daylight."

He dared to glance at Lucrezia but her eyes were taking in the crowded workroom.

Against the walls were assorted panels of various sizes, some covered in a thin layer of gesso, others close to finished. Along the northern wall, shelves held numerous glasses and ampoules filled with substances that reminded Lucrezia of the apothecary shops she'd visited in Florence. Chunks of purple hematite and clumps of malachite lay out in the open air on parchment, ready to be ground and mixed for pigment. An assortment of brushes, knives, and other pointed objects lay scattered on the table. Lucrezia recognized paint colors that matched the numerous splotches she had seen on the painter's hands during the week. To cover the stale smell, Fra Filippo had placed clusters of lavender and lemon balm throughout, which lent their fragrant notes to the room.

"Brother Filippo, it's delightful!" Lucrezia exclaimed, forgetting her shyness. "How hard it must be to leave each morning."

"Indeed, we're lucky to have you at Santa Margherita," Spinetta hurried to add.

"The good fortune is mine, Sisters." As Fra Filippo answered, he saw a slant of light fall across Lucrezia's face. "Look at the sun," he said. "We must begin as soon as we can."

The monk settled Spinetta at the small table in the antechamber, and Lucrezia stepped in front of the large window that faced the busy piazza.

As he came back into the room, Fra Filippo saw her tuck away an invisible wisp of hair. He felt alive in every muscle, intoxicated by the golden light that filled the room and created dapples of color on Lucrezia's robe.

"Sister Lucrezia," he said gently. "I am indeed blessed to have you here, when I am in need of something truly magnificent and beautiful for my patron."

"I'm glad to be of service." Lucrezia's words were stiff, her voice a whisper. She couldn't lift her eyes to the monk's. "And ready to begin."

The monk picked up a silverpoint and arranged a fresh sheet of parchment on his drawing table. He found the stylus, and checked its measure. He took his time in these tasks. The girl's face, framed in the white wimple, was pale.

"We'll follow the light," he said. "You'll sit here, and I, here." The monk motioned to a three-legged stool for himself, a straight-backed chair with a generous straw seat for her, in front of the window. Lucrezia stood where she was.

"Fra Filippo, I've often wondered—" she began.

Perhaps it was nerves that spurred Lucrezia to speak. Perhaps she wished the monk to dispel the disquieting rumors her sister had shared only a short while ago. Perhaps she simply wanted to hear Fra Filippo's soothing voice.

"I've often wondered about the mixing of paint, and what some call alchemy," she said.

The monk's eyes narrowed slightly.

"I'm sure it's not much different than what's done to mix the colors for silk," he replied with a small shake of his head.

"Forgive me, but at home I heard people—learned, pious people—speak against painters who mix strange substances to make their colors," she said. "It's said they tempt the devil."

"You are so curious," Fra Lippi said, approval softening his voice.

"I'm sorry," Lucrezia answered quickly. Her father had only allowed her to ask questions when she countered them with great modesty. "I don't mean to question your piety. I only want to know what you think of this practice, and if it's one you use."

"I do mix my colors in the new ways of the masters among us," he said, pleased to share his knowledge with her. "But God—not Satan—has passed this secret knowledge to us, so we might make His world more beautiful. Many great works that grace our churches have the most brilliant colors imaginable thanks to what others foolishly say is the devil's temptation."

Lucrezia could see she'd broached a subject that interested the painter. The warm, open quality of his features, even the hint of sadness in his eyes, made her feel peculiar.

"Yes, in some ways it is like the colors mixed in the *tintori's* vats, certainly I should have known that. My apologies again, Brother."

"Don't be sorry," he said. "It's better, I think, if I show you how this is done. It's not black magic at all, but simply the mixing of earthly materials provided by the Lord." Fra Filippo removed an assortment of jars and containers from the shelves. Holding an amber flask, he opened the cork.

"Smell this carefully."

She did, and her eyes filled with tears, her nose burned.

"Ammonia." The monk corked the flask and put it down. Next, he opened a clay canister that held a small bit of ground yellow substance.

"Careful," he said as he extended the canister toward Lucrezia. "This is worse than the first."

Gingerly, Lucrezia closed her eyes and used a hand to waft the odor toward her nose.

"It's vile!" Lucrezia cried, clapping a hand over her face. Her gesture delighted the monk.

"It's sulfur," he said. "Now, we put these two nasty substances together." He took a tiny dab of each and put them in a clean jar. "We add quicksilver. And then, a bit of tin." Fra Filippo added a few drops of thick liquid. "We stir them, then add the power of fire."

The *frate* lit a fat candle and held the jar over the flame until the substances began to melt. After a minute he removed the jar from the heat and swirled it. A beautiful, glowing yellow appeared. He held out the jar for Lucrezia to see.

"And this is not a sin?" Beneath the simplicity of her question, Lucrezia knew she was asking about more than alchemy.

"No. This is beauty. And beauty isn't a sin." Fra Filippo's eyes were warm. "This is mosaic gold. And it will be the color of your crown."

"Not mine." Lucrezia averted her eyes quickly. "The Virgin's."

There was a step behind them, and the two turned to see Spinetta in the doorway.

"It's beautiful, Brother," she said, approaching the table and looking at the gold in the jar. "But isn't it only God who can change the nature of things?"

Lucrezia stepped back, putting distance between herself and the monk. She was shocked at her sister's forthrightness, but the monk seemed to notice nothing unusual. He answered pleasantly, although there was none of the intimacy Lucrezia felt when he spoke to her.

"Yes, Sister Spinetta, it's God who transforms all things. Of course we know he transformed Adam's rib into the beautiful figure of Eve when he saw that Adam was lonely. But He does not hide this magic from us."

At the mention of Adam and Eve, the agony of their faces in Masaccio's fresco came into Lucrezia's mind. She had no idea that, as a boy, Fra Filippo had watched the master painter executing that very scene in the Brancacci Chapel.

"As Jesus turned water into wine, so we turn the raw skin of the silkworm into skeins of beautiful fabric," Fra Filippo continued. "We take the elements of the earth and make them into colors to adorn our churches. From the garden in the convent, to the walls of the church, beauty isn't lost, only transformed. This is the way of the world."

Fra Filippo went to a basin and washed his hands, then dried them on a rag. From one of his worktables he unfolded a small parchment with the preliminary sketches of the triptych in brown ink.

"Now, let me show you what we shall do," he said.

He described his plans for the triptych and, as he'd done for Ser Francesco, Fra Filippo brought out the panels of Saints Anthony Abbot and Michael for the sisters to admire. He described the Adoration scene in detail, his vision of the Madonna kneeling in the fertile woods surrounded by verdant flowers and trees, the Christ child shining like a votive candle against the dark night.

"There are many lemon trees in the land of Naples, and cypress grow along the river that runs beside Prato," the monk said. "I'll include these, a deer, and also an Apennine wolf that roams the hills, docile at the feet of the Christ child."

Outside, the bells tolled from the campanile of Santo Stefano.

"The day is moving on," Spinetta said softly. "I should allow you to begin."

Fra Filippo and Lucrezia watched her return to the antechamber.

"We can start now, Sister Lucrezia." The monk indicated the heavy chair he'd placed before the window. "Please, sit."

"But didn't you say you'd paint the Blessed Mother kneeling on the ground?"

"Yes," he said. "But I won't ask you to kneel, not here on the floor of my workshop."

"But the Madonna knelt," she said, thinking of the Virgin's humble sacrifice, and her absence of pride. "She knelt in humility."

Fra Filippo couldn't help himself. He reached out and gently placed two fingers under her chin, tilting Lucrezia's face upward. She felt the warmth of his touch spread to her cheeks.

"You are humble as the Virgin is humble," he said, staring. "Humble in your glory. Certainly, if you wish, Sister Lucrezia, you may kneel."

He stepped back and she fell to her knees. She folded her hands in prayer, assuming the pose of the Madonna that she well knew. After that, the only sound she heard was the scratch of Fra Filippo's silverpoint, filling the parchment.

Chapter Eight

Tuesday, the Twelfth Week After Pentecost, the Year of Our Lord 1456

When Fra Filippo saw the sun shine into his workshop window, he rejoiced. Lucrezia would soon be arriving.

Since Thursday he'd spent many hours sketching her face, imagining the novitiate's small body layered in rich robes, and carefully contemplating the colors the Madonna would wear in his painting. Of course he'd settled on a costume that would best complement Lucrezia's flawless skin, selecting a rich *morello* purple for her outer garment, white silk for the trim against her throat, a *benda* sewn with delicate pearls to ornament her hair. After deciding on these garments he'd gone back and forth to the convent only to fulfill his duties and secretly study Lucrezia as she bent in prayer or worked in the *giardino* under Sister Pureza's watchful eye. He'd gone out of his way to ingratiate himself to craggy Mother Bartolommea, reminding her that God readily welcomed into His Kingdom those who had offered Him glory through art, and promising that as soon as the Medici triptych was finished, the altarpiece with her kneeling at the feet of the Virgin with Saints Margaret and Thomas would be his next undertaking.

"I'm more concerned that there be no impropriety, Fratello, than I am with my own portrait," Prioress Bartolommea had said, narrowing her small eyes. She'd reminded him that many people had surely noticed the two sisters visiting his workshop twice during the prior week, and that their reputation was her chief responsibility.

"Then you may be assured that the honor of your novitiates is well guarded," he'd said. "Because I've invited the venerable Fra Piero d'Antonio di ser Vannozzi to visit with the sisters this Tuesday, while I work."

"The procurator of the convent?" The prioress had raised her eyes in surprise, for she'd believed the administrator was still visiting a new convent in Montepulciano.

"Yes, he's returned home for the *festa* and promised me the honor of his company. If you have no objections, Madre." Naturally, the prioress had offered none, for the procurator was of a rank and power above her own.

After this exchange, Fra Filippo had returned to his studio in the dimming light and retraced the curve of Lucrezia's cheeks, the fine bones around the eyes. He'd worked until the girl's beauty seemed to breathe on the vellum, and then he'd drawn the fields in which the Virgin would kneel, using silverpoint to convey the textured grass, the abundant flowers, and the graceful cypress trees.

He'd worked as if in a trance, his intuition ignited and his talents in full force. Fra Filippo had known the embrace of more than a few women: Magdalena di Rosetta Ciopri had taken him as a lover in the hills outside of Padua, and a wool merchant's wife in Florence had invited him into her bed many times. These women, and others whom he'd paid, had given the painter great pleasure. But they hadn't changed the very colors of the world to him, they hadn't turned even simple tasks into moments of heady satisfaction. Only Lucrezia had done this, and her power over him was evident in the confidence that guided his hand.

The bells of Santo Stefano tolled, and the sisters and their escort arrived. The young women entered modestly, as always, bringing the fresh scent of the convent gardens with them.

"*Bellissima*," Spinetta pronounced when she saw the new sketches. "You've captured something in my sister that lives beneath the surface of her skin."

The monk stared at the sketch for the triptych, which was propped next to the large central panel. He looked from his own handiwork to God's: from the vellum to Lucrezia's face. And he was pleased.

"It's difficult to look at my own face as you've drawn it, Fratello," Lucrezia said, turning her eyes from the drawing. Although she'd been curious about her reflection many times, the desire to see herself in a mirror or in the water of a riverbed had been tempered by her mother's sharp words against vanity.

"It's a true likeness, Lucrezia," Spinetta said warmly, looking from the monk to her sister. "I can promise you that."

Lucrezia put a hand to her wimple and adjusted the way it sat on her forehead. She looked again at the drawing of her own face, graced by a halo.

"But it's not meant to be me," she said. "The painting depicts the Blessed Mother."

"So it does," the monk agreed quickly. "You've only lent your beauty, so we might glorify the Holy Mother together."

The monk studied their faces as the sisters examined his work, and reveled in Spinetta's thoughtful observations about the details he'd drawn into the Madonna's lush surroundings.

"Last month, even before I knew where the face of my Madonna might be found, I walked along the Bisenzio River to study the cypress trees and clouds I saw under God's eye," he said quietly.

God's eye. Lucrezia looked at the monk and wondered if he mocked her. Was he warning her that God's eye was upon them, even now? Could he know how she felt in his presence?

She coughed, and turned away.

"You aren't ailing, are you?" the monk asked.

"No, praise God." Lucrezia crossed herself at the mention of illness, as she had been taught. She didn't look at him. "I only need a sip of water."

He handed her a ladle of water, and saw her face was strained.

"Perhaps you need to rest, Sister?"

"Perhaps," she agreed, but still she wouldn't look at him. "But when I sit for you, I'll be at my ease."

A knock at the door broke what passed between them, and a spry man in a cape swept into the room.

"Piero!" Fra Filippo rushed to embrace his friend, kissing him on each cheek.

Piero di Antonio di ser Vannozzi, procurator of a dozen convents in Tuscany, took an artful look around the painter's hastily tidied workshop, glanced at the young, lovely faces of the Florentine novitiates, and smiled warmly.

"Fra Filippo, God has been good to you," the procurator exclaimed. He let his eyes rest first on Spinetta, and then on Lucrezia. The novitiates averted their eyes until they'd been introduced, which Fra Filippo did with great formality.

"I'd received word that two new souls had joined us at Santa Margherita," Fra Piero said. "But since you only arrived after Pentecost, I hadn't expected the bond between you and our esteemed chaplain would be so strong, so quickly."

Lucrezia flushed.

"I don't mean to offend you, good sisters," the procurator said. "We're blessed to have Fra Filippo with us in Prato, and anything we can do to help his work is an honor."

The procurator was a man of the world, as kind and forgiving of the sins of others as he was indulgent of his own weaknesses of the flesh.

He'd long admired Fra Filippo's work and had made the painter's stay in Prato very comfortable, introducing him to the city's wealthiest men and helping him obtain their commissions. The monk had counted on this friend to bless his friendship with the novitiates.

"I wish I could visit longer, but I have important business today," Fra Piero said after he'd taken a glass of wine. "In addition to the preparations for the *Festa della Sacra Cintola,* I've been asked to say a blessing over the newborn son of Massimo di Corona." The procurator's face dimmed. "The child is safe now but the mother is clinging to her life."

"Poor woman!" Spinetta said. "I shall pray for her."

"*Per piacere,* Sister Spinetta." The procurator smiled when he spoke, and his crooked teeth gave him a slightly impish look. "If you would be kind enough to accompany me on my visit, your prayers and *simpatico* nature might do much good for the child and his ailing mother."

Spinetta's glance wavered across the sketches Fra Filippo had spread open on the table.

"Surely Fra Filippo can spare you for a short time," the procurator pressed on. "We won't be gone long."

Spinetta gave a questioning look to her sister, who nodded slightly.

"It's true, sister," said Lucrezia, hoping the others couldn't see how she felt at that moment. "No harm will come to me while Fra Filippo is working."

"If it won't be an imposition, I'd like to go," Spinetta said to the painter. "And I've already made fine progress with my copying of the Rule."

The monk looked at Spinetta, her brown eyes rounder versions of Lucrezia's blue ones, and said a silent prayer of thanks.

"That's fine, my child," Fra Filippo said. "Please, Sister Spinetta, go with my blessings."

As the door closed, Lucrezia tensed. She and the painter were alone.

"Is there something you'd like to see, Sister Lucrezia, something I might offer you?"

"No, Brother," she answered so quickly that her tone startled him, and he responded at once.

"Sister Lucrezia, are you all right? Does something displease you?"

"Oh, no, Fratello." She was glad to be alone with the monk, even though she was nervous. "Truly, I enjoy being here and being part of your work. It is only . . ." Her voice trailed off. She didn't want to offend him, but if he was guilty of the crimes Spinetta said he'd been accused of, Lucrezia needed to know. She swallowed, and continued.

"I've heard many things about you, and I'm confused. Please don't think me rude, Fra Filippo. I have so much fondness for you."

Fra Filippo looked into her troubled eyes.

"Many things are said about me, and you have a right to know what is true. There's no shame in seeking knowledge, especially if it's done without malice. Sit, Sister Lucrezia, and I'll tell you whatever you ask."

The monk indicated the chair by the window, and found another for himself. They sat with the sun behind them, illuminating Lucrezia's features and shedding a soft light on the monk's brow. The window was high enough so that they could not be seen by passersby on the street.

"If you've been told that I've broken God's laws, then it is true," Fra Filippo said. He spread his knees under his robe and leaned forward, palms on his legs. He sat so close, Lucrezia could smell the soap he'd used to shave his face that morning. "But I've been poor and in desperate circumstance, and only in those moments did I succumb to the temptation of dishonesty."

In faltering words, Fra Filippo described the months after his father's death when he'd been forced to scrounge for food scraps in the Florentine streets, and how those lonely childhood nights haunted him still.

"The Carmelites raised me, and in return I took the vow. You understand, Sister Lucrezia, how the cloth came to me, and I to God?"

"I understand, Fra Filippo," she said quietly.

"I tell you, honestly, Sister Lucrezia, that I didn't wish to cheat my assistant, Giovanni di Francesco. I had nothing to pay him with, but as soon as I did, I planned to give him all I owed." He shook his head. "I brought a mark of *vergogna* upon my name. I did not act like a man of honor. Or a man of God."

She'd broached the subject, and Lucrezia felt responsible for the regret that dogged his features.

"Even the best men are sometimes accused of falsehoods, and their good names blemished," she said. Her eyes filled at the thought of her proud father. "The silk guild accused *mi padre* of producing *strazze de seda filada*, silk of inferior quality, but it wasn't true. My father's silks were always *seta leale*, of the finest quality."

She leaned forward. The monk reached out and touched her hands. She didn't move, but she remembered the prioress's warnings.

"It must have given your father great joy to see you in his shops and to have you by his side," Fra Filippo said gently. "And his silks must have been very beautiful."

"So beautiful," she said. His compassion gave her the courage to continue.

"It was by my father's side that I learned to appreciate beauty," she said wistfully.

"Yes." The monk's answer was pregnant with meaning. "The beauty of this world, that mirrors God's heavens."

They looked at each other, and she pulled away her hand. But what had passed between them opened something inside of her, and Lucrezia's words came pouring out.

"My father had so many words for *blue*." She shook her head. "*Azzurro. Celeste. Blu scuro.* No two pieces of silk ever looked exactly the same to him."

She spoke of the flowered *appicciolata* and the rich red *baldacchino*, the *beche* with gold laces which her father had commissioned for her sister Isabella's trousseau.

"It was so beautiful," she said. "It was so beautiful, I ache when I think of it."

As she described the fine weaves of her dresses with their *bredoni* sleeves, and her first summer dress of white *damaschino* brocaded with gold flowers, the monk imagined a young Lucrezia dancing in her garden like an angel in white.

"And now," she said, looking down at her plain black garment. "There's only this robe."

Fra Filippo began to smile.

"Dear Sister Lucrezia," he said, barely able to conceal his delight. He was almost as pleased with himself as he was with her. "I cannot create a Virgin in a simple black robe for the illustrious Alfonso of Naples. He's expecting silk and pearls and velvet."

Lucrezia looked at him cautiously.

"Why are you smiling?" she asked.

"If it pleases you and doesn't offend your sense of modesty, I would like to have you model in fine clothing, proper for the Queen of Heaven. How much easier it will be for me to copy the folds of silk and the shimmer of real pearls, rather than only to imagine them."

"But it's impossible," she exclaimed. "I've given away all of my clothes."

"It's not impossible. I have fine clothes here in my workshop, courtesy of my great patron, Cosimo de' Medici."

The monk saw Lucrezia blanch.

"It is the custom, of course," he said gravely, checking his enthusiasm. "Models who sit for the great masters costume themselves in the appropriate garments."

"What garments would the Virgin wear? And how can you trust I'll do them justice?"

Lucrezia felt a heady excitement as Fra Filippo crossed to a small trunk in the rear of his *bottega* and began to remove delicate garments fit for a Florentine noblewoman. She saw him lift a *cotta* of *morello* purple, its sleeves decorated with small flowers and lined in silk, a *benda* sewn with pearls, and a thin gossamer veil.

"It's wonderful," she cried, thrilled at the thought of once more feeling the rush of silk against her arms, the gentle weight of a *frenello* winding through her hair.

The monk didn't trust himself to look at her face.

"If you will wear them, Sister Lucrezia, it will be of great help to me."

She carefully took the *cotta* from the monk and draped it over her folded arm. Gingerly she held the *benda* in the flat of her hand.

"I'm sorry I don't have a finer dressing room." Fra Filippo indicated the curtain he'd hung around the clutter in the back room of his workshop. "You may change there."

Quickly, before she lost her nerve, Lucrezia stepped behind the curtain and slipped off her robe. Standing in her *panni di gamba*, she felt the gentle weight of the silver medallion of Saint John the Baptist sewn into the hem, and a wave of doubt washed over her. Beyond the curtain, she could hear Fra Filippo moving something across the floor of his workshop, and an image of her father came into Lucrezia's mind. He was looking down at her, his dark eyes steely with disapproval.

"Stop," he whispered to her sternly. *"Disgraziata."*

Lucrezia's chest tightened.

"I followed your rules, Father, and look what's become of me," she whispered to herself.

Beyond the curtain Lucrezia heard the painter clear his throat loudly, and she clamped her lips shut.

I'm a novitiate consigned to God, she argued within herself. *I'm only modeling at the instruction of Mother Bartolommea to please the Medici. And to please the King of Naples.* Her fingers brushed over the velvet ribbons of the sleeves, which seemed to quiet her fear. *I can't be a signora, but I can pretend. There's no harm in pretending.*

She pulled the *cotta* over her head.

When he heard the gentle slide of the curtain, Fra Filippo looked up from his easel. The late afternoon sun illuminated the gold of Lucrezia's hair, wrapped tightly in a bun. Like a wreath of silk, the *benda* sat upon her head, the tiny pearls shimmering. The silk *cotta* stretched across her shoulders and chest, her sleeves swelling out like an angel's wings, the bodice hugging her waist and falling in heavy folds, just past her stockinged feet.

"Lucrezia." Fra Filippo breathed her name with such longing and disbelief, that he didn't need to say anything else. Lucrezia closed her eyes, afraid she might faint. As she did, the painter quickly picked up his pencil.

"Stop, please. Stay as you are," he said.

Lucrezia froze. The room, indeed the rumble of the streets of Prato outside his workshop, seemed to hush. The monk didn't take his eyes from her face or speak another word until he'd captured her expression, the gentle curve of her mouth, the way the *benda* sat perfectly on her forehead. When the sun passed over the neighbors' rooftop he touched a red crayon to the place where the Virgin's lips were parted.

"Enough," he said gruffly. "You must change back into your nun's robe."

Lucrezia didn't speak. She'd stood in one place for so long that she'd nearly forgotten where she was. Her muscles were stiff, and she ached. But the look on the painter's face was deeply satisfying.

"You've allowed me to see my vision come to life," Fra Filippo said. "Now hurry."

Behind the curtain, Lucrezia's fingers shook as she worked the buttons on the *cotta*. She pulled off the *benda*. She was being foolish, even more foolish than she'd been as a girl in Lucca, pretending to be a bride under her homemade bridal crown. To imagine the monk had looked at her with anything more than the eye of a painter entranced with his own heavenly vision was blasphemy—a terrible sin of pride and vanity. It was surely the urge of Satan in her.

Lucrezia tugged on the robe, and straightened her wimple. She had no looking glass, but when she stepped from behind the curtain, she knew the Lucrezia of splendor was gone, and she was bitterly thankful.

When the procurator and Spinetta returned she was sitting in the antechamber, waiting. She pressed at the wrinkles in her robe as Spinetta entered, her face drained.

"Oh, Lucrezia." Spinetta sighed. "I wish I could have done more for the poor woman, but I fear she will soon be with the Lord."

Lucrezia prepared to speak, but as she opened her mouth, the deep voice of the monk boomed forth.

"Sister Spinetta, I am sure you gave the new mother great comfort," Fra Filippo said from the doorway to his workshop. "Now you must return to the convent. Your escort will be here shortly."

Outside the *bottega* the skies were turning a deep blue. The de'
Valenti servant appeared, and the sisters said their good-byes hastily
before following him onto Via Santa Margherita for their brief walk
home.

"We are so fortunate," Spinetta whispered to Lucrezia as they
both breathed in the fresh evening air. "There is so much in this
world we don't know about suffering."

"Yes, Spinetta, it's true," Lucrezia replied, glad they were walking,
and that she did not need to meet her sister's eyes. "There is so much
that we don't know."

Chapter Nine

The Feast of Saint Bartholomew, the Year of Our Lord 1456

The sky went from midnight blue to deep black, and still Lucrezia tossed on the narrow cot in her cell.

Since sitting for the monk in a *donna's* fine dress, she'd been in the grip of an impossible fantasy. By day, when she busied herself in the garden, she was able to keep up the appearance of simple obedience. But alone, she thought constantly of the monk's face. When he'd seen her in the silken gown, it seemed to her that Fra Filippo had looked at her not as a nun, but as a woman. Of course he was a monk, she a novice, and any emotion that passed between them was shrouded by their robes. His affection for her could be nothing more than that of a priest for his flock, she knew. Yet she could not stop imagining his hands on her face, or pretending they might share what could never be.

Lucrezia heard an owl far off in the trees beyond the convent wall, and freed a hand to rub the aching muscles along her shoulder. In the days since she'd last visited the monk's studio she'd worked hard in the garden, cutting herbs and culling roots that would be mashed and fermented for Sister Pureza's healing tinctures. Only this morning she'd put on hard boots and used a spade to dig up a mulberry bush. She'd dug strenuously, bringing up calluses on her hands and a sweat on her brow. Such vigorous work had felt good to her young body, and she'd gladly taken the roots to the well and rinsed them thoroughly. Then she'd hauled them in a wheelbarrow to the chopping block next to the infirmary. A huge iron cauldron in the convent's kitchen had been fired, and the mulberry roots simmered there still.

After so much work, she'd expected to sleep well. And yet her mind raced. Lucrezia had never known a man such as Fra Filippo. The purpose and concentration he showed when he worked reminded Lucrezia of her own father. But the painter was a man who looked at her not as a father looked at his daughter, but as she imagined a man might look at a beautiful woman. Perhaps, even, at a woman he loved.

Secretly, she'd read the bawdy tales of Boccaccio's *Decameron*, which told of the fever a man and woman might feel in each other's presence. But she hadn't imagined how such a fever might feel, nor had she seen such evidence in her own life. There had been one stolen kiss with her betrothed, and it had raised only a sharp burn from his stubble on her cheek. But when she thought of Fra Filippo, and smelled his earthy musk, she imagined laying her cheek against his chest, letting him hold her in his arms and whisper all that he knew of art and beauty. And love.

Before her father's death, Lucrezia realized, she'd been a girl. Now, under the shadow of the veil that was to wed her to the Lord, she was becoming a woman. And there was no one with whom she might speak of such things. Her mother had never been her confidante. Her sister Isabella, to whom she might have spoken if they were near each other, had followed the monsignor's directions and refrained from writing to Lucrezia at the convent. Spinetta was too young, and too pious. It was impossible, anyway. Lucrezia knew that many clergymen consorted with courtesans and took lovers whose names were disgraced by their very surrender. And she was certain that a novitiate who felt this way in the presence of a monk was tempting the *malocchio*, the eye of the Evil One.

With no earthly women in whom she could confide, Lucrezia turned to the Virgin. In her cell, after the others shut their doors and extinguished their candles, Lucrezia prayed. For two nights she'd knelt on the rough stones and whispered what raced through her mind. Her words were no louder than the scamper of mice in the night stair.

"Holy Mother, forgive me for putting on fine clothes when I've pledged to follow in your ways. Forgive me for longing for what I can't have. Forgive me for what I feel under the painter's gaze. Help me, please help me, Blessed Mother."

Lucrezia prayed through the night and the monk's face floated through her mind; her father's hands, always at work, roamed across the expanse of her prayers. She saw a broken image of her own face under the crown of the Virgin and her body flamed with shame.

"Those who know such things say the painter's art is for your glory and for the glory of your Son," she prayed. "I humbly ask you to guide me, Mother Mary. I beg you to keep me on the righteous path."

Lucrezia remained on her knees as the moon rose. She prayed until the sisters assigned to Matins closed the dormitory door with a thud. Then she crawled into her cot, wrapped the blanket around herself, and tossed fitfully. Dragged from sleep by the bell that tolled for Prime, Lucrezia felt the grit beneath her eyelids and the ache of tired limbs. Her heart was heavy, yet at the same time she felt a joyful expectation. It was Thursday, and she would see the monk after Sext.

Robed figures rustled silently through the candlelit dawn as Lucrezia and Spinetta took their place in the church and knelt. The young novitiates bowed their heads in what seemed to be the same humble manner as before, and said their prayers with the same quiet vigilance. Yet everyone at the Convent Santa Margherita knew the escort had returned thrice for the sisters, and nuns who watched Lucrezia and Spinetta closely were aware that the novitiates had begun to change. Some thought it was vanity; others, pride; still others, who were generous in their assessment of human weakness, thought the sisters felt guilty about leaving the convent to visit the painter.

On her knees, Sister Pureza looked at Mother Bartolommea and waited for the prioress to turn.

"What is it, Sister Pureza?" The prioress's voice rasped with her first words of the day.

"Sister Lucrezia looks very worn. I fear the long hours with the monk are taxing her," she said.

"What trouble can it be to sit all day while the painter makes an image of your likeness?" Prioress Bartolommea snapped.

"I haven't had this experience, so I can't attest to its demands," Sister Pureza said. "But I have sat all day in contemplation of the Lord, and I know how tiring that can be. To pray all day is one thing, for at least it nourishes the spirit. But to sit for a painter must feed a sense of vanity and pride. Perhaps Sister Lucrezia is struggling in her prayers."

Prioress Bartolommea knew well the sin of pride, and how it could plague the spirit.

"She isn't the first novitiate who's struggled to adjust to the rhythms of cloistered life, and she won't be the last," said the prioress. "If she's troubled by her duties or by her conscience, she'll speak them in confession, and that will clear her mind."

"Perhaps," Sister Pureza said. "Although the monk is her confessor, and this will certainly come to bear on how she unburdens her soul."

Noticing the eyes of the others upon her, Sister Pureza shut her lips and finished the morning's contemplation in silence. When Lucrezia passed, the novitiate avoided her gaze.

At breakfast, instead of the usual buns and watered wine, the sisters found a generous fig *torta* and a pile of boiled eggs in a copper platter.

"Fig *torta*," Sister Bernadetta exclaimed. She clamped her hand over her mouth to silence herself, but the others voiced their appreciation.

"Blessed be the Lord, who sustains us with all good nourishment and sends us what we need to serve in His name." The prioress spoke from her position at the head of the table. "This morning, as we take in sustenance that is indeed glorious in the Lord's bounty, we thank the Medici, who sent this harvest of riches in honor of the Feast Day of Saint Bartholomew. We thank the bountiful family of Florence and pray for their continued prosperity."

At the mention of the Medici, all heads turned toward the novitiates, and Lucrezia reached under the table for Spinetta's hand. Despite the special food, she took only the smallest morsel of the fig *torta*, and was the first to rise when they were dismissed from the refectory.

"Certainly you won't send the sisters to Fra Filippo's *bottega* today," Sister Pureza said to the prioress after the nuns had filed out. "You see Sister Lucrezia is pale. And let us not forget she is in mourning for her father, who passed to Our Lord only some months ago."

The prioress's face darkened. What Sister Pureza said was true. But she also knew that Ser Francesco had arranged for the sisters to go to the painter's workshop every Tuesday and Thursday until the week of the *Festa della Sacra Cintola*. She'd accepted the gifts from the

Medici without question, and as long as she still had the Holy Belt under her bed, she could not turn away the escort when he came for the novitiates.

"Sister Lucrezia isn't fit for an outing," Sister Pureza continued. "Perhaps it's best if she remain in the convent today. I can prepare a tincture that will surely renew her, and if our good chaplain spends his day in contemplation as he should, then he won't miss her at all."

Mother Bartolommea nodded soberly. She knew her old friend was right. When the escort arrived she would send the monk a brief note telling him that Lucrezia would not be leaving Santa Margherita today.

The bells tolled as Lucrezia waited in the garden for Sister Pureza. She looked around at the bee balm in full flower and the coriander already going to seed. Kneeling on the narrow brick walk, she crumpled a vervain leaf and inhaled its scent.

"Good morning, Sister."

The novitiate stood when Sister Pureza arrived, and the old woman nodded. Her eyes were deep and kind. But they were commanding, as well.

"Sister Lucrezia, I fear we've taxed you too soon after your arrival at Santa Margherita," she said, gently taking the novitiate's arm. "The prioress has seen your fatigue, and believes it is best for you to remain here with us today."

Lucrezia held her breath. She was afraid that anything she said would reveal her confused feelings for the monk.

"I am terribly tired, Sister." She kept her eyes averted. "But our chaplain said the great Cosimo de' Medici expects the altarpiece in less than a year's time, so he might present it to the King of Naples. Surely if so much is asked of the chaplain, I can fulfill my own small role."

"Worldly matters aren't our concern," Sister Pureza said as she led Lucrezia to sit beside her on the garden bench. "There are always great matters in the world of men that press upon their duties. This is the world God made, and it is how men live within it. When you were with your father in Florence, you saw business conducted with great urgency, I'm sure."

The old nun waited for Lucrezia to nod before continuing.

"I, too, spent my girlhood among luxuries and those who live for them. There are few who know that I once wore fine dresses and attended wonderful gatherings in the homes of great men. But I did, child. I know how hard it is to leave that world behind."

Sister Pureza chose her words prudently.

"Prato is lively, and although some of our sisters do good works in the city, venturing out so soon after entering the cloister has presented you with what may seem to be a choice in the hand of your own fate. I'm old, but I remember how my heart was troubled when I arrived inside our walls. I remember wishing there might be some other way for me."

Lucrezia saw the woman's face go slack, as if remembering a great sadness.

"Did a tragedy fall on your family as it fell on ours?" Lucrezia asked.

"Yes." Sister Pureza didn't hesitate in her answer. "A tragedy befell my family. And I found refuge here with the good sisters of Santa Margherita. At first I resisted. But when God calls you to His cloister, it is best to accept His protection. When you let go of the world beyond our walls, only then can you see how vast the spiritual life is."

Lucrezia bowed her head.

"Going to the monk's workshop has taxed you," the old nun said. "I wish you not to return."

"But the prioress has made a promise to Fra Filippo. It is not mine to revoke." The thought of never returning to the painter's studio filled Lucrezia with dread. "I must do as I'm told, and go where the Lord sends me. Isn't that right?"

Sister Pureza saw a pallor spread across the novitiate's cheeks. Whatever God's will, she wouldn't allow the girl to become weak and ill.

"Come, Sister Lucrezia. You've worked many days in the garden, but haven't enjoyed the benefits of our labors."

Sister Pureza led Lucrezia to the bluestone that marked the entrance to the infirmary, and crossed to one of the small pallets against the wall.

"Sit," Sister Pureza said, and Lucrezia obeyed. In a few moments, the nun returned with a flask filled with a cloudy liquid.

"My head is very muddled, Sister," Lucrezia said. She let herself lean back on the cot. "I'm not certain why God has sent me here."

"You must trust that God knows what is best. All is in His hands." She gave the flask to Lucrezia. "This is vervain root and valerian. It will soothe you."

Lucrezia made a bitter face, but drank the tincture. Sister Pureza handed her a ladle of water, and the novitiate took that, as well.

"You must rest, Lucrezia. You must not allow yourself to grow weak, for in weakness the Devil finds and tempts us."

Lucrezia wanted to ask the nun if she'd ever been tempted by the Evil One, but she remained silent, and closed her eyes. She really was very tired.

As Sister Pureza watched the novitiate's chest rise and fall, she thought back to her own arrival at the convent so many years ago. She'd come to Santa Margherita with a child in her womb, and had done little but sleep, day and night. Like Lucrezia, she'd fought God's will. But in the end she'd seen His wisdom, and surrendered to it. Following her terrible loss, she'd turned to the midwifery skills she'd learned in secret at the side of her childhood nurse, and studied the medical works of Trotula di Ruggerio to strengthen her knowledge. After the Black Death claimed the best midwives in the valley, young Sister Pureza had found she was truly gifted in the birthing arts. For this she was ever grateful to the Lord.

Leaning over to loosen Lucrezia's wimple, Sister Pureza smelled the scent of chamomile. She slipped the wimple over the girl's head and patted at beads of sweat on her forehead. The old nun wished she could tell the novitiate how ferociously she, too, had suffered and fought in vain against her fate. But the secret shame of Pasqualina di Fiesole had been buried long ago, and her soul reborn as wise Sister Pureza. No one but the prioress knew the secrets from her past, and that was as she wished it to remain.

Chapter Ten

Seated in the confessional, Fra Filippo knew many of the nuns by their fragrance: Sister Camilla smelled of dust and camphor, Sister Maria of wheat and rosemary, Sister Pureza of the sage she used to smudge away impurities. Sister Simona, whose tooth ached perpetually, he knew by the clove she kept hidden in her lip, and he recognized the prioress by the whiff of sulfur from the candle that burned as she studied the convent's books.

When the scent of chamomile filled the small booth, Fra Filippo immediately knew Lucrezia had come to him. He strained to see her face through the cloth that hung between them.

"Fratello, please forgive me for not coming to your workshop," Lucrezia whispered as soon as she'd knelt. "I wanted to send you a message, but it was impossible. Sister Pureza insisted I rest, and she was right. I was troubled, Fra Filippo, and I am troubled, still."

Beneath the curtain she could see Fra Filippo's robe, his feet in their rough leather sandals. She rushed on, before he could speak.

"I fear that putting on the finery was a grave mistake, Fra Filippo, not because you gave it to me, but because of how it made me feel, and the vain thoughts I had when I wore it. Please, Fratello, I fear that what we've done—even in the name of the Virgin—is a sin."

Fra Filippo cleared his throat. He was determined to perform his role in the service of Lucrezia's soul.

"My dear sister, first I wish to grant you absolution for your sins in the name of the Father, the Son, and the Holy Spirit." He raised his hand, and made the sign of the cross. That done, he continued more gently.

"Surely the Lord moves among us in ways we do not understand," he said. "Sister Lucrezia, I, too, am torn."

The monk spoke tenderly. Lucrezia's mouth was dry.

"I can't pretend your beauty doesn't move me," he said. "I fear I can't be trusted to offer you the most holy guidance."

Lucrezia closed her eyes and saw flashes of red.

"What are you saying, Brother? Are you saying I was wrong to sit for you in the fine clothes?"

"Certainly not," Fra Filippo rushed to reassure her. "Others have dressed in appropriate costume so I might paint them in the fullest representation of the Virgin."

"There have been others?" Lucrezia asked. Her eyes flew open and she looked down at his hardened toenails and allowed herself to feel a small revulsion.

"There's never been another like you, Lucrezia." He faltered, but continued. "I can't trust my feelings. I'm unsure of my heart. That's why I cannot in good faith hear your confession. I'll ask the procurator to attend to your confession in the future. This is best, Sister Lucrezia. Please, let us not continue."

Lucrezia blinked, and spots danced across her vision.

"Forgive me. It is for the best," he said. "Now go in peace."

Silently, Lucrezia slid open the black curtain and hurried from the confessional, not daring to glance back.

*T*he procurator stood at the foot of the monk's bed, clutching a sketch of Lucrezia.

"You're being tempted, Filippo, I see it," he said. "Wake up, we must talk." Fra Filippo opened his eyes and stared into Fra Piero's scruffy face. Overhead, the crucifix hovered on the wall of his small bedchamber.

"Damn you," the monk grumbled. "Go away."

"Come on, Filippo, rouse yourself." Fra Piero shook the mattress and waved the parchment in his hand. "You can't deny what I see with my own eyes. You want the novitiate."

The procurator was turning the sketch this way and that, examining Lucrezia's luminescent beauty. "I see how you're spending your time—caressing the girl with your silverpoint, seducing her with every stroke of your charcoal."

Fra Filippo tumbled from his bed, used the chamber pot, and took his robe from its hook on the wall, pulling it over his head.

"I go away for two months, and return to find you this way," Fra Piero said. "Maybe you've forgotten your disgrace, but I haven't. I was there in Florence and again in Legnaia. If you're hungry for young flesh, let me find you someone less conspicuous, less risky."

The monk rubbed his face briskly.

"I don't want a whore," he nearly growled. "How dare you compare the virgin of Prato to a whore of Padua, to a *puttana* on the streets of Florence?"

"Calm down, Filippo," the procurator replied. "We're men, we have needs. I travel widely, I know chaplains and monks who indulge themselves with farm girls, courtesans—even a few who amuse themselves with boys."

Fra Filippo grimaced. He knew there were monks who preferred a man's body to a woman's soft flesh, but he'd never known any who admitted as much, and he was glad of it.

"I see the way you're drawing her face." Fra Piero whirled around. "If you won't deny your lust for her, then at least hide it better."

"That's just it," the monk said. "I fear this is far more than lust, *amico mio*."

Fra Piero was used to hearing the painter speak in grand superlatives. He ignored the last remark and walked from the kitchen into the *bottega*, which was filled with morning light. It was early, and the kitchen girl had not yet arrived to help with the morning's chores. There were soiled rags flung on the floor, jars of paint scattered about, and sketches propped everywhere.

Standing before a large wooden panel, Fra Piero examined a splendid throne and luminous angel's wings, and shook his head. Even the lauded works of Fra Giovanni the Dominican, beloved by the Medici and by many in the Orders, couldn't match this in sheer celebration of earthly beauty.

"This is the work for the Medici? This is why our friend Ser Francesco has come again?"

Fra Filippo nodded.

"You've surpassed yourself, Filippo. But you'll bring a great pain upon all of us if you're not careful. Prudence, maestro!"

The painter looked at the sketch in the procurator's hand, and recalled the haze of unreality that he often associated with his best work.

"Lucrezia Buti," Fra Filippo said. "I've never met a woman who could bring me to such heights."

"The girl is a novitiate, Filippo," Fra Piero exclaimed.

"I'm not a fool! I've already refused to hear her confession—you must go in my place, Piero."

The procurator sucked in a breath.

"So it's as I thought."

"It's much worse," the monk said. "When I'm near her, the very quality of the air and light seems to change. Everywhere I go, I see her face."

"For the love of Christ, protect yourself!" the procurator said. "If you must have a woman, Filippo, don't take a novitiate. I beg you, don't see her again. Not here—you have too much to lose."

Fra Filippo scowled at his friend.

"Only yesterday the provost complained to me about the progress of your frescoes," Fra Piero said. "Inghirami may have his own peculiar desires, but he's wise when it comes to the politics of the Church. I suggest you spend your time placating him, rather than entertaining yourself with the comely faces of young virgins."

"What peculiar desires?" Fra Filippo demanded. "I've never heard anything about the provost, save that he's stingy with the food he gives to the needy children."

"I heard it for the first time in Montepulciano, Filippo. There are men who say the provost looked at them the way other men look at a woman. It's only a rumor, but you know that even rumors can get a man in trouble. So be careful, Filippo. I can only do so much. The Medici can only do so much."

Shaking his head, Fra Piero paused at a small panel he'd over-looked. It was turned to face the wall, and signed on the back *O. de' V.*

"Is this de' Valenti's commission? Just yesterday, Ottavio was tell-ing me he's very eager to present it to his wife."

The procurator picked up the panel and turned it to reveal the no-vitiate's face again, a crimson hood emphasizing her beautiful mouth.

"It's magnificent. Luminous. But why is it still here? Why haven't you delivered it?"

"I can't part with it," the monk admitted. "I cannot bear to part with it."

"Oh, my friend," the procurator said. "I fear for you. Truly, I beg of you, do not have this girl in here again."

⋅~⊱⋅⊰~⋅

Fra Filippo walked to the convent that afternoon reviewing all the reasons why Lucrezia should not return to his *bottega*: she was a novice, and he was a monk; God had chosen her path, and he could not change it; she was an honorable young woman, and if he was alone with her again, he didn't know if he could trust himself.

Shutting the gate behind him, Fra Filippo vowed to tell Lucrezia his decision immediately after Nones prayers. He would be gentle, but inflexible.

With a heavy heart the monk called the nuns to the chapter house and watched them arrive one at a time, their faces haggard in the heat. Even Prioress Bartolommea sat with a deep sigh. But Lucrezia wasn't among them.

"In the name of the Father, the Son, and the Holy Spirit," he began.

He said the prayers dutifully, finishing with the benediction and urging the nuns to remain as long as they wished, enjoying the shady respite of the chapter house. Searching each face to be sure Lucrezia wasn't among them, he slipped out the door, determined to find her.

"Fratello." Her voice called to him as he was passing the garden well. He turned to see her mouth was pinched, her eyes sunken.

"Sister. You were not at prayers. Are you ill?"

"No." She dropped her gaze, and struggled to get out the words. "I believe I'm to come to your *bottega* one more time, and I look forward to seeing all the work you've done. I—"

"Sister Lucrezia." He tried to interrupt her, but she put out her hand and continued.

"I trust I've done nothing to hinder your work," she managed to say. From the corner of her eye she saw Spinetta approaching. "Fratello, I pray you won't keep me from all the beauty you've shown me," she said in a rush. "In your work. Your work for the Lord."

She knew they were consigned to God and there could be nothing between them. But everything of wonder and beauty that she'd found since coming to Santa Margherita led to him. Even her tasks tending the herbs with Sister Pureza led to the colors that were ground with his mortar and pestle. The splendor he'd shown her was sustaining her spirit.

"Please," she said softly. "Beauty isn't a sin. You told me this yourself."

Fra Filippo blinked. He was transfixed by the movement of her lips.

"Don't take it from me," she said, her voice low. "Please."

"Sister Lucrezia," Fra Filippo said gently. "I hear your plea."

"Then I may come again?"

He meant to say otherwise. Instead, he nodded mutely.

When Lucrezia and Spinetta arrived the following afternoon, Fra Filippo met them at his doorway.

"Today, *sorelle mie*, I'll take you on a small outing," the monk said, forcing a smile. He stole a glance at Lucrezia, whose blue eyes were radiant in her somber beauty. "I can go no further with my work on the altarpiece until I have some fresh pigments and supplies delivered, and it is too fine a day to remain in the *bottega*."

If Lucrezia wanted to see art and splendor, he would show her all that he could. In this way he would honor Fra Piero's advice and Lucrezia's sincere plea at the same time.

"With your consent, we'll go to the *pieve di Santo Stefano* and check on the progress of the frescoes." He bowed, hoping Lucrezia would understand he meant this to be his gift to her. "That is, if it pleases you to do so."

Lucrezia and Spinetta glanced at each other and then at Fra Filippo, their wimples fluttering slightly.

"*Si,* Fratello," both sisters said, and then Spinetta laughed. "It would be a great pleasure for us," she added.

The monk shut the door and the three walked briskly across the Piazza della Pieve. Together, they created a study in contrast: Fra Filippo's heavy brows and dark stubble stood out sharply above his floating white robe, while the nuns' tunics seemed even blacker against their pale complexions.

It was a busy day in the square, filled with trotting horses, the smell of cured meats from a nearby butcher, and a pair of dogs yapping in pursuit of a chicken. Wheels scraped against cobblestones, the chink of a blacksmith's hammer rang out, and the light footsteps of street urchins flew across the narrow alleyways. Men and women hurried by carrying bundles and talking loudly as the green and white striped basilica rose dramatically above them.

"It's beautiful," Spinetta exclaimed, looking up and shading her eyes against the sun. "It does justice to God's glory."

Fra Filippo pointed up to a rounded pulpit that jutted out from the side of the church, overlooking the piazza. The putti carved on it were gilded and appeared to be dancing wildly in the sunlight.

"The Pulpit of the Sacred Girdle was designed by Donatello and Michelozzo," he said, knowing the names of his celebrated contemporaries would be familiar to the Florentine sisters. "Provost

Inghirami will stand up there during the *Festa della Sacra Cintola* when he holds the Holy Belt for all to see."

Entering through the heavy church doors, the three made the sign of the cross and let their eyes adjust to the dim light. The noise and activity of the piazza quickly vanished, replaced by the scent of incense in the still air.

"Look here." Fra Filippo directed their attention immediately to the left, where the novitiates saw an enclosed chapel surrounded by an ornate bronze gate. Candles flickered in sconces hung from chains overhead.

"The Chapel of the Holy Belt," he said solemnly.

"La Sacra Cintola della Madonna," Spinetta exclaimed. She and Lucrezia had heard much talk about the celebration that would overtake the city on the eighth day of September. Both sisters pressed their hands to the tall gate, its delicate trefoils locked against their entry, and peered up at the colorful scenes on the chapel walls.

"The frescoes were painted by Agnolo Gaddi, son of the Florentine artist Taddeo Gaddi," Fra Lippi said. He gestured to an elaborate golden coffer that sat on the altar. "And the reliquary is remarkable."

Lucrezia stifled a sigh.

"They say the belt offers protection and good health for women who are with child," she said softly, again regretting the vows that condemned her to a barren womb.

"I've heard the Virgin's blessings extend to all who touch it," Spinetta said. "And we'll be given the chance to do so on the day of the *festa.*"

They stood in solemn contemplation, each praying for what he or she most wanted from the Virgin on this day. Then the sisters followed Fra Filippo toward the front of the basilica, passing a few lone souls who knelt on the elaborately tiled floor, and circling a grand bronze candelabrum filled with tallow candles. The chaplain paused below a tall wooden statue of the Virgin and Child, then beside another of Saint Elizabeth, before mounting two sets of white steps in the presbytery, genuflecting in front of the high altar covered in a red cloth for Pentecost, and passing behind it into the chapel where he spent most of his days.

As they stepped onto the wood floor, their eyes took a moment to adjust to the bright sunlight that flooded the *cappella maggiore*. The sisters were surprised by the maze of scaffolding filled with men, tools, and buckets of paint, but Fra Filippo smoothly nodded to his assistants, who greeted the visitors without stopping their work. Tomaso and Young Marco stood together on a low scaffolding, laboring carefully on the dark green leaves in the scene of Saint John's mission and speaking in quiet voices. Another assistant, Giorgio, was using a small brush to add tiny touches of white to the dusty rocks in Saint Stephen's scene.

Fra Filippo had not been to the church in many days, and in his absence Fra Diamante, his senior assistant, had overseen the application of the first layers of *intonaco* to the scenes in progress. At Fra Filippo's arrival, the *frate* turned from the table where he'd been poring over the fresco designs, and opened his arms to greet the painter. His face was lively, his brown monk's robe splattered with paint.

"I must show you all that we have done," Fra Diamante said, indicating the careful lines he'd added to the scene of Saint Stephen's mission.

As the two men consulted, Lucrezia straightened her back and looked around the chapel. Her eyes roamed over the scaffolding, the thick plaster and chalk lines on the walls, the buckets of paints, and the string of candles that ran along the floor. She hadn't realized there were so many artisans under the painter's direction, and the enormity of his undertaking here only increased her admiration for him. She smiled shyly as he climbed carefully down the makeshift wooden steps, and came toward her and Spinetta.

"Here, on this wall, is the life of Saint Stephen," Fra Filippo said, touching her elbow so she would turn toward the north lunette. "It begins on the top tier, with his birth, and ends at the bottom, with his funeral."

Lucrezia looked at the lively figures indicated in sinopia, and marveled at the lifelike quality of their gestures, the careful proportion of their bodies.

"What's over here?" Spinetta moved nimbly among the strewn tools, between the stubs of many candles, and gestured to the freshest chalk lines drawn over a smooth patch of plaster.

"That wall is dedicated to the life of Saint John the Baptist." Fra Filippo moved closer and inspected the progress there, noting that all had been done as he'd instructed. He waved a hand toward a corner of the chapel, where the eastern wall met the southern one.

"This panel will depict Saint John kneeling at the moment of his beheading," the monk said. "The scene will turn the corner and continue here, where his head will be placed on a platter and carried into Herod's banquet on the southern wall."

Fra Filippo couldn't keep the excitement from his voice as he described the way he'd conceived the scene, how the figures would seem to inhabit the very space in which the viewer stood, and how the tragic end of the saint's life would appear almost as a performance on the walls of the chapel.

"The *effetti* are masterful, Brother Lippi." Lucrezia uttered her first words since entering the chapel. "I can almost see what you're describing." She was about to say more when she was startled by a loud cough.

Turning quickly, she saw a sharp-featured man in a red robe moving toward them from the rear of the altar. He seemed to glide on invisible feet, his robes dragging on the floor behind him.

"*Buongiorno,* good provost," Fra Filippo said, greeting Provost Inghirami. "I thought you were presiding at a funeral."

Fra Filippo noted the deep furrow between the provost's brows and the way he clenched his right hand. He thought about the rumors of the provost's unnatural longings, and wondered if it could be true.

"And I've returned," the provost said crisply.

"I see that, and I'm hoping you are well. I have brought two of our novitiates from Santa Margherita, so they might see your church and all its wonders. I've just finished showing them where your portrait will go."

Turning his shoulder away, the provost scowled at Fra Filippo.

"Why have the novitiates been brought here?" Inghirami demanded.

"Your Excellency, I beg your pardon, but this has all been carefully arranged with Mother Bartolommea. She has given her permission for their travel, especially as she has been asked to do so by the emissary of the Medici." Fra Filippo spoke the name of his powerful benefactor decisively. "Their assistance has been indispensable in my completion of an important commission for the Medici, and in return, I've offered to show them around your magnificent chapel."

"I see."

The provost was, of course, aware that the Medici's emissary was in Prato. But until this moment he had not been sure why the sealed missive directing him to surrender the Holy Belt to Ser Francesco had come directly from Rome. Now, Inghirami began to see the force of the hand that had stripped his church of its most prized possession. The *Sacra Cintola* would not be gone for long, but the provost was nevertheless keenly disturbed by its removal. Allowing the belt to leave the church could only endanger it and, by extension, endanger him.

When Inghirami spoke again, it was with a new hostility in his voice.

"It's my understanding the novitiates were to be carefully chaperoned, and only leave the convent in service of the Lord," he said.

From under the fold of her wimple Lucrezia glanced from his thin lips to the provost's clasped hands. She saw they were small and smooth, so different from the large and well-worn hands of the painter. Glancing sideways, she could see that her sister was staring at the ground, her cheeks pink with embarrassment. Her heart sank as she heard the provost speaking sharply in her direction.

"You shouldn't linger here any longer," the provost said, training his eyes on the space between Lucrezia and Spinetta. "Novitiates should remain cloistered. The world is a dangerous place, as you know. The walls of the convent exist for a reason."

"You are right, Your Excellency." The painter moved as if to shield the sisters from his glare, and cursed himself silently. Once again, he'd acted rashly. He could hear Fra Piero's warning echoing in the back of his mind, and he doubled his efforts to placate the provost. "We must go, as the escort will arrive shortly to return the sisters to the cloister. Please excuse us."

Inghirami stepped aside to allow Fra Filippo and the novitiates to pass. Lucrezia felt his eyes burning into her back even after she'd dipped her fingers in the font of holy water and left the church.

When they reached the *bottega*, the escort was already waiting for them, fidgeting in his loose tunic. Spinetta stepped beside him, wishing to return to the convent as quickly as possible. But Lucrezia lingered. Fra Filippo moved close enough for her to smell the alcohol and rough soap he'd used to clean his hands.

"*Arrivederci*," he murmured.

She gave him a small smile.

"*Grazie*," she barely managed to say before she turned and followed the escort.

Avoiding her sister's glance, Lucrezia brushed the limestone dust from her fingertips. The bells of Santo Stefano began to ring as they left the Piazza della Pieve behind, and soon the steady tolling from every corner of the city filled the air as Lucrezia walked slowly beside her sister without speaking.

Chapter Eleven

With the Feast of the Sacred Belt only two days away, the city of Prato was bustling with preparations. Bakers kneaded dough and shaped corded rolls, butchers quartered smoked meats, youngsters readied their costumes and practiced their dances, candlemakers brought out their best beeswax, and shopkeepers doubled their wares for the visitors who would flood the narrow streets.

The belt was honored on four other days in the year, but never with the pomp and celebration that accompanied the *Festa della Sacra Cintola* on the Virgin Mary's Feast Day on the eighth of September. On this day the gold reliquary would be opened, the Holy Belt of the Virgin displayed from the pulpit of Santo Stefano, and all of Tuscany would turn its eyes toward the city. There would be games as well as prayers, and every nun and monk in Prato would raise their voices in praise of the Holy Virgin.

At the Convent Santa Margherita, Sister Maria chopped cheese and raisins to make the traditional stuffed eggs, the nuns rehearsed the psalms they would chant, and on a rare visit to the kitchen, Sister Pureza prepared the herbs that would be rolled into savory cakes the sisters would eat in the evening after the *festa*.

Alone in her chambers while the others worked furiously, Prioress Bartolommea pulled the wooden box holding the *Sacra Cintola* out from under her cot and knelt before it.

"Blessed Mother," she prayed in a shrill voice. "Smile down on us in recognition of all that I—and the others—have done in your Holy Name."

The prioress stayed on her knees through the morning, ignoring the call to prayer, the knocks on her door, and even the gruff voice of Sister Pureza, asking if she needed a tincture to revive her energy.

"No," the prioress called, raking her fingers through her gray hair. "Leave me be, I need solitude for my prayers."

She ignored the bell at the gate, which rang incessantly with second requests for cream from the dairy man, and many extra deliveries for the kitchen. The prioress had only two more days before the belt would be secreted back to the church and returned to the reliquary, and she'd yet to see the blessings it was said to bring.

Fearing that she might have been tricked with a forgery, the good mother waited until she'd heard the prayer for Nones. Then she lifted the wooden lid and carefully held the soft folds of the belt between her fingers. She felt the worn goat's wool and studied the golden stitches that had circled the waist of the Blessed Mother. It seemed real enough, she thought. And yet she felt nothing.

⚬~✦~⚬

*W*ith a heavy heart Lucrezia worked in the *giardino*, picking through the prickly rosemary that tore at her fingertips. She could hear the nuns practicing their vocals for the *festa* parade, and Lucrezia was glad that it was too late for her to learn the notes for the procession. She preferred to be alone with her thoughts in the garden, where tender shoots of ferns poked between the bricks and there were no demands that couldn't be resolved by propping a stick or snipping a branch.

She was cutting a shoot of rosemary when the shadow of the prioress fell across the ground where she knelt.

"Sister Lucrezia, I wish to introduce you to Prior General Ludovico di Saviano, the head of our order."

Lucrezia brushed her hands on her robe, and stood. The sun was behind the prioress, putting her in silhouette. Lucrezia could barely make out the face of the tall man next to Prioress Bartolommea, but knew by the finely cut black robes and tall headpiece that he was a worldly man. Lucrezia lowered her eyes.

"God's grace to you, Prior General," she said softly.

"Are you the novitiate who has been going to Fra Filippo's workshop?" the man asked in a sharp voice.

Startled, Lucrezia looked at the prioress, but the woman's wimple obscured her face.

"There is no need to look to Mother Bartolommea," said Prior General Saviano. "She has shared everything with me. I only wish to be reassured that you have gone willingly, and that you have not been compromised."

The man's head moved left and right as he spoke, and after a moment he blocked the sun so that she could see his face, the angry look about his eyes. He was nothing like the painter; he was stern, with an air of entitlement. Lucrezia nodded.

"Is there anything you wish to say about the monk, or the circumstances of your visits with him?"

Images from the *bottega* came rushing to her: the Virgin's golden halo, the painter's brush flying across the canvas, the soft sound of his pencil on parchment. Lucrezia shook her head faintly.

"Nothing?" the man asked, this time perhaps a bit more patiently.

She remained silent, struggling to hide her nerves. When the man spoke again, he enunciated his words clearly and she heard the years of seminary training in his diction.

"I welcome you to the convent, Sister Lucrezia. I will keep you in my prayers."

He turned, and the prioress ran after him to keep up with his long strides as he left the garden and walked into the grassy patch behind the chapel.

"Prioress Bartolommea." The prior general's voice was cold. "I do not approve of the unconventional practices you allow in Santa Margherita. If I hadn't received notice from Provost Inghirami, I would have had no idea you'd allowed the novitiates to go into Prato."

Prioress Bartolommea stared up at the prior general's profile, but what she saw in her mind was the altarpiece she'd been promised, and the small wooden box hidden under her bed.

"I can assure you it was out of my hands," she stammered. "The arrangements were made at the explicit request of the Medici."

"You should have come to me out of respect."

"Of course," said the prioress. "You have my apologies, Prior General."

"I trust your dealings with the Medici in this matter are finished," the cleric said.

"Perhaps," Prioress Bartolommea said tentatively, for she knew that a Medici messenger would arrive the following morning to retrieve the belt. "Of course, we do have other business with the Medici, Your Grace."

"What other business can you have with the Medici of Florence?" Saviano snapped. "Santa Margherita is our humblest cloister."

"We've been praying for them," the prioress said. "For their concerns in Prato, especially those of Ser Cantansanti."

Prior General Saviano stared at her.

"Yes." The prioress nodded. "We've been praying for Fra Filippo's timely delivery of the altarpiece to the King of Naples, so that peace may reign between men."

The prior general shook his head in disgust, and waved for his carriage.

"See that the souls in your care remain so," he said. "Pray for *that*."

⁂

Three loud raps sounded on Fra Filippo's door and startled the painter.

"*Aspetta!*" the monk yelled, wiping his hands on his apron and pushing back his stool as he stood. "Wait."

He was expecting Niccolo, the butcher boy, bringing his monthly supplies of ox bones to be ground into binder for the paint. Annoyed at the disturbance, Fra Filippo swung open the door, a sour look on his face. Prior General Ludovico di Saviano filled the doorway.

"Wait?" Saviano asked icily. "What should I wait for?"

"Pardon, Your Grace," Fra Filippo said, recovering from the surprise. "Pardon and welcome."

He stepped aside quickly, allowing the prior general to enter. As he turned, his heart sank. If only he'd known Saviano was coming he could have gathered up the drawings of Lucrezia, and covered the sketch for the altarpiece.

"I was lost in my work, and not expecting anyone, Prior General. Of course, you're always welcome."

"All right." Prior General Saviano responded with an air of impatience. "And how is your work going, Fra Filippo?"

"I suppose you mean the frescoes at Santo Stefano?" Fra Filippo asked. "It's been going rather slowly, but with two new assistants, the pace has picked up in these last weeks. Praise God."

"New assistants?" Saviano shook his head. "I'm certain the provost told me your budget allows only for two, Filippo. You'll dismiss the others at once."

Including Young Marco and Fra Diamante, he had four assistants at Santo Stefano, all paid directly by the *Comune di Prato*, in accordance with the terms of his contract. The monk opened his mouth to speak, but Saviano waved his hand irritably and moved on.

"I've heard there are things of great interest going on in Santo Stefano," the prior general said. He ran his hand along the heavy table where the painter had his jars of colors and supplies. "But I see you have plenty to keep you busy right here in your *bottega*."

Prior General Saviano eyed the dried jar of green paint, the dirty rags, and the piles of parchment. Scanning the room, he fixed on the detailed sketch for the Medici altarpiece and saw the face of the novitiate he'd met at Santa Margherita's that morning. She was drawn kneeling in a fine gown that exposed her lovely collarbones, her arms in sleeves covered with tiny flowers, her hair wrapped in a *benda*. Every inch of Sister Lucrezia's face had been rendered faithfully, but seen through a veil of such love that she no longer looked entirely mortal.

Fra Filippo registered the shock on Prior General Saviano's face.

"I've begun the altarpiece in earnest now," the painter said quickly. "The Medici have been keeping the pressure on me and the prioress was kind enough to send me a model to hasten the work along."

"Why, yes, Brother Filippo, I am aware that Sister Lucrezia has been here several times, walking the streets of Prato for all to see."

The monk made a gesture as if to speak, but Saviano raised his voice and continued.

"Today, I've had the pleasure of making the novitiate's acquaintance."

"Ah, now I see," the prior general said softly. He held the *benda* up to his face, and inhaled a long breath of chamomile.

"You see nothing at all," Fra Filippo snarled in disgust. "What can you see?"

Prior General Saviano took the *benda* and held it in front of the sketch. He held the empty silken *cotta*, and ran it through his hands as if it were a naked woman's skin.

"You're even more clever than I thought, Fra Filippo. I hope you've enjoyed her while it lasted."

The monk felt his rage flame. He reached for the garments.

"I'm painting her for the glory of Florence. It is my duty."

The cleric flared his nostrils, like a steed at the start of a long run, and gripped the finery in his thick palms.

"What's in your mind is wrong," Fra Filippo said heatedly as he tore the garments from the prior general's fists.

"What is in my mind is not the issue, Fratello." Saviano stood shoulder to shoulder with the monk. "What is at issue is what is in *your* mind. This will not go unpunished, I assure you. "

The prior general strode angrily from the *bottega*, slamming the door fiercely behind him. Fra Filippo watched a tumbler fall from the easel, his hands just barely missing it before it hit the ground and cracked into a dozen pieces.

⁂

Lucrezia sorted the birthwort, her mind on the chaplain and the man who'd come into the garden that morning. Fra Filippo was a monk of formidable talents and skills, and this made people humble in his presence. But the man who'd been in the garden today seemed to be someone whose power could overwhelm both friend and foe.

"The work goes well today, I see," Sister Pureza remarked.

Lucrezia paused only a moment to greet her mentor.

"You're lucky you won't be singing the psalms in the *festa*," Sister Pureza said. "It's a strain to memorize new psalms each year, only to forget them by Advent."

The old nun lowered herself onto the bench alongside the novitiate, took up a fistful of the birthwort, and began to snap the leaves and stems. Her wrists were thick and her movements less limber than Lucrezia's, but her fingertips knew just where to find the joint of the leaves and she made quick work of it, falling into the side-by-side rhythm that the novitiate had come to enjoy.

"There's a full moon," Sister Pureza said after a long silence.

Lucrezia looked up and followed the nun's gaze. She'd caught only the sliver of the moon through her window, and was surprised to see it brightly visible in the blue sky to the east.

"I've had word from the de' Valenti house that the child is coming."

"Yes?"

"Before I came to the convent I'd received some training as a midwife. After the dark days"—Sister Pureza made the sign of the cross as she thought of the terror of the plague—"there were few of us left in Prato who knew these female ways, and I was called upon to assist at many partum bedsides. I've attended many difficult births since that time."

She kept her hands moving steadily as she spoke. "Signora Teresa de' Valenti and her husband are generous friends of the convent, and this will be the good wife's seventh labor."

Lucrezia shivered at the memory of her sister's partum screams.

"I'll need the birthwort, and some licorice root. And I'll need an assistant with me at the palazzo," Sister Pureza said. "I shall bring you."

"Yes. He asked me about the chaplain." Lucrezia avoided saying the painter's name aloud, and spared herself the fluster that came at his mention. "He seemed to be agitated."

"Agitated?" Sister Pureza leaned forward, her face puzzled.

Lucrezia saw the prior general's abrupt movement as he crossed the courtyard, and felt a stab of apprehension. But she was with Sister Pureza, and took comfort in the old woman's presence even after the cleric disappeared from their sight.

"No. I spoke out of turn, Sister," Lucrezia said, shaking her head. "He was only in a hurry. We spoke briefly, for barely a moment, and then he was gone."

"Never mind," Sister Pureza instructed. "We have much to think about, not the least of which is our duty at the Valenti palazzo. After Terce you must pack your things, and be ready to go with me when we are summoned."

⁂

*S*ister Pureza came for Lucrezia after dark, swiftly whisking her to the de' Valenti carriage that waited in the courtyard. The streets were empty, and they quickly arrived at the fine palazzo that filled an entire block on Via Banchelli, the golden hue of its stone exterior illuminated by lanterns.

A servant in a blue cap greeted the women and led them through a low back door. They passed through a busy kitchen with rough beams painted with intricate patterns of red and green. Although it was a mild evening, a bright fire blazed.

Following the servant up a narrow stair lit by a chain of sconces, the nuns entered the private *appartamento* of the Valenti family and were ushered into Signora Teresa's elaborate birthing chamber.

"*Grazie*, Maria," Signora Teresa cried as soon as she saw them. Her face was puffed and she was sitting in her large bed propped against a mound of pillows and surrounded by five women: two serving her, two related by blood, plus the midwife who'd been in charge until Sister Pureza's arrival. Robust under her white *cuffia da parto*, Signora Teresa groaned.

"Not a moment too soon," she cried. "My waters have already come."

Lucrezia looked around the chamber that had been prepared for the lady's confinement and spared no expense. It was furnished with an enormous carved chest upon which sat a luminous *maiolica* pitcher, heavy gold silk curtains that hung around the bed and covered the windows, and the *sedia da parto*, the birthing chair, which stood in a place of honor next to the fireplace. On the other side of the room a large *cassone*, decorated with images of Venus, stood open, more sheets and linens visible in its deep recesses.

"Sister Pureza—" Signora Teresa's sentence was cut off by a spasm that took her breath away.

The old nun withdrew a sage smudge stick from her bag and lit it. She handed the smoking herbs to Lucrezia, and instructed her to walk the perimeter of the room to cleanse the air. Lucrezia did as she was told, keeping her face turned away from the laboring woman even as she breathed in the smell of her sweat, sharp and fetid under the perfume of lavender water.

"Mother of God," the woman moaned.

"Recite your *Ave Maria*," Sister Pureza instructed the woman. "Put your mind on your prayers."

The pains were only minutes apart, and Sister Pureza was worried. The younger midwife knelt in a corner of the room, holding a pair of forceps in her hand.

"Dear Mother in Heaven," the woman in the partum bed screamed.

Her hair was matted, her teeth gritted together. Sister Pureza turned to see dark, clotted blood gush from between the mother's legs.

Quickly, the old nun grabbed a towel and a flask from her bag. She warmed her hands by the fire and took a bit of liniment in her palms, rubbing them briskly together. She carried a copy of the *Practica Secundum Trotam* in her bag, but it had been years since she'd needed it. She knew where to lay her hands on the laboring mother, how to apply the ointment to the perineum, and where to massage the woman's belly to help the child through the birth canal.

She worked confidently, using her fingers to measure the woman's opening, counting the duration of the spasms, keeping her palms on the mother's body. Signora de' Valenti groaned again and her belly hardened, her hands flailing for something to hold on to. Sister Pureza spoke to Lucrezia in a deep, strong voice.

"Stand next to her. Let her take your hand."

Lucrezia moved quickly, positioning herself next to the bedpost for support and reaching out for the mother. The woman grabbed hold of her hand and screamed. The howl frightened Lucrezia.

"It's all right," Lucrezia said, as much to console herself as to console the woman. "We're here with you."

Signora de' Valenti looked up and saw Lucrezia's face—the face of the Madonna—over her bed.

"*Bella Maria,* Blessed Mother." She raised herself off her pillow and arched her neck toward the vision. It must surely be a miracle, for the face of the Madonna was here. The Virgin's own cool fingers were between her hot ones. "Help me, *Madre.* Help me."

Sister Pureza looked up from her place between the woman's legs and stared at Lucrezia. Sometimes it was said that the sick and the ailing had a hand already in heaven, and could divine what others could not.

"Leave me on earth, Mother Mary, don't take me away yet."

Sister Pureza frowned, fearing the woman was having delusions that could only be explained by a great sickness of body.

"Focus on your child, Teresa," the old midwife said. "Close your eyes and think about the child."

A shriek, followed quickly by another, sent Sister Pureza into a squat between the woman's bent knees. She beckoned for the first midwife to stand beside her, ready with the forceps.

"Bear down," Sister Pureza instructed. "Bear down, use your strength." Panting, Signora de' Valenti squeezed her eyes shut and bore down. In her great effort her eyes flew open and she cried out in agony and in ecstasy.

"Mother Mary, Mother Mary," she wailed. Tears blinded her as she grabbed for Lucrezia's forearm and dug her nails into the novitiate's flesh. "Mother Mary, deliver me," the woman cried. There was a gush of mucus and blood, and the head of the child crowned.

"Don't stop, Teresa," Sister Pureza instructed firmly. "You must keep pushing, do not stop."

Lucrezia looked down at Sister Pureza's wimple, bobbing between the woman's bent legs, and smelled the sharp odor of blood that filled the chamber. The birthing mother panted with her eyes closed and sweat pouring down her forehead, her dark hair matted. Then her eyes opened, she moaned, the bed shook, and Lucrezia felt herself grow faint.

There was a pounding on the door, and Sister Pureza, gruff as a stableman, shouted, "Not now, this is the moment." In the same voice she shouted at Signora Teresa, "*Pronto*, now, it must be now, the child must come now, push with all your strength."

She put a quill filled with mustard powder up to the mother's nos-

tril, and blew. Signora de' Valenti's startled eyes opened, she began
to sneeze violently, and in the convulsions of the sneezes her uterus
contracted, the hip bones opened the final space necessary, and the
baby burst from between the wishbone of her legs into the warm
linen blanket Sister Pureza held to catch him.

The old nun put her mouth over the baby's face, sucked off the
mucus that covered his nose and mouth, spat into the *tafferia da parto,*
the wooden bowl that was by the bedside, and checked the infant
quickly. He was whole, round, and fat.

Sister Pureza gave the child to Lucrezia and told her to have the
basin of water moved just outside the bedroom, near the warm fire
that roared in the hallway. Servants immediately sprang into action,
tugging the heavy basin through the doorway.

"You must use the swaddling bands," Sister Pureza said, fingering the ends of the linen *fascia* that she'd wrapped around the child.
"Only uncover the part that you're washing, and you must bundle
him quickly again to keep off the chill. When the babe is clean, give
him to the wet nurse. Tell the *balia* to put him to the breast to see if
he'll suckle."

As quickly as she gave her orders, Sister Pureza returned her attention to the mother. The child was pink and robust, but Signora
Teresa was delirious, her skin broken in a patchy fever. She continued
to call out the name of the Virgin even as Lucrezia shut the door
behind her.

"*Dominus spiritus sanctus,*" Sister Pureza prayed. She put her hands
out and held them over the mother's breast. "*Veni creator spiritus, mentes
tuorum visita, imple superna gratia, quae tu creasti pectora . . .*"

As Lucrezia stepped out of the room with the infant, the servant
who'd led them up the stairs came to her, tense and pale.

"It's a son. An heir," Lucrezia said. She looked down at the child. His face was puckered and red, his eyes squeezed shut, his hands balled in tight fists.

"And my lady?" The servant peered into Lucrezia's face, but before words could pass Lucrezia's lips, the woman's mouth opened in a wide circle.

"*Dio mio,*" the servant cried, raising her hand to her forehead and making the sign of the cross. "You have the face of the Virgin."

The servant turned and pointed. On the wall opposite the bedroom hung a painting Lucrezia had never seen before. It was a painting of the Madonna in crimson robes trimmed in gold, holding the Christ child and seated upon a green throne, a delicate pearl *benda* wrapping her hair. The Virgin's face was her own.

"How?" Lucrezia cried. "How did this come to be here?"

"It is a gift from the master to the mistress. It was delivered by the painter Fra Filippo only this week."

The servant looked from Lucrezia to the painting and back again.

"The resemblance is impossible," she said, and stared again at Lucrezia.

Tightening her hold on the child, Lucrezia stepped closer to the painting. She felt a strange, dizzying sensation, the same sense of unreality that filled her whenever she thought of the painter.

"Sister!" Lucrezia heard the sharp cry from inside the bedchamber. It was Sister Pureza's voice, but she'd never heard it sound this way before. "Sister Lucrezia, I need you at once."

The mother groaned and shrieked, the babe in Lucrezia's arms opened his mouth and wailed. Lucrezia's head was fuzzy with fatigue and confusion.

"I am needed," she said to the servant, whose face had crumpled. Lucrezia passed her the child, and hurried back into the birthing chamber, where Signora Teresa was flailing her arms and legs. Sister Pureza was prostrate across the woman, trying to keep her from falling off the bed. The first midwife was on her knees, praying.

"You must find a cloth and tie her," Sister Pureza instructed. "I can't minister to her this way, I can't get her to drink anything that will calm her."

Lucrezia hesitated.

"Do what I say, child. Take a long piece of sheeting and twist it like a rope."

Lucrezia took a clean sheet from the pile in the corner, coiled it into a makeshift rope, and brought it to Sister Pureza.

"Tie her before she hurts you," Sister Pureza commanded. Lucrezia's hands shook so badly that the twisted sheeting slipped from them.

"Please," Lucrezia said. "I cannot do it. I'm sorry, Sister, I'm too frightened."

Sister Pureza looked at Lucrezia from head to toe.

"Come, take her hands," Sister Pureza said. "I'll tie her, you hold her."

In her fever, Signora Teresa felt herself fading, and she was afraid. She turned toward the candlelight, and saw the face she'd seen before.

"Is it you?" she whispered to Lucrezia. "Is it you, Blessed Virgin? Have you come for me?"

"I am Sister Lucrezia," the novitiate said. She felt strange, and wise beyond anything she'd felt before. "Don't be afraid. The likeness in the painting is only a coincidence. I'm not the Virgin. I haven't come to take you. You have a strong, healthy heir. He's in the hands of your servant and he's being washed now for the nurse."

Signora Teresa, long devoted to the Blessed Virgin, heard Lucrezia's words and let herself be calmed. Everything was all right. She took a deep inhale, and her limbs went limp. When Sister Pureza put the cup of chamomile and vervain to the new mother's lips, she drank quietly. A short while later the fever lifted, and Signora Teresa de' Valenti slept under two blankets while the women of her family prepared the rich *desco da parto*, the painted birth plate, heaped with oranges and sweets. Signor Ottavio drank a glass of port in honor of his new son, Ascanio di' Ottavio de' Valenti. And in the hall outside the confinement room, Sister Pureza stood staring at Fra Filippo's *Madonna and Child*.

"The signora was fading. She was halfway to heaven," said the younger midwife, who'd come to stand beside Sister Pureza. "Your novitiate has the Virgin's blessing, Good Sister."

Chapter Twelve

Friday of the Thirteenth Week After Pentecost, the Year of Our Lord 1456

The waning moon seemed to follow Sister Pureza and Lucrezia back to the convent. The women were exhausted, and the swift carriage rocked them even as the cradle lulled the newborn to sleep under the terra-cotta roof of his family's palazzo.

Behind her closed eyelids, Sister Pureza contemplated Signora Teresa's health, the miraculous cooling of her skin, the soothing of her spirit. The herbs from the convent garden had never seemed more potent as on this night. When it had appeared the mother would slip into the delirium that befell so many others, Signora Teresa had looked at Lucrezia's sweet face and her blood, her humors, the very fever in her body had been cooled.

Of course the servants had seen this transformation; Signora Teresa's sister-in-law had witnessed it, as well. *A miracle*, they'd said among themselves until Lucrezia had turned and said, "There is no miracle here, I beg you not to say such a thing." They'd all nodded, of course, but crossed themselves before leaving the confinement chamber. And when the nuns packed up their things and prepared to return to the convent, it was with the parting words of Signor Ottavio in their ears.

"Any *servizio* I can do for you, at any time," the wealthy man had said, taking Sister Pureza's old hand in his.

Now, Sister Pureza sighed without realizing she stirred.

"I'm sorry, Sister Pureza," Lucrezia whispered, touching the midwife's robes. "I'm sorry. I don't know what to say about the painting. I had no knowledge of it until tonight."

Sister Pureza turned and looked at Lucrezia. Even after a harrowing night, the girl's physical perfection was unmistakable.

"To have such beauty cannot be easy," Sister Pureza said gently.

Lucrezia was silent. At home there had only been a single circle of polished silver, and Signora Buti had let the girls look at their reflection only on Saturdays when they washed their hair and bathed in preparation for the Lord's day. Other young ladies of Florence primped before their reflections daily and some, Lucrezia knew, sat outside in the sun to bring the yellow and gold colors out in their hair. But the Buti sisters had never been permitted or encouraged in even harmless vanities such as pinching their cheeks or biting their lips for a touch of color.

"I don't know." Lucrezia's voice quivered. "No one has ever said such a thing to me. But I've often wished to hide my face because of the way men look at me."

Lucrezia had never admitted this to anyone. She thought of Fra Filippo, and the pleasure his gaze gave her.

"There's no shame in your beauty, dear child, nor is it your only virtue. It couldn't have been your face alone that soothed Signora de' Valenti tonight."

Lucrezia was close enough to feel the warmth of Sister Pureza's small body. She was grateful for the darkness.

"Like the flowers in our garden, your beauty has a purpose," Sister Pureza went on. "I've been thinking about this since I learned that Fra Filippo would paint your likeness. If your face can become the face of the Madonna, and it can keep a woman such as Signora de' Valenti from being claimed by the evil spirits that gripped her, then I believe there is much goodness in it."

Sister Pureza turned in her seat as much as her old body allowed, to look Lucrezia full in the face.

"Treasure your beauty, Sister Lucrezia, but guard against its corruption."

Lucrezia nodded. She was reminded again of the words Fra Filippo had spoken to her in the confessional, when he'd said beauty in the world is a mirror of God's kingdom. A *speculum majus*.

"The chaplain said the holiest of men believe beauty in this world pleases God because it brings our world closer to His. But if this is so, then what about Christ's suffering, and the Virgin's?" Lucrezia asked.

The carriage crossed a mound of stones in the road, and Lucrezia's body bumped against Sister Pureza's. She felt the old woman steady herself.

"If suffering brings us closer to God, then how can beauty do the same?" she tried again. "Surely something comes from Satan, Sister Pureza. Is it suffering, or is it beauty?"

Sister Pureza was tired. She wished only to close her eyes, but sensed there was something important behind the novitiate's questions, something that made the young woman terribly unhappy.

"Beauty is from God, vanity is the Devil's work. And as for Christ's blood, Sister Lucrezia, you were at the birth tonight, you know the suffering that Eve's curse brings to women. There's always blood." Hearing the harshness of her words, Sister Pureza tried to soften them. "But remember, child, that while the Virgin paid in innocence for the sins of others, She was crowned queen in heaven."

Lucrezia couldn't begin to untangle her tongue or her prayers fast enough to ask any more questions.

"Your beauty and goodness are a gift," Sister Pureza said gently, her voice growing dim as Lucrezia closed her eyes. "But beauty fades. The soul must grow stronger and wiser."

When Lucrezia opened her eyes the carriage was pulling through the convent gates. It left them in the courtyard, and the nuns hurried to the low dormitories, the gray stones glowing eerily in the moonlight.

"You did well tonight, *mia cara*," Sister Pureza said. "Now sleep."

But once she was alone, Lucrezia's head began to buzz again with the talk of blood and beauty, the recollection of the signora's screams, and the portrait of herself as the Virgin, painted by Fra Filippo's hand.

Lucrezia paced her narrow cell for a few moments—the room was too small, too airless. Slipping her boots back on, she lit a candle and slid down the dormitory hall to the night stair. Descending into the narrow passage, she moved quickly past the spiders, which she'd learned to ignore, and didn't even look down at the tiny mice that scampered out of her way.

Reaching the church steps, Lucrezia blew out her candle to save the wick. Hearing a footfall in the landing above, she thought one of the nuns was up to say Lauds before daybreak, and Lucrezia prepared to greet her with a somber nod.

"Well." Prior General Saviano stepped in front of Lucrezia. The door to the night stair closed behind her. She and the prior general were alone in the narrow corridor that led to the apse.

He moved the candle between them and looked at her from head to toe.

The prior general had slept poorly, and his eyelids burned. The girl's beauty, brilliant even at this hour, seemed to mock him—just as the painter's disrespect had mocked him, and Prioress Bartolommea had angered him.

"General." Lucrezia bowed and hesitated, unsure of the proper way to address him. "Fratello Saviano."

"Fratello?" Prior General Saviano was certain the girl meant to ridicule him. He had been belittled all day—slighted and humiliated at every turn. The fine garments in the painter's room and the sketch showing the girl's bare collarbones flashed through his mind.

"I am Prior General Ludovico Pietro di Saviano." The man recited his full name and title in his deepest baritone. As he spoke, Lucrezia saw the hem of his black robes move and sway. She saw the candle he held throw strange shadows across the bricks on the floor. "Surely you're not confusing me with your good friend, the painter? *He* is a *frate*, a mere *frate*, despite what you may have been led to believe."

Lucrezia's mouth grew dry. She was afraid of this man. Recalling Sister Pureza's words in the carriage, Lucrezia tugged her wimple down and tried to turn away. But the prior general put his hand on her arm.

"Why do you hide from me, Lucrezia?"

She could smell the long night in the odor of his body.

"I'm tired, Prior General Saviano. I've come only to say a prayer before I sleep."

"Lucrezia." Saviano spoke her given name, and it felt sublime and sensuous on his lips. "You are not yet of the veil, you haven't taken the vows. They call you Sister Lucrezia, but that is not true yet, is it?"

Lucrezia stiffened. The prior general didn't let go of her arm. As she twisted away, he stepped closer. His thighs, firm under his robe, pressed against her hip.

"Prior General," Lucrezia stammered. "Please, sir, let me pass."

"I've been to the workshop of your friend *Frate* Filippo. I know that you took off this robe." The prior general pinched the fabric of her gown. "I know you disrobed for him, you put on the fine clothes of a Florentine *donna*."

Pressing his face against hers, he gripped her arm higher, near her bosom. Years of denial raged in his loins.

"Lucrezia. Are you Fra Filippo's lover?"

"I'm not." Terrified, she tried to wrench away.

"He's had many, you know. Many lovers." Prior General Saviano tightened his grip. "You're nothing special to him." He pursed his lips. "But you could be special to me."

"No!" Lucrezia twisted away and kicked at his legs. His candle fell to the ground and sparked at the edge of his robe. As he looked down at the candle she rushed past him.

"Come back," the prior general called, but she only shrieked again, stifling a sob. He heard revulsion in her cry, and it stung him.

"You've made your lot, now," he called, his voice rising. "Nothing good will come of it, you'll see. This is my convent—*my* convent. Remember that."

Lucrezia burst through the church door and stumbled into the cloister garden. The prior general knew she'd taken her clothes off in Fra Filippo's *bottega*, he knew about the fine silk *cotta*. She yanked open the first door she came to, and ran through the latrine to the dark hallway in the nuns' dormitory.

Hearing the girl's sobs, Sister Pureza opened her cell door. She'd already removed her wimple, and her long gray hair was loose. She put out an arm and grabbed Lucrezia as she passed.

"What is it?"

"The prior general," Lucrezia sobbed. She pulled up her sleeve and showed Sister Pureza the angry marks the man had left there.

$\mathcal{S}$ister Pureza waited until the cock crowed three times, and then walked across the courtyard. The old midwife didn't try to deny what had happened, or make excuses for the prior general. Men took advantage of women; she knew this was the way of the world outside the church walls. But inside the convent a woman, even a beautiful woman, should be able to find sanctuary.

Assuming the prioress was still sleeping, Sister Pureza knocked softly on her door and then pushed it open. But Prioress Bartolommea was already awake. She was kneeling at the foot of her bed with the Bible open on her cot. By the dim light of a single candle, Sister Pureza saw the stout figure bolt and rise. Around her waist was a green and gold belt of such finely woven wool that even in the candlelight, it glowed and sparkled.

"Sister!" The prioress raised her hands to block Sister Pureza's approach. "I am in prayer, you have interrupted me. Please leave at once."

Sister Pureza stepped forward. She did not take her eyes off the belt.

"Is that the *Sacra Cintola*?" she asked as Mother Bartolommea tried to hide the sash with her elbows.

The prioress shook her head vigorously.

"That's the Virgin's Holy Belt, isn't it?" Sister Pureza knew the belt was kept behind a locked gate in Santo Stefano, and that papal orders forbade its removal from the sanctity of the chapel. "The Holy Belt, here, in your cell. How can it be?"

The prioress, who had not yet put on her wimple, brushed a clump of gray hair away from her eyes and flashed an angry glance meant to intimidate the old nun.

"This doesn't concern you, Sister Pureza. As I have said repeatedly, all that goes on in the convent is not known to you. I have plans that will enrich our coffers with the blessing of the Holy Mother."

"Plans?" Sister Pureza stood her ground, neither backing up nor moving forward. She was old, but she was not weak. "Plans that include the Holy Girdle of the Virgin Mary?"

"And myself," the prioress sputtered.

"And yourself." Sister Pureza thought for only a moment more. "And the novitiates, I presume? Perhaps in exchange for compromising their welfare, you are now in possession of the city's most precious relic."

"That's enough, Sister Pureza." The prioress advanced toward the midwife. "I will not hear any more. You must leave at once, so that I might return the Holy Belt to its secured storage place. And you must not tell anyone that the belt is here. By the time the sun is up it will be gone, and any appearance of impropriety concerning the *Sacra Cintola* would be a travesty our convent might not survive."

"My good Mother." Sister Pureza looked from the prioress's bare feet on the stone floor, to the robe she'd slung sloppily over her plump shoulders. "The convent's sanctity has already been compromised. This is what I have come to tell you."

"I shall not hear it," the prioress said. "You have been behaving very strangely."

"You must hear me." The old woman shook with anger. "The prior general does not respect the sanctity of these walls. On this night he has forcefully and improperly approached the novitiate Lucrezia, with unspeakable intentions."

The prioress stood, paralyzed. She had her hands on the Holy

Belt, and blasphemy was being uttered in her own cell. She turned her back on Sister Pureza.

"You must leave," she said in a low voice, as she began to open the long golden ties that secured the belt on her waist. "You must not allow your good sense to run away with you. You must think very carefully. The prior general is an important man, and you cannot make slanderous charges against him. There are hands more powerful than his directing what happens here in Santa Margherita."

She removed the belt, and turned.

"Leave my chambers." The prioress raised her voice. "I am your superior and I order you to leave my room at once."

Sister Pureza passed the dawn praying outside the door of Lucrezia's cell while the girl paced inside. When she heard braying on the road and the convent gates open before the bells rang for Prime, the old nun hurried to the window at the end of the hallway and saw a fine Medici steed in the courtyard, tamping a circle of dirt outside the prioress's study. She watched the prioress meet the messenger and hand him a velvet pouch. The relic, Sister Pureza imagined.

Lucrezia stayed in her cell while the nuns filed into the church for Prime, but Sister Pureza stationed herself stiffly next to Prioress Bartolommea and kept her eyes open at all times, even when the prioress closed her own. The prior general left the church as soon as the last note of the morning chants ended, and when Sister Pureza reached the convent refectory she found him sitting alone, calmly eating a boiled egg. He eyed her coolly as she approached, bowed, and met the man's gaze.

"Here in the cloister, Your Grace, women come and go in the service of God." Sister Pureza chose her words carefully. "We must feel we may move freely, unmolested, and without fear of a fellow clergy interrupting our task."

She paused, waiting.

"And what has this to do with me?" Prior General Saviano asked dully.

"Everything," she said. She began to formulate a narrative of the scene in the church corridor. "I returned before Lauds this morning, after the novitiate Lucrezia and I delivered a child at the home of the merchant Ottavio de' Valenti."

She saw the prior general's mouth stiffen, and continued hastily.

"You know what happened, as well as I do," she said. "I will not—"

At the hard touch of a hand on her shoulder, Sister Pureza turned to see the pasty face of Prioress Bartolommea.

"Do not trouble the prior general," the prioress said, stepping between the two of them.

"Excuse me, Mother." Sister Pureza put out her arm and tried to move the prioress from the place where she had planted herself. "I am in the middle of speaking with him."

The prioress pivoted, and stared at Sister Pureza's elbow, which was pressing roughly into her side.

"Excuse *me*, Sister," said the prioress in a clipped tone. "But you are hurting me."

Sister Pureza became aware of the other nuns watching the three of them. She stepped close to the prioress, so her voice would fall on her ears only. The two women had come to the convent at the same time, some fifty years earlier. They had known each other as novitiates, called each other by girlish names. Sister Pureza used one of those names now, to remind the prioress of what they'd once shared.

"Bartolinni, my friend. You must ask him to leave."

"Then it's no surprise why I've asked her to sit for these portraits. She makes a very fine Virgin."

"Certainly," the prior general agreed. "But to have her here is improper, and a mockery of my Order. I will not have it."

"I've done nothing wrong." The monk struggled to avoid the appearance of guilt. "At the request of the Medici, I've commenced work on a magnificent altarpiece, one that sings the Madonna's praises. If she's beautiful, it is a reflection of the purity and beauty within the novitiate and the Mother."

"Filippo, you, of all men, can ill afford even the whisper of indiscretion. And I will not tolerate it."

Fra Filippo had known Lucrezia's visits to his *bottega* would end; the prior general was only announcing the inevitable. And though he felt it might break his heart, Fra Filippo could do nothing but bow to Saviano's orders. Even the Medici's influence would go no further to secure their meetings when anyone could see that he had more than captured the young woman's likeness already, many times over.

"Your will is done, Prior General. I'll not see the novitiate here again."

Satisfied, and weary from his long morning, Prior General Saviano prepared to leave. But as he turned to exit the workshop, the flowered sleeve of a *cotta* caught his eye from under the crooked top of a wooden chest. His robes rippled as he walked to the storage box and lifted the top. A deep purple dress with flowered sleeves lay crumpled in a pile. Gingerly, he lifted the dress. A *benda* and a pair of silk stockings fell out of its folds.

The prior general swung around and stared at the sketch of Lucrezia, his eyes moving back and forth from her image to the pile of wrinkled clothing in the chest. A purple, as deep as that of the gown, spread on his cheeks and climbed to the tip of his forehead.

"Really, Sister." The mother spoke as if their intimacy had been erased decades ago. "You must stop telling me what I must do."

The prioress had a moment of regret when she saw the hurt in her old friend's face. But then she thought again of the Holy Belt. She imagined her own likeness in a painting glorifying the Virgin Mother. She thought of the glory this could bring to the convent, and of the many hours she'd spent on her knees praying for just such good fortune to reach her here, on the long road outside of Florence. And she was silent as her friend blinked and turned away.

Within the hour, Sister Pureza settled on a plan of action. She sent a hurried note to Ottavio de' Valenti, advising him that Lucrezia was available to help care for his wife and child, and suggesting it was of some importance that he extend an invitation to the novitiate as soon as possible. She hoped and prayed that de' Valenti would welcome their virgin with open arms, and she was right. A message came that same afternoon, with the request from Ottavio de' Valenti sent directly to Mother Bartolommea. Along with the note, he sent four gold florins.

Prioress Bartolommea clapped her hands when she opened the pouch. Then she called Sister Pureza to her chambers, and said to her in a hurried whisper, "You see, the Sacred Belt is doing its job. The miracles are happening already. Look, Sister Pureza. I know what I am doing."

Sister Pureza nodded as if the prioress had indeed been responsible for the content of the note, the gold florins, even the miracle of the birth itself. The prioress summoned Lucrezia at once, and while the tear-streaked face of the young woman hovered before her, ghostlike, Prioress Bartolommea congratulated herself on the good fortune of the Lord's ways.

"You will return to the home of Signora de' Valenti and help care for her," Prioress Bartolommea said. "She believes you have a gift for healing, but you must not let this go to your head. Any gift you have is from God, as all blessings come from Heaven."

Lucrezia was distraught. So much had happened so quickly, and all of it seemed to turn on what people saw in her face and what they imagined they knew of her. She did not know about the gold florins, but she had seen the splendor of the de' Valenti home, she had heard wondrous praise from everyone in the birth chamber. Beauty and gold were as much a part of fate and fortune as were prayer and piety, Lucrezia realized. Perhaps they were even more important than God's will. If, as Sister Pureza had said, beauty was a gift from God and there was no shame in it, then she had nothing to fear. And yet, she was afraid.

Hands clasped, Lucrezia fought against tears. She felt in some way the prior general's rough attentions were a warning, but whether they were from Satan or from the Lord, she couldn't decide.

"You have been summoned," Sister Pureza said quietly. She stood between Lucrezia and the prioress, showing allegiance to neither. "Is there anything you wish to say to Prioress Bartolommea?"

"I will go where I am needed, Mother," Lucrezia said, willing humility and calm to come to her.

The prioress nodded. "Go pack your things," she said, thinking of the sour faces of the other nuns, who were beginning to grumble about the many privileges given the beautiful novitiate. "You will leave quietly tomorrow, so there won't be jealousy among the others."

Prioress Bartolommea didn't think it prudent or necessary to tell the women that Prior General Saviano had forbidden her to grant

Lucrezia gasped, dropping the herbs she held in her hands.

"But I'm not trained in midwifery," she exclaimed. "I have no knowledge of childbirth."

"Your training has already begun," Sister Pureza said. "Birthwort, for the bleeding. Vervain, for the humors. Sage for purification, wintergreen for the pain."

"But there's so much more," Lucrezia said. "So much more that I don't know."

"You'll learn," Sister Pureza said. "It's sharp medicine for a young woman to see the pain of childbirth, even a young woman bound for the veil."

A flash of white cloth moved on the other side of the cloister garden and caught Lucrezia's eye. She tore her gaze from Sister Pureza's and peered through the cloister arches, hoping for a glimpse of Fra Filippo. Seeing the look that passed across the young woman's face, Sister Pureza turned also, and saw the cleric. But it was not Fra Filippo. The man's robes were black, ornamented with a white vestment that waved as he walked briskly toward the refectory.

"The prior general," Sister Pureza said, squinting across the hedge and past the wall of the barn, to where the man hurried in the direction of the prioress's study. "I saw his horse earlier."

"Yes, he arrived this morning, when you were practicing the psalms with the others," Lucrezia said. "Mother Bartolommea brought him to the garden."

"The prior general was here, in my garden?"

Sister Pureza always found the prior general's presence disturbing. He lingered too long in the refectory after meals, and stayed in the convent's guest room longer than necessary while he dined with important merchants in Prato. In short, he seemed far more concerned with power than with piety.

special visiting privileges to the novitiates. Nor did she see reason to deny de' Valenti's generous request. The prior general would soon be gone, and if he noticed Lucrezia's absence and inquired about it, the prioress knew what she would do: she would simply show him the gold, and smile. Four florins were worth a great deal; even the prior general would not be able to deny it.

Chapter Thirteen

Feast of the Sacred Belt and the Nativity of Mary,
the Year of Our Lord 1456

Filing into the church for Lauds on the morning of the *Festa della Sacra Cintola*, the nuns whispered feverishly about the birth at the Valenti household, and the strange tension that had invaded their private world.

"I heard Lucrezia weeping all night, and the prioress was up well before dawn," Sister Maria said.

"Maybe Prioress Bartolommea is displeased with Lucrezia," said Sister Piera, who immediately made the sign of the cross to protect against the sin of jealousy.

"The novitiate is proud of her beauty," surmised Sister Maria, who blushed at her bold statement. "You know Sister Pureza and Prioress Bartolommea do not approve of pride or vanity."

"I wish I knew what made Sister Lucrezia weep," said Sister Bernadetta softly as she padded behind them. "I'd help her, if I could."

Among the troubled and curious souls, only Spinetta and Paolo, the shepherd boy, knew the plans that had been made for Lucrezia. For the promise of bread, and herbs from Sister Pureza's garden, Paolo had agreed to lead the novitiate to the Valenti palazzo when the time came.

"But why is it a secret?" Spinetta whispered to her sister as they filed into the church. "If there's nothing wrong, why is it a secret that you're going to help Signora de' Valenti care for her new baby?"

Although Lucrezia suspected Sister Pureza had arranged to have her removed from the convent to keep her away from Prior General Saviano, she could only guess at the intentions of the old nun and the prioress. She gave Spinetta a terse shake of her head and then bowed in silent prayer.

As the nuns filed toward the refectory for a quick breakfast, Lucrezia pulled her sister into the dormitory and pressed her prayer beads into her hands.

"I'm returning them so you can have their comfort while I'm away," she said.

Spinetta took the beads, still warm from the folds of her sister's robe.

"Lucrezia, I'm afraid. There's something you aren't telling me," Spinetta said.

"Don't be afraid, Spinettina." Lucrezia's fingers worried the hem of her *panni di gamba* until she found the silver medal she'd sewn into its cloth. Using the tip of a fingernail she broke open the loose stitches, slipped the silver medallion into her palm, and held this, too, out for her sister.

"Until I return, keep my medallion safe," she said. "I won't need it at the home of Ottavio de' Valenti. I have been there, Spinetta, there's no need to worry. It is a grand palazzo full of people and servants and warm fire."

Spinetta searched her sister's face, but Lucrezia revealed nothing.

"I'll return soon," Lucrezia said recklessly. "If I'm not back within two days, I'll ask the mistress of the house if you can come to help me."

"Yes." Spinetta brightened, slipping the medallion into the fold of her robe along with the beads. "We had such fun together in Fra Filippo's workshop. Didn't we?"

"Yes, *mia cara*. I haven't forgotten anything that happened at the painter's *bottega*," Lucrezia said. As she spoke, she wondered again what the painter had told the prior general, and what had led the angry man to believe she and Fra Filippo had been intimate. At the memory of the accusation, Lucrezia shuddered. "But I do not think we will return there again."

⁘⧂⧃⧂⁘

The good citizens of Prato awoke on the morning of the Feast of the Holy Belt to find the day bright and the sky clearing. Shopkeepers swept their floors, hearths sparked, kettles warmed, and mothers wove their daughters' hair with ribbons and told them the story of the Holy Belt of the Virgin Mary.

"And so the Holy Virgin passed her belt to Thomas as she ascended to Heaven," Teresa de' Valenti recounted from her partum bed, the sheets pulled up under her chin, her eyes still sleepy. Her four daughters, Isabella, Olivia, Francesca, and Andreatta, all washed and dressed, sat on the plump bedding listening to the story of the Virgin's ascension.

"Her beautiful belt, which had many sacred powers, was kept safe in Jerusalem until it was acquired by the merchant Michael Dagomari of Prato, as part of his wife's dowry," Teresa de' Valenti told her girls. As she spoke, she looked at the face of the Virgin in the portrait that had been moved to her bedside. Her children's eyes followed hers. "When the good man returned from the Holy Land with his bride, he brought the treasure with him and gave it to our church for safekeeping. For three hundred years the Blessed Girdle of the Virgin Mary has been here, and many important men have entered our great city walls to beg the Virgin for favor and holy intercession."

All over Prato, children listened in rapt attention to the story of the Holy Belt, and waited impatiently until the church bells rang and every doorway and window in Prato was flung open and the streets finally flooded with people making their way toward the church square.

※

*L*ed by Prioress Bartolommea, the nuns walked through the convent gates and into the streets of Prato.

"Mother of Heaven, it's a beautiful day," Sister Antonia declared, and the others agreed.

Throngs of early-morning faithful, pressing toward the piazza, stepped aside to let the nuns pass, their habits gently rippling in the soft breeze. Prioress Bartolommea began chanting the Gloria and soon the others joined her.

As they drew closer to Santo Stefano, the sisters heard trumpets blowing and horses neighing. Some of the nuns grew increasingly delighted, intoxicated by the music and laughter, while others were unnerved by the riot of color and the sound of marching feet and blaring horns; shy Sister Piera even felt a little panicky and wished, for a moment, she was back in the safe terrain of the cloister.

Patting their robes and straightening their spines, the nuns joined the crowd behind the *pieve*. With Sister Pureza in the rear, they took their places in pairs along the southern edge of the square, a few feet in front of the handsome Pulpit of the Sacred Girdle, just as the high notes of the trumpet were sounded. The crowd hushed, and the procession began.

Provost Inghirami and Prior General Saviano sat on sleek black horses draped in gold and green silk, bracketed by young boys carrying Medici flags. Behind them walked a handsome Ottavio de' Val-

enti, his dark hair slicked with oil. He was followed by his eldest
daughters and two rows of young girls dressed in white *gamurre,* gold
and green ribbons wound through their braids. Young town boys
dressed in bright *farsetto* doublets and silk stockings sounded trumpets, their thick curls blowing softly with each note, and two of the
tallest carried a large banner with the image of the nursing Madonna
painted in bright colors, followed by a procession of proud mothers—some pregnant and others carrying fat, squawking babies who
clapped their hands with delight or cried for their mother's milk.
At the rear of the procession came the members of the Orders—
Augustinian, Dominican, Franciscan, and Carmelite—who lined the
square, their brown, black, and white robes quivering like quiet notes
against the reds, greens, and purples of the citizens' festive attire.

As the parade ended, the crowd turned to face the Pulpit of the
Sacred Girdle, cheering wildly as Provost Gemignano Inghirami
stepped out upon it. He raised his spindly arms and held the green
belt above his head and instantly, as if choreographed, the men,
women, and children made the sign of the cross and quieted so the
provost could speak.

"Holiest Mother, Queen of Heaven, Divine Virgin, we come here
today to honor you and praise your name. Mary, Full of Grace, we
bestow our love and adoration upon you. May the divine grace of
your *Sacra Cintola* protect us and keep us as we honor you in the name
of your Son, the Lord Jesus Christ. Amen."

The people squeezed closer to the pulpit, holding up their arms
to be nearer to the sacred relic. Although that would be as close as
many got, the sisters of Santa Margherita would be permitted the
supreme blessing of touching the belt within the chapel. As best she
could, Mother Bartolommea began to shepherd her flock toward the

church doorway along with the tumult of many others in monastic tunics and nuns' robes. So many people swelled toward the entrance that Spinetta grabbed Lucrezia's hand to be sure she stayed close. Lucrezia squeezed her sister's fingers and brought them to her lips, then forced them away. As she did, Sister Pureza slid alongside her and said, "This is for the best, my dear. May the Lord watch over you tonight."

Then the old nun melted back into line with the others and Paolo appeared at Lucrezia's side, his thin hand sliding into hers. Wordlessly she left Spinetta and the others and followed the boy as he slipped nimbly through the crowd. At the edge of the square he paused to look up at her, flashing a gap-toothed smile.

"Sorella," he said. "You're very lucky to be going to the fine house of Signor de' Valenti. You can eat as much as you want there."

Lucrezia smiled in spite of herself, and followed Paolo through the narrow streets, moving against the flow of people who filled the small shop doorways and crushed toward the church. She was sorry to be missing the celebration, for it reminded her of *festa* days at home with her sisters and parents. But she forced herself to keep up with Paolo, who'd let go of her hand and was flying ahead on fleet feet.

Amid the mad bustling, Fra Filippo at last spotted Lucrezia. She was hurrying away from the *pieve*, with Paolo leading.

"Sister Lucrezia, wait," he called out.

Lucrezia turned to see the monk moving toward her.

"Keep going, Paolo," she said. "Signora de' Valenti is at home with her child, and they are waiting for me."

"Sister Lucrezia," Fra Filippo's voice rang out again. "Please stop!"

Paolo looked up at Lucrezia. His sister was the monk's kitchen girl, and both children were accustomed to doing as the man instructed.

But Lucrezia quickened her step. As the monk's heavy footfalls caught up with hers, she remembered the prior general's rough grip, his harsh words. She spun around and faced Fra Filippo, her eyes blazing.

"Keep your distance, Fra Filippo," she said. "Please, leave me in peace."

She gestured for him to stay away, and as she did, the sleeve of her robe flew up, revealing the bruises the prior general had left there.

"You've been hurt!" The monk tried to reach for her, but she snatched her arm away.

"I beg of you," he said. "Whatever has happened, you must let me help you."

"Help me?" Lucrezia began hurrying past the shop doorways, with Paolo beside her. The monk followed. "You've put me in the position of running from the prior general," she said. "Now I must hide from him. Do you realize what he thinks of me?"

"Lucrezia." Fra Filippo leaned over Paolo and reached for her hand again. "For the love of God, will you tell me what is happening?"

Lucrezia stopped to catch her breath, curling her hands up under her long sleeves. A group of nuns from Sant'Ippolito turned onto the street, heading toward her.

"I'm going to the home of Ottavio de' Valenti," she said. "I'll stay there to help his wife with their child until—until it's safe for me to return to the convent."

"Until it's *safe*?"

"I believe I will stay until the prior general is gone."

Fra Filippo's ears burned.

"But Saviano will be at the de' Valenti home tonight, perhaps for several nights," he said. "He's going there for a grand dinner in honor of the merchant's newborn son."

The sounds of the parade filled the streets, and the merriment seemed to draw closer. The nuns approached, chanting softly.

"If he's hurt you, you can't go there," he said rapidly. He turned to Paolo, who was bouncing on his toes, waiting.

"Paolo." The monk took the boy by his thin shoulders. "The plan is changed. You must take Sister Lucrezia to my *bottega*. Your sister is there, and you must ask her to stay. Tell Rosina I'll give her an extra silver piece for her trouble. Do you understand?"

"No." Lucrezia shook her head. "Prioress Bartolommea sent me to the Valenti palazzo, the signora has asked for me."

The painter grew agitated, and seemed to stand taller in her path.

"I know Prior General Saviano, Sister Lucrezia, and if the nuns think it best to keep you away from him, then you cannot go to the Valenti palazzo until he is gone."

"Then I'll return to the convent," she said.

"And if he looks for you there?" Fra Filippo asked.

Lucrezia didn't move.

"Go with Paolo," Fra Filippo commanded. "I'd accompany you myself, but I'm expected at the *pieve* and am already late. We will do what we can about the prior general when the *festa* is over."

Lucrezia's head was spinning. If she went to de' Valenti's, the prior general was sure to find her there. Yet if she went back to the convent, the prior general could just as easily return to prey on her again. Santa Margherita was not a refuge for her now.

"*Sì*. All right, Fra Filippo, yes, I will go, but only until I've found a better place."

The monk put a reassuring hand on her arm.

"This is best," he said. "The prior general will be reprimanded. He will not come near you once I have spoken to my powerful friends."

"Please, you've done enough," she said, regaining the strength that had eluded her this morning. "I will stay until it is safe to go to Signora Teresa's bedside, and with God's will, no one will know where I have been."

"As you wish," the monk said. He instructed Paolo to take Lucrezia around the long way to his *bottega*, so she would not have to pass through the crowded piazza again, and bade them haste.

In their heated exchange, neither the painter nor the novitiate realized the nuns from Sant'Ippolito had clearly seen Fra Filippo—so unmistakable in his large white robes—stop Lucrezia and send her down a different winding street, in the opposite direction of *la pieve*.

Chapter Fourteen

After Nones, Feast of the Sacred Belt, the Year of Our Lord 1456

Lucrezia sat in a sturdy wooden chair next to Fra Filippo's hearth, watching a girl in a ragged dress stirring the fire. Her arms were thin, but she poured water into an iron kettle effortlessly, raising the heavy pot shoulder height to hang it over the flames.

"I'm Rosina," the girl said. Her hair was dark, her face plain and sweet. "I'm Paolo's sister."

The sounds of the *festa* reverberated outside, but all was quiet in the painter's studio.

"Why aren't you at the *festa*?" Lucrezia asked.

"I come every morning to help Brother Filippo in the kitchen," Rosina said. Dark eyelashes grazed the top of her cheeks. "I'll go to the *pieve* when my work here is done."

The girl looked at Lucrezia's robe and wimple.

"Soon I'll be of age," she added. "Then I will enter the Convent Santa Margherita."

Rosina handed Lucrezia a heavy mug. As she drank the sweet wine, the novitiate felt fatigue settle into her body. She hadn't slept all night. It wouldn't hurt to rest, she thought as she set the cup on the floor and closed her eyes. She was safe here. Surely she'd feel better if she prayed for guidance and surrendered to the sleep that is the Lord's best medicine.

Lucrezia woke on soft bedding. The room was dark and silent and for a few confused seconds she thought she was home in Florence, in the walnut bed that she'd shared with Spinetta.

"Is anyone here?" she called out.

She lifted the blanket and sat up. Someone had removed her boots and stockings. Vaguely she remembered Rosina's small, strong hands. Lucrezia rubbed her eyes until they adjusted to the darkness, and looked around at a small bedroom of rough-hewn beams and uneven walls. The ceiling was made of a thatched straw that could barely be expected to keep out the spring rains. She strained to listen, but the *bottega* and streets beyond seemed quiet.

"Is anyone here?"

She was still wearing her robe, and her wimple was tangled. As she removed the head covering Lucrezia looked around the bedroom, peering through the darkness at the outline of the large wooden bed, a simple chest, and a small washbasin. Above the basin she could make out the thick lines of a cross. She wondered if the monk had returned from the *festa,* and if Rosina was still in the kitchen. But before she could rouse herself, Lucrezia fell back onto the bed. She was as far from the prior general as she could be, in the protection of Fra Filippo, chaplain of her convent.

Tiptoeing into the kitchen the following day, Lucrezia was grateful to see Rosina in a clean blue dress covered by a pale linen apron.

"*Buongiorno.*" Rosina held a large wooden spoon, and her apron pockets were brimming with rags.

Taking a piece of bread from the girl, Lucrezia lifted the curtain that led to the monk's studio and peeked into the workshop. Morning light filled the *bottega* and the monk turned from his easel, paint-brush in hand.

"You've slept a long time, Sister Lucrezia," Fra Filippo said, his face brightening at the sight of her.

"I must leave here," she exclaimed. "I must at least present myself at the Valenti palazzo, where I'm expected."

"Don't worry." Fra Filippo held a hand under his dripping paint-brush. "They've received word that you are detained."

"But what reason did you give?"

"The note said you aren't feeling well." The painter took in the tight lines of her face, the shadows beneath her eyes. "Which seems to be true."

"You told them I'm here?" She took a step backward, and realized her head was bare.

"The note was sent by our friend Fra Piero, the procurator," the monk hurried to explain. "It doesn't say where you are, only that you won't be arriving for at least another night."

"Then the procurator knows I'm here?" Lucrezia looked behind her, through the curtain that separated the *bottega* from the kitchen. She could see Rosina stoking the fire. She reached a hand up and grabbed the length of her hair, nervously twisting it into a knot. "I asked you to speak of this to no one."

"Fra Piero is a trusted friend, *mia cara,* and he agrees we must protect you from the prior general. When Saviano leaves the Valenti home, of course you will go there."

Lucrezia looked away, wrapping the knot of her hair more tightly.

"The prior general misunderstood," the monk began. He faulted himself for allowing Saviano to bully his way into the *bottega* and then leave with wrongful assumptions. "He saw the painting of the *Adoring Madonna*, and the robes you wore while I worked, and he misunderstood."

"I'm ashamed." Lucrezia dropped her voice. "He thinks I've given away my purity. Please, Fratello, you have to tell him it's not so."

"I told him quite insistently, Sister Lucrezia. But he's not a man who listens to reason." From where he stood, Fra Filippo could see the vellum on which he'd drawn her face, the studies he'd made for her likeness on the Medici panel. His pen, he saw, did her justice. "In time, the work which you've helped me create will be finished, God willing. When the altarpiece is received and praised in Naples, the prior general will understand his error."

"And until then?"

"Until then, you're under the protection of the procurator. A note signed by him gives full sway over any instruction you have from the prioress."

"It isn't proper," Lucrezia insisted quietly. "You know I can't be here alone with you."

Fra Filippo's face darkened.

"Of course I've taken this into consideration," he said. "Rosina will stay until Spinetta can come. It's only for a day or two, until the prior general is gone."

"Under what claim will you send for my sister?"

"The procurator has already sent for her. He wrote to Prioress Bartolommea, asking that Spinetta be permitted to join you at the de' Valenti palazzo. But of course he will see that she is brought here, where the two of you will stay under my protection. I'm the chaplain of the convent, and there's room enough in my small home for us to keep separate quarters. Everything is completely proper."

"So much deception," Lucrezia said. "It's sinful."

"The first sin comes from the prior general," the painter said. "When he's gone, you will carry on with your business, and none will be the wiser. What else can you do, Sister Lucrezia, given his reprehensible behavior? Here, no one will know where you are, and you will be safe."

Lucrezia gave a small nod. It seemed the monk knew what must be done, and had taken charge of everything.

"As long as Spinetta is coming soon," she said. "As long as I'm not here alone with you, Fra Filippo."

The monk nodded brusquely. Above all, he wanted Lucrezia to know he would protect her honor. He moved to the panel with the figure of the kneeling Madonna, and pretended to study it.

"I'll need to work while you're here, of course." From the corner of his eye he saw Lucrezia's gaze roaming the studio, her hands pulling at her knotted hair. "Please, Sister Lucrezia, cover your head and you'll feel more comfortable."

Alone in the bedchamber, Lucrezia used the painter's basin to rinse her face. Checking the door, she removed her robe and stood in the silken *panni di gamba*, washing quickly with a rag and remembering how kind Sister Pureza had been to let her keep the undergarments. Slipping her robe back on, she combed her hair with her fingers, and wound it back under her wimple, securing it carefully. Her boots were not in the chamber, and so she went back into the kitchen, bare feet padding against the straw scattered across the floor.

"Sorella, I've just cleaned your boots, let me get them for you," Rosina exclaimed. She ducked through the door of the kitchen and returned with the boots. When Lucrezia returned to the *bottega* her wimple was in place, all of her lovely yellow hair tucked away, and the painter was at his table looking at a small sketch. He spoke without looking up at her.

"Do you know the story of Saint Stephen's life?" he asked. "It was fraught with suffering and doubt, but it was a colorful life, and an exciting one."

The painter pointed to his sketch as he described the scenes he was re-creating in the chapel frescoes.

"There's the stoning of the saint," he said, indicating the group of men with their arms in the air, the cowering figure of the saint in a corner of the sketch. "And there's his funeral, with his disciples kneeling by his corpse."

Lucrezia had shown great interest in his work, and a fine understanding of art and beauty. As long as she was here, Fra Filippo wanted to share his knowledge with her.

"When I paint the funeral I have to think of all the sad things I've known in my life," he explained. "I have to pour every sorrow and every moment of lost faith into the piece. It's the only way to show the humanity of the saint's life."

The novitiate turned to him, her face registering surprise.

"When have you lost faith, Brother Filippo?"

"There are dark moments in every life, Sister Lucrezia. You're still young, but in time you'll understand."

"I'm not as young as you might believe," she said. "Since losing my father, I've aged a great deal. At least, that's how I feel."

She made a gesture with her arm, and the sleeve of her robe lifted to reveal the bruises. The monk put a hand out as if to touch her, but she pulled away.

"Tell me about the life of Saint Stephen," she said quickly. "Please."

Fra Filippo cleared his throat and found the voice that he used during worship, speaking in a tone that was both warm and commanding.

"He was the first martyr," the monk said quietly. "But after his death he saw the Father and the Son. That was his reward for suffering in good faith."

He brought Saint Stephen's life into clear relief, culling facts and stories from his many hours of study. He recounted the saint's trial for blasphemy, his public stoning, the scene of his magnificent funeral. When he'd clarified for himself the images that he wanted to capture, Fra Filippo shuffled through his parchments and spread the largest one across his oak table. He anchored it in place and silently, almost with his eyes closed, sketched the general outlines of the scenes and indicated in his rough handwriting what he would place within each frame.

Lucrezia sat on a stool and watched his fluid movements, the way he fell into the dream of his work and seemed to forget everything: the sounds of activity in the piazza beyond the curtained window, even her very presence in the studio. Her father had been the same, capable of submerging himself in a book of figures, or drawings and colors, emerging hours later as if he had been in a distant place that was closed to her. But in the *bottega,* she didn't feel far from the painter. Somehow she felt she understood what he was doing as his hand flew across the parchment, making deft strokes and scribbling notes on the margins.

With a few final marks he'd completed two new figures, their heads perfect ovals, their robes flowing in sinuous arabesques. Then Fra Filippo stood, propping the large parchment against the wall, and stepped away to study what he'd done.

"*Bene,*" he noted with satisfaction. He drank from the ceramic jug and held the wine out to her. She shook her head.

"I remember, in the confessional, how you gave me permission to seek beauty," Lucrezia said, forcing out the words she'd been rehearsing in her head. "I can't tell you how that lightened my heart. I'm very grateful to you, Fratello."

The monk smiled and they looked at each other until Lucrezia turned away.

"And of course, I am most grateful for your protection," she said.

⋘⊰◦⊱⋙

*I*n the de' Valenti palazzo, Prior General Saviano woke from a long night of celebratory eating and drinking and joined Ottavio in his dining chamber. They took a leisurely meal together, and the prior general asked the merchant about his position concerning the politics in Rome, the illness that was reportedly consuming Pope Callistus III, and whom he supported as the next pope.

"I favor the Archbishop of Rouen," said Saviano. "I do not believe the Medici should control all of Florence and the seat of Rome as well."

"But think of Piccolomini's diplomatic skills," argued de' Valenti. "Certainly the Bishop of Siena will do more for us than d'Estouteville can, coming from Rouen."

Prior General Saviano frowned and de' Valenti, ever the gracious host, offered his guest more wine, and then changed the subject.

"I pray, Your Grace, you might visit my son in his chambers," the merchant said. "A final blessing, before you return to Florence?"

Agreeing, Prior General Saviano followed his host through the *piano nobile*, up the main stairway graced with tapestries and frescoes depicting scenes from the Old Testament. Ottavio greeted his wife's many attendants with a gracious air of indulgence, and they parted to let him pass. At the entrance to her birthing chamber, the merchant paused in front of the portrait he had commissioned for his wife, and gestured to Fra Filippo's painting. But it was unnecessary. The Virgin's face had already caught the prior general's eye.

"Ottavio, can you explain this?" Saviano asked in a low rumble. "This is the novitiate from the convent."

De' Valenti nodded, and rested his hands on his full belly.

"I've only seen the novitiate once, Your Grace, but I can tell you the picture barely does her beauty justice." Ottavio clapped a silk-covered arm around the shoulder of his guest. "Teresa claims the painting has holy powers. She believes it is the girl herself who kept her alive on the night my son was born. Everyone in my house is calling this piece our *Miraculous Madonna.*"

De' Valenti pushed his *berretto* up on his head and scratched at his temple.

"My wife has given me four daughters and three heirs, but the devil took each of my sons before his first earthly breath. Only this one survives, and if my wife believes there was a miracle in her birthing chamber, who am I to deny it?"

Making his way into his wife's private apartment, Ottavio de' Valenti found Teresa propped on many plush pillows. He kissed her cheek, and she greeted him fondly.

"Ottavio, didn't you send for the novitiate?" she asked. "I thought she was to arrive last night."

"I wrote immediately to the prioress." The merchant knelt at his wife's bedside and took her hands in his own. "This morning we received word that she is delayed. But it's only for a day or two. Then she'll be here with you."

Behind him, Prior General Saviano screwed up his face. He'd expressly said the girl was not to leave the convent.

"The novitiate? The Virgin of the painting is to come here?"

Teresa de' Valenti smiled and nodded.

"My husband is good to me. He's good to all of us. The Lord has given us many blessings, and now we have our own *Miraculous Madonna.*

It is a blessed omen that she is here among us, don't you agree, Prior General Saviano?"

⁓⊱⋆⊰⁓

"*P*lease, Fra Filippo, don't let me keep you from your work," Lucrezia said after their moment had passed. "I'm content to sit and watch, especially if you have something to keep my hands busy."

Fra Filippo's eyes fell upon the lavender he'd taken from the convent garden two weeks earlier. The flowers had dried, and could be ground to make fragrant oil.

Gathering the herbs and a wooden bowl and pestle, the monk settled Lucrezia at his table, where she nimbly separated the kernels as he talked about his plans for the frescoes.

"There's also the life of Saint John the Baptist, who is the patron saint of the wool guild in Prato," he said. "I'll show his birth, his parting from his parents, and the banquet when his head is brought to King Herod on a platter. Many church patrons have paid to have their likenesses among the faces at Herod's banquet. It's said that when a patron is depicted in a painting that serves God's glory, it takes him one step closer to heaven's gate."

His voice trailed off, and Fra Filippo turned to his fresh parchment, imagining where he might place the faces and bodies of the banquet revelers. As she sifted through the lavender, the colorful grains falling easily from the stems, Lucrezia wondered if her likeness as the Virgin Mary also brought her closer to heaven's gate.

"Do the paintings act as an absolution?" she asked softly. "Is that why the patrons are brought closer to heaven when they're depicted in your work?"

Absently, the monk answered.

"*Si, si.* A man may pay the church for forgiveness of a sin already committed, or become a patron and earn leniency for future transgressions. At least"—he glanced sideways at her—"at least, that's what they say in Rome."

Lucrezia thought about his reply, and wondered if Fra Filippo might agree to paint Spinetta's face in one of his fresco scenes. Spinetta wasn't a sinner, but it couldn't hurt to have extra assurance of God's good favor.

"It is past Sext," Fra Filippo said after a time. "You must be hungry."

The two had a light meal of bread and cheese in the kitchen. Rosina poured them each a cup of watery wine, and tidied up the hearth as they ate in strained silence.

"If there's nothing else, Fratello, my mother needs me at home," Rosina said after she'd wiped their small plates.

Lucrezia looked up in alarm.

"Of course." Fra Filippo stood and brushed the crumbs from his hands. "And I must go to the chapel to check on the progress there." He reminded Rosina to be sure her brother had gone to the convent and delivered the procurator's message.

"Yes, Fra Filippo," the girl replied, "my brother has done as you asked."

"*Si,* he's a good boy." The painter removed a silver coin from a jar on the shelf, and slipped it into her hand. "Bring your mother something from the market."

"*Molte grazie.*" The girl pressed her cheek against his hand, bowed to Lucrezia, and slipped out the door.

It was still early afternoon. Standing in the doorway to the antechamber, Fra Filippo turned to Lucrezia.

"I'll work in the chapel until the light fades," he said stiffly. "Please pass the time as you like, and I won't bother you again until dusk. By then I trust Spinetta will have arrived."

After he'd gone, Lucrezia moved restlessly around the studio. She lifted a sheet and saw a darkly painted pietà, the face of the Virgin taut and gray. Lifting another cloth draped over a large panel, she found a kind-faced friar with a halo above his head. When she couldn't make out his identity, she dropped the sheet and picked up a pile of parchments. She turned them over and found her own likeness looking back at her. It was her face, her cheeks, her eyes. Yet by the monk's hand she'd become something precious and holy. She'd become the Madonna, the Blessed Mother.

Spinetta had said the likeness was flattering, but Lucrezia wanted to see for herself if this was true. Although she'd worn splendid dresses, and been adorned with delicate *bende* made by the finest weavers in Florence, here in Prato she'd been told for the first time that she was a beautiful woman. She couldn't help but wonder what changes showed now, in her face. Her eyes moved quickly across the monk's cluttered worktable, sure that there would be a reflective surface among his many tools.

The monk wasn't a tidy man, and his table was piled with many instruments. She reached over a cluster of large vessels and pots toward a glass canister near the wall, and her sleeve caught on a paintbrush, tipping a jar of color. Lucrezia cried out and jerked her arm back. But instead of steadying the container she upset another, which tipped into a bowl of paint.

She jumped back, but it was too late. The viscous liquid streaked down her robe from waist to knee, and it smelled of rotten eggs.

Lucrezia grabbed a crumpled rag, but wiping at the *verdaccio* only smeared it further. She tried water, but it beaded up on the oily surface of the paint. Lemon did the same, and wine vinegar bubbled and turned the green mess into brown and purple the color of an old bruise.

When it was clear the thick paint wasn't lifting, Lucrezia remembered that Fra Filippo used ammonia to clean his brushes. She bent to the low shelf where she knew he kept the flask, and carefully removed the stopper. The sharp odor burned her eyes. Looking quickly around the workshop, assured that no one passing by could look in and spy her, Lucrezia slipped the robe over her head and stood in her undergarments. She laid the robe onto the floor, where she could be sure nothing else would spill on it, and blotted the black fabric with the foul-smelling ammonia. But instead of lifting the color, it seemed to suck away the pigment. The robe was ruined.

Surveying the sloppy mess she'd made, she thought bitterly of the beautiful dress she'd worn on the day she left her home. Lucrezia replaced the stopper in the flask, returned the ammonia to the shelf, and went into the kitchen, where a bucket of water sat on the floor beside the fireplace. Wearing only her wimple and her *panni di gamba*, Lucrezia knelt, dipped the rag in the bucket, and dabbed furiously at the green splotches and grayish pools of color where the ammonia had leached the dye from the fabric.

The terrible smell made her dizzy. Sitting back on her heels, she fingered the hem of her silken chemise, where she'd secreted her medallion before giving it to her sister, and wished she had it now. Her eyes were closed when the knock came, three quick taps that she barely heard before the door opened and the wind came in with the imperious figure of Prior General Saviano.

"Brother Painter," he cried into the *bottega*, his voice a mockery. "*Frate Dipintore*, I wonder if you can solve a mystery for me?"

Lucrezia pushed her slight figure into the small space behind the kitchen doorway.

"Is anyone here?" The prior general's voice brayed in unison with his horse, which neighed at the post outside the doorway.

He clomped through the *bottega*, treading across the splattered green paint. He would tell the painter that he was forbidden to paint Sister Lucrezia's likeness again, and then he would go directly to the convent where he would upbraid the insolent prioress for disobeying his explicit orders that the novitiate not leave the convent.

"Fra Filippo," he called in a snarl.

His temples pulsed and his boots made wet footprints as he entered the kitchen and spotted the crumpled robe, and then the small toes of Lucrezia's stocking-covered feet. He turned slowly to his left, and Saviano's heart began to pound when he saw her figure, crouched behind the door. His eyes climbed up the coil of Lucrezia's body, taking in her white silk undergarments, her bare arms. Stepping closer, he put a hand out and touched her wrist. She flinched.

"Sister Lucrezia!" His lips were tight. He looked right and left, around the small kitchen. "Why are you here?" he demanded.

Lucrezia didn't speak. Her eyes burned and brimmed with tears.

"Where is the monk? Are you alone?" The prior general's gaze changed from angry to bright as he took in the gravity of their circumstance. "You don't need to hide, my dear." He wrapped his long fingers around her arm, and pulled her from behind the doorway. "Come here, let me see what the monk has done to you."

"No." Lucrezia's lips tried to form words, but no sound came. She lowered her eyes and resisted as the prior general pulled her into the center of the kitchen. Holding her with a strong grip, he reached for her chin with his other hand. Her heart sank, and she trembled. She willed herself to move away, but her feet wouldn't obey.

"You know how beautiful you are," Prior General Saviano said.

She thought of Daphne, the Greek maiden who'd turned into a tree so Apollo couldn't have her body, and Lucrezia stood still as a tree as the prior general roughly ran his thumb along her chin and tugged at the brim of her wimple. He pushed it back, then tugged it off, letting a long piece of hair spill out from under her hairnet. He fingered it gently.

"The devil has made your beauty bewitching," Saviano said. He held her arm tightly with one hand, and used the other to trace the bone up to her cheek, past her tiny earlobe, down the length of her white neck.

She could hardly breathe.

"Bewitching." His voice was husky. "Beautiful, bewitching Lucrezia. This is how the painter touches you, isn't it?"

Lucrezia's eyes moved toward the doorway. Where was Spinetta?

"He doesn't," she said weakly. "He doesn't touch me."

"You're lying." The prior general's voice was low but harsh, and drops of spittle sprayed her cheek. "But your lies won't do you any good."

Under his robes, the general felt his lust fueled by envy and anger. Why should the painter take liberties of the flesh while he did not? Why should he deny himself when the girl had already compromised her virtue and given the sweetest bit of it to Lippi?

He clamped her hair firmly, locking her in his grip. Lucrezia felt his cold hand reach up and pull at the silken bloomers, the *panni di gamba* she'd sewn in her father's home. The cloth ripped away as if there had been nothing there but cloud and air.

"Don't fight me," he said gruffly, his breath hot on her face. "Give me what you've given to the painter."

He pushed her backward, lifting her off the ground and pinning her against the kitchen table. Lucrezia could smell onions and cheese on his breath. Her stomach was on fire, her body was numb. His hips pressed against her from the front, the wood table cut into her back. Breathing loudly, he pulled his robes up and fumbled under them, then roughly parted her legs. Lucrezia squeezed her eyes shut as he pressed between her thighs. There was a chafing, a dry heat, and she felt herself tear in two as he thrust harder, deeper. She cried out. Her head snapped back and hit the table, and she bit down on her lip and tasted blood. The prior general grunted loudly, the sound of an animal roared in her ear, and he thrust furiously until he shuddered, and for a moment everything in the room was still.

Then he reached between them to separate his body from hers, and when his hand came up wet and rusty with the smear of new blood, his eyes widened. He cried out a final time.

"You were—" He couldn't bring himself to say the words.

Lucrezia turned away and covered herself with her bare arms. The cleric stood upright and when he didn't reach for her again, she pushed past him into the monk's bedroom, slamming the door and falling against it onto the ground, sobbing.

In the kitchen, the prior general wiped the blood and his seed on the hem of his black robe. He folded himself back into his undergarment, and looked around at the disheveled studio. Without another word, he turned and left.

Fra Filippo took a last look at the sketches he'd made on the plastered walls in Santo Stefano, brushed the red chalk from his palms as best he could, and said good night to his assistants as dusk fell. Looking behind him at the stained-glass windows of the church, he felt wonderfully happy. It had been a fine day's work, but all afternoon his mind had been in the *bottega* with Lucrezia. How lovely it was to have her there, even if only for a day or two. He knew she'd be in nuns' robes, but when he thought of her, he pictured her wearing the silk dress of *morello* purple, the *benda* sewn with small pearls.

He went out of his way to stop at the baker for two sweet rolls, one each for Lucrezia and Spinetta, before turning for home. As he hurried back across the piazza he saw that his *bottega* windows were dark. He reprimanded himself for failing to show Lucrezia where to find the candles and lantern, and quickened his pace until his steps crunched on the gravel in the walkway and he pushed the door open, calling her name.

There was no reply. He fumbled in the darkness, the smell of ammonia and something else burning his throat.

"Sister Lucrezia?" He felt a sudden alarm at the strange smells, the slick dampness under his feet as he reached for the candle on the worktable and sparked a match.

The flame flared. He held the candle high to see around the studio.

"Sister Lucrezia? Sister Spinetta?"

Wildly, he thought Lucrezia might have run off, leaving behind her nun's robe and slipping away in the silk costume he kept in his chest. Pausing at the wooden chest, he lifted the lid to see the purple and blue silks folded carefully in their place. A chill went through him. He parted the curtain and stepped into the kitchen, his boot skidding on a lump of black fabric, his eyes and nose pierced by the stink of ammonia and something foul and unfamiliar. He reached down and recognized the cloth as Lucrezia's convent robe. Next to it, like the soul of its dark shadow, he saw the torn silk undergarment. As he bent to touch it, a sob came from the bedroom.

"Dear God." He nearly wept the two words. "Dear God." Quickly, he pushed against the door and into the room, holding the candle high.

"Lucrezia!"

Her immobile form was curled on the bed, wrapped in a blanket. At the sound of his footfall and his voice, Lucrezia cried out.

"Go away," she sobbed, curling into herself. Fra Filippo imagined the worst. The face of a whore in Venice, her cheeks and nose disfigured with angry slashes, came into his mind.

"What is it?" He fell to his knees at the bedside, put the candle on the floor. "What's happened? Tell me what happened to you."

Her sobs were her only answer. She couldn't imagine what words she could use to tell him such a terrible thing.

The monk's hand touched her shoulder. She flinched, but didn't move away. Her body was numb.

"Please, let me see you. Let me see your face, Lucrezia." Every bit of love and tenderness the monk had been hiding came out in the way he spoke her name. He didn't care anymore. In his heart he prayed, *Please, God, let her be all right and I'll do whatever I must to protect and love her.*

He dared to touch her hair, to lift the wet tangles from her face. She turned her body away, but let him see her hot cheek. It was unmarked.

"All this, for a ruined robe?" he asked gently.

"Not a ruined robe," she managed to choke out. "It's me. I am ruined. I'm ruined."

He pushed her hair from her neck, and saw the angry scratches.

"What's this?" His anger rose. "Did you go out? Did something happen in the street?"

"No." She rolled her body away from him. "The prior general," she said, and her weeping took away the rest of her words.

In an instant, Fra Filippo knew what it was that he smelled in the small chamber, mixed with the sour odor of ammonia and blood. And he knew what had happened.

"Prior General Saviano did this?"

Lucrezia's hands flew to cover her ears.

"Don't say his name," she cried. She began to shiver. "I'm cold," she whispered. "Very cold."

Realizing she was naked beneath his blankets, Fra Filippo reached his strong arms under her small body, wrapped the blankets around her tightly, and lifted her from the bed. She felt herself rise, and for a moment she was terrified that she would fall, fall and never stop. She clung to his shoulders.

"Let's get you warm," he said. Her face was very close to his. He could see everything now, the wound on her bottom lip, the bruise against her left eye, the wet matting of her hair. "Let me take care of you."

She closed her eyes. The monk carried her to the kitchen, and gently placed her in the heavy chair next to the hearth. He piled several pieces of kindling and wood onto the smoldering embers, and fanned them until a small flame caught. He did everything without moving more than an arm's length from her.

"Where's my sister?" she asked solemnly. The fire roared at his back, throwing an orange light across her face. "Is she not coming? Have you lied to me?"

"I promise you, Lucrezia, I haven't lied to you. I'd never lie to you."

Her gaze, filled with such pain and longing, released something inside the painter.

"I couldn't lie to you, Lucrezia." He reached a hand out as if to take her chin in his palm, just as she'd imagined he might. "I love you."

Her eyes widened.

"I speak the truth, more than any other truth I've ever known. I love you. I nearly told you so in the confessional, Lucrezia. I'd rather die than see you suffer, I love you—I'm so sorry I left you here alone."

Lucrezia pushed away his hand and put her palm to her mouth.

"Why are you saying this now, Fra Filippo? Why now that I'm ruined?"

His blue eyes blazed.

"You aren't ruined, Lucrezia. Your purity isn't lost unless you surrender it willingly." Drawing on the words of Saint Augustine, he tried to offer her comfort. "Chastity is a virtue of the mind as well as the body. It's not lost if you don't yield willingly. Saint Augustine said it in Rome, it's what the Order teaches."

She wanted to believe what he was saying, but she couldn't.

"You said it yourself, Fra Filippo. You said it's my face, you said—" The prior general's words came back and she covered her face with her hands. "Even *he* said the devil made me beautiful, that's what he said."

Fra Filippo shook his head.

"Your beauty is a gift from God," he said. "God damn the prior general. And damn the Church that's made of arrogant men like him."

"Stop it, stop it," Lucrezia cried. "Stop saying such things."

The monk tried to pull her close but she turned away.

Fra Filippo found the thick white robe he wore in the coldest winter months and brought it to her. He poured a bowl of water from the cistern and handed her a clean linen cloth.

"*Mia cara,* you must wash yourself, please," he said. "Call to me when you're finished."

Alone by the fire, Lucrezia gingerly touched the moist cloth to the place where she'd been torn. She didn't look down at her body, but kept her eyes steady on the ground. When she was finished, she pulled on the robe. The monk's garment fell far below her feet, and she tugged it up in a bulky drape, wrapping his rope belt twice around her waist. She combed out her hair and braided it as she'd done when she was a girl. She was sitting, waiting, when Fra Filippo came back into the room.

"How can I go back to the convent now?" she asked.

"Maybe there's another way," the monk said quietly. What had happened made no sense. It made no sense that she should be so beautiful, and so sad. It made no sense that he should love her as he did.

"And what if I'm to have his child?" A fresh sob escaped her throat.

"You won't have his child," Fra Filippo said. "I'll send for Sister Pureza. She'll know what to do."

"No, you can't tell anyone," she cried. "If you do, he'll speak against me, you know he will. Even powerful friends can't protect a woman from the lies of a man like him."

Fra Filippo had heard the tearful stories of many young women who'd lost their innocence in an act of violence, then lived in silence with the secret for just this reason.

"You'll stay here," the painter said. "You'll stay with me and I'll take care of you."

"It's impossible," she said. "Don't promise what can't be."

"But it can be, Lucrezia. Nothing is impossible if God wills it." He took her cold hands and rubbed them between his warm palms.

"It's wrong," she cried.

Fra Filippo squatted so that they were face-to-face.

"What was done to you is wrong," he said. "But not love. Love is never wrong."

He looked at her steadily, and she began to weep.

"Will you pray for me, Fra Filippo?" she asked, falling on her knees. "It's my fault, Fra Filippo. I don't know what to do. Please pray for me."

Chapter Fifteen

Monday of the Fourteenth Week After Pentecost,
the Year of Our Lord 1456

Lucrezia woke to the sound of pots rattling in the next room, and her eyes flew open.

The devil made your beauty bewitching.

She was ruined. She could think of nothing else.

Give me what you've given the painter.

She felt shame in the pain between her legs and in the bruises on her neck. The prior general's words haunted her, and she could still feel his hands burning on her body.

Wrapping the heavy robe tightly, she put her crushed wimple over her head and crept to the bedroom doorway. Only the dimmest light was visible through the small kitchen window, and there seemed to be no one stirring in the streets. The monk stood by the hearth with his back to her. He was dressed, and he'd folded away the bedding from his makeshift pallet. She saw he'd washed her *panni di gamba* and laid it on the hearth to dry. The garment was in shreds.

"Good morning," she whispered. Her throat was raw. "Where is my sister? Why isn't she here?"

Fra Filippo turned to see her engulfed in his winter robe, her face puffy, her head hastily covered by her wimple. She looked small and lost.

"*Buongiorno,*" he said gently. "I don't know what has detained her,

but I trust Sister Spinetta will be here soon. If not, I will ask Fra
Piero to fetch her himself."

The bruise on her eye was gray and soft green, and there was a
spot of dried blood on her lip. She put a hand out and grabbed his
arm, feeling the strength beneath his white robe. It was the first time
she'd ever reached for him.

"Please stay with me until she arrives." She blinked, and wouldn't
meet his eyes. But she asked again. "Please don't leave me alone."

He bent and put his lips to her forehead, resting them for a
moment on her cool brow.

"I'll stay with you, Lucrezia," he said.

"And work," she said. "Please, you must work. You must show me
something beautiful."

He could only get her to swallow a bit of wine and bread before he
began to gather the materials he needed for his work. He did everything carefully, moving slowly as the sun rose over the city. He'd
stored the triptych panel behind a bench in the corner, where no
harm could come to it. Now he put it on the easel and placed the
sketch on the table beside him.

"Come, look," he said. Lucrezia stood next to him and quietly
studied his plans for the Medici's *Adoring Madonna*, which would be
the center of the three-part altarpiece. Around the kneeling Virgin,
Fra Filippo had drawn dense, beautiful woods and a sky brimming
with angels and penitent saints. Mary knelt in a clearing before the
Child, who rested on her silken veil.

"The wilderness is a place of meditation and redemption," the
painter said.

He showed Lucrezia the barren tree that would stand on Mary's left, the young sapling that would stand on her right.

"The bare branches evoke death. The young tree reminds us of the fertile womb."

As she listened, Lucrezia dimly remembered Sister Pureza telling her which herbs cleansed the womb and robbed it of its contents. Her head was too addled to recall anything clearly.

"Before the birth of the child, there's hopelessness. After the child there's renewal and light," the monk said quietly. His hand followed the shape of the Madonna's body where the sunlight would fall on her shoulders. "The Virgin is kneeling in adoration as she welcomes the Savior. She's kneeling in humility," he added.

Both Lucrezia and Fra Filippo thought at the same moment of the way she'd insisted on kneeling when she'd posed for him that first day in his *bottega*. She'd knelt in humility. And he'd touched her chin.

"Yes," Lucrezia said. The place between her legs was raw. She tried to keep her mind on anything but the smell of blood, the memory of the prior general's heavy body and his animal groans.

"And what will this be?" she asked, holding her finger above the sweeping lines in the background.

"That will be a sturdy elm, holding the vine." He paused and waited. "The vine represents the wine, of course."

Rosemary. Lucrezia remembered the old nun's words. *Too much rosemary can rid the womb of its blessed contents.*

"The wine." She spoke slowly. "The wine is a symbol of Christ's blood."

She looked at the elm, its branches spread in the shape of a cross.

"Is the elm the cross on which He died?" she asked.

"*Sì.*" The painter nodded with a sad smile. "I never tire of painting her," he said. "Our Blessed Mother comes to us in so many guises. The Queen of Heaven, the Madonna of Humility, the Bride of Christ, the Annunciate Virgin. She suffered even in her innocence. When I paint her, all of this must show in her face. Compassion. Sadness. Purity. Love."

Fra Filippo took Lucrezia's hand gently.

"Purity," he repeated, kissing her fingertips, looking into her wounded eyes. How much he wished to lessen her pain. "Love."

Rosemary.

"Fra Filippo, do you have any rosemary?"

He squinted in confusion, but he didn't let go of her hand.

"Rosemary," she said again. "I'd like to have some bread, made with rosemary. If I may. If it's possible."

"Anything," he said, gently squeezing her fingers. "With love, Lucrezia, anything is possible."

⁓

*S*orella, it's me, Spinetta. Please open the door."

Lucrezia swung open the *bottega* door and looked directly into Paolo's dark, shining eyes. Spinetta stood behind him, her small face pale against her white wimple.

"Spinetta!" Lucrezia pulled her and Paolo inside quickly, and shut the door. "At last, you've come."

Spinetta looked quizzically at the large white robe Lucrezia wore.

"Why are you here, Lucrezia? And what have you done with your habit?"

"*Vieni*, Spinettina." Lucrezia tugged on the sleeve of Spinetta's rough robe. "You, too, Paolo."

Checking the latch, Lucrezia hurried them through the antechamber and into the studio.

"Signora de' Valenti sent a note to the convent asking why you hadn't arrived," Spinetta said, struggling to catch her breath. "Very soon after that, the prioress received a note from the procurator, asking that I be sent to join you at the palazzo. There was a great stir at the convent, and a visit from two nuns from Sant'Ippolito, and finally Paolo confessed that he'd brought you here."

Spinetta shook her head, her eyes brimming.

"Of course Mother Bartolommea wouldn't let me leave. I had to sneak away. I ran with Paolo, as quickly as I could. What's happening, Lucrezia? And what have you done with your habit?"

"Paolo," Lucrezia said, avoiding her sister's eyes. "Go into the kitchen with Rosina, and have something to eat."

The boy nodded and slipped through the narrow curtain. As he did, Spinetta looked around the workshop. She saw Fra Filippo busying himself in the back room, and she grabbed Lucrezia's hand.

"Fra Filippo hasn't been back to the convent since the day of the *festa*," she whispered. "I listened at the door, and heard the nuns from Sant'Ippolito say they saw him pulling you away from the parade against your will. Is it true?"

Lucrezia shook her head.

"It wasn't safe for me at the convent," Lucrezia said, stroking her sister's arm. "Fra Filippo brought me here to look after me."

"You can't stay here, Lucrezia. Don't you know what they'll say about you?"

"A terrible thing happened." Lucrezia couldn't look at her sister. "The prior general was very rough."

"Is that why you left Santa Margherita so suddenly?"

Lucrezia nodded.

"But he's gone now," Spinetta said. "He came for his things yesterday evening and left with barely a word to anyone."

"He was here, yesterday. Fra Filippo was gone." Lucrezia spoke quietly, her hands clenched together. "The prior general came in when I was alone and he—"

"He what?"

"He forced himself on me."

Spinetta whimpered, and pulled Lucrezia against her.

"It's all right, I'm all right now." Lucrezia pushed her sister away gently.

"We have to tell the prioress," Spinetta said. "She'll see that the prior general is punished."

Lucrezia's eyes were sad and deep. Her resolve had strengthened during the night. It was a resolve born as much of pride as of shame.

"No, it would be his word against mine, and I'm nothing, only a novitiate. You mustn't tell anyone, sister. Fra Filippo has promised to make it right and I trust him."

The young women turned to where the monk was holding a sketch up to the rear window, pretending to focus on his work.

"But the prior general must be punished!" Spinetta cried again.

"Fra Filippo has promised to take me away from here as soon as he can. Until then, I'll stay here with him." Lucrezia spoke quickly. She put her lips against Spinetta's ear. "Spinettina, what I tell you now you mustn't speak of to anyone. This very day Fra Filippo is to see the Medici's emissary, to ask for special dispensation from the pope. And when he gets the news he wants from the Curia, he's promised to marry me."

Spinetta turned pale.

"What about your vows?"

Lucrezia looked into her sister's eyes.

"Imagine, Spinetta, if a child is to come of this." Lucrezia hurried through her words. "I must have some way of standing the shame.

Fra Filippo has offered to help me. And remember, *mia cara*, I'm not blessed like you, with a soul made for the cloister."

"What if the pope refuses? That is likely, isn't it?"

"I don't know." Lucrezia pressed her palms together, her lips tightened. "I only know that I can't go back."

Spinetta threw her arms around her sister and began to weep.

"But Lucrezia, a novitiate living with a monk is a terrible sin, and a shame to our family's good name."

"Please, Spinetta, he says he loves me," she whispered. "If all is as God wills, how do we know that *this* isn't God's will?"

Spinetta blinked into Lucrezia's stricken face.

"And you? Do you love him?"

Lucrezia bit her lip. How could she explain all that she felt at this moment: fear, shame, sorrow, gratitude, and love?

"Yes." She nodded, looking into her sister's dark eyes. "I love him."

"*Sancta Maria, Mater Dei, ora pro nobis peccatoribus, nunc, et in hora mortis nostrae. Amen.*" Spinetta slipped her hand inside the pocket of her robe and pulled out Lucrezia's silver medallion of Saint John the Baptist, pressing it into her sister's hand. "I don't understand, Lucrezia. I don't understand. But I'll stay as long as you need me. I'll stay until word comes from Rome."

❦

When Ser Francesco Cantansanti showed up at the *bottega* shortly after Sext that afternoon, Fra Filippo was ready.

Lucrezia and Spinetta were in the monk's bedroom, hidden from sight. The sketch for the Medici centerpiece stood on an easel, illuminated by the light from the large front window. Next to it, the nearly finished panel of Saint Anthony stood on one side, the finished panel of Saint Michael on the other. Saint Michael's silver breastplate and shield glittered like true warriors' armor, and Saint Anthony's face was kind and humble. Fra Filippo was pleased with these portraits representing the patron saints of King Alfonso of Naples, and he felt certain Ser Francesco would see their great worth.

"I'll try to finish the work before the date on the contract, if possible." Fra Filippo bowed his head as the emissary surveyed the work. "It is my sole intention to please my honorable patron, the great and illustrious Giovanni de' Medici."

"This is far better behavior than I've seen from you in some time, Lippi," Cantansanti said, moving closer to inspect the panels. "Perhaps you can explain what's brought you to your senses?"

At that moment a clatter came from the bedchamber, followed by a muffled whisper. The men's eyes met, and Cantansanti's filled with a new light. The whisper came again. The voice, faint though it was, surely belonged to a female.

"Ah, Fra Filippo, there's nothing like a pretty girl to spur you in your heights of creativity," the emissary said, turning to him with a half-smile. "I like the soft flesh of a woman as well as the next man. But I wish you wouldn't bring women to your *bottega* when the eye of the Medici is on you."

Tall in his boots, he folded his arms over his chest. Fra Filippo hesitated only a moment. The emissary had helped him before. He was a strong man, opinionated but fair.

"Of course I never forget the eye of the Medici is upon me, as you say," he replied. "The sketch you see is complete, and I've begun transferring the image onto the wood panel. You may take the vellum with you when you leave."

Casting a satisfied glance at the sketch, the emissary nodded, and Fra Filippo continued.

"The woman you heard has played an important role in helping me to conceive the piece for His Eminence. She arrived here yesterday. She seeks my protection."

At this, Cantansanti arched his eyebrows in mock surprise.

"Your protection? Then she must not know you well."

"Please, this isn't a joke. The novitiate fled the convent to protect her honor." Fra Filippo slid a ceramic jug of wine toward Cantansanti. "Good sir, you've helped me before and I need your help again, perhaps more than ever. And so does the girl."

Fra Filippo lowered his voice, and nodded at the Virgin in his sketch.

"Do you see her face?"

Cantansanti nodded. "Breathtaking."

"It's the novitiate, Lucrezia, recently arrived at Santa Margherita with her sister."

Cantansanti's face darkened.

"The novitiate who's been coming and going at my bidding?" he asked tightly. "She's a nun, Filippo. Tell me the whisper in your bedroom isn't from her lips."

"She's not a nun," the painter quickly said, again pushing the wine in Cantansanti's direction. "She's only a novitiate, and that against her wishes."

The painter paused. What could he barter that he had not yet traded against in his life? His soul and heart went into his work. His flesh went into his work. He'd lost sleep and meals, given whole years of his life to create art in the glory and praise of God and Cosimo de' Medici. He'd given almost everything he had. And yet there was more. At the bottom of the well, instead of despair, he'd found a new river of hope.

"This isn't a whim—believe me, I haven't known her, not as you imagine," Fra Filippo said. He fell to his knees in front of Ser Francesco, and the man, who'd seen all sorts of hubris from Fra Filippo and never expected anything but pride and audacity, was aghast.

"For God's sake, get off your knees," Cantansanti said. He grabbed the jug of wine and drank. Fra Filippo shook his head.

"I won't get up until you've heard me, good Ser."

"Then speak." The emissary kept an eye on the monk, another on the sketch for the altarpiece, and wished he had a third to train on the doorway to the kitchen. If the novitiate appeared, he wanted to see her in the flesh.

"Don't drag it out anymore, Fratello, just tell me what you want—and don't ask for money, there are no more florins until the work is complete."

"I want nothing as base as money," the monk scoffed. "For this girl I would give away my money. I'd sell my flesh if I had to, to see her heart satisfied."

"We don't want your flesh, either, Filippo. We want your masterpiece, and we want it in Naples. Now tell me why you're on your knees, or I'll leave."

Fumbling in his pocket, Fra Filippo withdrew the letter he'd carefully written and sealed with his blue wax.

"I want to marry Lucrezia," he said, holding out the note. "All is explained in this letter beseeching the aid and endorsement of my great patron. I beg of you to deliver it to Ser Cosimo by your own hand."

Cantansanti took more wine. He drank until the jug was empty. He didn't reach for the letter.

"You've lost your senses." His voice was cool. "You're a monk."

"I'll give it up. I'll give up whatever is asked of me."

"The Medici family is best served by your continued service

to Rome," Cantansanti said. He put the jug down. "I'll make no promises."

"All I ask is a petition in my name. You know that many exceptions have been made when the great Medici family has requested it."

Cantansanti's eyes narrowed. The power of the Medici was to be respected, not invoked. He put a hand on the painter's elbow and pulled him up from his knees. Then he took the sealed note.

"I'll do what I can. And you, Fra Filippo, you'll do what you must."

Cantansanti tucked the letter into his pocket and turned on his heels. Outside the *bottega*, he shook his head and almost laughed. The monk had even more audacity than he'd imagined.

*In Florence, a very weary Prior General Saviano climbed two wide steps and entered the Barbadori Chapel of Santo Spirito, crossed himself, and knelt at the marble altar. This private chapel had long been the prior general's place of penitence, prayer, and worship. The light was dim but the scent was pleasing, as the prior general had the chapel rails polished with lemon oil each day, and the candles fragranced with frankincense each evening.

Clasping his hands, Prior General Saviano lifted his eyes to the predella beneath the altarpiece. It had been created by his nemesis, Fra Filippo Lippi, at the behest of the Barbadori family of Florence, and depicted an ecstatic Saint Augustine at the precise moment the Lord had pierced his heart with faith.

"My great sainted brother," Saviano prayed. "You know I've long held my lust at bay, and you know how difficult this has been for me. Now this girl, this daughter of Eve, has led me astray. I beg you, show me what I must to do to cleanse myself of this sin."

Eyes open, knees on the padded step, the cleric looked at the brown folds of the saint's robe, the books and inkwell on his desk, the fine golden light of Saint Augustine's study. Although he had little patience for its creator, Prior General Saviano had long loved this painting. Before, he'd been able to meditate solely upon Augustine when he gazed at the altarpiece. Now, try as he might, the cleric was unable to push the painter's name and face out of his mind. Each time he saw the monk's bulky frame, he saw the novitiate beside him; the monk's eyes filled with reproach, the novitiate's full of horror.

"She was surely put there to test me, and I failed," Saviano said.

Closing his eyes, the prior general sickened at the memory of what he'd done. His nostrils seemed to fill with the foul scent in the small kitchen, the memory of her virgin blood. Quickly he opened his eyes and inhaled the cleansing scent of lemon oil and frankincense. He reminded himself, as he'd done so many times during his years in the clergy, that it was Saint Augustine who'd given the most generous and forgiving of all saintly commands: love the sinner, hate the sin.

"With all the strength of my faith, Lord, I detest my sin," Prior General Saviano said, bringing his gaze to the arrows that pierced the saint's breast. "And I hate the man who brought me to the sin. I will not let Fra Filippo be the ruin of me."

Anger filled the man's knotty limbs. He stood to his full height and eyed the self-image that Fra Filippo had painted into the altarpiece. In it, the painter's face was young, and he looked like one of the *ragazzi* of Florence, as surely he had been.

Prior General Saviano vowed that the painter would not make a mockery of his Order, nor of the blessed Convent Santa Margherita. If there was a sin that demanded recompense it was the sin of the man who'd brought the novitiate into his *bottega* and kept her there; it was the sin of temptation, the sin of Eve. Yes, yes, Saviano told himself:

Lippi was the snake, Lucrezia was Eve, and he, Prior General of the Order of Saint Augustine, was the victim of their devilish temptation.

Making up his mind, the man crossed himself and strode through the halls of Santo Spirito to his office chambers. There, he rang for his secretary.

"Bring me a pot of cheese and some wine," Prior General Saviano said, remembering it had been many hours since he'd last eaten. When the refreshment came, he used a dull knife to cut large hunks of cheese, which he crammed into his mouth. When the cheese was gone, he dictated a missive to Provost Inghirami of Prato, to be announced by *il banditore* in the central piazza of Prato.

Fra Filippo Lippi is hereby dismissed of his duties as chaplain at the Convent Santa Margherita, he wrote. *By decree of the Order of Saint Augustine on this tenth day of September in the year of our Lord fourteen hundred and fifty-six.*

Chapter Sixteen

"Perhaps you could go to Signora Valenti," Spinetta said, her small hand reaching across the table, "and explain why you were delayed."

"What explanation will I give?" Lucrezia asked. She was weary of this question, which she'd answered many times. "Will you have me tell her that I've been compromised and ruined?"

"You needn't tell everything, Lucrezia, only that you are afraid to go back to the convent."

"No." She bent closer to the needle she was threading through her *panni di gamba*. Soon they would be mended, although they would never be flawless, as they had been before. "I cannot face the terrible lies and rumors that are out there, especially if they come from Signora Valenti's lips."

"Lucrezia, forgive me." Spinetta had to force herself to speak gently. "But I think perhaps you simply *want* to stay, even if it means bringing our ruin."

Lucrezia knotted the thread, and snapped it with her teeth. She could barely admit it to her sister, or even to herself. But it was true. She did not want to leave Fra Filippo. Not only because he would protect her, but because his love and his promise gave her the strength to rise each morning. If this was a sin, she prayed God would forgive her.

"Please, Spinetta, be patient. It will not be long until we have word from Ser Cantansanti, or from Rome. Have faith, I beg you."

The days were quiet, and Fra Filippo spent them working on his altarpiece or studying Lucrezia's face. The bruise over her eye was fading, the place where she'd bitten her lip had healed to a dark red. But since the *Festa della Sacra Cintola,* something more had changed. Her smile came more slowly, and the expression in her eyes was heartbreakingly close to the Madonna he'd always sought. Although Lucrezia was young he could see that she understood what the Blessed Mother had known: the link between suffering and joy, death and birth, fragility and strength.

"Your beauty's even more compelling than before," he said as he studied the shadow in her eyes.

"Is that why you love me?" Lucrezia asked quietly. She'd washed her hair that morning, and was dressed in a simple pale dress she'd found among the costumes the monk used for his paintings. Under the dress she wore her mended *panni di gamba.* "Do you love me because I'm beautiful?"

Fra Filippo had felt many things in the last week. He'd felt rage, regret, and a desire for revenge. But above all there was the need to protect and nurture Lucrezia. Yes, he loved her beauty. He'd made it his life's work to understand beauty and he knew, perhaps more than most, that beauty was always more than what met the eye. Just as his paintings were made luminous by layering colors one upon the other, he saw that Lucrezia's beauty came from a wellspring that could only be found in the depths of a complex soul.

"There are many beautiful women in the world, but none has ever moved me as you do," he said gently. "Even before I saw you, Lucrezia, I knew your face somewhere in my heart."

For the first time in his life, the monk shared his private fears and pains. He told Lucrezia about the nights he'd dreamt of his mother's voice and awakened bereft on the narrow pallet in Santa Maria del Carmine; of the years he'd struggled to create with pencil and vellum the wonder and awe he felt.

"When I was a young man, painting was all I had," he said quietly. "It was all I had, and so it had to become everything to me."

She watched as his eyes clouded.

"In the monastery, it saved me from despair. In prison, when I feared for my life, I imagined all the paintings I'd create in God's honor, if He would let me live," the monk said. "For years I've painted as I prayed; I've prayed as I painted. After a time there was no difference between one and the other."

Lucrezia nodded silently.

"All my life I've been searching for something," he said with deep conviction. "I don't love you because you're beautiful. I love you because you're the answer to everything I've looked for."

He knelt before her.

"For me, to see beauty is to see God," the monk said thoughtfully. "Beauty on Earth is a mirror of God's love in heaven."

"A *speculum majus*," she whispered.

"Yes, that's right. A *speculum majus*." He put a hand on her cheek, and she didn't move away until she heard Spinetta's step in the doorway.

⁘

Mother Bartolommea was clear: she wanted the novitiates back in the convent before Santa Margherita became the subject of mockery and the target of the prior general's wrath. Already, she had to make do with Fra Piero acting as chaplain to her nuns. Who was to say the prior general wouldn't remove her from the post as prioress, also, when he heard of this new scandal?

"I don't care how you do it," she said to Sister Pureza. "I want you to bring them back here. You've spent more time with Sister Lucrezia than any of us. You're the one who insisted I send her out of the convent for her own protection. Now you must bring her back."

The old woman left the convent alone the next day, just after Terse. Walking along Via Santa Margherita, Sister Pureza vowed to bind the novitiate to her even more tightly than before. She would offer Lucrezia her protection, and she would be firm in her resolve.

At the Piazza della Pieve, she asked a boy where the painter lived.

"Fra Filippo?" The boy pointed to a house with a thatched roof. "He is there."

Sister Pureza squared her shoulders and marched up to the door.

"It is Sister Pureza." She rattled the latch. "Let me in."

Spinetta jumped up and ran into the bedroom, followed quickly by Lucrezia, who'd picked up the *cappello* she was embroidering, and dropped it over her bare head.

Fra Filippo waited until both young women were safely out of view before opening the door and looking down into the wrinkled face of Sister Pureza. Her anger was evident in her pinched mouth and the hard squint of her eyes.

"I know the novitiates are here, Chaplain." She put a special emphasis on his title, spitting it through her lips. "Let me have them."

"Sister Pureza," he said calmly. "You know I am no longer chaplain of the convent."

"Precisely," she said. "The novitiates have no business here with you. Release them to me."

"I am not holding them against their will." Fra Filippo's body blocked the doorway, his heavy hand held the door in place.

"They belong in the convent."

"But you sent Lucrezia away." The painter steadied himself, and spoke gently. He would get nowhere with the old nun unless he could settle her down and send her away without incident. "You sent her away for her own protection."

"I sent her to the home of Ottavio de' Valenti, Fratello, I didn't send her into your hands to ruin her."

Lucrezia listened from the bedroom. She put her lips to Spinetta's ear, and whispered, "Please remember your promise to stay here with me."

"Sister Lucrezia is an angel," Fra Filippo said quietly, in the doorway. "I have only the deepest reverence for her."

"Then let her come with me," Sister Pureza said. "Prioress Bartolommea will forgive her if she comes now. Both of the novitiates must return at once."

"Lucrezia doesn't want to go back," Fra Filippo said.

He slackened his stance and Sister Pureza, spry even in her advanced age, slipped under his arm and into the workshop. She moved quickly and found herself staring at a tangle of wool and silk cloth laid out on the floor in a series of cutting patterns.

"What is this?" she demanded. "Have you taken up the work of a seamstress as well as that of painter and monk?"

Sister Pureza leaned over and picked up the yellow silk of a sleeve Lucrezia had cut that very morning from an old piece of *strazze de seda filada* she'd found.

"I demand to know what's going on here."

"The girl will not be safe at the prior general's convent," the painter said. "She cannot go back now."

Lucrezia moved toward the doorway. She didn't want to be found hiding, and she was afraid the monk's anger might compel him to reveal her bitter secret. Straightening her spine, Lucrezia tucked her hair under the *cappello*, pulled on the needle until it snapped from the thread, and stepped into the workshop.

"Sister Pureza, I am here."

The nun and the monk turned to stare at Lucrezia. In her pale *gamurra*, locks of hair spilling from under the cap, a blue shawl slung round her shoulders, she looked as if she'd stepped out of a painting.

"Lucrezia!" Sister Pureza gasped. "Why do you look this way? Where is your robe?"

Seeing the nun who'd given her only friendship and protection, Lucrezia's throat filled.

"Sister," she cried. "Oh, Sister, forgive me."

Lucrezia wrung her hands, and in this single motion Sister Pureza read far more than the young woman had intended. She stepped across the fabrics and seized Lucrezia by the arm.

"Are you hurt? Have you been harmed or soiled against your will?"

Lucrezia's eyes widened.

"No, Sister Pureza, you misunderstand," she said, shaking her head. Wildly, her eyes sought the painter's, sending him a pleading glance. "Nothing's happened against my will."

Sister Pureza's grip on Lucrezia's arm tightened.

"You and Spinetta will come back to the convent with me," she said. "You can't stay here, and certainly not like this. You'll ruin your name and your father's name, and then you'll have nowhere to turn."

"It's not true." Fra Filippo spoke in his deepest baritone. "I can care for her."

It was Sister Pureza's turn to drop open her mouth, and stare at the monk.

"Have you lost your mind, Fra Filippo? You are acting *senza ver-*

gogna, without any shame at all! This is absurd. You mustn't ruin the girl with your devilish notions."

Fra Filippo stared at Lucrezia and spoke to her directly.

"I'll marry you, Lucrezia, as I promised. I'll renounce the cloth and marry you."

"It's the devil in her beauty," Sister Pureza said angrily. "I told you, Lucrezia, to guard your beauty carefully."

Lucrezia's hands flew to her face. "No," she cried.

Fra Filippo stepped forward.

"Go away," he said loudly, towering over Sister Pureza. "Go away, old woman."

Sister Pureza glared at the monk, and looked beyond him, to Spinetta.

"Sister Spinetta," she said. "Save yourself, at least."

Spinetta's face crumpled. She very much wished to hurry into the old nun's arms, and tell her everything. Only her promise to Lucrezia kept her silent.

"I'm sorry, Sister," Spinetta said weakly. "I cannot."

Sister Pureza looked from one face to the other. Fra Lippi stepped toward her.

"You'd best be going, Sister Pureza," he said firmly.

The old nun stood a moment more, looking from one to the other.

"Will you not change your mind?" she asked Lucrezia a final time. When the girl shook her head, the old woman turned and left the *bottega,* defeated. Lucrezia might believe the monk had the power, the will, and the worldly talents to look after her. But when the painter felt the wrath of Rome or the anger of his patrons, Sister Pureza doubted his resolve, or his lust, would be strong enough. And Lucrezia would suffer, just as she, Sister Pureza, had suffered so many years ago.

Chapter Seventeen

The Sixteenth Week After Pentecost, the Year of Our Lord 1456

More than a week passed with no word from Florence or Rome. Lucrezia and Spinetta slept and woke together in the monk's bedroom, and each day they wrapped some bread and cheese for his lunch before he went off to work on the frescoes at the *pieve*.

Rosina's mother was sick and the girl stayed away, but Paolo ran small errands for them in the afternoon, and after breakfast the two walked to the water pump and carried fresh water back in the monk's heavy wooden buckets. Alone in the house, the sisters swept the corners of the rooms and prayed, or stitched a proper dress for Lucrezia from the silk and linen scraps they'd found in the storage chest. They kept their hands and minds occupied, but it was a time of great anxiety. Spinetta continued to pray that her sister would relent and return to the convent, while Lucrezia prayed her monthly bleeding would come, and worried when she saw her face filling and her cheeks softening. Yet, in her heart, Lucrezia was also joyful. She looked forward to the painter's return every evening, and he never failed to bring home a small gift: one day a comb for her hair, another day a sack of oranges. Only this morning she'd put on a new *reta* to cover her head.

Between chores and the ritual of liturgical prayers that Spinetta insisted they keep, Lucrezia spent hours studying the paintings and sketches the monk had stored and stacked in every corner of his *bot-*

tega. She didn't dare move things too far from their places, but she tidied the shelves and straightened the panels, and as she did so she found a dozen small studies of the Mother and Child, and a large collection of drawings for the *Annunciation* he'd painted as a gift for the church of San Lorenzo in Florence. Seeing how many years Fra Filippo had spent working for God's glory only made it more wondrous to her that she was here with him now, and that he said he loved her. She prayed that word from Rome would come quickly, and that it would be favorable.

❧

*I*n the *cappella maggiore* of Santo Stefano, where his assistants were busy grinding azurite and malachite, Fra Filippo stood in a doorway with the procurator. The men leaned against the limestone wall, a font of holy water between them.

"My love for her is sincere," the painter said in a strained whisper. "Every day she lives without word from Rome is a torment to her, I can see it. I can't bear to have her suffer, and I can't wait any longer to hear what the pope will say."

Fra Piero studied his friend's face.

"They say Pope Callistus is gravely ill," said the procurator. "But he's never been a friend to the Medici, nor a patron of the arts. It's doubtful he'll grant what you've asked."

"I know," Fra Filippo said solemnly. "But I've been reading about matrimony, and there may be an alternative, Piero."

The monk walked to his worktable and retrieved the book he'd been studying all week. It was blue, with a title engraved in gold, *Concerning the Sacraments of the Christian Religion.* He opened to the page he'd marked, and held it out for his friend to read.

"In the time of Pope Innocent III a simple sentence was enough, it says it right here." Fra Filippo indicated the page he'd noted. "See, one only needs to say, 'I receive you as mine, so that you become my wife and I your husband,' and it's done."

The book specified that it was the act of sexual union that consummated the marriage and made it binding according to law, but the painter was silent on this subject.

"What do you think, Piero?" He laid a hand on the procurator's sleeve.

Fra Piero was a practical man. He'd made the best of life by utilizing all the Church could offer, and finding ways to compensate for what Rome would neither abide nor provide. He knew his friend was permitted an even wider berth around the rules, as long as his work remained in favor. But it was a lot to put on a man's God-given talents, and the procurator was hesitant to be an accessory to what Rome might consider a grave affront.

"Why do it at all, Filippo? Saviano's gone, no one's bothering you. Why not let things stay as they are, or let the girl return to the convent?"

Fra Filippo glanced over at the far wall of the chapel where Young Marco was adding shadows to the face of the young Saint Stephen. The apprentice was barely past puberty, and had the sweet, dark looks and deep eyes of a young Roman.

"It's not enough," Fra Filippo said. "I don't want to trick her, or keep her with me as a concubine. I want to be her husband. I want to offer her as much protection as I can."

"And if you're thrown in jail? How will you protect her then?"

"The Medici won't let it happen, not with so much riding on the triptych, not as long as I'm in the good graces of Ser Francesco Cantansanti."

Fra Piero groaned. "Did you have to fall in love?"

"Do you think I had a choice?" Fra Filippo retorted. Again, he held up the blue book. "It says here that a union sealed by mutual consent and the blessings of a priest are enough to turn it into a sacrament. Plenty of others have married far from Rome but with the righteous knowledge of Jesus Christ. You know it's true, Piero. My God, even Piccolomini has two bastard children, and he's the Cardinal of Siena."

Fra Piero's sharp eyes wavered.

"As long as Prior General Saviano is alive, she can't go back to Santa Margherita, you know that." The painter lowered his voice. "At least I can offer her the protection of my name."

"If you've figured everything out, why do you need me at all?"

"As our confessor, and as a witness. If anything happens to me, you can step forward and profess that she's my wife, bound to me by vows of love."

Fra Piero shrugged and shook his head.

"Does it really mean anything?" he asked. But even as he looked at his friend's face, filled with determination, the procurator knew the answer.

"It means something to me," the painter said. "And it will mean everything to her."

"It will only afford you as much protection as your work affords, you know that, Filippo."

"Then thank God for the work," the painter said. "And pray that it's good."

⟡

Although only the pope can grant you and Fra Filippo dispensation to marry, I can bless the union of your souls privately, so that you may have peace and live as man and wife in the eyes of the Lord."

Lucrezia was alone with the procurator in the kitchen, and her head was reeling.

In her hands she held a copy of the blue book, its title stamped in gold.

"Fra Filippo's name means a great deal throughout Florence and the surrounding regions," the procurator said. He put a palm on her forehead. "You've put aside your wimple; you haven't taken the vows that make you a bride of Christ. It's unusual, Lucrezia, but I believe there is merit in such a union. If it's what you want."

"I want to be with him. I want to be his wife, if you say it's possible."

"Then let it be so," Fra Piero said.

Lucrezia knelt and began the confession that would prepare her for the sacrament of matrimony. In halting words she spoke of the prior general's violation, and of her own shame and guilt. It was the first time that Fra Piero was told, directly, what the prior general had done, and in his outrage the procurator vowed silently that he would do everything he could to ensure Lucrezia's future safety and happiness.

"I'm not only angry at the prior general," she whispered. "I'm angry at God, and at the Church. And at myself," she said. "I was looking for a mirror when I spilled the paint. My vanity is what destroyed the convent robe. If not for that, he wouldn't have found me in my *panni di gamba* and then . . ." She faltered. "And then maybe none of this would have happened."

"Perhaps," Fra Piero said gently. "But we can't guess at God's will, Lucrezia. We can only bend to it."

When Lucrezia and the procurator parted the curtain that separated the monk's quarters from the *bottega,* they found Fra Filippo had just finished covering his large worktable with a clean white cloth. A candle burned next to a silver chalice filled with deep red wine. Spinetta stood near the front window fingering her prayer beads. She refused to meet her sister's eyes.

"I know this isn't the wedding day you imagined," Fra Filippo said as he came to stand beside Lucrezia. She could smell the fresh soap he'd used to wash his hands, mingling with the sharp smell of paint.

"There's no contract to sign, no *sponsalia*, no procession, no feast," the painter said. "I can't give you those things, although I wish I could. But I wish to marry you and to offer you all I have. We will be one, and no harm will come to you ever again."

Lucrezia closed her eyes.

"Are you ready, Lucrezia?" The painter touched her elbow. She opened her eyes. They were still and deep.

"Yes," she said. "I'm ready."

Holding up the blue book, Fra Piero began.

"All things are possible with the blessing of the Lord," he said, nodding at the two standing side by side, the painter a half *braccia* taller and several stones heavier than the young woman. Lucrezia kept her eyes on the procurator and avoided looking toward Spinetta, who stood reciting the rosary, her lips moving silently.

"In goodness and with holy intentions, this man and woman come together to be united in the sacrament of matrimony on this twenty-fourth day of September," said Fra Piero. "There can be no happiness without a wife, and no one should be judged wise, as Aristotle says, who spurns so great a good of nature, so great a pleasure of friend-ship, and the usefulness of so great a gift."

From his pocket, the painter withdrew a small velvet pouch. With thumb and index finger he carefully removed a ring, and held it out to

Lucrezia. It was a thin gold band, polished to a warm shine, embedded with a small red stone.

"Red jasper, for love and fidelity," he said.

Lucrezia's eyes grew moist as his large fingers slid the ring onto hers. The red jewel caught the light from the window, matching the color of the spiced wine.

"I take you to be my wedded wife and I espouse you; and I commit to you the fidelity and loyalty of my body and my possessions; and I will keep you in health and in any condition."

Lucrezia recited the vows back to him. "I take you to be my wedded husband and I espouse you; and I commit to you the fidelity of my body and my possessions."

Fra Piero made the sign of the cross over their bent heads.

"You are married in the eyes of the Lord. May He bless your union and protect your lives."

The painter reached over and held up the chalice. He placed it tenderly against Lucrezia's lips and watched her drink from it. Then he kissed her sweet, moist mouth.

Spinetta was relieved when her sister came into the bedroom that evening, as she'd done every other night. Lucrezia took off her dress and slid under the blanket beside her, putting her cold feet against her sister's warm ones.

"Please try to understand, Spinetta," Lucrezia whispered.

"It's done," Spinetta said simply. "Now we must continue to pray for what is right."

Hours later, lying in bed listening to Spinetta's deep breathing, Lucrezia could still feel the painter's lips on hers. She put her hand on the blue book from which Fra Piero had read their vows. By the light of a dying candle, she found the words she sought and read them again, then again.

Slipping out of bed, she crept into the kitchen to Fra Filippo, who was lying on his pallet next to the hearthstones. With her chemise skimming the floor she knelt and touched his blanket.

"Fra Filippo," she whispered. "Filippo," she tried again, using only his Christian name.

Waking at the brush of her breath on his cheek, the painter sat up. The blanket fell to his waist, exposing his bare chest.

"What is it? What's wrong?"

"I've read the book," she whispered. "The blue book, *Concerning the Sacraments of the Christian Religion.* I saw the page you marked."

His heart seemed to stop. Did she think their vows were insincere? Was she going to leave him even when he could still taste her kiss and smell the chamomile in her hair?

"I want to be your wife," she said softly. She looked down at his bare chest and reached out her hand, almost touching his dark tuft of hair. She felt a longing that wasn't desire, but need.

"I read what it said, Filippo," she continued. "We aren't yet truly man and wife. We haven't consummated our promise."

The monk put a hand out and cupped her chin.

"Do you know what you're saying?"

She leaned forward, her head almost resting on his shoulder.

"Yes." She touched the hand that held her chin, her palm smooth and delicate. "I want to be your wife. Tonight."

"Lucrezia." Her name filled his throat and he gently pressed his mouth to hers.

His lips were dry and cool but as they lingered, she felt them swell and grow moist. Eyes closed, she saw his face in her mind, his searching blue eyes, the protective largeness of his frame, the strong, capable hands. She tried to calm her nerves, to trust that what came next would be no more frightening for her than it was for every new bride.

"Filippo," she whispered. "Do you love me? Truly?"

"I love you, Lucrezia."

Gently, the painter turned his body and lowered her onto the pallet next to him. He lifted the blanket, and pulled her under it with him. His chest was covered with soft, dark hair, and she buried her face against it. His lips roamed from her cheek, to her ears, down to her neck. He paused at the place where the prior general's hard grip had left a string of bruises, and kissed each one.

"I love you," he said again. "I love you."

Fumbling, he opened the clasp that held back her hair and pulled it softly around her face, kissing the ends, letting it tickle his cheek. Then he lifted her arms and began to slide her shift over her head. She felt his hands on her shoulders and then on her breasts. His fingertips lingered on her nipples.

Still kissing her, Fra Filippo slid her chemise off her shoulder. Her breath was coming in short gasps now. Nothing mattered more than their bodies, together. She would be his wife, and she would no longer be afraid.

He drew back and looked at her in the soft firelight. She forced a smile, and nodded. The painter ran his hands from her shoulders to her thighs. For a moment she remembered the prior general's hot breath, and she recoiled. As if he could read her thoughts, the painter murmured words of reassurance, all the while holding her closer, pressing himself more firmly against her, covering her with his own warmth.

She felt his thick fingers touching her, and inhaled deeply. The monk brought his hand to his mouth and wet his fingers on his tongue, then slowly brought them under the blanket, moving them back and forth across the lobe that seemed to grow under his touch. A low moan escaped Lucrezia's lips, and the sound of her pleasure excited the painter. Softly, he parted her legs and rolled between them. She cried out.

"Is it all right, *mia cara*?" The monk's voice was throaty and deep.

She opened her eyes. His face was close, and the love in his eyes reassured her. She pressed a palm against his cheek and nodded.

Gently, slowly, a great heat pressed into her, filling her in a place she'd never realized was empty. Lucrezia drank in the painter's familiar scent of wine and gesso and realized what it was to be in love. Until this moment she hadn't known what it meant to be joined to another, body and soul, and the gratitude she felt more than made up for the pain that grew stronger as her body opened and he thrust more deeply. He kissed her eyes, her brow, her cheek; his breath rasped in her ear. His body stiffened, he shuddered, and Lucrezia held him more tightly, astonished by his complete surrender. She felt a soaking between her legs.

"Lucrezia." He pulled back to look into her face. His eyes were bright, lit from the inside.

"Now we're truly married," she whispered, surprised at how much sorrow she felt along with her joy.

"I love you," he said. "Lucrezia, don't cry. I love you."

Chapter Eighteen

The Nineteenth Week After Pentecost, the Year of Our Lord 1456

Lucrezia's bruises healed until they were barely shadows on her body, wiped away by the painter's love. Autumn blazed and cooled, and the woodpile outside the *bottega* grew smaller. She began spending more nights on the pallet with Fra Filippo, letting his hands roam the length of her body, his palms press lightly against her mouth to muffle her cries of pleasure. He was patient and kind, and in the dark she found it easier to push the prior general from her mind.

As the Feast of All Saints' Day approached, Spinetta complained of a chill at night, and asked if she might sleep on the pallet by the hearth.

"Thank you," Lucrezia said quietly. "Thank you for your love and understanding."

"I do not know what is right any longer," Spinetta said, her eyes darkening. "I pray every night for your soul, *mia cara.*"

"As do I," Lucrezia said.

She said nothing about her monthly bleeding, which had not come for nearly two months now, but each morning, after the painter left her, she knelt by the bed and prayed for the Virgin Mother's guidance.

Lucrezia knew from the past that emotional turmoil could interrupt her regular bleeding, but the prior general's violation gave her different cause for worry. If there was to be a child, more than ever she and Filippo would need the pope's blessing. And if, God forbid, the child was the prior general's, she would need the Holy Mother's protection and perhaps more love than the painter had for her.

"Do you hear anything from your patron?" Lucrezia asked Fra Filippo one evening, as he was cleaning his brushes.

Fra Filippo didn't meet her eye. He'd received a note from Ser Francesco Cantansanti two days earlier, delivered to him at the Church of Santo Stefano.

> *Day and night Pope Callistus III is surrounded by his cardinals, who seek every opportunity to ingratiate themselves with His Holiness and discredit one another. The time is not favorable for a dispensation from the Vatican. I suggest you direct your passions to your work, and leave matters of love to those who do not wear the robe. Remember what harsh penalties the Archiepiscopal Curia can inflict when it wishes. And remember that you cannot marry the novitiate and also retain your title as Frate. Without it, you will renounce all the protection the Church affords you.*

"Filippo?" Lucrezia repeated. "What have you heard?"

Clearing his throat, Fra Filippo kept his eyes on his brushes, and his hands busy. He'd replied to Cantansanti in haste, and dispatched the letter that very morning.

> *My friend and honorable emissary, I respect your good judgment and trust you to know when the time is right in Rome. Meanwhile, I am in need of more gold leaf and lapis, which you know is very dear. I beg you to send me what funds you can so that I may finish the altarpiece in the fullest glory that Naples requires and the honorable Cosimo expects.*

"The Medici want to see the altarpiece in Naples as soon as possible," he said. "When it arrives, I believe good things will come to us."

Lucrezia's face clouded. The central panel of the triptych hadn't been touched in days. Although her image was sketched and already filled in with an underpainting of *verdaccio* and a bit of *cinabrese* to warm the Madonna's cheeks, it clearly wasn't close to completion.

"Then I pray you'll finish it quickly," Lucrezia said, her voice more terse than she intended. "So that good things will come to us soon."

But good things did not come quickly. In a week's time the painter was forced to admit the loss of his chaplain's wages meant he could no longer afford to pay Rosina. The girl, who'd just had a birthday, happily went off to Santa Margherita to begin her life as a novitiate. But the morning after she bade them good-bye, Lucrezia found Spinetta weeping in front of the hearth.

"I want to go back to Santa Margherita, too," Spinetta said, turning away from her sister. She was no longer angry, only sad. "Soon it will be Advent season, and I want to be with the others in the convent."

"I know," Lucrezia answered. "But I'm afraid of what people will say if I'm living here alone with Fra Filippo."

"Then come back with me," Spinetta said. "People are talking, Lucrezia. You must know that. He's still a monk; no matter what he's said to you, he puts on his white robe each morning and walks through the piazza with his head held high."

"But I love him," Lucrezia said, lowering her gaze. "And my curse, Spinetta, my bleeding."

Spinetta turned pale. When her own curse had come the week

prior, she'd used a small pile of clean rags, boiling them and then stacking them behind her few private belongings in a shelf by the hearth. She'd assumed her sister had been doing the same.

"Your bleeding hasn't come?"

Lucrezia shook her head, refusing to look up at her sister.

"How long has it been?" Spinetta asked.

"Not since we left home, Spinetta. Not since July."

Spinetta muffled a cry.

"You see why I'm praying for word from Rome?" Lucrezia whispered.

Spinetta pressed her lips together.

"I'll stay with you a bit longer," she said, reaching inside the pocket of her robe for her prayer beads. "But I must at least practice my duties as a novitiate, and serve the poor and ill in the *ospedale* when I can."

Lucrezia's beauty and love gave Fra Filippo all that his heart needed, but the world demanded payment for food and firewood, and feeding three people taxed his meager resources until they were nearly gone. The food he brought home each evening grew more sparse, and while Spinetta was across town at the *ospedale* on a cool afternoon, Lucrezia went into the small patch behind the *bottega* to dig for some root vegetables to fill their stomachs.

Advent was upon them and it was cold, even in the sun. Squatting heavily, she tugged at the tubers pushing their way up through the hard ground. Her back ached and her breasts felt heavy, the raw wind cut against her bare hands, and her eyelids were nearly shut. In an hour's time she'd dug only three onions and a rutabaga.

Inside for the afternoon siesta, she wrapped herself in the rough woolen blanket that smelled of Fra Filippo, and fell into the cocoon of sleep. She'd never felt so tired, it seemed, in all of her life. Even after she'd slept deeply, she barely kept herself awake through the evening meal of thin onion soup.

The painter helped her into bed that night, bringing her an extra glass of wine as she combed out her hair. She was pale, he saw, but her eyes were somehow bluer than they'd ever been before.

When she woke in the morning, Lucrezia rushed to the chamber pot and retched. The painter brought her a rag and wiped away the bile that wouldn't stay down. He said nothing of what he suspected, and neither did Lucrezia. But when she went into the kitchen, Spinetta was standing at the hearth, staring at her with wide, frightened eyes.

"Are you ill?" Spinetta whispered, shaking her head even as she asked.

Lucrezia looked at her sister. How stark their differences appeared: Spinetta in her black robe and wimple, starched and fresh, while Lucrezia's *gamurra* hung damp from perspiration under the plain blue robe she'd pulled over her head.

"I don't think I'm ill, sister."

They could hear the painter moving around in his workshop and they spoke quietly to each other in urgent tones.

"I must stay here and have the child."

"The child of a monk." As the bitter words left Spinetta's mouth, the far worse possibility was reflected in the expression on her face.

"Whatever God wills," Lucrezia said, dropping her eyes to the rough floorboards. Spinetta crossed herself and sat heavily on the stool opposite Lucrezia.

"What did Fra Filippo say?"

"I haven't told him yet," Lucrezia said. "But he must know. In truth, sister, I'm afraid of what will happen now."

She closed her eyes and pictured a fat-limbed, blue-eyed child with Filippo's broad features. But each time she remembered the prior general's face, nausea took hold of her.

By the time Spinetta went to the market for a bit of ham, leaving the two of them alone in the *bottega*, Lucrezia was exhausted from worry. She found the painter in his studio, and cleared her throat to get his attention.

Turning from his palette, Fra Filippo guessed exactly why she'd come to him. He'd suspected her news for some days now, and although it had consumed his thoughts, he was still unsure of his feelings.

"Filippo?"

She saw his face was grave, and tears stung her eyes. The painter reached for her hand and held it tightly.

"What is it?" He touched her cheek. "Why are you crying?"

Outside, the streets stirred with the sounds of horses pulling carts, but the *bottega* was perfectly still. Lucrezia said nothing. She guided the painter's hand to her belly, and placed it there, gently.

"It's been many months since I suffered the curse," she said. She laced her fingers through his, and watched his face. He blinked, but didn't move. His hand stayed where it was, warm and immobile.

"I'm going to have a child," she blurted. "Tell me, Filippo, is it a blessing, or is it a punishment?"

As she voiced her fears, what spread over the painter's face wasn't horror or dread, but something much closer to happiness. Fra Filippo didn't take his hand from her belly, but simply pressed more firmly.

"A child from my Madonna will be a blessing," he said.

"I'm not your Madonna," she said weakly. "I am not any Madonna. To say such a thing is blasphemy."

Fra Filippo knelt and pressed his face against her belly. He had no child on earth, only one poor soul born too soon to the woman he'd known in Padua. Long ago he'd come to accept that while even cardinals had illicit children, he would have none.

"I've always longed for a son," he said. "I can't feel sorrow at such news."

"But we're not married in the eyes of Rome. When they see me in the streets they will speak ill of me, and just think what they'll say at Santa Margherita! Filippo, now more than ever we have to pray that favorable word comes from Rome."

"I don't care what they say in Rome," he said passionately. He stood and took Lucrezia's face in his hands. "Since the moment I saw you, Lucrezia, I've seen and felt many things I'd never believed I would see on this earth. We'll pray and work fervently for word from Rome. But no matter what, I'll never let you live in shame."

Bolstered by his words, she let his joy wash over her.

"And if Rome says it is impossible?" she asked, putting her cheek on his chest.

Fra Filippo knew that what happened in Rome would depend on the goodwill and influence of the Medici. God governed heaven, Satan ruled over hell, but it was Cosimo de' Medici who willed what happened on their peninsula.

"Remember, nothing is impossible if God wills it," the painter said. "If God wills it, nothing is impossible."

Despite the monk's happiness, he heard the echoes of Ser Cantansanti, his face stern as he warned Fra Filippo not to flaunt his romantic dalliance under the watchful eye of the Medici.

⁓⁂⁓

*Y*ou are following God's will, Lucrezia," Spinetta said one morning. "But I, too, must do what God asks of me. I must return to the convent to celebrate the Lord's birth."

"You've been very good to me," Lucrezia said bravely. "I know Fra Filippo will care for me. Please tell the others I am sorry if I have caused them pain."

On the eve of the Nativity, Lucrezia said a tearful good-bye to Spinetta and watched through the window as her sister followed the wiry figure of Paolo through the streets, heading toward the gates of Santa Margherita. When the two disappeared from view, Lucrezia put on the simple dress she'd stitched from the remnants Fra Filippo had brought to her, and stood outside until she was able to catch the eye of a woolgatherer's wife.

"I would like to take in the air today," Lucrezia said, with a sad smile. "And would be ever grateful if you would accompany me."

The woman, called Anna, was one of many in the city who'd heard rumors of the miracle at the palazzo de' Valenti, and believed in Lucrezia's goodness. She was simple but devout, and walked beside Lucrezia to and from the banks of the Bisenzio River, speaking little. Lucrezia hid her face with her hood, but when she returned home her cheeks were pink, and she felt the strength of a new resolve.

"I don't want to hide," she said to Fra Filippo. "It's the eve of Our Lord's birth. I want to go to church and receive the sacrament."

Fra Filippo sent a note to his friend Fra Piero, who hadn't visited the *bottega* since the day the two had exchanged their vows. Their friend arrived at the house at sunset, carrying a ham in a sack. Bird-like and full of energy, his nose red from the cold, the procurator tossed his gift onto the table, crossed the room, and opened his arms to embrace Lucrezia.

"You're radiant," he said, his warm smile displaying his crooked teeth.

Grasping her hand, he drew Lucrezia into the kitchen, where he sat her close to the fire, took a seat on a stool, and guessed at her news.

"A child is a blessing," he said kindly. Although he wondered about the source of the child's seed, he remained silent on this question, and reminded himself that the vows he'd pronounced for his friends had the Lord's legitimacy, if not the pope's approval. "How wonderful that you've received this gift during this joyous season."

After he'd said a prayer for mother and baby, the three of them ate heartily, put on their warmest cloaks, and set off for Mass at Sant'Ippolito.

Stepping through the great arched doorway of green marble, Lucrezia felt swept up by the glorious joy of worship. She'd been hiding in the *bottega* too long. It was good to be back in church. She walked between Fra Filippo and Fra Piero, and sat with the other parishioners. She listened to the voices chanting in prayer, and she sang along in her heart. When she walked up to the altar behind Fra Filippo, and took the holy body of Jesus Christ into her mouth, she felt nearly faint with satisfaction and piety.

She was walking back to her place in the nave when someone whispered, *"la donna,"* as she passed. She looked up to see the curious eyes of a fine lady upon her.

"It's her," the woman said to her companion as she held her hand out toward Lucrezia. The woman wore a dress of double silk, a *berretto,* and a velvet *mantello.* Her fingers shimmered with rings and emitted a gentle perfume.

"Do you know me?" Lucrezia asked, flustered. She peered into the woman's face, sure that she would see hatred and anger.

"I know that yours is the face of de' Valenti's Madonna," the woman whispered, making the sign of the cross. "The *Miraculous Madonna*. They say that you're blessed."

Walking home after Mass, Lucrezia slipped her arm through the monk's and pulled herself toward him. The sky was black, and she could read the constellations.

"There it is," she said, pointing overhead. "The star the three kings followed."

Fra Filippo put his cheek next to hers and followed the direction of her finger until he, too, saw the bright star. There was the promise of snow in the air.

"I'm happy," she said.

Fra Filippo beamed down at her.

"The world is so beautiful tonight," she said quietly. "I know we have many worries but still, Filippo, I am very happy."

Chapter Nineteen

Tuesday of the Sixth Week After Epiphany, the Year of Our Lord 1457

"I wouldn't have believed it if my Luigi hadn't delivered a piece of leather to Fra Filippo's *bottega* and seen her with his own eyes," the cobbler said to the men gathered in his *bottega* on the Piazza Mercatale. "Now I'll have to beat it into my boy that nuns aren't for the taking."

The others laughed, their mouths full of black teeth and brown bread.

For months, Lucrezia had kept her condition concealed under a cloak, but by late February the child in her womb was visible to anyone who stopped to look. She'd seen the way the boy stared at her that morning when he delivered the piece of leather she needed to fashion a harness for her partum belt. She knew that soon word would be all over Prato.

"The white monk must be busy at work painting his own *desco da parto*," the baker joked, slapping his hands against his apron and sending a cloud of flour into the air. "He can do the baptism, too, and he won't have to pay that greedy Inghirami!"

The cobbler spat on the ground. He held a shoe between his knees and hammered off a broken heel.

"His bastard and his whore will need all the blessings they can get," the man said, shaking the hair out of his eyes.

Warming themselves by the cobbler's fire, the tradesmen and artisans whose *bottegas* lined the city square stood together eating from their pockets and enjoying the pleasure of a bawdy tale. The fishmongers, who'd seen Fra Filippo hurrying to snatch up the unsold fish they were required by decree to dump into the street at the end of each day, chuckled in disbelief at news of Lucrezia's pregnancy. The leatherworkers hiked at their tooled belts and wondered why men of the Church could take mistresses when they had to make do with the scrawny whores who lived behind the market plaza.

"As bad as they are in Rome, at least they don't make a public display of their sins," said Franco, whose younger brother was the stable boy at the palazzo de' Valenti.

"That's right," the others agreed, nodding their heads. "It will cost him plenty to buy the indulgences for this in Rome."

News of Lucrezia's pregnancy circulated from the Piazza Mercatale to the Piazza San Marco, and from there to the Piazza San Francesco. By Vespers, the entire Valenti household had been told. Two kitchen maids laughed spitefully, but the others wept when they heard that the model for their *Miraculous Madonna* was soiled. Signora Teresa de' Valenti, who'd remained convinced of Lucrezia's goodness and chastity even after she'd heard the girl was living with the monk, was horrified.

"It's nothing to smile at, Nicola!" the signora scolded the maid.

Until the information was whispered to her as she sat by the fire, Signora Teresa had somehow believed the girl was still pure in spite of the place where she laid her head at night. Even now, the *donna* felt certain that Lucrezia had been led astray by Satan, seduced or perhaps taken against her will, as happened to so many young women.

"It's tragic," she said later to her sister-in-law, who had been present at Ascanio's birth and been the first to call Teresa's survival a miracle. "One so fair is at the mercy of the world after she's lost her father's protection."

The merchant's wife pushed herself onto her feet and walked purposefully to stand before the painting that all in her household now called the *Miraculous Madonna*. For a moment she allowed herself to wonder if perhaps the girl's virtue was still intact; maybe Lucrezia was innocent, even as the Holy Mother had conceived without surrendering her virginity.

"Blasphemy!" she said aloud, shaking the thought from her mind. But Teresa de' Valenti couldn't wholly dismiss her impossible notions. The young woman had saved her life. Sister Lucrezia's face had become the one that Teresa prayed to, the one she saw in her mind when she said her *Ave Maria*. Surely there was something she could do to help Lucrezia now.

"I'll send a note to Sister Pureza," Teresa said. As the wife of the city's wealthiest merchant, she knew that her word swayed opinion on the streets. Perhaps, considering how generous her husband had been to Santa Margherita this year, she could wield her wishes inside the convent walls, as well. "I'll remind her how the girl assisted me and ask her to be kind and merciful."

Turning to Nicola, who was putting a stack of clean linens away in the birthing chest, the merchant's wife called for vellum and a pot of ink.

❧ · ❧

By the dim sunlight that bled through the high window of her cell, Sister Pureza read the letter that had arrived at the convent along with a small pouch of lire. The coins had been snatched up by Mother Bartolommea but the note had been given to Sister Pureza with the seal unbroken.

If it is true, I beg you to have mercy, Sister Pureza read. *She, too, is a child of God, and in need. I implore you to bear in mind, Sister, she is only a helpless woman in a world of strong men.*

The old nun didn't want to believe the rumors that had reached the convent, but it seemed impossible to deny them any longer. She dropped the parchment onto her writing table and paced her small cell.

She'd done all that she could think of, and still the girl had fallen to sin. She'd come to think of Sister Lucrezia as her own charge, almost like a daughter to whom she would pass on her knowledge of herbs and midwifery. Of course the world was full of strong men; this is why she'd begged Lucrezia to return to the convent. But the girl had refused. Sister Pureza was heartsick, and she was angry.

She remembered how small and frail the novitiate had looked in Fra Filippo's kitchen, yet how stubbornly she'd refused to return to Santa Margherita. Even when Spinetta had come back, Lucrezia had remained with the monk, alone. She'd stayed of her own volition and now, instead of using her healing hands and soothing words to help others, Lucrezia would cry out in the agony of Eve's labor. Her bastard child would come into the world covered in blood, and wrapped in shame. And the Lord, who didn't look kindly upon children born of lust, might well inflict the same loss upon Lucrezia that He'd inflicted upon Pasqualina di Fiesola so many years ago.

———

*I*n his wood-paneled studio in the southern wing of Santo Spirito in Florence, Prior General Ludovico Pietro di Saviano tossed the offensive letter into the fire and watched it blaze.

Once again, Provost Inghirami had been the bearer of bad news. *I am sorry to disturb you with news of such a sordid nature, but it is my duty.* Indeed, the provost carried out his duties well when they involved delivering embarrassing news to the prior general. What a good laugh they must be having in Prato, Saviano thought sourly: the half-mad monk walking arm in arm with the pregnant novitiate, thumbing their noses at the Carmelites, the Augustinians, and the Lord Himself. It was small consolation, but at least everyone would now know what a wicked seductress hid behind that angelic face.

"Damn her and damn the monk." Saviano's words ripped from his mouth, although there was no one there to hear them. "And a curse on their bastard, too."

The prior general froze. *A bastard.* The child was most certainly a bastard, but was it Lippi's bastard? He did a quick calculation of time, remembering Lucrezia's thin wrists twisting beneath his hands, the gurgle of pain from her throat as he entered her. He couldn't deny the possibility. He felt a moment of manly pride at his virility, followed quickly by the horror of what might be.

But the prior general wouldn't allow himself a moment of pity. The woman had chosen her lot. She'd proven herself a harlot by living in sin.

He stood taller in his costly vestments from Rome. It was bad enough the novitiate had shamed him and shamed the convent, but parading through Prato with a huge belly for all to see was too much. The monk had the protective shield of Cosimo, but this *puttana* was still an Augustinian charge. And he was still in control of her.

As the smell of singed paper filled his nostrils, Prior General Saviano contemplated his next move. Only he knew what was best for the Order. He would do what he had to do for himself, for Santa Margherita, and for the sanctity of the Augustinians.

Rumors continued and the foot traffic along Via Santa Margherita swelled as the curious and the outraged tried to peer inside the monk's *bottega* for a glimpse of the pregnant Madonna. Afraid and ashamed, Lucrezia hung the largest piece of cloth they had across the window that faced the street. The cloth was red, and bathed the inside of the *bottega* in a pink light that would have pleased Lucrezia if it hadn't been there to hide her from the world.

Occasionally one of the woolgatherers' wives knocked shyly on her door to see how she fared, and Nicola came from the Valenti palazzo each week with a basket of fruit or some sweet rolls from Signora Teresa. But for the most part Lucrezia was alone while Fra Filippo worked on the frescoes at Santo Stefano, and she sat in the pink light pretending she didn't hear the people on the road outside.

"Maybe it's an admission of sin," said one woolfuller to the other, as they passed in the morning and saw the red curtain in the window. But when they returned that afternoon, Fra Filippo was taking the curtain down so he could paint inside by the natural light, and the passersby began to speculate that the red curtain, appearing and disappearing in the window with no apparent logic, was meant to send them some message or sign.

"Maybe it's red to tell us the child is purged from the womb," said one of the old merchants' wives who believed Satan had taken up residence along Via Santa Margherita.

"Maybe it's there to keep the Evil One away," said another.

"Or to welcome Satan," said an old crone, whose body was twisted under the rags she gathered in the marketplace and wove into ropes to sell.

Some people crossed themselves as they passed the *bottega*, a few spat; others left small offerings for the pregnant Madonna. Lucrezia took the unwelcome attention with as much fortitude as she could muster, squaring her shoulders and trying not to look out the window too often.

"In time they'll forget us," Fra Filippo told her gently. Even when she clapped her hands at a small basket of brown eggs left by the doorstep, he reminded her that in a city so full of sickness, birth, death, and prosperity, the leering eyes of the curious soon would be focused elsewhere, and tongues would be wagging over someone else's change of fortune.

"Of course." Lucrezia smiled. "And when word comes from Rome, we'll no longer need to hide," she added bravely.

Her composure didn't crack until the day she saw Paolo passing on the road and waved to him from the doorway.

"Come inside, you can tell me what you hear from Rosina," she called, beckoning.

Paolo hung his head and stayed on the street. Lucrezia pulled a shawl from a hook near the door, and hurried toward him. Heads turned to watch her.

"I'm sorry," Paolo said when she'd gotten closer. "*Mia madre* forbids it."

⁂

As Fra Filippo predicted, with the coming of carnival that marked the start of Lent, well-wishers and gossipmongers alike stopped haunting the street outside their door. Fat Tuesday was celebrated with a boisterous procession led by Provost Inghirami with a confraternity of Church dignitaries and civic officials from the *Comune di Prato*. Children danced in the streets, men and women wore masks they'd fashioned by hand or bought from merchants who'd brought them from the shops along the canals of Venice. Everyone feasted, and the air was filled with the scent of roasting pig.

But there was no fattening of the larder at Fra Filippo's house, where his silver pieces numbered no more than ten, and Lucrezia woke on the first day of Lent pledging to keep her body from the painter for the forty penitent days of *Quaresima*.

"For the child's sake," she said, planting a shy kiss on his cheek. "I love you, but I must be strict in my Lenten penance."

Her eyes moved in shadow, and Fra Filippo couldn't read what they said. But he knew she worried for the child's soul, and agreed that penitence in the time of Lent was always prudent.

"I'd like to speak with Sister Pureza," Lucrezia said to Fra Filippo over their small *cena* that evening. The bells for Nones had rung long ago, and there were ribbons of blue paint running through the monk's hair. His thoughts were elsewhere, and Lucrezia did her best not to let that discourage her.

"There's no one else who knows so much about childbirth. I want to be prepared, Filippo."

By her own calculations the child had taken root any time between the ninth of September and the first day of December. If the child came in June, and was a healthy size, she would know Fra Filippo was not the father—and so would he. Despite his reticence, she knew the monk also carried the secret of her stain. He swore he loved her, and she believed him, but sometimes she lay awake all night, afraid he would refuse to claim her child as his own if she did not carry it long enough.

"Sister Pureza is not our friend now," the monk said heavily.

"She was my friend once." Lucrezia hung her head. She'd eaten only a few pieces of bread, but her stomach felt full. "Maybe she'll be my friend again, when all is right."

Fra Filippo gazed at the place where her dress swelled under her breasts. He pictured the robes of the Madonna, still full after the birth of the child, and wondered at the ample breasts he might paint in his altarpiece. He rubbed his eyes, to secure the vision there, and finished his meal in silence.

Lucrezia slept long and hard as the cold stone of the moon rose that evening, but Fra Filippo could not rest. He'd written again to Ser Francesco Cantansanti but heard nothing for two weeks. With Lucrezia's large belly in his sight even while she slept, the monk gnawed at the end of his quill and composed a lengthy, suppliant letter to the Curia in Rome.

Your Blessed Holiness, Pope Callistus III, whose face is always closest to the Lord's, he began.

For two pages, Fra Filippo poured out his reverence, his dedication, and all he'd done to honor and celebrate the Lord in churches from Rome to Naples. He listed his patrons, beginning with his days at Santa Maria del Carmine and the *Madonna and Child with Angels* for the Carmelites of the Selve Monastery, followed by the tabernacle and frescoes for the Antonians of the Basilica del Santo in Padua, through to the *Coronation* he'd completed for the church of Sant'Ambrogio.

Fra Filippo wrote:

Your Holiness,

In my lifetime of gratitude and in service to the Lord, my requests never have been sent to trouble or worry but only to honor the Church and the great office of the Holy See. Now I prostrate myself at your feet and beg that in

Your Great Mercy and Your Holiest Power you might grant absolution and dispensation to me, a humble servant of the Lord, so that I might enter in the Sacrament of Matrimony with one Lucrezia Buti, fourth daughter of Lorenzo Buti of Florence, who comes to me with no dowry and for whom I renounce all claim to one now or henceforth. Ut in Omnibus Gloricetus Deus.

Chapter Twenty

The Second Week of Lent, the Year of Our Lord 1457

Fra Filippo labored every morning on the frescoes, and every afternoon he hurried home to work on the *Adoration* altarpiece. Sometimes he skipped lunch, and often didn't stop until long after the sun went down. He'd promised Giovanni de' Medici something truly new, and in the past it had never been difficult to conceive and execute a fresh concept. He'd been the first to paint matching portraits of a couple gazing at one another as if through the window of a confessional. He was the one who'd continued his landscapes from one wall to the next, coaxing the viewer to follow the thread of a storyline. And it was he who'd been inspired to use the impish faces of the *ragazzi* for the angels in his heavens.

Now he strove to depict the wilderness as a scene of penitence, with the Madonna kneeling over the newborn Christ in the open air. To paint a Madonna under God's sky, without the walls and buildings that man had built around her, was a bold idea that had never been done before: not by the great masters of the earlier centuries, not by Masaccio, not even by Fra Giovanni the Dominican. It wasn't in the Gospels, nor even in the apocryphal legends.

The open landscape would put the Madonna in the natural world, showing her divinity and closeness to creation. And to be worthy of all that he'd staked upon this single work for the Medici, the Madonna had to be a simple woman whose beauty suggested the strength and grace needed to bring the Christ child into the world. She had to be convincing and meditative, sad and hopeful at the same time.

As he worked, Fra Filippo imagined the pope reading his request for dispensation to marry Lucrezia, and he prayed the Virgin would help to sway the ailing prelate. He tried not to dwell on the Curia's silence. He tried not to remember the feel of the lash on his back, or to feel the pressure of Lucrezia's blossoming belly, her hungry beauty, the beseeching look in her eyes every afternoon when he returned from the market with an ever-smaller sack of food for their meal. He tried to focus only on the Madonna, on the Child, on the hope the birth brought to the world.

Yet when he put down his brush at the end of each day, and stepped back to see what he had accomplished, Fra Filippo knew that he was failing.

The Madonna's body wasn't sufficiently beautiful; the trees and animals he'd so carefully sketched, the fat angels in the clouds, even the clouds themselves weren't potent enough to delight a king. The weeks of working on the painting, adding one troubled brushstroke after another, hadn't made the piece better, clearer, or more power-ful. With so much at stake, his inspiration had been muddled and confused, and this was evident in the work.

Fra Filippo had come to this painful place before, when the only thing to do was to begin again. He knew what must be done, and as dawn broke on the second Thursday of Lent, Fra Filippo stole into his workshop while Lucrezia slept, and quietly mixed a sticky batch of white gesso.

He acted in detached defiance, splattering gesso on the floor, on his robe, and across the unformed wilderness on the panel. With a dozen broad strokes, he blotted out eight months of work.

"I will," he said as he rubbed his hands across his face, streaking his cheeks and scalp with white until he looked like one of the figures carved on a church façade. "I will."

He began again that very day, deciding on three angels to hold up the plump body of the Christ child, the hands of God reaching through a cloud that hung over the blue-green forest. There would be a midnight sky and, above it, a blue sky framed by a rainbow, emblematic of God's promise.

He woke early the next morning and briskly executed his sketch, prepared the panel, and opened his container of woad to grind blue pigment for the sky.

But the corked jar was empty.

He opened the pewter canister of buckthorn, thinking he'd work at least on the deep green of the forest leaves. That, too, was nearly gone. Even the powdered *margherita*, which he'd taken from Lucrezia's hand on that June day in the convent garden, was nearly finished.

The painter bent over his worktable and hung his head.

For two years he'd been relying on Sister Pureza to supply him with many of the herbs and plants he needed for his work. But he hadn't set eyes on the old nun since September, when she'd turned her back on them and left the *bottega* in silence. It would take days to get materials from Florence, not to mention payment which he could ill afford to make. His money was almost gone. Only yesterday, he'd counted the last five pieces of silver hidden in the pouch he kept under a hearthstone.

Without supplies, he could not paint. Without money, he could not buy supplies. And if he did not paint, he would be ruined.

Running quickly through his commissions, Fra Filippo realized his only hope was to complete a significant portion of the frescoes at Santo Stefano, and hope he'd be able to cajole a few more florins from the *Comune di Prato*.

Saying nothing to Lucrezia, who was dressing in the bedroom, he grabbed a piece of dried salami and went out. In the church he found his assistants in the *cappella maggiore*, just beginning to layer the color in the scene depicting young Saint Stephen taking leave of his parents.

"*Buongiorno,*" he said, glaring at the yawning young men.

Fra Filippo stared up at the wall, where he'd labored for weeks on the birth scene of Saint John. He'd lovingly drawn the gentle smile of Saint Elizabeth and the sure hands of the nursemaids who washed the infant. He'd pictured Lucrezia's gentle glow as she reached down to feel the soft skin of their new child, and in his mind he'd replaced the orange and gray interior of Saint John's birth chamber with the simple rooms of his own home.

"I've mixed the *intonaco* for the new *giornata*, maestro," said Tomaso, coming up behind him. "What colors will you need for the background of the funeral scene?"

The morning was cold, and Tomaso's words formed clouds in the frigid air. The painter whirled around to face him.

"The work is not going quickly enough!" Fra Filippo snapped. The months of speaking to his assistants with quiet approval were gone. "Work faster!"

He directed Fra Diamante to take over the background scenery for the missions of Saint Stephen and Saint John.

"The white caves and stones for Saint John, the deep woods for Saint Stephen," he instructed, indicating where and how the colors should be placed for the best effect. "They must be done now. They must be done so I can paint in the figures."

He put each assistant to work on a different *giornata*, placing the buckets of paint roughly in front of them, barking his instructions, urging them on.

"Do you want to eat? Then you must work!" he said, spinning around the chapel from wall to wall, looking at the incomplete versions of his dreams.

"God, you ask more of me than I can give," he muttered to himself as he leaned against the heavy worktable and hastily drew the figures that would people the frescoes. "I can't paint without color, without supplies, without lire."

The assistants saw his lips moving and assumed he was praying. They made wider circles around him, and each time he glared at them, they worked faster.

"Veloce!" he said, watching Young Marco taking his time with the folds of a leaf. "Faster."

The day passed in a frenzy. No one stopped for lunch. They worked until the light was gone and Fra Diamante put a tired hand on Fra Filippo's shoulder.

"We've done all that's possible in a single day, maestro," he said. "We must go home now."

After the others had left, Fra Filippo threw down his brushes, climbed off the scaffolding, and snuffed out the candles. He made his way down the nave to where the *Sacra Cintola* was kept. He'd been in proximity to the Holy Belt of the Virgin for many years, but had never felt the need to call on its powers until now.

Kneeling before the locked gate that guarded the holy relic, he sank to his knees and wrapped his hands around the bronze bars.

"Hail Mary, full of grace." He whispered the words of the Virgin's prayer, suffused with more feeling than ever before. "The Lord is with thee."

When he finished the prayer he began again, and then again, finding solace in the rhythmic repetition of the words.

"*Madre mia*, forgive me if I've wronged you. Forgive me."

As he prayed, Fra Filippo recalled that day in the confessional, when he'd searched for just the right words to comfort Lucrezia in her weeping.

"Virgin Mother, I cannot fail," he whispered. "I must be able to work and take care of Lucrezia, or all will be lost."

The candle beside him burned down until it was extinguished, and the monk was surrounded by darkness. As he tried to get his bearings, he heard footfalls from the direction of the altar. Turning, he made out a red-robed figure, carrying a candle, passing through the transept.

"Inghirami?" he whispered hoarsely into the dark. "Good provost? Are you there?"

The figure seemed to move more quickly. He heard one, maybe two men. Standing abruptly, the monk rushed up the nave, toward the altar. The flame vanished around a corner to the right of the presbytery. Fra Filippo heard a door open.

"Who's there?" His voice echoed through the church, past the silent wooden statues of the Virgin Mary and Saint Elizabeth, across the high altar where the heavy crucifix stood in darkness. He thought of Lucrezia, alone and vulnerable.

Seized by an unnamed fear, the painter spun around and ran from the church, white robes whipping from the wind of his own movements. From the church steps he saw his *bottega* windows were dark, as they'd been on that terrible night many months before.

"Lucrezia?" He shouted for her as he stumbled through the dark workshop into the kitchen. "Lucrezia?"

The bedroom door was closed. He flung it open.

"Lucrezia?"

Her sleeping body rolled toward him in the dark. Panting, he put a hand on her forehead. Her eyelids fluttered, and she spoke as if from a dream.

"What is it, Filippo?"

The painter dropped to the floor, his head at her side, all the worry he'd been carrying for months finally bringing him to his knees.

"Is everything all right?" She was so deeply asleep that her eyes didn't open.

"Yes," he said, barely choking down his fears. "Everything's fine."

❦

After that night in the church, it seemed Fra Filippo saw red robes everywhere. He saw a flash of red rounding the corner in front of him as he walked to the market in the morning, and the edge of a red robe seemed to flash beyond his vision every afternoon. Of course Provost Inghirami couldn't be everywhere at once, and yet it seemed he was haunting the painter even in his dreams: grimacing as Fra Filippo counted the silver pieces that ran through his fingers like fish slipping through a stream.

"Have you seen Provost Inghirami?" the painter asked Tomaso one morning. He'd slept badly again, and woke determined to ask the provost to authorize the *Comune di Prato* to advance him more florins for the fresco work. He was already in arrears to the church and the city for money he'd used to pay back debts to the Augustinian Order, and knew it was highly possible that the provost would refuse. But without something, he and Lucrezia would starve.

"He comes when you're not here," the assistant replied. "And he never says a word, only stands behind us and watches."

Fra Filippo thought he saw Young Marco blush, but he couldn't be sure.

"Young Marco, have you had some problem with the provost?" he asked.

"No, maestro, nothing," the soft-spoken young man assured him, his eyes dewy and sweet.

Fra Filippo set everyone to their work before settling at his table to review the rough plans for King Herod's banquet scene. He was sketching the silver platter that would hold the head of John the Baptist, and mentally composing the words of supplication he would use with the provost, when a messenger arrived from the home of Ottavio de' Valenti.

"My master wishes to see you at the palazzo today. It's a matter of some urgency."

Filled with foreboding, Fra Filippo gave a few hurried instructions to Fra Diamante, and stopped before the chapel of the *Sacra Cintola* to say a quick prayer to the Virgin once again.

"Good Mother, I'm nearly without hope," he whispered. "Please don't let me fall into ruin."

Fra Filippo was greeted at the Valenti palazzo with the same civility as always, and shown into the merchant's study, with its rich intaglio carvings, where he accepted a glass of *vernaccia* from Ottavio's decanter. Perched on the edge of a chair beside the fire, the painter offered his patron a weak smile.

"You don't look well, Brother Lippi," de' Valenti said, frowning.

Fra Filippo straightened his spine as best he could, and leaned across the mahogany table. "I have many worries, but they aren't your troubles, good friend, they're mine."

Ottavio de' Valenti was a formidable ally, one of the few people in the painter's life to whom he currently owed nothing. The monk raised his glass to the merchant and drank half of it down in a fast gulp.

"And our Madonna?" De' Valenti smiled. "Is she well?"

Fra Filippo was taken aback, startled by the fear that perhaps he owed de' Valenti some work he'd forgotten. When he realized the merchant was speaking of Lucrezia, he bowed his head in a grateful nod.

"She's well enough, praise the Lord," he said cautiously. He couldn't help but let his eyes wander around the magnificent room, noting the ample pile of firewood next to the hearth. Without realizing it, Fra Filippo put his hand to the coin pouch at his belt, and felt for the single piece of silver there. De' Valenti got right to the point.

"I'm in the position to offer you a commission, one that will come with a sizable windfall. Forty florins," the merchant said, a glass of honeyed wine in his well-manicured hand. He took a slow sip. "Enough to provide for *la donna* and *il bambino*, at least for some time."

The monk was astounded. His prayers to the *Sacra Cintola* had been answered quickly, and with good fortune.

"An enormous altarpiece, for the Bankers' Guild. They want a nursing Madonna surrounded by angels, with their patron Saint Matthew kneeling in honor at her feet," de' Valenti said.

He pulled a paper from his desk and read the complete request of the Arte del Cambio. Below the central panel with the nursing Madonna, the *predella* was to contain scenes of Saint Matthew's life; the side wings would have images of Saints Matthew and Jerome. The altarpiece was to be grand, costly, and, as de' Valenti emphasized, rapidly executed in time for the summer celebration of the Feast of Mary Magdalena, when the Arte del Cambio's new guild offices would be opened and blessed.

"They proposed another painter, but I assured them you are the best. This is true, *amico mio*," de' Valenti said. He wasn't one to offer indiscriminate praise. "They'll pay you the florins when the work is complete. They want it three weeks after the Solstice, in plenty of time for the feast."

"It is not possible," Fra Filippo cried, more forcefully than he meant to.

"The time doesn't suit you?" De' Valenti frowned.

"No, the timing is fine, it's most agreeable, Ottavio. But I must have supplies, gold leaf, lapis lazuli, a fresh set of poplar panels. All of these are costly, and can't be obtained on credit, you understand. I must have resources if I am to reflect God's glory in the work."

De' Valenti nodded.

"If there's no other way," he said hesitantly. He knew the guild wouldn't be patient. "They'll pay you half the florins up front, but they'll expect to see regular progress in return. And they'll be after you, Filippo."

As de' Valenti spoke, Fra Filippo imagined Lucrezia dressed in the finery she deserved, their baby swaddled in real silk rather than scraps and coarse cloth. He imagined new thatch on his roof, perhaps a strong bed with wooden posts and an embroidered coverlet. For a moment the unpainted walls in Santo Stefano and the half-finished panels for King Alfonso flashed through his mind, but he brushed them away. Clearly, this commission was a gift from the Virgin Mother, bestowed upon him through the powers of her Holy Belt.

"You can sign the contract and get your money tomorrow at the guild offices," de' Valenti said, leveling his gaze at the painter. "But as I said, these men expect the work on time. And they are not gentle men, Filippo."

"*Grazie.* Thank you, Signor Ottavio," Fra Filippo said as he clasped the merchant's hand. "May God grant you mercy and profit."

Fra Filippo went to the guild offices early the next morning to collect twenty gold florins, signing a contract in his heavy hand and solemnly accepting the money from the notary of the Arte del Cambio. He passed by a row of offices and lingered at the doorway long enough to see a small man in a red robe eyeing him over a pile of papers. As he exited the wooden doors of the building, guarded by two porcine men in black tunics, the hefty bag of florins pulled reassuringly on Fra Filippo's belt.

In good cheer, he stopped and visited the butcher, picking out the fattest rabbit for their evening meal. Lucrezia cooked the rabbit that afternoon, stewing it with yellow onions and the last piece of ruta-baga, and they ate an early *cena* by a newly fed fire. They hadn't had fresh meat since Lent had begun, and Lucrezia was radiant. Seeing her happy, Fra Filippo couldn't bring himself to tell her about the new piece for the Bankers' Guild—he knew another commission would only make her worry.

"Your long hours of work have brought their reward," she said, smiling across the table.

"Soon Lent will be over," he said, wiping his mouth with the back of his hand. "We've abstained, as you asked."

Lucrezia bowed her head.

"We have to be very careful of the baby, Filippo."

He pushed back his chair and stood behind her. Then he breathed a kiss onto the back of her neck.

"Always," he said, inhaling the scent of her chamomile. "Always."

Chapter Twenty-one

Holy Week, the Year of Our Lord 1457

In small niches along the streets of Prato, parishioners festooned their Madonna statuettes with white flowers, and white sashes were cleaned and readied to be hung over church doorways in preparation for the celebration of Easter. Lines from the Gospels rang out in the piazzas at night, where the confraternities mounted passion plays and the long-faced cobbler, chosen to represent the Son this year, dragged a heavy cross supplied, as always, by the Woodworkers' Guild. The streets leading to the Church of Santo Stefano were turned into the *Via Dolorosa*, Christ's road of misery, and despite the short patches of grass that had already begun to grow, the small hill that led to the sheep meadows north of Prato became a terrifying Golgotha.

As she'd done every year since reaching womanhood, Lucrezia attended Mass on Holy Thursday. She'd rarely ventured out of the *bottega* since her pregnancy had begun to show, but the Mass before the *Triduum Sacrum* was a treasured ritual she didn't want to miss. With her head covered by a generous hood, she walked slowly to the Church of Santo Spirito and joined the others who waited on the side of the nave. When there was a free spot at the altar, Lucrezia knelt and began her *Ave Maria*. She was aware of her belly's heavy low sling and bent over it protectively. When she had finished she rose slowly, her hands on the low arch of her back. Lost in prayer, she nearly walked into the woman heading toward her. It was Sister Bernadetta from the convent.

"Sister Lucrezia!" the nun exclaimed, gazing at Lucrezia's belly. "I've been praying for you," the nun said, dropping her eyes.

Although she was startled, Lucrezia was pleased to see the young nun.

"What are you doing here?" she asked.

"I was coming from the *ospedale* with Sister Simona, and we stopped here to say a prayer," the nun answered softly.

"Sister, please tell me if Spinetta is all right. She hasn't written to me."

"Yes, she's in fine health." The nun hesitated. "But your sister's taken a vow of silence and speaks only in prayer." Seeing Lucrezia's confusion, she continued. "She's pledged to remain silent until she's taken the full veil."

At the kind expression in the nun's eyes, Lucrezia's own eyes filled. She'd endured much loneliness, and couldn't bear to have the sisters at the convent think ill of her.

"Look, Sister Bernadetta." She thrust out her left hand and displayed the golden ring she wore.

"Are you a *monna*, a married lady?" Sister Bernadetta squeezed Lucrezia's hand, and the young woman wanted nothing more than to tell her friend that she was properly wed.

"We're awaiting word from Rome, and pray we'll hear from His Holiness, Pope Callistus, soon. Until then we've exchanged the promise a man and a woman can give one another, and have the blessing of a priest."

The nun smiled kindly, but Lucrezia could see it was a smile of pity. She didn't ask any more questions, and Sister Bernadetta seemed

eager to go. She saw the nun looking past her, to pale-faced Sister
Simona who waited near the narthex.

"I'll pray for you and the child," Sister Bernadetta said after
she'd kissed Lucrezia's forehead. "God's grace to you. And blessed
Easter."

*t dawn on Easter morning, Lucrezia knelt at the foot of the
bed singing a hymn praising the resurrected Christ, and
repeating her *Ave Maria*.

"*Ave Maria Stella, Dei Mater Alma, at que simper virgo, felix coeli porta.*"

When she'd finished, she rose slowly and walked into the empty
kitchen where a fire already roared. She warmed her hands, arching
her back against the pressure of her growing belly. Silently, still lost
in the reverie of her chanting, she drew back the curtain that led into
the workshop, and gasped.

There was a rainbow of silks in the *bottega*, the likes of which she
hadn't seen since the heyday of her father's shop in Florence.

"Oh, Filippo." Her eyes took in several *braccia* of the finest blue
silk from Lucca, the richest browns and golds, the jewellike purple
and red. "They're beautiful."

The painter rose from his worktable and crossed to her. His robe
was brilliant white amid the color.

"Where did this treasure come from?" she asked.

He smiled. The effort and promises it had taken were worth it,
simply to see the joy on her face. He lifted a piece of blue silk and
held it out to her. Her hand grasped his, the silk rippling between
them like water.

"I've gone to my friends and begged what favors I'm owed," he said. "My only wish is for you to be happy. For you, and the child."

"But each piece must have cost many florins—"

"The child will have a proper baptismal gown, Lucrezia, and you will have a silken pillow to rest your head upon when you labor."

Lucrezia closed her eyes and fingered the blue silk, imagining their child swaddled in a length of *seta leale,* lying in a cradle lined with rich fabrics and plush pillows.

The painter touched her face. There was a wrinkle on her skin where she'd been lying against the blanket's fold. He touched the ridge there, put a hand on her shoulder, moved the white cloth of her sleeping gown.

"I did this for you," Fra Filippo said quietly. "Because I love you."

He took her face in his hands and turned it this way and that.

"You've been very understanding," he said, desire deepening his voice. "Very patient. Very beautiful."

He buried his face in her neck and kissed her, fell to his knees and pressed his face against her belly. Lucrezia was startled at the way her body responded, with heat and longing that began between her legs and radiated upward.

"Filippo." She ran her hands across the top of his head, along the rim of his short hair and the stubble on his cheeks.

He stood and gathered her into his arms. Even with the baby, she was light. He carried her to the bedroom and carefully laid her on the soft bed. The blue silk was still in her hand. He spread it on top of her like a blanket, watching her face come alive at the feel of the silk against her skin, the surprise in her eyes as he worked her *gamurra* up over her belly and shoulders until all that covered her was the lake of blue silk.

He swiftly unknotted his belt and stripped off his robe. Her belly was the blue sea beneath him and he reached for it, feeling the length of her body, seeing the delicate veins that ran in her arms as she touched him. He stroked her face, touching her above the silk and then sliding his hand below it, across her full breasts, the taut, swollen belly, the brush of hair between her legs, her soft thighs. Gently he pressed her knees apart, using the strength in his arms to protect her from his weight as she opened.

Lucrezia had never felt such desire. She felt her breath grow shallow, her eyes roll back. The painter watched her face. Her lips parted and she began to moan softly. He moved in her, whispering her name, thrusting slowly.

Lucrezia let herself go. She felt herself grow from the single point between her legs to the depth and width of the earth. She cried out. Her moaning turned to deep sighs, and Fra Filippo knew that no matter what other men said of his sins, God had chosen to allow him into heaven.

Lucrezia dressed for Easter Mass in a simple blue *gamurra*. She could still feel the painter's hands on her skin, his body's gentle pressure, the surprise of her desire.

She brushed her hair languidly. It smelled of the chamomile she'd rinsed through it, but also of the smoke from the hearth, and the plaster dust that was always in the painter's robes. She ran her fingers across her belly's tight drum, waiting for the child's kick. When she felt it, she smiled and called out.

"Filippo?"

She went into the kitchen, and heard him folding away the silks in the next room. She pulled aside the curtain at the doorway, looking for the tenderness in his eyes. But before their gazes met, a movement caught her eye and she looked past him, to the window that opened toward the piazza.

A flash of red robe appeared, followed by a hand reaching into the window. Lucrezia screamed. Fra Filippo dropped the stretch of purple silk in his hands and whirled around. He ran to the door and flung it open. As he'd expected, there was no one there.

"Who was that at the window?" Lucrezia asked, shaken and pale, both hands below her belly, as if she could cradle it in her arms.

"I'm sure it was nothing," Fra Filippo said.

"It was someone," she insisted. "Someone in a red robe trying to climb up to the window."

"Whoever it was, he'll be sorry if I see him here again," the painter said.

His words hid his growing fear, and replaced the gentle calm that Lucrezia's body had brought him. It was Easter—surely it wasn't Inghirami spying at his window on a day when there was so much to do.

Chapter Twenty-two

The Fourth Week of Easter, the Year of Our Lord 1457

Fra Filippo was at the center of activity in the *cappella maggiore*. Fra Diamante had been called away again, and there was much to accomplish before the *intonaco* could be mixed and the sketches transformed into the colorful figures of King Herod and his banquet guests. The painter felt the power of a king in his very fingertips, and wanted to get to work before the feeling slipped away.

"Andiamo," he snapped at Tomaso. "Prepare this surface so we can begin."

Giorgio was stretching a cord across the wall to check the accuracy of the perspective line, while Young Marco ground the pigment for yet another batch of *giallorino*.

"You, too, Giorgio, hurry up. And Young Marco, how long does it take you to mix some binder?"

Frustrated by the slow progress of the frescoes, the painter turned his thoughts to the Bankers' Guild altarpiece. To quicken his progress, he planned to copy two of the figures he'd already sketched for the frescoes, using a rabbi from the synagogue as the figure of Saint Matthew beside the nursing Madonna, and two others from the same scene for the figures of the saints on either side panel. It was a common practice, and one the men of the Arte del Cambio would never notice.

The painter was contemplating the figures of Saint Jerome and

Saint Matthew when he felt the air beside him stir, and looked up into the solemn, gray face of Provost Inghirami, whose red robes swirled around him.

"It's been too long," Inghirami said, his voice cold and measured.

Fra Filippo stiffened, shuffling a blank piece of parchment on top of the sketch in his hand. He hadn't seen the provost for many weeks. He tried to take a measure of the man, to determine if his were the red robes that seemed to be haunting him.

"What are you working on, Fratello?"

Moving aside the silverpoints and parchment, Fra Filippo picked up the sheet on which he'd drawn Inghirami's face. He held it up for the provost and saw he'd been too kind. In the sketch the man looked sharp and graceful, fully alive.

The provost narrowed his eyes.

"It's fine," he said. "The *Comune di Prato* has approved my likeness. But we have heard you've taken an additional commission, Fratello." The provost let his eyes roam the clutter on the worktable. "Remember, you're indebted to Santo Stefano."

"How can I forget?" Fra Filippo smelled the sardines the provost had eaten for lunch. "You seem to be everywhere. Reminding me."

The provost raised himself even taller, his spine erect. He glanced beyond the painter to where the assistants were busy at their work, safely out of hearing.

"I don't like your tone, Fratello," Inghirami said. "Remember, the *comune* gets its reports from me. Don't let the Bankers' Guild supplant your obligations to the Church. It will not bode well if you do."

With a nod, the cleric slipped away again, his red robes hissing along the limestone floor as they dragged behind him.

He'd barely left the chapel when Fra Filippo felt a hand on his shoulder and turned abruptly to face his friend Fra Piero.

"You startled me, Piero," he said, trying to hide his unsteady hands. But the procurator knew him well, and pulled him into the nave, where fresh air entered from the open doors beyond the narthex.

"What's the matter, Filippo? You look terrible," Fra Piero said.

The artist shook his head and forced a smile.

"*Mio amico*, you know how it is when I'm puzzling over something in my work." He shifted his body, craning to see the mouth of the *cappella maggiore*. Fra Piero followed his gaze.

"Something's troubling you," the procurator said. They stood beside the wooden statue of Saint Elizabeth, the row of votive candles flickering around the base of the pedestal. "What is it?"

As Fra Filippo prepared to answer, he caught another spark of rippling red fabric, and his body twisted. The motion came from a doorway that led to the stairs accessing the church's crypt. A tall figure in red slipped quickly through the door, shutting it silently behind him.

"Inghirami?" the procurator asked.

Fra Filippo was hesitant to speak. "I seem to be seeing red robes everywhere."

"What do you mean?"

Reluctantly, the painter told him about the figure at the window on Easter morning, the man in red who seemed to shadow him through the streets.

"The provost doesn't move with ease. He's old and slippery, not quick and strong," Fra Piero said. As he spoke, the procurator wondered if his friend, who was under a great strain, was letting his imagination get the better of him. "Probably it's just someone who's curious about your affairs, Filippo. Don't let it trouble you."

Still gazing across the nave, Fra Filippo put a hand to his temple and rubbed his eyes.

"My head's pounding," he said.

"You should rest. Go home, check on Lucrezia."

"*Sì, sì*, I will," Fra Filippo said. "But first I must go to the apothecary and get a tincture for my head." He blinked, and there were dark spots in front of his eyes. "I'll have to come back later, but an hour of rest will do me good."

The painter hurried toward the apothecary, taking a shortcut through an alley behind the cobbler's shop. He was looking down at the street, aware only of the throbbing in his temples, when he felt the rush of a man on either side of him. He turned right, then left. The men moved in front of him, blocking his way.

"*Buongiorno*, Fratello."

"*Buongiorno.*" He nodded. He barely gave them a second thought until the oafs stopped, forcing him to yield.

"We've come from the Bankers' Guild," said one. Fra Filippo looked from one man to the other. The first was short, his face covered in stubble that barely concealed an angry purple scar. The other was tall and thick, with arms the size of a horse's flank.

"What is it?" the painter asked irritably.

The short one stepped closer. The painter's heart began to race.

"Our master would like to see the work you've done for the altarpiece," said the short man.

Fra Filippo's head was pounding.

"I don't have it with me," he said, irritated. "It's at my workshop."

"Take us there," the tall one demanded. "Show it to us."

The painter tried to pass the larger of the two, but the man moved in front of him and uncrossed his arms. Fra Filippo could see he was strong as a bull, and probably just as mean.

"We're not the Casa del Ceppo, we're not a charity house," the man said. "The painting is due soon after the solstice. The guild wants to see that you're working on it."

"If the Arte del Cambio wants to see what I've got, tell them to come to my *bottega* in a civilized manner."

"We know what you've done." The man spat at Fra Filippo's feet. "If you've got something, show it to us now, and we'll report back to the guild."

Shaken, the monk tried to move back, but he bumped up against a building. The two men in black parted, and a third, in red, stepped forward. Fra Filippo felt a chill of recognition as the red robes rippled.

"I'll gladly come to see what you've done." The man addressed him in a far kinder tone than the others had used. Fra Filippo thought he heard an accent from the north of Italy, perhaps somewhere near Milan. "Shall I come now?"

Fra Filippo's eyes moved left and right, casting about in his mind for some other sketch he might pass off as the one for the bankers. But there was nothing.

"I thought so, Fratello," said the small man. Fra Filippo remembered him sitting behind a table at the guild offices, on the day he'd signed the contract. "We may not be men of high art, but our money is good, and you have our twenty florins."

Fra Filippo was silent.

"Either you deliver the altarpiece on schedule, or you give us back the money while there's still time to commission someone else. Maybe even your friend Fra Diamante."

"Do not threaten me," the painter exploded. "I am under the protection of the eminent Cosimo de' Medici!"

"Not in Prato," the man said. He put out a hand, much larger than Fra Filippo had expected, and pushed against his shoulder. "Do we understand each other, Brother Lippi?"

The monk clenched his jaw. His head felt like it was about to explode.

"Do we? Or shall I stop in at your *bottega* tomorrow, and take some things to guarantee you'll give us what we want?"

"Don't you dare!" he said as he clenched his fists. "You stay away from my home."

"Don't test us," the man said, stepping away and letting his shadow cover Fra Filippo's. "We are not patient men."

Half asleep, Lucrezia entered the workshop with a cup of watered wine for the painter, and instead of the altarpiece she'd been watching him coax into life, she saw the rough painting of her own face and hands floating in a sea of white. Everything else was gone, covered by streaks of white.

"What have you done?" Lucrezia cried. She put the cup down on the worktable and cradled her belly with her arms. "The altarpiece is our only hope—you told me yourself, the dispensation from Rome won't come without it!"

The monk swung around, the flat gesso tool clutched in his hand.

"It's not good enough for a king," he said sharply. "Our dispensation won't come with muddied colors and vague lines! I can't send this in the Medici's name."

The painter wiped a hand over his face, smearing gesso across his forehead. Lucrezia looked at the scraps of paper and dirty rags he'd tossed onto the floor during the long night.

"Tell me what's happening, Filippo," Lucrezia said. "Tell me what to do."

His eyes were staring past the panel, at a place on the wall where there was only a crack in the plaster.

"Do you still love me?" she asked, her voice breaking. She looked down at her bloated stomach, her once-slender hands puffy and stiff. The ring he'd given her in December now cut into her finger. "Am I not beautiful to you anymore?"

"You're the most beautiful woman on earth," he said fiercely. "Your face on the panel is the only thing worthy of the king. It's the only thing worth saving."

"Please, Filippo, you'll begin again, won't you?"

Chapter Twenty-three

The Sixth Week of Easter, the Year of Our Lord 1457

Lucrezia was stitching a small sleeve onto an infant's gown when the pain ripped across her belly. She cried out—but there was no one to hear her cry, and she was glad. It was only May. The child couldn't come yet.

She pushed aside the pile of silk pieces, dropped her head between her legs, and lifted up her skirt. There was no water, no blood. Lucrezia gripped the edge of the table and panted.

"Not yet, God. Please, not yet," she gasped.

The tightness pulled across her belly, expanding beneath her partum belt. Lucrezia reached for the belt she'd fashioned from soft leather, and loosened the laces. She squeezed her eyes shut and prayed aloud.

"Mother Mary, give me strength," she groaned, grabbing at a ream of blue silk. She'd been saving it for a special dress but now she put one end between her teeth and bit down to keep from screaming. She tasted the fabric and a vivid memory of her father's robes flashed in her mind. She gnashed her teeth and writhed in the chair. Just when she thought she couldn't bear it anymore, the pain stopped. Lucrezia lifted her head and blinked.

Outside her window, sun was sparkling on the road that opened to the Piazza della Pieve. The silk pieces cut for baby clothes were on the floor where she'd pushed them, together with the needle, thread, and sewing hoop.

Wiping her forehead with a rag, Lucrezia drank a cup of cool water from the cistern. Next to the hearth was the basket of delicacies Teresa de' Valenti had sent that week, along with a note promising to send a midwife to Lucrezia when her time came. The signora hadn't said whom she would engage, or how the midwife was to be sent for, and Lucrezia was sorry she'd waited so long to ask. For all of her careful praying, the cutting and sewing of the baby's clothes, the drinking of herbs to ready her for labor, Lucrezia was alone and unprepared. And the pains were strong. Strong enough that she feared her time was here.

When she could stand, Lucrezia gathered her cloak, prayer beads, and the soft yellow *cotta da parto* she'd nearly finished. She tidied everything as best she could, put the pile of necessities on the bed, slipped the circle of beads into her pocket next to the medallion of Saint John, and prepared to find Fra Filippo at the church. She was nearing the door when the pain came again, bringing her to her knees. It took several minutes to pass, and many more until she was able to look up and take a true breath.

She'd fallen at the foot of the Medici altarpiece, which stood on a large easel near the doorway. At first the image was unclear to her, but as the pain faded, the scene on the large panel came into focus. Her own likeness was at its center, but Lucrezia didn't study her face. In the months of living with the painter, she'd tried not to look at the Virgin's image and think of herself. Instead, she looked at the woods and flowers Fra Filippo had painted, pleased to see how much progress he'd made—not only in the Virgin's swelling blue robes but in the sunlight that shone through transparent leaves in the field, and the light from the holy dove radiating across the kneeling Madonna.

Lucrezia's gaze wandered to the panels that stood on the floor next to the easel, with their lifelike images of Saint Michael and Saint Anthony Abbott. The panels were finished, and she studied them closely for the first time, seeing Saint Michael's armor pitted and gleaming with silver, the fine brown fabric of Saint Anthony's costume, his clothing the same color as the earth.

"Per piacere," she whispered to strong, gentle Saint Anthony Abbott, who knelt humbly on the ground. "Don't let the child come now. Not yet."

Even as she prepared for another wave of pain, she promised herself that she would do everything possible to keep the baby inside her until late June, so that Fra Filippo might claim the infant as his own.

After that day, Lucrezia moved about very little. She sat with her feet up on a stool with her face turned to the sun when it came in through the window on a right angle, a shawl around her shoulders when the sun fell below the city's rooftops. Spring was everywhere, in the onion grass that grew along the paths in and out of Prato, in the mewl of new calves in a neighbor's pen, and in the smell of freshly turned earth where the woolfullers' wives hoed their modest gardens.

Lucrezia sat in the wooden chair by the hearth sewing and praying as the sun rose and fell. She had nothing to do but sew, and wait. And what she waited for—the child, word from Rome, a note of loving kindness from her sister at Santa Margherita—could not be rushed. She was in the chair when Ser Francesco arrived at the end of May to check on the Medici altarpiece, and she was there embroidering two silken panels of a pillow when the emissary came again in the heat of midday on the Feast Day of Saint Thomas the Apostle, in early July.

The smell of Ser Francesco Cantansanti's horse outside the window turned Lucrezia's stomach. She heard his boots hit the ground, and the clink of the harness as he tethered the horse. Ser Francesco paused at the doorway long enough to knock and call out, and then swept into the *bottega* without waiting for an answer. As he bowed to Lucrezia, his eye took a quick inventory of the rich cuts of silk cloth that filled the workshop.

"Fratello." The emissary nodded, and stopped to study a sketch the painter had made for the design of the triptych frame.

"Ser Francesco," the painter greeted the emissary warily. Cantansanti's presence further taxed his time, and Fra Filippo was already spread thin. He reached for his jug of wine and stayed where he was.

"Are you still at work on the halo?" Cantansanti demanded when he saw the small brush the painter held to the panel, making tiny dots of color. "The halo was finished last week, Filippo. Why are you laboring over small details when there's still so much to be done?"

"It is not as simple as it looks!" the painter snapped, but quickly softened his tone. "I must keep layering if we want the halo to shimmer like real gold. If King Alfonso is to be pleased, the work can't be rushed."

Wiping his brow, Fra Filippo thought recklessly of the altarpiece for the Arte del Cambio, which was due in one week's time. Ser Francesco's ever-watchful eye had diverted the painter from that work even as the Bankers' Guild had sent their messengers twice more, demanding to see the progress he'd made. The answer, regrettably, was that he'd done little. The altarpiece needed to be done in a fury, or he would know the guild's wrath.

With the Feast of Mary Magdalene only two days away—and the altarpiece more than a week late—the monk slipped out of bed before dawn. The heat was already unbearable. He put a cup of honeyed water and some bread by the bed, and brushed a kiss across Lucrezia's damp forehead.

"I have to go to the chapel," he said. "If Ser Francesco comes, tell him he can find me at Santo Stefano. I'm bringing the Medici pieces with me, so I can study them while I'm working."

After making sure the paint on the Madonna's halo was completely dry, he carefully wrapped the triptych panels in smooth cloth and piled them into his wagon along with three large pieces of poplar he'd cut for the Cambio's altarpiece. Each blank panel was nearly as tall as he stood, and the central piece was wider than the spread of his arms.

In truth, Fra Filippo was bringing the Medici altarpieces with him so he might study the effects he'd achieved there and roughly replicate them on the panels for the Arte del Cambio. He had less than two days to pull together the triptych of the nursing Madonna surrounded by Saints Matthew and Peter. It wouldn't be good but it would be big, and with a bit of the Virgin's luck he thought that would more than satisfy the rough men of the guild.

❦

When the bells of Nones rang that afternoon, Lucrezia's fingers were deftly sewing a nightshirt for the baby. Nicola was across the table, eating one of the sweet rolls she'd brought from Signora de' Valenti and laughing merrily at a story she was telling about the Valentis' daughters.

"And the ducks chased the girl back to the water!" Nicola said.

She was laughing heartily when Lucrezia heard footfalls and heavy breathing outside.

"Open the door, Filippo!" a gruff voice growled at the door.

It couldn't be Cantansanti, Lucrezia knew, but she called his name anyway.

"Stop stalling, let us in." A hand rattled the iron latch, the heavy wooden door banging against the frame.

Lucrezia stood, pressing her hands against the small of her back. Terrified, she stood in the antechamber and opened the door to find three men filling the doorway. Two were dressed in black, a third wore a red robe. She smelled wine, onion, and a spice she couldn't recognize. Her stomach turned, the child kicked.

"We're from the Bankers' Guild," said the shortest of the three, arms crossed in front of his chest. He had a dark beard that barely hid a long scar that sliced his cheek from eyebrow to chin. "Where's the painter?"

"He's not here." She tried to keep herself calm, but the men's anger was palpable. She felt her knees begin to buckle, and clung to the door.

"Get him," the largest one said harshly. "Get. Him. Now."

"Nicola," Lucrezia called out to the servant. "*Veloce*, run and get Fra Filippo!"

She heard movement, and the servant brushed past her and the men, her feet moving nimbly down the pebbled path.

"He'll be here," Lucrezia said, avoiding the men's eyes. She forced herself to stop shaking. "You only need to wait a few minutes."

"We don't like to wait," the man in red said curtly. With a chopping gesture he moved her aside, and the three men entered the *bottega*. "We've been waiting for months. We've come for the altarpiece."

Lucrezia looked at the man in panic. "The altarpiece? Are you from the Medici?"

"The Medici?" The men in black looked at each other and gave her a wily smile. "Yes, we're here to fetch the Medici paintings. Give them to us."

Lucrezia paled. The men spread across the room like a stain, their odor bringing up bile in her throat.

"Where's the altarpiece? It was due yesterday." The bearded man stopped at Fra Filippo's table, scanned the drawings, and begin tearing them into uneven pieces.

"He's been working on it," she said, confused and dizzy. "Ser Francesco has been here almost every week. Surely you must know."

"Olivio, it's not nice to lie to a nun," said the short man in red, putting a special emphasis on the word *nun*. He turned to Lucrezia. "We're not the Medici, we're from the Arte del Cambio. We've come for the commission."

"The commission?" Lucrezia reached behind her, and fell back into a chair. "The commission?" she asked faintly.

"It's late," said one.

"But it's not here, is it, Sorella? The painter's been lying to us, hasn't he?"

Lucrezia's whole body froze. She looked wildly around the studio and then she remembered Filippo had taken the *Adoring Madonna* and the panels of the saints to the church, pulling them in a little cart.

"I don't know what you're talking about," she said tearfully. "Please, ask Fra Filippo yourself, I'm sure he'll give you what you want."

"We've done that already. Either we get the altarpiece, or we take whatever we can. He owes us many florins."

With his right arm, the tallest of the three knocked over a neat row of jars.

"Please be careful," Lucrezia said faintly.

The short man opened a large black sack and began to dump chunks of pigment into it, while the other noisily stacked poplar and other wood panels by the door.

"These should bring something for our troubles," he grumbled.

With a drunken stagger the short man fell against a stool, and it crashed to the ground. Paint splashed across Lucrezia's robe and she ran into the kitchen, listening to the men trampling through the workshop.

"Please," Lucrezia shouted. "Please be careful."

She listened to the men cursing and laughing as they stomped in and out of the *bottega*, trampling her little garden and attracting the attention of the woolgatherers' children, who stood around the house, their mouths open, watching.

"The gold must be somewhere," she heard one of the men growl.

"He's hidden it well, the bastard," said another, as he flung the last pieces of wood onto the pile.

"Lucrezia?" Out of breath, Fra Filippo pushed through the men and strode through the messy *bottega*. "Lucrezia, are you all right?"

Her reply was drowned out by the men's shouts as they swarmed him, the two in black grabbing his arms.

"Lucrezia?" He shouted her name again, struggling against the men's rough grips. "Where is she?"

"She's in the kitchen," said the red-robed man in his clipped Milanese accent. "We're not interested in your *puttana*, Brother. We've come for the altarpiece."

"Bastards!" the monk shouted, kicking out with his heavy sandals. "Get out of here. Get out or I'll kill you!"

The tallest of the three clenched his fist and swung up.

"The altarpiece, or the money," he shouted as he struck the painter's chin. Fra Filippo's head snapped back. "We told you we aren't patient men. Where's the painting, eh, Fratello? Where is it?"

"I'm working on it," Fra Filippo answered, his mouth bloodied.

"It's too late. It should be done."

"It's at Santo Stefano," he said, pushing out his chest. "Let me go and I'll show it to you."

"You're lying. We've been there. We know there's no panel for the Cambio."

"You fools." The painter pulled a hand free and struck out blindly. "You know nothing."

The tall man laughed again, bending back Fra Filippo's wrist until he cried out in pain.

"We know that artists who bed pretty nuns don't keep their promises, we know that much."

The painter roared against his captors, but they only held him tighter. The tall man landed a short blow to Fra Filippo's right eye, another to his belly, then a third and a fourth in his gut. In a flash the monk remembered the gap between the memory of physical pain and its reality. A hard kick to his thigh, another blinding shock in his groin, and he fell to the floor, the men's hard boots cracking into his ribs.

"Do you think the Bankers' Guild runs on charity? We've been patient. You're lucky we don't break your arms."

As he writhed in pain, they took Lucrezia's silks, and a rough hand grabbed her yellow *cotta da parto* and wrapped it in a long bolt of blue silk.

"You filthy son of a begger, how dare you touch that dress!" Fra Filippo raged. There was a boot planted firmly on the small of his back but he arched himself up as high as he could, and swore as the man piled up all of the beautiful fabrics.

"I'll kill you," he raged. The man pressed his foot deeper into his back, and the monk couldn't move. The man in red bent down, his face as red as his clothing, and spat his words at the painter.

"Finish it. Or I'll kill you."

It was the last thing Filippo heard before the left side of his head exploded in pain and his mind went blank.

Lucrezia waited until the men had retreated down the gravel path. When she was sure they'd gone, she stumbled across the rubble, locked the latch, and pushed the broken stool in front of the door-way. Then she sank down on the floor next to the motionless painter, and put her head on his breast to listen for a heartbeat. She touched Fra Filippo's bloodied cheek, and she wept. But behind her tears there was anger, and despair.

"You didn't tell me there was another commission," she cried into Fra Filippo's expressionless face. She held his head in her hands. "You lied to me, Filippo. You lied to me."

Lucrezia stayed on the floor next to him, waiting for him to wake. She was tired. So very tired.

She woke in the dark, with sharp pains in her belly.

"Filippo, something's wrong," she cried, reaching out to shake his shoulder. "The baby, Filippo." She called his name louder, and slapped at his cheek. He moved at last, slowly and with difficulty, and reached for her hand. It was freezing cold.

"I'm bleeding."

Shaking the sleep and pain from his head, the painter groaned and rose to his knees. Lucrezia's face was pale. She shifted her hips to the side, and he saw a small, dark stain on the floor.

"The baby, Filippo. The baby's coming."

The painter dragged himself to the kitchen hearth, where he moved aside the loose stone, and reached for his bag of florins. Thank God the bankers hadn't found his gold.

"Filippo." Lucrezia's voice was panicked. "Hurry."

The painter staggered to her side.

"I'll get someone," he said. "I'll send word to Signora de' Valenti, she'll send the midwife."

"No, there's no time, Filippo. Please, take me to the convent. Sister Pureza will help me."

The color was leaching from her face, and the smell of blood frightened him. Struggling to think clearly, he rushed into the dark street until he reached the fencemaker's *bottega*. Under the moonlight, he saw the craftsman's wagon hitched to his shack and heard the braying of the donkey behind the house. The sound of his footsteps roused the fencemaker, who appeared bleary-eyed at the window.

"For the love of God, let me have your cart and donkey tonight."

His battered ribs pulsing with pain, Fra Filippo quickly yoked the donkey and hitched the cart. He led the animal back to his *bottega*, wrapped a blanket around Lucrezia, and carried her outside. He placed her gently in the back of the cart, using blankets and torn silk to cushion the hard wood.

Under the blanket, Lucrezia watched the stars over the rooftops and prayed. It was late July. She'd done what she'd wanted. She'd kept the child inside of her long enough to know that it belonged to Fra Filippo.

Chapter Twenty-four

Last Day Before the Feast of the Magdalene, the Year of Our Lord 1457

Prioress Bartolommea clutched the three gold florins in her hand and stared at the painter. There was just enough moonlight to see his battered face.

"Remember, I'm waiting for my altarpiece, Fratello," she said. "The one you promised me almost a year ago."

"Yes, the painting," he answered warily. "After the child is born."

Across the dark courtyard Fra Filippo could see Spinetta and Sister Bernadetta leading Lucrezia under the stone archway into the cloister garden. A stooped figure hurried toward them, carrying a candle.

"She'll be safe here. Now go," the prioress said. "The prior general has barred you from the grounds."

Sister Pureza put a palm on Lucrezia's belly and reached between her legs. Lucrezia winced at the probing fingers.

"You're not ready," the nun said, wiping her fingers on her apron. "Rest now. You're going to need your strength."

Lucrezia touched the old woman's hands. The nun's familiar lavender scent, her quiet certainty, filled Lucrezia with gratitude. Her eyes welled with tears.

"Thank you, Sister Pureza," she managed to say. "*Molte grazie.*"

She was surprised when Sister Pureza turned quickly away, reaching for a tray of herbs she kept in a cool shelf dug into the thick infirmary wall.

"It's too soon," Sister Pureza said gruffly.

"Too soon?" Her voice shook. "Too soon for the child?"

"Too soon to thank me."

Lucrezia's heart began to pound. "But he's all right, isn't he? The baby's all right?"

The old nun's back stiffened.

"Why do you say *he*, Sister Lucrezia?" She swung around, her hands empty. "What makes you think the child is a boy, and not a girl?"

Lucrezia felt certain the child she carried was male. For months, she'd believed it was a boy. A son for Filippo. Stung by the nun's sharp words, she only shook her head.

"A girl will suffer, as all women suffer." Sister Pureza's voice was surprising in its strength. It seemed to echo off the walls. "Do you think the fates will be kind to a child you've carried in shame?"

Lucrezia's eyes filled, blurring the old woman's angry features.

"I don't know," she gasped.

"Of course you don't know." Sister Pureza didn't even try to tamp her anger. "You know nothing about suffering and pain. You're a fool—a vain, foolish girl."

Lucrezia didn't try to stop the woman's words. She deserved whatever reproach the old nun gave her.

"Please, Sister Pureza." Her voice cracked. "Don't blame the child for my sins. Don't punish him."

"Boy or girl, it's God who'll do the punishing, not I."

Stunned at her own outburst, the old nun's hands shook among the vials on the tray. She opened a cork stopper, smelled the bitter vervain and thistleroot, poured some into a cup of water, and stirred.

"Drink this. It will help you rest," she said sharply. She held it out, but Lucrezia didn't take it.

"Do as you wish." The old nun shoved the small cup between Lucrezia's clenched fists. And as she did, she saw the girl wore a band of gold, ornamented by a red jasper stone. Red jasper, for love.

❧

*T*he prioress wrote the letter herself. She wrote it that very morning, while Sister Camilla and Sister Spinetta were in the church for Terce prayers. She didn't need them snooping into her business; she was sure that what she did was good and righteous.

In the name of the Lord, the twenty-first day of July, 1457

Your Grace, the most Revered Prior General Saviano,
Lucrezia Buti has returned to the convent this morning, in the pains of labor.
I share your outrage at this shame, but have done as you wished, and allowed
her to enter.

The prioress looked at the three gold coins on the desk.

She came with two gold florins, which will be added to the convent coffers.
As you are aware, our funds grow ever smaller. May Christ keep you well,
and in His favor.

As Prioress Bartolommea folded and sealed the note, doubt flickered through her. She couldn't fathom why the prior general wanted

Lucrezia back in the convent; she'd certainly been no asset to Santa Margherita. But Saviano was a potent man, and she was in no position to challenge him on the matter. Instead, she'd made up her mind to use Lucrezia's presence to coax—even to force—the painter to deliver the altarpiece he'd promised her.

Although the prioress tried to hide it, she'd grown frail over the winter, and her strength hadn't returned with the summer warmth. She felt her time on earth coming to an end, and wanted to leave this world with all the assurances she could accumulate. Her image in the altarpiece with the *Sacra Cintola* was something she'd been counting on to weigh in her favor when God took her measure on the stairway to heaven.

Prioress Bartolommea looked down again at the letter in her hands, and it seemed the words she'd penned only moments ago were nearly illegible. She held the parchment close to her eyes, but that only made her vision worse. She moved it away from her face, as far as she could reach, and was just barely able to make out the prior general's name where she'd written it.

"I must remember not to write so small," she muttered to herself.

⁂

After he'd returned the wagon and donkey to his neighbor, Fra Filippo bandaged his head and wrapped his chest with rags that were trampled with dirty footprints. Cautiously he felt his ribs, relieved that they hadn't been broken. He tidied his *bottega* as well as he could, but there was little left that he could salvage. Most of his supplies were gone, and what hadn't been taken was smashed on the ground.

The monk found a splintered quill, and a pot of ink the men had missed, and wrote to Giovanni de' Medici on a torn paper.

My honorable Giovanni, I have worked like a slave to make the painting just as you wish—I will do everything I must to complete it to your liking.

His hand shook. He'd been foolish, spending the money from the Bankers' Guild as if there was no end to it.

Please do not leave me without hope—without supplies or money I cannot continue.

Fra Filippo knew he sounded desperate. But his reputation and honor were less important than replenishing the supply of pigments and other materials so that he could work.

I vow the work will be finished by the twentieth day of August, and in good faith I am sending you the drawing of the frame so you can see how the wood-working must be done and what style the frame will be, and I beg you to pledge to me the one hundred florins I need for the design. It is a fair price, you can ask anyone you like, I only pray you see my labors are in good faith.

It wasn't too soon to ask for the frame to be ordered and started. If God wanted more than he could do in one lifetime, and if he was to please the Medici and the King of Naples, then Fra Filippo needed other men to be laboring along with him.

I must leave Prato. I beg your reply for I am trapped, and also ask your forgiveness for writing to you in my desperation.

The painter spent the rest of the day and evening drawing out the plans for the altarpiece's ornate frame, with Gothic arches and gilded finials. He finished and sealed the letter as the moon rose. And he prayed that Giovanni de' Medici would be understanding, and generous.

But the elder Medici son was not so inclined. In two days' time, the monk heard the news from Ser Francesco Cantansanti's own imperious lips.

"There will be nothing more until the work is finished," the emissary said, standing in the monk's doorway and surveying the empty studio. His eyes narrowed. "I pray to God those thugs didn't take the altarpiece."

The monk's eyes were red, as if he hadn't slept in many days. Scabs had begun to form on his face, where he'd taken the worst of the beating.

"No, it's safe, thank God," Fra Filippo said.

"You're lucky. You should have avoided those men, Filippo." Ser Francesco planted his feet and looked around at the debris Fra Filippo had missed when he swept. "Where are the paintings for King Alfonso?"

"At Santo Stefano, where they'll be safe. I'm guarding them with my life, Francesco." Fra Filippo addressed the emissary by his given name, and his voice cracked. "But I must have more gold to finish the Madonna's robes. I must at least have that."

Cantansanti reached in his pocket and pulled out two gold pieces. The painter was trying his patience. But it would do him no good to see the monk fall into despair.

"Buy only what you need. Show me when you've made progress, and I'll help you if I can."

As he turned to leave, Cantansanti looked back into the studio, to a single sketch on the painter's wall. It was the girl who'd modeled for the monk's Madonna. The sketch showed her in the fullness of pregnancy, her face looking up as if beseeching the heavens.

"I hear the girl's gone back to the convent, Filippo. Is it true?"

Fra Filippo nodded. "Only until the child comes," he said.

The emissary ground his boot in the doorway and shook his head. "And then?"

"We're still waiting for word from Rome. So much depends on that. On what my patron and his family can do for me."

"What they can do for you will depend on what you do for us, Filippo. I promise you'll get nothing more if you fail us with the altarpiece."

⚬≈❦≈⚬

*N*ews of the raid on Fra Filippo's *bottega,* and of Lucrezia's return to the convent, reached Fra Piero as he traveled along the road from Lucca.

As soon as he reached Prato, he hurried to Santa Margherita and sat in the stifling convent study listening to Prioress Bartolommea run through a litany of complaints and demands. She seemed to squint when she spoke to him, and Fra Piero found himself growing impatient with her self-importance, her petty needs. He had no idea how Fra Filippo had tolerated his chaplain's duties here for two years. In just a few months, the same duties had exasperated Fra Piero's patience.

"Sister Lucrezia has come back to us full with child and in need of our care," Prioress Bartolommea said at last. "What are we to do, Fratello? The painter has brought his stain upon us but we're bound by Christ's teachings to offer safe harbor to all who ask forgiveness for their sins."

The procurator nodded thoughtfully. "I will speak with her myself," he said. "I will hear her confession, and then hear the others'."

—◦◦◦◦◦◦—

The procurator found Lucrezia lying on a pallet in the infirmary, her feet propped on a pillow, belly high and full, face puffy and pale.

"Fra Piero." Lucrezia smiled weakly when she saw him, and he was relieved at the strength in her grip when he took her hand.

"You saw us exchange the vows." Lucrezia spoke through dry lips. She saw Sister Pureza standing in the doorway and she pulled the procurator closer to her, dropping her voice to a whisper. "If I am dying you'll give me Extreme Unction, won't you? And will you promise not to let the child live as a bastard?"

"You'll be fine," Fra Piero said, putting her hand back on the bed beside her body. "Pray and be brave, Lucrezia. You are in good hands with Sister Pureza."

He heard Lucrezia's confession, granted her absolution, and made the sign of the cross on her forehead. Then he stopped to speak with Sister Pureza, who was clearly pained by the novitiate's condition.

"Sister Pureza, I beg you to remember that there are many secrets that can change the fate of a beautiful young woman," he said. He was surprised when the nun's features hardened at his words.

"You forget I'm an old woman and I've lived a long time," she said roughly.

The procurator blanched, and she continued.

"The world is full of suffering, Fratello," she said. "If we show sympathy to the novitiate, she won't be prepared for the pain that's sure to come."

Fra Piero studied Sister Pureza's face, certain she didn't know what the prior general had done to Lucrezia or how much Fra Filippo truly loved the young woman. If he hadn't been bound by the confidentiality of Lucrezia's confession, he would have told the old nun all that he knew. Instead, he summoned Christ's words, hoping to invoke at least a small bit of mercy.

"Remember, the weak will enter God's kingdom first, Sister Pureza," he said. "And the righteous will be last."

From Santa Margherita the procurator went directly to the painter's *bottega*. It was empty, the lock on the door broken, the hearth cold. The studio was littered with debris, and there was a single parchment with a drawing of a pregnant Lucrezia, her face looking toward the skies, propped against the wall.

Fra Piero found the painter up on the scaffolding at Santo Stefano, his arms a fury of movement, buckets of paint at his feet. It wasn't even close to Vespers, but the painter had sent his assistants home, and was alone in the *cappella maggiore*.

"Fra Filippo." It took the procurator several tries before he caught the painter's attention. When he did, the large man moved dangerously quickly down the scaffolding.

"Do you have news?"

"I've seen Lucrezia. The child will come soon, Filippo, you have to prepare yourself."

"I am preparing," the painter said. "I delivered the altarpiece to those bastards at the Arte del Cambio yesterday—they refused to give me the rest of the money because it was late, God damn them— and you can see I'm working furiously."

The painter gestured wildly to a dark corner of the chapel, where he'd stored the Medici triptych.

"I want to leave here, Piero, and take Lucrezia with me. As soon as the child is born, as soon as the frescoes are finished, as soon as I've been paid, I want to leave this city."

He spoke with such speed, the procurator was alarmed. He laid a hand on his friend's shoulder. A wasted look haunted his face.

"Are you eating, Filippo?"

"Eating? My God, Piero, look at the feast of King Herod, here on the wall." He pulled his arm, and Fra Piero followed him to the right of the scaffolding. "Look at this banquet scene."

The procurator took in the details of the frescoed banquet table, the chessboard of green and red floor tiles painted across the bottom of the wall, the strained faces of the banquet guests, the gray head of martyred Saint John. He followed as the painter moved several feet to the left and held the lantern above a hazy white space on the red and green tiles.

"My Salome," Fra Filippo said, his voice thickening as his words slowed. "This will be my Salome."

Fra Piero climbed up the scaffold and looked carefully at the face that was sketched faintly on the wall. The woman looked like Lucrezia, ripe in the fullness of her pregnancy. But there was something in the dancer's faint expression that he'd never seen on Lucrezia.

"Salome performs a harlot's dance," Fra Filippo said, coming so close that Fra Piero could smell the many unwashed days and nights on his soiled clothing. "She dances so that King Herod will give her whatever she wants, and then—"

Fra Filippo stopped.

"And then?" Fra Piero waited. The lamplight flickered on his friend's face, making strange shadows.

"And then with a single dance, a single request from her lips, Saint John is martyred. His head is delivered on a platter."

Fra Filippo fell silent. He'd been here for days, it seemed, thinking about Salome. At last he understood—her dancing figure would anchor the entire fresco cycle. He would paint her in layers of white, in ghostly motion, only slightly more present than a mirage. Salome's body would flow with snakelike grace apart from everything else, swaying to an inner rhythm.

Forgetting his friend, the painter took a red crayon from his pocket and sketched Salome's figure in the form of a perfect arabesque against the fixed lines of the tiled floor. Men and women would condemn Salome as a heartless harlot, but they would look at her with longing and envy, and understand the bewitching spell she cast over her audience.

"Filippo?"

The painter turned at the sound of his friend's voice, and blinked. How long had the procurator been standing there with him? He looked at his work and waved his hand across the scene, his eyes wild as he gestured to the spot where Salome's pointed foot would barely skim the surface of the floor in the banquet hall.

"You see, Piero, Salome is beautiful but she's capricious. She has a ghostly power no man can hold on to," he said. "Anyone who looks at her will understand that Saint John's strength, his very life, was destroyed by a woman who seemed no more substantial than the fleeting smell of her perfume, a woman with only one delicate foot tethering her to this Earth."

The procurator put his hand on the painter's shoulder again.

"Filippo, don't worry. I'll watch out for Lucrezia."

"Of course." Fra Filippo nodded furiously at the mention of her name. "But truly, Piero, she's in God's hands now. We're both in God's hands."

Chapter Twenty-five

Tuesday of the Twelfth Week After Pentecost, the Year of Our Lord 1457

There was no mistaking the pains this time. Water rushed between Lucrezia's legs, her belly hardened, her bowels emptied, and spasms ripped through her. It was just past Nones on the twenty-seventh day of August, a day so hot she could barely breathe.

"Help me, Mother Mary," she cried. "Help me."

The novitiate was the first at her bedside.

"Rosina." She grabbed the girl's small hand. "Rosina, please get Sister Pureza."

Sister Pureza came in silently, rinsing the garden dirt off her palms and depositing a fresh bunch of parsley into a cup of cool water. She dried her hands on a clean rag and told Rosina to fill the wooden tub with warm water from the kitchen cauldron. The old woman folded back Lucrezia's gown and reached between her bent legs. The mouth of her womb was beginning to open.

"Stand up, Sister Lucrezia." The old woman took her by the elbow and lifted her to a seated position. "The child is coming, you have to help it along."

Lucrezia's eyes were dark blue, the whites shot with broken blood vessels.

"I don't know if I can." She hooked an arm around Sister Pureza's shoulders and let her feet fall to the floor.

"Rosina, hold her other side," Sister Pureza said when the girl returned with the warm water and poured it into the tub. "Now walk," she ordered Lucrezia. "Walk."

Lucrezia dragged herself back and forth across the infirmary until the sun passed over the west wall of the convent and Sister Pureza let her collapse onto the pallet at last. Rosina came to her with a cup of fennel stew. Her mouth was dry from wailing, her body weak.

"I can't do it," she said, panting. "I'm sorry," she said to Sister Pureza's back. "I can't do it."

"Don't waste your strength," the old nun said. "Eat."

Lucrezia labored into the night, far longer than she thought she could endure. Spinetta hovered outside the infirmary door and twice Lucrezia called to her, but her sister didn't answer.

"Please, bring Spinetta to me," Lucrezia begged. In the month since she'd been at the convent, Spinetta had been to see her only twice, and she'd refused to speak or even to meet her eye. "I want to see her."

"Rosina is the only help we need," Sister Pureza said, her jaw tight.

The old nun warmed a dab of lemon oil and lard between her hands, rubbing her palms swiftly. Then she reached between Lucrezia's legs and smoothed the balm onto the tender pink skin that was stretched nearly to the point of ripping.

"My God," Lucrezia screamed. Her breath came in rapid gasps and she bore down, shrieking.

"Now's the time," Sister Pureza said. "The child's coming now."

Rosina held Lucrezia's legs in the air and a dark head crowned the torn skin.

"Bear down," Sister Pureza instructed. "Bear down."

Lucrezia screamed, her cries filling the night and reaching the ears of the nuns who cringed in their cells. With a final heave, Lucrezia's body let go of the child and it slid into a blanket in Sister Pureza's waiting arms.

Sister Pureza took the knife in her hand and sliced the thick chord that bound the child to the mother.

"Is it a boy?" Lucrezia had barely enough energy to ask that simple question. When she heard only silence, she began to wail. "What's wrong? Is something wrong with my baby?"

Sister Pureza looked between the child's legs to the small purple scrotum, the plug of his penis. She turned him over, held him by the feet, and swatted him on the back, then on the bottom, twice. He coughed thick mucus from his lungs, and his wail filled the chamber.

"Thank God." Lucrezia began to weep. "Thank you, God."

"It's a boy," the midwife said quietly. She rinsed him in the tub, wiping his face and body, and running her finger across the strange mark on the boy's left buttock. She used the corner of the blanket to rub him clean, taking an extra minute at the deep red cross. But the birthmark didn't smudge. Sister Pureza glanced across the room at Rosina, and saw the girl's dark eyes taking everything in.

"Let me hold him," Lucrezia said, stretching out her hands weakly. But the old woman ignored Lucrezia's cries as she swaddled the child tightly in a blanket worn soft and gray from years of washing. She put the child into Rosina's arms, and pushed down on Lucrezia's swollen belly until the afterbirth slid from her. The young woman had lost a lot of blood. Her limbs were shaking dangerously, and her arms were cold to the touch. Sister Pureza pressed a poultice between her legs, and covered Lucrezia with a heavy woolen blanket.

"Let me hold him." Lucrezia reached a pale hand toward the novitiate. "*Per piacere*, give him to me."

Sister Pureza watched for the beads of perspiration that would mean Lucrezia's body was warming, then brought her a thimble of calendula and nettle tea.

"Drink this," she said.

Lucrezia pursed her lips and swallowed obediently.

"Bring him to me," she begged, reaching out her arms. But Sister Pureza had already taken the child and turned away.

"Sister, where are you going?" Lucrezia watched the woman's wimple and dark robe sway through the candlelit chamber. Sister Pureza stopped near the wooden crucifix that hung on the wall, and held a sheet of parchment up to the candlelight.

"Baptize him, please, Sister," Lucrezia said, her voice weakening.

The old nun was already doing exactly that, making the sign of the cross on the infant's forehead, dripping water from her damp fingers and murmuring the words that would cleanse his soul of original sin.

"Be sure his head is warm," Lucrezia heard the midwife say to Rosina. "He may be traveling far."

"*Bambino mio,*" Lucrezia called out. "Where is he going? Where are you taking him?"

Neither the old woman nor the young girl turned.

"Bring him to me," Lucrezia cried. She saw Sister Pureza opening the door and Rosina leaving with her baby.

"Spinetta, are you there?" Lucrezia called frantically. She tried to sit up but her arms were too weak, the pain too great. "Bring him back," she wailed. "Bring him back to me."

The door closed. The child and Rosina were gone. Only Sister Pureza remained, her face pinched and impassive.

"Where is he going, Sister Pureza? I beg you, bring him back to me."

All these weeks, the old woman's coolness had seemed a just

punishment for her sins. But this was something Lucrezia hadn't imagined.

"I came to you in good faith, Sister Pureza, I thought you were my friend."

The old woman didn't answer. She walked quickly around the room, rolling up soiled bedsheets, dragging the washtub of blood-tinted water into the herb garden.

Squaring her shoulders, the midwife held a match to a bundled stick of dried rosemary and sage, spreading a thick plume of smoke that burned Lucrezia's eyes. The girl's weeping grew more heart-wrenching.

"I tried to show you what comes of carnal knowledge," Sister Pureza said through the darkness. The girl stopped wailing, and Sister Pureza could tell she was listening. "But you didn't take my warning. You didn't believe me. Now you'll know, Sister Lucrezia. Now you'll know."

"Why are you doing this?"

"I've followed the prior general's orders."

"The prior general," Lucrezia shrieked, and moved as if to rise. "*Dio mio,* don't let him do this to me. You know he hurt me, Sister Pureza, you know the prior general hurt me."

"It's not in my power to go against his orders. You've conceived and carried a child in sin. Now your sin will be erased, and the child will be raised by a Christian family. Consider yourself blessed."

Lucrezia couldn't answer through her tears.

"This is best," the midwife offered. "We've delivered of you a healthy son, but we won't speak of him again. You'll see, this is best," she said as she shut the door.

Lucrezia wept alone, her eyes fixed on the wooden crucifix on the wall.

"Jesus Christ and Mother Mary," she cried into the sage-smoked darkness. "Protect my son until we're together again. I beg you to watch over my baby."

She waited, letting the darkness envelop her. Then she whispered the baby's name so the saints and the Virgin and Jesus Christ Himself would know this babe was her own.

"Filippino. Watch over my Filippino and bring him back to me. Jesus, Mother Mary, can you hear me?"

She looked to the crucifix on the wall, and it seemed even Christ, in His suffering, had turned away.

The next morning Lucrezia sought sympathy in Sister Pureza's gray eyes, but the old nun refused to speak of the child. Briskly she changed the poultice and rags between Lucrezia's legs, then brought her a warm broth and urged the girl to eat.

"Please let me see the procurator," Lucrezia asked after she'd sipped some broth and was certain there would be no mercy from Sister Pureza. "I want him to hear my confession; I need to atone for my sins."

The old nun brought the procurator to the infirmary after Nones prayers. Lucrezia waited until they were alone, then clutched desperately at Fra Piero's hand and put her lips to his ear. She barely trusted herself to speak the few necessary words without wailing.

"Do you know they took my baby?" She could see in his eyes that he already knew.

"You let them take my baby? You knew and you let them?" Her voice was a ragged sob as she shook her head wildly from side to side. "Please, Fra Piero, don't let the prior general do this to me."

Fra Piero took Lucrezia's small hands in his, holding them still.

"I'm sorry, I have no real power in the Order," he said. "If I cross the prior general he'll strip me of my post and I'll be of no use to you at all."

"No!" Lucrezia tugged her hands free and fell back against the pillow, weeping. "You were there when we took the vows, you know the child isn't born out of wedlock, Fra Piero, don't turn away from me now, I beg you."

She took a deep breath and a new sense of fury filled her lungs. Her face contorted.

"Tell Filippo they've taken our son," she said fiercely. "Tell him to call on his friends, now. His powerful friends."

Seeing Sister Pureza returning, Lucrezia clasped her hands together and the procurator made the sign of the cross on her forehead with his thumb.

"You'll do it, won't you, Piero?" she whispered feverishly as she watched him go. "You'll do it."

Sister Pureza and the procurator came face to face in the doorway. Before Fra Piero could speak, the old woman cast a hard look into the sickroom.

"You've tired her," Sister Pureza said curtly. "She must rest, or she won't get her strength back."

Then she closed the infirmary door, leaving Fra Piero alone in the garden.

Fra Piero went directly to the *cappella maggiore* in Santo Stefano. He found Fra Filippo standing in front of his dancing Salome, adding white to the wisp of her flowing gown.

"You've come with news?" The monk's robe was frayed and he needed a bath.

"Come walk with me," Fra Piero said, looking around at the

chapel. Fra Diamante waved a greeting from the scaffold, Giorgio and Tomaso nodded, and Young Marco, whose hands were as slender as a girl's, was using a feather brush to put light clouds in the sky over the scene of Saint Stephen's martyrdom. "We must speak alone."

The two monks hurried from the room, and at the entrance to the nave Fra Filippo stopped.

"Has something happened?" he asked anxiously. "Has something happened to Lucrezia?"

"Lucrezia's fine. I've only just come from the convent," Fra Piero said cautiously. "The child was born at dawn. It's a boy. A fine boy."

The monk's face broke into a broad smile, and he clapped his friend on the shoulder.

"A son." He threw both arms around him. "I have a son. Come, Piero, let's have a glass of wine and praise the Lord."

They walked into the sunlight, turning east into the Piazza Mercatale, where Fra Piero picked out a cask of wine from the covered booth of the Vintners' Guild. He uncorked it and passed it to his friend. Fra Filippo held the bottle toward heaven, thanked God, and took a long swallow.

"There's something else." The procurator watched the painter lower the cask and narrow his eyes. "It's not good, Filippo."

By the time his friend had told him everything, the painter had guzzled most of the wine, sending rivulets of crimson down the sides of his mouth and onto his robe as he worked himself into a rage.

"They can't do it, they can't do this to her," Fra Filippo growled, kicking a stone in the road. He tipped the bottle and swallowed the last drops. "God damn Saviano."

Fra Piero bought another jug of wine and walked Fra Filippo to the bridge over the Bisenzo River, past the silk dyers' vats and the fishermen's shacks that lined the riverbank. Fra Filippo drank the second flask more quickly than the first, reeling between rage and despair. He stood beside the tallest cypress along the river and held on to it as if he might fall off the edge of the earth. Then he begged a third bottle of wine from Fra Piero, which he drank as they stumbled back toward the Piazza della Pieve.

"I'll kill him," he said as he walked up the pebbled path to his *bottega*. "He's the devil, that's what he is."

The painter's front door was unlocked, and the air inside was stale. He picked up the sketch he'd made of Lucrezia, and carried it with him as Fra Piero led him to the bare pallet in the bedroom.

"My altarpiece, I can't leave it at the chapel." The monk's speech was slurred as he grabbed Fra Piero's robe at the collar and tried to pull himself to his feet. "I'm going back for it."

"I'll go," Fra Piero said, pushing the painter away. "You stay here. Don't go off and get into trouble," he said. But he could see there was no danger. The monk could hardly walk.

Fra Filippo let his friend leave, and surrendered himself to the swirling darkness. Once he was alone, the last of the painter's bravado slipped away. His lungs tightened, his stomach turned, and his throat began to burn. It had been many years since he'd wept, and his tears came in great hollow sobs that shook his body as they echoed in the empty bedroom.

The hour of Vespers had arrived as the procurator approached the rectory at the Church of Santo Stefano. He went the long way to the *cappella maggiore*, pulling the painter's sturdy little wagon to the rear of the chapel and entering the church through a side door. All of the lanterns had been extinguished in the empty church, and he stopped to let his eyes adjust to the dim light.

From somewhere near the altar, Fra Piero heard the sound of metal clinking, the rushed rustle of robes. He stopped and held his breath as he listened, the sound becoming more distinct. His eyes adjusted to the darkness and Fra Piero was able to see moonlight coming through the large window behind the altar, the wooden statues of the Virgin and Saint Elizabeth standing impassive above the tiny votives that flickered around their pedestal bases. He crept forward, toward the muffled sounds. Whoever was there was moving quickly, and furtively.

Quietly, Fra Piero slid along the cool tiles of the church floor, turning the corner toward the bell tower door. He made out one voice, then a second, much fainter. He moved closer, on silent feet. The door to the bell tower was open, and through the narrow space he saw the hem of a dark robe trailing up a short flight of broken steps.

Fra Piero stopped and held his breath, waiting. He saw the dark robe swaying to and fro, back and forth.

"You're an angel, Young Marco." He heard the sharp voice of Provost Inghirami, full of something hot, something the procurator hadn't heard in a long time.

Fra Piero pressed himself against the wall, out of view, and peered around the doorway. In the dim light he saw the provost reach down and yank off the belt at his waist, jangling the keys that hung there. The fingers were milky white in the darkness as the provost's hands slid up, exposing the bare flesh of smooth buttocks bent in front of him. With a jerky motion Inghirami reached behind him, hooking the belt and keys over a spike in the wall before hoisting his own robes above his thighs.

Fra Piero couldn't tear his eyes away. The provost's long hands gripped the boy's flesh, his body thrust, he moaned unintelligible words above the soft gasps of Young Marco.

When he'd seen more than he wanted, Fra Piero tiptoed silently back to the *cappella maggiore*, where he grabbed the altarpiece and slipped out of the church the same way he'd entered.

Chapter Twenty-six

"Please, Lucrezia, just a little bit." Spinetta spoke her first words in many months, her voice thick. "Eat a little bite for me."

Sitting in the infirmary, Spinetta gently brushed the hair from her sister's forehead with one hand, while holding out some raisins and a handful of shredded partridge Sister Maria had saved from the soup. Lucrezia's eyes hadn't recovered their light, nor her complexion its color. Her thin wrists poked from under the white balloon of the plain *guarnello,* and lay flat on the blanket.

"*Bambino mio,*" Lucrezia whispered, her voice hoarse. She shook her head from side to side and Spinetta could see her full breasts pushing against the light fabric, the gentle mound of her still-swollen womb beneath the blanket.

"*Mia cara,* you must eat and drink." Spinetta brought her sister's hand to her lips and her tears spilled onto them, wetting the raisins in her palm. "You need your strength."

Two days had passed since the birth, and Lucrezia seemed to be getting weaker instead of stronger. As she watched her sister's eyes flutter and close, Spinetta remembered the strength Lucrezia had shown that day in the *bottega,* after her violation. Spinetta had given her promise, then, never to tell what had happened, and she'd been silent all these months simply to keep the truth inside of her. But so much had come to pass, and now it seemed Lucrezia's very life hung in the balance. Sister Pureza had turned a cool eye on Lucrezia's suffering, and this made Spinetta angry. The very people who were supposed to protect them had failed Lucrezia in every way—they were hurting her still.

Dropping the food on a cloth, Spinetta rushed from the infirmary. As usual, Sister Pureza was busy at work, trimming the white roses that rimmed the edge of the garden. The old woman looked up as Spinetta approached, but didn't slow in her task. She gave the slightest nod, then looked across the garden to where Rosina knelt among the shade plants, digging up morels that grew between the mossy stones.

"My sister refuses to eat or to drink." Spinetta didn't stop for niceties. She blurted out her words. "I've never seen her so weak."

The nun squinted up at her.

"Lucrezia will eat, and she will heal. She's young and healthy." As the old nun answered, she clipped a white blossom, which fell perfectly into the basket at her feet.

"How can you be so untroubled by her suffering when you've caused it, Sister Pureza?"

The old woman flinched, but her voice was calm.

"No, Sister Spinetta, your sister made her own choice. She sinned willingly, surrendered her chastity of her own volition, broke her vows knowingly."

"No!" Spinetta's voice filled with emotion. "Her innocence was stolen from her, her chastity was violated."

Sister Pureza stood up and shaded her eyes from the sunlight, to get a better look at the girl.

"I was there." Sister Pureza measured her words slowly, carefully. "She told me herself that she'd remained with the painter at her will. I asked if he'd forced her to stay, or violated her, and she swore he hadn't."

"Because he didn't, Sister Pureza. The painter didn't. It was the prior general. He took her by force. He's the one who stole her chastity."

Sister Pureza felt dizzy. The cloying heat in the garden seemed to suck all the air from her lungs.

"What are you saying?"

"I'm saying the prior general found her and forced himself on her," Spinetta answered. "He took her virginity. I would have told you before, but she begged me not to."

Sister Pureza thought back to the day in the painter's *bottega*, when the novitiate had appeared in her white *gamurra*, her hair around her face like a golden halo.

"Why didn't she come to me?" Even as she asked the question, Sister Pureza already knew the answer.

"She was ashamed," Spinetta said quietly.

Sister Pureza felt a wave of nausea. She wiped her hand across her mouth.

"Is it the prior general's child?" Sister Pureza asked grimly.

Spinetta took a moment to answer.

"No. I don't think so."

Sister Pureza's answer was fierce.

"Then she has sinned willingly, no matter what the prior general did to her, she sinned knowingly with the painter."

Now it was Spinetta who felt dizzy. Lucrezia had said that blame would fall on her, despite the prior general's deed.

"The painter promised to protect her. He said he loved her," Spinetta cried. "Ask Fra Piero, Sister. He was there when they exchanged the vows, he saw them become man and wife."

Sister Pureza's face folded into a frown.

"Only the Church can bless the sacrament of marriage, Sister

Spinetta. And the Church cannot, under any circumstance, condone the marriage of a monk and a novitiate."

"But the Church can let the prior general go unpunished?" Spinetta cried. "I begged Lucrezia to come to the convent, but she said that blame would fall on her, no matter what was true. And she was right."

With that, Spinetta turned and ran from the garden, tripping over her feet and leaving the gate to swing open in the still summer air.

The scent of roses was everywhere, and dust from the leaves covered her fingers. Sister Pureza sat alone on the stone bench in the garden.

Lucrezia wasn't the first young one she'd known to lose her virginity by force. It happened all the time, in every city, to women of every rank and station: housemaids, kitchen girls, merchants' daughters. Even nuns. It happened in an instant, often in silence, always in secret. Then the men carried on, salved by a moment's pleasure, while the women bore the stain as if it were a natural part of Eve's curse.

Weakened and ashamed, Sister Pureza let herself fall back into the memory of her own youth. For decades she'd pushed away every sound and smell reminiscent of her own surrender on a summer night in a lush Roman garden, when the roses were in full bloom and the heady smell of mint and moss underfoot filled her with thoughts of love and pangs of longing.

Like Lucrezia, she'd been a young beauty on the cusp of womanhood. But Pasqualina di Fiesole hadn't been taken by force; she'd surrendered willingly to a young man who belonged to one of Rome's finer families. And when the evidence of her sin had begun to show in her belly she'd panicked, and she'd lied. She'd claimed her virginity had been taken against her will, and begged her father to go to the young man's family and insist on marriage. Instead, her mother had sent her to the Convent Santa Margherita, where she'd lived with her secret, alone, as the child grew in her womb.

Remembering the rank smell of the infirmary when the child had been delivered into this world, Sister Pureza felt her lungs fill with long-suppressed sorrow. God had punished her for her passion and her lies. He'd punished her, and He'd punished her daughter, too. What other reason would have compelled the Lord to take the beautiful girl back to His kingdom only hours after her birth?

Sister Pureza's tears stained her browned skin. She couldn't change the ways of the world, or what had happened. She couldn't undo the terrible sin the prior general had committed against Lucrezia, or the secret she'd lived with for so long. But she knew where Lucrezia's babe had been sent, and she could find him. At least she could repair this one wrong deed.

Sister Pureza slipped away from the convent right after Terce, while Prioress Bartolommea was in her study, going over the account books. The sun was hidden behind a cloud as she made her way toward Porta Santa Trinità, where the streets turned into narrow footpaths. A gaggle of hens came to peck at the hem of her robe as she walked. Several low buildings squatted at a tilted angle, and the air was filled with the stench of cabbage and old fish.

She'd prepared herself to knock on many doors, but stopped at only a few before she heard the high wail of a newborn through the window of one of the lowest hovels. His cries grew more pitiful as she approached the doorway and began to knock steadily. The *balia* pulled the door open. The child's mouth was attached to the nipple that poked between the folds of her dress, and he suckled furiously as his sobs subsided.

"Yes, Sister?" the *balia* barked when she saw her. "What are you doing here?"

The *balia*'s dark hair was wrapped in a brown rag, and streaks of yellowed milk stained the front of her thin dress. Behind her, Sister Pureza could see several children crawling among the baskets on the floor. The baby made soft mewling noises as he drank, fat hands reaching for her bosom.

"God's grace to you," the nun said, looking the woman in the eyes. "I've come to relieve you of your duties. The child's mother is healed; she can nurse him herself now."

"Eh?" The *balia* frowned. "The man said I might see two years' worth of wages for this babe. This is good milk he's paying for!"

The old nun reached for the small purse that hung on a cord around her neck, and shook out a gold coin she'd secreted away so long ago that she'd forgotten how she had come to acquire it.

"Take this for your troubles, *balia*. It isn't two years' wages but it will help until you find another *bambino* to feed." Sister Pureza pressed the coin into the woman's browned fingers. As soon as she did, the woman pulled the baby from her breast and thrust him into the old woman's hands. The child gave only a meek protest.

"Take him, then. Go on." The *balia* turned her back on the nun and shut the door.

There was a crude stool beneath the lone window of the shack. Sister Pureza gingerly lowered herself onto it, holding the baby tightly. Gently she began to unwind his dirty blue swaddling cloth. The *balia* hadn't trimmed his pale fingernails, nor bothered to remove the dirt that had settled in his tiny creases of fat. When they returned to the convent, she would make her special balm to soothe the raw skin around his scrotum, she thought, as she turned him over to see how bad the rash was on his buttocks.

Then she gasped.

There were a few tiny red bumps, but otherwise the skin on his bottom was clear and smooth. There was no birthmark.

"Balia!" She stood and banged on the door. "You have the wrong child."

It took the rest of the coins in Sister Pureza's small purse to extract the full story from the irritated wet nurse. The baby that had arrived on her doorstep in the night had indeed had a cross-shaped birthmark on his buttock and he'd suckled with a hearty appetite. But the next day a messenger had come with a sealed letter from the Church of Santo Stefano, and another small child in his arms. The *balia* couldn't read, but the messenger had shown her the seal of the provost of Santo Stefano, and she'd surrendered the first *bambino*, accepting the coins and the second child.

"And where was the first child taken?" Sister Pureza asked.

"I don't know, it made no difference to me." The *balia* swatted at a child who'd grabbed onto her apron. "One hungry mouth's the same as another."

In a daze, Sister Pureza turned and walked through the streets of Prato. She passed women resting their tired bodies against rusticated walls, and others who sat outside their huts pulling nits from their children's hair. A few asked her to pray for them and she nodded blankly. When she passed by the Palazzo Comunale she broke down and cried.

Dio mio, don't let the prior general do this to me, the girl had begged, her face strained with the hours of laboring. *You know he hurt me, Sister Pureza, you know the prior general hurt me.*

Sister Pureza wept for what she'd done, for what had happened to the novitiate, and for what had happened to her so many years ago. The wounds felt so fresh she could almost smell the blood of her own laboring as she imagined the face of the Virgin, at the foot of the cross, watching helplessly as her Son called out for his Father.

⁓⊱❦⊰⁓

*L*ucrezia felt the damp rag between her legs, the rough blanket scratching her neck. Fra Piero and Spinetta were by her side, praying and forcing bits of food into her mouth. Her body was growing weaker, and Lucrezia lacked the strength even to lift her arms. But without her child, she didn't care.

"What if he's hungry?" she whispered, her face turned to the limestone wall.

Fra Piero saw her lips moving, and bent over her.

"What is it, my dear?"

"What if he's cold?" she whispered. "What if he's sick?"

Her breasts ached beneath the cloth Sister Pureza had wrapped around her chest to staunch the flow of her milk, and sometimes she swore she could feel the baby kicking as if he were still safe in her body.

"Please, Lucrezia, *mia cara*, eat something," Spinetta begged, offering her plump raisins, ripe figs, the thinnest broth.

Spinetta wondered bitterly where Sister Pureza was hiding. It had been many hours since she'd confronted her in the garden, and Spinetta couldn't imagine what the old woman was doing.

"A little broth, please," she begged, but Lucrezia's lips were clamped shut.

As Fra Piero prepared to leave, he bent over the limp girl and whispered into her ear. "Filippo sends his love. He begs you to keep up your strength."

"What for?" Lucrezia asked, her breath hot and hollow. "Has he called on his friends? Has he found our child? Does he think I'm still waiting for word from Rome?"

She saw the procurator's shadow move along the wall as he left the infirmary, and felt Spinetta's hand on the curve of her hipbone. But Lucrezia didn't turn. She didn't eat, even when Rosina crept to her side with a small cooked egg cupped in her palms.

"No," she whispered, barely looking at the girl. "No."

As evening descended over Santa Margherita, Lucrezia remembered the first time she'd knelt in the convent chapel and studied Fra Filippo's painting. She thought of the pleasure she'd felt when the painter praised her beauty. And everything became clear to her. Sister Pureza was right—her sins were great, her foolish pride even greater. Others had imagined her as the Blessed Mother, even mistaken her for the Virgin, and she'd allowed this flattery to shape her thoughts and color her actions. Her vanity had offended the Virgin, and now she was in misery.

Mother Mary, don't let the child suffer for my sins. Forgive me, please.

Lucrezia prayed as she fell into a troubled slumber. She prayed as she saw the drawn face of Sister Pureza hover over her in the dark, checking the cloth that bound her breasts, and changing the bloody rag between her legs. She prayed as the dawn broke through the fading night.

"Virgin Mother." Her words came out in feverish mumblings. "Please accept my humble sorrow. Through my sorrows I've come to know your pain. Dear Mother, please help me and help my baby."

Fra Filippo watched Thursday dawn through his *bottega* window. He'd promised Lucrezia no one would hurt her again, and now she was suffering. The prioress had taken his gold, then turned against him; Sister Pureza had betrayed them. Lucrezia was refusing to eat. She was growing weaker.

The painter imagined himself storming the gates of Santa Margherita and taking Lucrezia away with him by force. But of course it was impossible. Without work his gold would quickly run out, and the prior general, or Inghirami, or the Medici, or the Curia—perhaps all at once—would come after him, and demand he pay for his transgressions.

Fra Filippo pulled on his soiled robe. He sharpened his razor and shaved carelessly, nicking the side of his chin. He'd believed his talents would get him what he wanted. He'd believed the Medici would help him. Now he saw that he'd been using his God-given gifts as if they were currency, exchanging them for whatever he could get a man or woman to promise him, whatever it was that he wanted.

Distracted by the Medici's incessant demands for their altarpiece, he'd let the true Virgin Mother slip from his sights. But her *Festa della Sacra Cintola* was approaching, and Fra Filippo resolved to please her. Somehow he would beg supplies and begin the altarpiece he'd promised Prioress Bartolommea, making it a magnificent offering to the Virgin. In this way he hoped to humble and ingratiate himself to the Holy Virgin Mary, protector of women and children.

A rooster crowed in the neighbor's yard, and cartwheels began to turn along Via Santa Margherita. As Fra Filippo grabbed a piece of bread, there was a faint knock on the door.

"Fratello, it's Paolo. I have a message for you."

The monk anxiously opened the door and looked down into Paolo's face. In the months that his sister had been at the convent, the boy looked as though he'd grown several inches. Fra Filippo put out his hand.

"Give it to me, please," he said, with a wave.

"There's no note, only a message from the convent."

Fra Filippo paled. "Hurry up, out with it."

"Sister Pureza said you must come. It's urgent," Paolo stammered. He thrust a ragged black robe into the painter's hands. "Put on this robe, and toss a stone over the wall into the garden. Then wait for her by the old pear tree."

When the rock fell into the garden, Sister Pureza put aside the basket of tall basil stems she carried, and slipped out the convent gate. She smelled the bruised fruit that rotted on the ground, and found Fra Filippo near the twisted pear tree that grew where the orchard had been. If not for the painter's distinctive features, she would have thought it was another man who waited for her. The painter she knew was strong, vibrant, and sure-footed, but this man was thin, the skin around his eyes the sallow color of an old bruise.

"What's happened to Lucrezia?" he asked.

The old nun was filled with shame and regret.

"Her recovery is slow, but she's young, and she'll mend," Sister Pureza said. She looked directly into the monk's bloodshot eyes. "Don't worry, Fra Filippo, I've sent for you as a friend."

Sister Pureza didn't have the luxury of choosing her words carefully. "Spinetta told me everything, Fratello," she said. "We don't have time now to discuss the wisdom of why or how you took Sister Lucrezia into your heart and your bed. Only that you did."

"Because I love her," Fra Filippo blurted. "I love her. I told you that day in my *bottega,* I'd give up the cloth and the Church, I'd give up everything to be with her."

Sister Pureza had ceased believing in earthly love long ago. She'd believed, instead, that all love was spiritual, and belonged to God. Yet here was a man of great passion, who was willing to surrender everything for the sake of love. When she looked at him again, and saw the naked anguish in his face, she knew that what he said was true. He was in love with the girl.

"I have no idea what goes on in the world of men," she said. "But I want to help you."

Sister Pureza recounted the prior general's cruel orders, her visit to the *balia,* and the provost Inghirami's treachery.

"I don't know where the babe's been sent," she said. "But I'll try to find him."

She looked into the painter's lined face. He was twice the novitiate's age. Yet such a difference in years was common between husbands and wives.

"If the Medici will help you, perhaps you have a chance, Fra Filippo."

The monk felt himself soften toward the old woman, whose eyes were kind and wise, and who surely must have been beautiful when she was young.

"Thank you," he said, bowing his head. "Thank you, Sister Pureza."

Sister Pureza and Fra Filippo sneaked into the convent just after Sext, when the nuns and the prioress were gathered in the refectory for their midday meal. Everyone ate heartily, and no one glanced out the doorway to see the white hem of the monk's cassock beneath the plain black robe as he hurried across the grounds, and into the infirmary.

"Filippo." Lucrezia raised a hand toward him, then let it fall. She was ashen and nearly lifeless under the white sheet. "They took the baby away."

He gathered her in his arms, and pressed his face to hers.

"Lucrezia." He took a deep breath. She smelled of sour milk and unwashed sheets. Her sobs were small quakes against his chest. "Lucrezia, *mia cara*, I'm so sorry for everything. But you have to eat. You have to keep up your strength."

"What for?" she said, weeping. "The baby's gone—what do I have to live for?"

"Sister Pureza knows everything now," he said. He brushed her limp hair from her face, ran his palm across her wet, hot cheek. "She knows what happened to you," he whispered. "And she's going to help us."

"How?" Lucrezia dimly recalled Sister Pureza rubbing a balm on her belly and legs during the night. "Has she told you where she sent the baby?"

Fra Filippo's throat closed and he choked at the pain in her face. "He was sent to a *balia*."

"Have you seen him? Have you brought him back to me?"

He shook his head, but the painter couldn't bring himself to tell her the child had been switched by Inghirami.

"We're doing everything as quickly as we can. You mustn't give up, *mia cara*."

Lucrezia saw the strain in Filippo's eyes, how lined and tired his face had become. She put her hand to his cheek, and let herself rest against his arms.

"I don't care about anything else, only the child. Bring him quickly, Filippo."

Chapter Twenty-seven

Wednesday, the Thirteenth Week After Pentecost,
the Year of Our Lord 1457

Prioress Bartolommea reached for her new spectacles, which had been sent from Rome at the cost of a single gold florin. She held Fra Filippo's note between her two fingers, and read it with a grimace.

Mother Bartolommea,
I intend to keep my promise and paint the altarpiece for Santa Margherita.
It will depict the Virgin at the moment she gives the Sacra Cintola to Saint
Thomas. With your permission I will come to the convent, to be sure the sketch
of your face captures your likeness. I am at your mercy, and await your word.
In faithful humility to Christ and the Virgin—Fra Filippo Lippi.

It had been nearly a year since the prioress had prayed with the Holy Belt of the Virgin wrapped around her hips, and still no good fortune had blessed the convent. If she'd been a different kind of woman, Prioress Bartolommea might have taken it as sign of her own shortcomings. Instead she accepted the fact, as she did nearly everything, with a large dose of annoyance and not a little petulance.

As she stared out her study window over the top of her spectacles, her eye caught the full quince tree with its gilded fruit and she remembered how eagerly she'd seized on the idea of getting the relic, of holding its luminous green and gold threads in her own hands. She'd believed good luck would visit them, and had been modest in her prayers, asking only for a new desk for the convent study, large iron pots for the kitchen, and some padding in the coffers from which she might treat herself to a small jeweled ring. But their fortunes hadn't changed. Relations were strained within Santa Margherita, the divide growing between those who felt a deep sympathy for Lucrezia and those, like herself, who understood that Lucrezia had brought about her own suffering.

She'd had to use her own florin for the spectacles that balanced now on her nose and pinched her face at the slightest movement. And worst of all, more than three times this month she'd seen a strange reddish tint in her urine, which surely meant the humors in her body were imbalanced. Although the prior general had forbidden him to enter the convent gates, it was time the painter got to work on the altarpiece; her time on this earth was surely running out.

"Sister Camilla, I need some ink," the prioress said with a determined flourish. "We'll write to Fra Filippo and tell him to start my altarpiece immediately."

Sister Pureza saw Fra Filippo arrive just after Lauds carrying a piece of rolled parchment and wearing his familiar leather pouch across his shoulder. She watched his white-robed figure move slowly to the study of the prioress, then she sent Rosina to the kitchen for some broth. After it cooled, Sister Pureza sat at Lucrezia's side and spooned it into her mouth.

"The *Festa della Sacra Cintola* is approaching," Lucrezia said softly. "I'd like to be strong enough to go and pray to the Virgin, as I should have done last year."

Lucrezia looked into the old nun's eyes and saw that they were guarded.

"What is it, Sister Pureza?" she asked. "You're going to bring back my baby, aren't you?"

"I'm doing all I can," Sister Pureza said. She took measure of Lucrezia's face. "I've already gone to the *balia* where the child was sent."

"Yes?" Lucrezia's breath caught in her throat. "And he's there?"

"No, *mia cara*, I'm sorry. He was taken away, but I don't know where."

Lucrezia pushed away the spoon that Sister Pureza held to her lips.

"Then you don't know where he is, and you don't know if you can find him," she said, anger blotting out her fear. *"Mio bambino."*

"There are many women in Prato who'll help us. But it takes time," Sister Pureza said, trying to soothe Lucrezia.

"But he needs me, Sister Pureza." Lucrezia's eyes shone with a steely glint. "He needs me now."

It seemed to Sister Pureza that a pall hung over Santa Margherita, slowing the very bodies that slept in the cells, worked in the barnyard, and prayed in the chapel. Yet in a cruel reversal of the lifelessness that haunted the convent, the *giardino* was in the full bloom of late summer. For the first time in many years the honeysuckle and the pole beans were growing in wild abundance, their vines tangled together along the low garden wall.

As she showed Rosina how to snap the long beans from the vines and let them drop into the basket at her feet, Sister Pureza tried to imagine where the child could have been sent. The prior general was cruel and shrewd enough to have sent the *bambino* anywhere in the hills, perhaps anywhere within the states of Italy. But news of a bastard child spread even more quickly than the sores on a leper, and news of a child born to the novitiate was surely on the lips of every merchant and scullery maid in Prato. She needed a friend who could be her eyes and her ears in the city, keeping watch over what happened and listening for what was rumored. For this, Sister Pureza could think of none better than the women at the de' Valenti palazzo, where many messengers and merchants visited each day.

Leaving Rosina to her work, Sister Pureza walked back to her cell, smoothed a parchment out on her desk, and composed a note to Signora Teresa.

When she'd finished and sealed her note with candle wax, Sister Pureza quietly found the man who came to fetch the convent's milk and cream to market, and asked him to deliver it to the palazzo that very afternoon.

"Take an extra bucket of cream for your children," she said to the ruddy man as she pressed the note into his fat palm.

The man returned the next morning with a fine linen envelope sealed with the Valenti family crest. The signora wrote that Nicola, whose ears never missed a word of gossip, had heard that two children had been brought to the hospital of the Casa del Ceppo earlier that week, a bell ringing for each of the poor squalling souls.

The signora had written:

I pray you may find the child. Lucrezia is deserving of a child. I have sensed her goodness, and this small transgression may be God's way of bringing humility and forgiveness to those of us who have been blessed with much more than she. If it may be of help, I offer the gift of a single fat pig to whoever leads us to the child.

Folding the note into her robe, Sister Pureza found Rosina and instructed her to gather another basket of pole beans from the garden and then to trim the buckthorn. She stopped to see the prioress in her study, nodding to Prioress Bartolommea from the doorway.

"What is it?" the prioress asked, looking up over her spectacles.

"A laboring mother in the Falconi family has been taken with fever," Sister Pureza said. "They've sent for me, and promised a new pig for our barnyard if I come right away."

"A new pig?" the prioress said weakly.

"God willing, I'll be back before Nones," Sister Pureza said, before quickly ducking out the convent gate.

The *ospedale* of Prato was not as grand as the foundling hospital in Florence, nor as famous, but had been built by the same good merchant of Prato, Francesco Datini, in the final spate of generosity that had poured forth as his death approached. The building stood in the southern quarter of the city, its façade marked by a simple loggia, the colorful crest of the Datini family, and several roundels with carved putti. As Sister Pureza approached the building she saw a group of older children gathered around two nuns who wore the brown robes of the Franciscan Order. Each child clutched at a crust of bread, and no one paid any heed as the old nun in black mounted the stairs and entered the building.

Sister Pureza had birthed many children, but had only been inside the *ospedale* twice before. As she stepped into the small rotunda, she was greeted by the sound of babies crying and the sharp smell of urine. Sister Pureza stopped a nun who hurried through the halls, and asked where the newest babies were kept. Without breaking her stride, the nun nodded in the direction of a small room behind the main staircase.

Alone in their makeshift cradles, three tiny babies squawked, each bright red with hunger, all waiting for the sole *balia* who served the foundlings. Looking at the mewling infants, Sister Pureza couldn't help but think of Teresa de' Valenti's ornate birthing chamber and the many attendants who bathed, swaddled, and fed her child.

Gingerly, the old nun picked up the first baby, whose minute head was covered in a fuzz of red hair. A quick peek under her swaddling revealed that the child was a girl. Kissing her forehead, Sister Pureza laid the child back down and reached into the cradle for the second child. She waited for his spray of urine to finish before she turned him over, praying for the telltale red mark on his buttocks. It wasn't there.

"Please, Blessed Mother, let this be the one," Sister Pureza said as she gently lifted the third baby. He was large and healthy, and for a moment the nun's heart quickened as she thought of the painter's sizable frame. Already this babe's tiny buttocks were dimpled with fat, but aside from that, his skin was clear. He was not the child she sought.

There was still an hour of daylight left when Sister Pureza returned to the convent and made her way back to the herb garden. Rosina had left the buckthorn she'd trimmed in a neat pile, and the smell of steamed green beans filled the air around the refectory. Tired and discouraged, the old woman reached for her garden shears to finish the day's work.

She'd tried what she could, followed whatever small leads she could find, but it was not enough. Lucrezia was right: the child needed her now. The longer he was away from her, the farther he could be sent, and the less likely it became that he would be found and returned.

"Mother of God," Sister Pureza prayed. "Help me to make it right."

She put down her shears and paced the garden, running her hands along the tops of the flowering basil, the spikes of lavender that had grown to a thick swatch of tall plantings since her first years in the garden. When the answer came, the nun nodded her old head and left it bowed in thanks. She let the warm August breeze blow over her, and she breathed in the thick perfume of the abundant lavender.

In the morning, when Fra Piero came to say Mass, Sister Pureza pulled him into her garden. They hadn't spoken since that day in the infirmary, when she'd been too angry to be forgiving. But since she'd resolved to help find the child, she'd sensed the procurator waiting for her to approach him. When she did, his face was alert, his eyes receptive.

"I've done everything I can think of," she said. "But it's come to nothing. The prior general and the provost are powerful men. Only God Himself, or the Blessed Virgin, could move them to return the child." .

The procurator nodded. Perhaps he'd overestimated the old woman. His eyes wandered around the garden. He could smell the sharp aroma of thyme drying in the sun along the rocks.

"The *Festa della Sacra Cintola* is coming, and all of Prato will be focused on the relic," she said. "I've prayed on this a great deal, and I believe the intercession of the Virgin and the power of her Holy Belt may help bring about the miracle we need."

She glanced around to be sure they were alone, and lowered her voice to nearly a whisper.

Fra Piero bent closer. As he listened to the old nun, his mind raced. He willed himself to carefully trace the lines of the apse, the nave, and the chapel in the Church of Santo Stefano. He thought back over the mounting preparations that were being made for the *festa*. In the past month, he'd spent a little more time than usual in the *pieve;* he'd seen the shadow of Provost Inghirami and the smaller form of Young Marco moving through the church together, and spied them slipping down the stairs that led from the bell tower to the crypt.

"I think I can help," the procurator said slowly. His eyes darkened, then danced. "Yes, if I may have a day or two, I believe I can get what you need."

Lucrezia was half asleep when she heard the steady step of Sister Pureza in the infirmary. She opened her eyes and saw the old nun standing next to her pallet, carrying with her the scents of the garden, as always.

"Lucrezia, I know you're suffering." The old woman held a small cup toward her and shook it slightly. "This is Saint-John's-Wort. It will soothe your pain and help lift your spirits." She paused. "I know this, child, because it helped me once."

The nun sighed and slid the wooden stool closer to Lucrezia. The young woman looked at her warily.

"I know this, because it helped me once," the old nun repeated. "Long ago, when I was young and beautiful, I made a terrible mistake. I sinned and I paid for it dearly."

Lucrezia rubbed the sleep from her eyes, and listened.

"I've known the hands of a man on my body, and the quickening of a child in my womb," Sister Pureza said slowly. "All my life I've carried this shame."

A look of sympathy crossed Lucrezia's face, and the nun put a callused hand under Lucrezia's chin. With the girl's face tipped up to hers, Sister Pureza poured out the long truth.

"I confused passion for love," she said, steeling herself against the memories. "I've seen many others suffer in this same way, Lucrezia. Mistaking passion for love, and then paying for their sins in blood."

She shook her head, remembering how she'd lain in this very room, so long ago, and vowed never again to succumb to lust, or weakness, or lies. Her tongue tripped over the memories and she spoke to Lucrezia in a long, rambling confession.

"If I was harsh to you, it was because of this." The nun's voice broke, and Lucrezia felt her own tears spilling. "It was because when I saw you, I saw myself. And I was afraid."

Sister Pureza saw Lucrezia's wet cheeks, and remembered that first day, when the novitiate had begged to keep her silken *panni di gamba* from home.

"Don't cry, Lucrezia. It's not too late for you. We'll pray to the Virgin. We'll find your son."

Lucrezia shook her head.

"Sister Pureza, do you honestly believe the Virgin will help me, even now?"

Sister Pureza paused. She believed the Virgin surely saw and took pity on the young woman's suffering. She believed the Virgin was good and merciful, and that she would help Fra Piero carry out the task that her plan depended upon. But she couldn't say this to Lucrezia.

"I believe the Virgin knows the sorrow in your heart and that she loves your child." With rough brown fingers, she wiped the girl's cheeks. "Now drink this herb. We need you to be strong."

Chapter Twenty-eight

Friday of the Thirteenth Week After Pentecost, the Year of Our Lord 1457

Candles and oil lanterns flickered and hissed as the painter paced before his frescoes and studied them carefully. He'd lived with this cycle for nearly six years now, and its stories and images had come to resemble those of his own life. In Saint Stephen's separation from his parents, the painter saw the pain of losing his own mother and then his father; in the birth scenes he saw the luxuries he'd wished for Lucrezia; in the martyrdom of Saint John the Baptist he saw his own desperation; and in Salome, who was ripe and full in her sensuous beauty, he saw a seductive rendering of his own beloved Lucrezia.

He'd been working through the night, but the monk squared his shoulders and stared at the scene of Saint Stephen's birth. A *balia* sat on the ground of the birthing chamber, the infant in a basket next to her. Yet these figures didn't adequately illustrate the legend of Saint Stephen in peril—a tale that Fra Filippo had begun to realize was terribly close to his own son's life.

As the sun made its first faint appearance in the east, Fra Filippo stirred a fresh jar of *terra verde* and dragged a ladder across to the northern wall of the chapel. He climbed the scaffolding that abutted the lunette, and began to paint *a secco*, putting a new layer of paint onto the dried plaster. His brush created a spectral green image in the midst of the placid birth scene: a winged demon, hunched over the infant's cradle. The demon held the infant saint in his left arm as he placed another, ordinary child, into the blessed infant's basket. In a moment the green demon would carry the true Saint Stephen away from his mother, even as she lay blissfully unaware on her high bed.

For hours Fra Filippo worked on the green satanic figure, making it as real as the other figures in the scene. Then he stepped back and studied the evil creature. It was even more deathly, more horrible, than he'd pictured in his mind. With this new creation, no one who looked at the fresco could fail to see the demons that haunted the painter's life.

He heard Tomaso arrive, and Fra Filippo bellowed for a bucket of plaster. As soon as the assistant scrambled up the scaffolding, the painter took the bucket and began to smear a fresh, large circle of *intonaco* on the outer limits of the scene. With facile strokes he created an orange-robed nursemaid, her simple gown falling in heavy folds. In her outstretched arms she held a small baby, his rounded head a perfect, foreshortened sphere. She passed the child to a waiting clergyman, whose green robe matched exactly the *terra verde* demon. The connection between the two figures was unmistakable, impossible to ignore. Although the cleric's robe was green instead of the red of Provost Inghirami's cassock, Fra Filippo was certain he'd painted an image that would stab at the man's heart.

Inghirami will burn with shame when he looks at this scene, the painter thought, and for just a moment his misery was eased by something approaching satisfaction.

He used a rag to wipe the splatters of paint from his hands, leaving the brushes and buckets for his assistants to clean. It was still early, and he didn't want them to know he was leaving for the day; perhaps for many days. He had to be alone to devote himself to the altarpiece of the Holy Belt in penitence and humility. For him, praying was painting, and he intended to pray with all his might.

With a pack on his shoulder the painter hurried away from the church, carefully pulling the small cart with his work behind him. Only Fra Piero knew where to find him.

───※───

*P*rior General Saviano's carriage rolled into Prato and stopped at the *Pieve di Santo Stefano.* Brushing past women scrubbing the steps, he marched through the front door and demanded olive soap to wash his hands, peppermint oil for his feet, and silk sheets for his bed.

"Right away," he said. "Send them to the guest room in the rectory, along with your finest wine."

The prior general had postponed his arrival for the *festa* as long as he could. He had no desire to publicly associate himself with the painter's escapades, and when he'd learned Lucrezia was still lying in at the convent infirmary, he'd made up his mind to forgo the comfortable room at Santa Margherita and stay instead in the tiny guest chamber at Santo Stefano.

The prior general drank the wine as soon as it was brought to him, then went to Inghirami's private kitchen and ordered a full meal, sending the kitchen maid back twice for more bread and gravy. He nodded coolly to Father Carlo, who came looking for Inghirami, and refused to let himself become worked up when the provost appeared and brought up the drama unfolding in Rome, where Pope Callistus III lay gravely ill.

"Never mind what's happening in Rome," Prior General Saviano snapped as he wiped gravy off his lips. "I want to see the *Sacra Cintola* straightaway. I've got my own prayers for the Virgin."

"Of course," Inghirami said as agreeably as he could manage. "Of course, if you wish, we can go immediately."

The church was filled with workers polishing the woodwork with lemon oil, sweeping the floors, brushing cobwebs and hornets' nests from the hidden spaces under stairwells. Stopping in front of the altar, Saviano strained to see what progress had been made on the frescoes, and barely missed tripping over a bucket of soapy water.

"Should we have a closer look at the fresco cycle?" the provost asked.

Prior General Saviano glanced around, noticed the white robes of the painter were nowhere to be seen, and consented. Fra Diamante and Tomaso stepped out of their path as the two clerics entered the *cappella maggiore* to survey the work.

"The scene of King Herod is quite fine," Prior General Saviano acknowledged with a begrudging nod. "Don't you agree?"

"Yes, yes," the provost answered as he squinted into the shadows under the scaffolding. He was hoping to see Young Marco and signal for the boy to meet him in the stairway of the bell tower later. Otherwise he'd have to hang his rope belt by the campanile door, and then wait in the meeting place for the boy to see the sign.

"What is the meaning of this?" Saviano demanded.

Provost Inghirami turned to see the red-faced cleric waving a hand toward the wall under the northern lunette.

"Is something wrong?" Inghirami asked.

"Look for yourself," Saviano snarled as he made an angry gesture.

It took a moment for Inghirami's eyes to find the green demon, and to discern the message Fra Filippo had inserted into his painting. His eyes moved from the green cleric's robes, to the green wings of the demon, to the trim of green around the bottom of Prior General Saviano's rich cassock. Although legend said the infant Saint Stephen was nursed by a doe and then brought back from the wilderness and put into the arms of a benevolent bishop, it seemed clear that Fra

Filippo, in painting the cleric and the demon the same color, wished to imply a connection between the two, an evil thread that linked them in their intent to do harm.

"It's nothing, Your Grace," the provost whispered. He gave a meaningful glance in the direction of Fra Diamante and Tomaso, who'd stopped what they were doing and turned their attention to the two men. "Just the reckless imagination of a crazed artist."

Inghirami was loath to take the prior general's arm and lead him away, and was greatly relieved when the prelate took his cue, turning his back on the fresco and leaving the *cappella maggiore* with a great flourish of his robes.

"Who does he think he is?" the prior general growled.

"He's got the devil in him," Inghirami whispered. "He'll be sorry."

As the two hurried to the Chapel of the Holy Belt, Provost Inghirami fumbled among the keys on his belt for the one that would open the bronze gates. The two men were silent as the chapel opened with a slow creaking.

A stream of light fell through the circular window in the rear of the chapel, and dust rose, swirling and shimmering as it caught the sunlight. Incense was burning nearby, and the air smelled of myrrh as the two approached the coffer that held the sacred relic.

As he did whenever he was about to open the reliquary box, Provost Inghirami genuflected and made the sign of the cross.

"*Sancta Maria, Mater Dei, ora pro nobis peccatoribus, nunc, et in hora mortis nostrae.*"

"Amen." The prior general's voice was loud in the hushed chamber. He nearly snatched up the coffer himself; only Inghirami's quick movements prevented it. The provost bent, laid his hands on the reliquary lid with its gilded volutes, and used his thumbs to release the clasps that held it shut. He took a deep breath, and lifted the lid.

The box was empty.

The provost gasped, and drew himself up in horror.

"What's the meaning of this?" Prior General Saviano demanded for the second time in an hour.

"My God, I have no idea." There was a tremor in Inghirami's voice. He stared into the coffer, and quickly snapped it shut.

"Do I have to remind you that your most important duty here is to keep watch over the Virgin's relic? If the *Sacra Cintola* isn't here, where is it?"

"I don't know." The provost ran a thin finger inside the neck of his robe.

"You have the only key, and it falls to you to explain what the devil is going on," snapped the prior general.

"I don't have it, I can assure you of that." Inghirami dropped to his knees.

"Dear Virgin Mother," he prayed. "Please tell me what has happened."

The prior general glared at the provost.

"Get off your knees," Saviano hissed. "This isn't a time for prayer, it's a time for action. Stealing the belt is a crime punishable by death. If there's no other culprit, the blame falls to you."

The provost closed his eyes and took a deep breath. He'd never intended to tell a soul that he'd surrendered the *Sacra Cintola* to Cantansanti last year. But surely, if pushed, Prioress Bartolommea would confess to having had the belt in her possession, and she would implicate him in its disappearance. Better to tell all that he knew now, while he had the prior general's attention. And it was possible, he thought, just possible, that the prioress and the Medici had conspired to take the belt a second time.

Steeling himself for Saviano's ire, Inghirami quickly recounted the day Cantansanti had come to Santo Stefano and requested—no, *demanded*—the temporary surrender of the belt.

"Cantansanti carried a sealed directive from Rome, instructing me to surrender the *cintola*," he said. "I have good reason to believe the Medici took the relic to the convent, to the secret keep of Prioress Bartolommea."

"What?" asked the prior general. "How could such a thing happen without my knowledge?"

"It was for the painter, I'm quite certain," the provost said in a low voice. "The same day the belt left the chapel, Sister Lucrezia left the convent. The next month, the painting they call the *Miraculous Madonna* appeared at the Valenti home."

⁂

Prioress Bartolommea heard the bell at the convent gate, and gave a startled glance in Sister Camilla's direction at the sound of steeds on the road.

"Who's that?"

Sister Camilla ran to the window.

"It's the prior general," she reported.

The prioress removed her spectacles and hid them in the pocket of her robe.

"Prior General Saviano? Is he expected?"

"I'm here now," the prior general said, sweeping into the room with the provost close behind. "What does it matter if I'm expected?"

The prioress stood and stepped out from behind her desk.

"Sister Camilla, you will leave us alone," Saviano commanded. His temples pounded as he waited for the secretary and provost to leave. Then he shut the door behind them. He and the prioress were alone.

"How dare you take the Holy Belt?" He enunciated each word carefully.

The prioress forced herself to meet the man's angry glare.

"I assure you, Prior General, I don't know what you're talking about."

"Do not lie to me." He pulled himself up to his most imperious height. "The belt was here in the convent; now it's missing again. You must return it at once."

Prioress Bartolommea felt overheated. The prior general seemed to be taking up all of the light and air in her study. But her discomfort didn't change the fact that she didn't have the Sacred Belt of the Holy Virgin, nor had she seen it in nearly a year. She explained as much to Saviano.

"Only the Medici's emissary could arrange for such a transfer, and Ser Cantansanti hasn't been in Prato for more than a month," she said, trying to keep her thoughts straight and appeal to the prior general's sense of reason. "If the sacred relic isn't in the locked case, then only the provost can know where it is."

"Is that your final word, Mother?"

"I can't tell you what I don't know," she said, her chin quivering.

"Very well." Prior General Saviano flung open the door, and nearly knocked over the provost. He hissed into Inghirami's pale face.

"For your own sake, Gemignano, if you know where the belt is, tell me now."

"I swear on my soul," the provost stammered as he retreated. "I saw it safely returned behind the locked gates of the chapel nearly a year ago." Inghirami remembered the terrible fate of the two men who'd been hanged in the square for the attempted theft of the belt in the prior century. "It must be here," he insisted. "Search the convent, I beg of you."

The prior general turned to the prioress.

"If we find it on the convent grounds, Prioress Bartolommea, you will answer to Rome."

Stunned, the prioress felt her bladder release, and a warm trickle slid down her leg as the prior general marched into the courtyard.

"Prior General, we're humble servants of the Lord," she called as she hobbled after him. "There is not a thief among us."

The prior general looked around, and she followed his gaze. The nuns had gathered at the windows and doorways of the chapter house, and under the arches of the cloister garden. Sister Isotta was swaying like a tall cedar, and plump Sister Maria was wringing her hands in a kitchen rag.

"You know we have taken the vow of poverty, and humility," she said weakly.

"Where are the novitiates?" Saviano asked.

"We have three novitiates," the prioress said. "I presume they are all in the infirmary, where Sister Lucrezia is resting."

The prior general's eyes narrowed.

"Bring them to me," he said.

"I'm afraid Sister Lucrezia still hasn't recovered from her ordeal," the prioress said.

The prior general leaned closer.

"Last time the belt left Santo Stefano, it was brought here on her account," he said. "If you won't tell me where the belt is, maybe she will."

"Sister Maria," the prioress called. "Go to the infirmary and fetch Sister Lucrezia."

The plump nun nodded solemnly, and began to turn. But from behind the cloister archway, Sister Pureza appeared. All eyes watched as she walked directly to the prior general and stood on his shadow.

"Sister Lucrezia has suffered a great trauma. She cannot be disturbed," Sister Pureza said.

The prior general clenched his jaw.

"Who are you, to speak to me in such a way?" he demanded in a hard voice.

Sister Pureza didn't flinch. She didn't even blink.

"The novitiate was a pawn for the belt once, but she won't be a pawn again," she said.

The cleric stared down at her. She stepped closer, and lowered her voice.

"You won't find the Holy Belt here," she went on. "Only the provost has the key, and as you can see, the key never leaves him."

Prior General Saviano followed the old nun's sharp gaze, and looked at the ornate iron key that hung from the belt on Inghirami's waist.

"If the belt wasn't removed by the use of that key, then there's no earthly explanation for its disappearance."

She watched a cloud pass over the provost's face, and took two steps toward him.

"Provost Inghirami, no one but you can be held responsible for the belt, and the Curia knows this. But there is another possibility, perhaps one you haven't considered."

"And what is that, Sister?"

Although he kept the disdain in his voice, Sister Pureza could see the provost was shaken.

"For hundreds of years the Virgin of the Belt has interceded on behalf of women and mothers," she said. "She appeared to the Bishop of Medina and frightened him nearly to death when he offended one of her faithful."

Sister Pureza turned, to be sure both the provost and the prior general could hear her. She knew by their expressions that her words had them riveted.

"The Madonna of the Holy Belt is the patron saint and protector of mothers and children. If the belt is not in the coffer then perhaps the Virgin Mother has removed it as an earthly expression of her righteous anger. And for good reason."

No one moved. Even the prioress, who very much wanted to step closer so she could hear what the old nun was saying, stayed where she was.

"The Virgin speaks through the *Sacra Cintola*," Sister Pureza said. "Her miracles are conducted through the belt. Her desires are communicated through the belt, Provost Inghirami."

"You're an old, foolish woman," the prior general said, finding his voice at last.

Sister Pureza turned to him. Although she was small and stooped, the difference in their size seemed suddenly insignificant.

"What else can it be, but that the Virgin Mary of the *Sacra Cintola*, protector of mothers and children, is unhappy with what has come to pass here in Prato?"

She leveled her gray eyes at the prior general, then at the provost.

"The belt isn't here. I suggest you look inward, and prayerfully consider what's been done to offend Our Holy Mother."

Having spoken her piece, Sister Pureza stepped back, her eyes not leaving the provost's. The horses stamped the earth, the pigs routed in the mud, and overhead, falcons circled.

The prior general turned to the prioress. He thought he smelled urine as he approached her.

"We'll be back, Prioress," he said. "You had best take care of how you, and your charges, speak to me."

As their horses trotted along Via Santa Margherita, Provost Inghirami felt faint with anxiety. He slowed alongside the prior general's black steed.

"What if the old woman is right?"

"Don't be a fool." Prior General Saviano didn't even look at him as he shook his head.

"In the name of God, I can't dismiss what she's said. I've witnessed the belt's power many times. I've seen the *Sacra Cintola* cure a child of leprosy, and stop the bleeding of a mother who'd lost three sons before she was delivered of twins two months after she touched the *cintola*. I can't ignore what Sister Pureza said."

The prior general's mind raced. He felt sure the old woman had somehow hatched a plot to put the fear of God into Inghirami. But what if she hadn't? What if the Virgin Mary herself had actually removed the belt? In Florence, he'd seen the miraculous Holy Mother bring a child back from the brink of death, and cure an old man who had the rage of Satan in him. The power of the *Sacra Cintola* was legendary throughout the land, and was widely known to have cured the noble *donna* Josefina da Liccio di Verona of a weak womb when she'd traveled to Prato for the *festa* some years ago.

"The feast is in three days," Inghirami said as the bell tower of Santo Stefano came into view over the rooftops. "If the *Sacra Cintola* isn't here on the morning of the *festa*, we can be certain the Curia's guards will be here by evening."

Prior General Saviano reared his steed to a stop in the Piazza della Pieve. The falcons that had been circling the field beyond the convent seemed to have followed them. Now a swarm of gnats hung in the air around them in a humming brown cloud, and merchants and messengers in the plaza made a large circle around them. The prior general waved his hands to cut through the swell of insects.

"A pox on the old nun," he cried, and his horse snorted and stamped. "She can't command what we do."

"With all respect, Prior General, the Virgin's strength is greater than any man's, and her power extends from earth into heaven." The provost swatted a gnat from his cheek. "Imagine reaching the gates of eternity only to find the Blessed Mother was angry at you."

The two men shuddered. They nodded to each other in wordless agreement.

---

*L*ucrezia sat up when Sister Pureza entered the *infermeria*. The old woman's cheeks were red, her eyes alert.

"Rosina told me the prior general is here," the young woman said, a catch in her throat. "Is it true?"

"He's gone. Don't worry, my dear, he won't come near you." Sister Pureza squared her stooped shoulders. "He came because the *Sacra Cintola* is missing."

"Stolen?" Lucrezia gasped. "Who would do such a thing?"

"Not stolen." Sister Pureza took Lucrezia's hand. "I think this may be the miracle we've hoped for," she whispered. "The Virgin has indeed seen your plight, and heard your prayers. And I believe she's speaking now."

Lucrezia's eyes stung. She gently removed her hand from Sister Pureza's, and pushed the covers off her legs. She slid out of bed, barely feeling the ache in her groin, and knelt on the hard floor. She made the sign of the cross, and began to pray.

Outside, near the well in the chapter house garden, Sister Bernadetta and Sister Maria heard Lucrezia through the open door of the infirmary.

"Hail Mary, full of grace, the Lord is with Thee." Her voice was loud and clear. "Blessed art thou among women, and blessed is the fruit of thy womb, Jesus."

"She's praying," Sister Maria said, feeling a flood of joy at the strong sound of Lucrezia's voice. She made the sign of the cross and fell to her knees beside the well.

Moved by Sister Maria's compassion, Sister Bernadetta also fell to her knees and began praising the Virgin Mary.

"Holy Mary, Mother of God, Virgin of the Holy Belt." Their voices joined together and rose on the wind that wafted through the doorway of the infirmary, over the high walls of the convent, into the streets of Prato.

Lucrezia prayed all day, and on through Vespers. Rumors of the missing belt passed from the mouth of the convent's stable boy, and spread like fire through the humblest homes of Prato. The stars came out, and the moon witnessed Lucrezia's devotion. Her plea was felt in the fingers of the solitary weavers in Prato who worked beside the last embers in their hearths; it stirred the housemaids in the Valenti palazzo, who'd eavesdropped at the door of their mistress's room and learned of the young woman's misfortune. Lucrezia's vigil, and news of the missing belt, moved the hearts of expectant mothers, and even Rosina's mother, who was eating the last of her thin gruel before bed, found herself praying more fiercely than usual for the benevolence of the Mother of the Holy Belt.

When Teresa de' Valenti kissed the forehead of her son, Ascanio, that night, remembering his birth nearly one year ago, she said a special prayer of thanks to the Virgin of the Belt and asked her to bless Lucrezia and her child.

"The babe is gone, and now they say the belt is missing," Signora Teresa whispered on her knees, fingering her fine prayer beads. "Dear Mother, make the world right, I beg of you. *Ave Maria, gratia plena.*"

Not one of the women who prayed that night knew for certain

that the missing child and the stolen relic were linked. Not one saw Fra Filippo sketching by candlelight in the old stone waterhouse beside Fra Piero's small dwelling. Not one visited Provost Inghirami or heard his desperate prayers to the Virgin.

But if any one of the women had pulled on her cloak, walked to the edge of the Bisenzo River, and looked up into the branches of the tallest cypress, she might have seen the dark cloth that was hidden among the thick leaves of the tree. And if she'd reached up, as far as the height of two men, and tugged a loose thread that hung from the black silk, the *Sacra Cintola*, glowing in the moonlight, might have fallen out of the wrapping and dropped into her waiting arms.

Chapter Twenty-nine

Dawn was still far away when an invisible hand pulled the bell at the convent gate, but Sister Pureza was already awake, and listening. She rose quickly, her eyes scanning the dusty hall of the dormitory as she hurried into the cool night. The old nun heard the cows and pigs grunting in the dark barnyard, and snores greeted her as she rustled past the prioress's private quarters.

At the gate, Sister Pureza slid open the small peephole.

"Who's there?" She wasn't surprised when her question was met with silence.

Sister Pureza turned the lock and opened the gate. There was a basket on the flagstone step, and in it lay an infant wrapped in a blanket. The old nun looked right and left, but whoever had delivered the child had vanished. Dawn was breaking in a dim line on the horizon as the baby let out a weak cry.

The midwife heard softly padding footsteps, and turned to see Lucrezia approaching.

"*Mio bambino.*" Lucrezia pushed past Sister Pureza and fell to her knees. She lifted the child into her arms and held him tightly. He smelled of milk and the cool mist of dawn.

"At last," she cried, fumbling in the folds of the blanket to find his small hands. "He's cold, Sister Pureza," she exclaimed, laughing and weeping at once. "My little Filippino's hands are cold."

She pressed the child against her and rocked back and forth, falling immediately into the natural sway and rhythm of motherhood. Lucrezia had no doubt: the Great Mother had protected her child, heard her prayers, and returned her son to her.

"Thank you, Blessed Mother. Thank you," she said.

But Sister Pureza was not so easily satisfied. Locking the convent gate, she gently reached for the baby.

"What is it?" Lucrezia's voice rose to a high pitch. "You can't have him, Sister Pureza. He's mine. The Virgin returned him to me."

"Hush, hush, it's all right, Lucrezia. I just want to be sure it's your son."

"Of course it's my son, the Virgin sent him, it's the miracle we prayed for."

"Yes, of course," Sister Pureza said as she stroked the young woman's damp hair. "There's a mark, Lucrezia. The Lord gave your child a birthmark, so you might always know him, wherever he was sent."

Lucrezia's grip loosened a small bit. "If it's a boy, it must be Filippino," she insisted, her eyes clouding. "It must be him."

Opening the child's blanket without taking him from Lucrezia's arms, Sister Pureza pushed the folds to one side. The baby wore a cloth wrapped around his bottom. She loosened the knots and turned him over.

"Yes." She bared the small red cross so that Lucrezia could see it. "This is your son. The Virgin of the *Sacra Cintola* has indeed returned him to you."

When Fra Piero came to the infirmary at Prime, the baby was at Lucrezia's breast. She made a small effort to cover herself, but was too peaceful and delirious to be unduly modest.

"Please tell Fra Filippo." Her voice was thick. "Tell him the Virgin Mother has returned the child to me, and the Lord has marked him with the sign of His blessing."

She smiled gently, her face glowing. The child was warm in the crook of her arm, his body nestled against hers, the skin of her breast and the plump warmth of his cheek pressed together as one. She put a finger against the baby's damp palm and Filippino wrapped his hand around it, the translucent fingernails pumping with his blood. His eyes were shut, his cheeks filling and emptying, his lips pursed with the steady work of suckling. His eyelids, moist and purple, fluttered as he broke his mouth from her nipple. Lucrezia turned her blue eyes away from the infant, and sought the procurator's.

"Fra Piero," she said. "Please ask Filippo to come and take us home."

For at least the tenth time, Mother Bartolommea looked through the basket that had been left outside the convent gate. She shook her head, and muttered to Sister Camilla.

"There must have been some gold, something in the basket, a sign of gratitude from the Virgin," she said. "The child entered the world here, we gave his mother shelter, we've endured the anger of the provost and the prior general."

The prioress shivered at the thought of Prior General Saviano. What would he say when he heard the infant had been returned to Lucrezia and the two of them were here together, against his direct wishes?

"Sister Camilla," she called with certainty. "The prior general has been very clear. He doesn't want the child here on the consecrated grounds of the Order."

Sister Camilla's nose was bright red. Prioress Bartolommea looked at it twice. She certainly hoped the secretary wasn't moved by the return of the child, or sympathetic to Lucrezia's foolish plight.

"The mother and child must go," the prioress said. "As soon as they're able. There's no place for fornicators in our midst, Sister Camilla."

"What about our altarpiece, Prioress?"

The prioress blinked and reached for her spectacles. She thought she saw a smirk on Sister Camilla's face.

"It's already begun," she said. She fumbled for a parchment which she unrolled and held up to the sister with a flourish. "The painter has agreed in writing. It's as good as a contract."

*

*I*n his friend's modest house beyond the city walls, Fra Filippo stepped back and looked at the two works he'd propped against the wall. One was the prepared poplar with the detailed sketch for the convent's altarpiece; the other was the *Adoring Madonna* for the Medici.

He'd spent the better part of the last two days hiding from Cantansanti and sketching out the piece for the convent, with the Blessed Virgin handing the *Sacra Cintola* to Saint Thomas. He knew the altarpiece would be beautiful, the Virgin in a *mandorla* against a teal sky, Saint Thomas kneeling at her feet with his hands holding the green and golden belt. The prioress would be present, too, as she had to be, her pinched features and clenched hands stark against the black robe as she, too, knelt at the feet of the Virgin beside Saints Margaret, Gregory, Augustine, and two others. The Virgin, in whose honor he'd labored on the piece, would be spectacular. And Saint Margaret, namesake of the convent, would bear the lovely countenance of Lucrezia.

The plans for this piece had excited him at first, as he'd poured his penitent prayers to the Virgin into its design. But now, his eyes kept returning to the Medici's *Adoring Madonna.* He couldn't hide from the emissary for much longer.

Bowing his head, Fra Filippo leaned closer to study his lovely Virgin kneeling in the woods. She had Lucrezia's face, the purple *morello* of the robe and the *benda* of delicate pearls she'd worn that first day she'd come to his *bottega.* The Virgin smiled softly as she adored her Child and all the light of the world seemed caught beneath her glowing skin. In the depths, the elm tree held tight to its vine, and the forest floor was strewn with the most delicate violet blossoms.

Only the Child's face was missing now.

A year ago, he'd longed to see the face of his Madonna, and God had shown it to him. Now, he longed for the face of his son. Ser Francesco could bring an army to his doorstep, he could beat him with his own hands, but as long as Lucrezia remained in the convent and his son was gone, Fra Filippo knew he would never be able to finish this altarpiece. He could not paint another infant until he saw the face of his own.

"Filippo, good news, praise God."

The monk turned at the sound of his old friend at the doorway. Fra Piero's face was ruddy, his crooked smile beaming.

"I've just come from the convent. Your son has been returned, strong and healthy—"

"*Robusto*? My son?" Fra Filippo wasn't sure if he'd heard the procurator correctly. "My son is returned?"

"*Si,* today, just this morning mother and child are together."

"I must see them, *pronto.*"

The monk began to push past the procurator, already imagining the blessed scene that awaited him at the convent.

"Stop." The procurator put out his hand.

"Is something wrong?" Fra Filippo's face darkened. "What aren't you telling me?"

"The prioress will not allow you to take them away with everyone watching. You must wait till the *festa*, when Lucrezia and *il bambino* will be alone at the convent. Then you can bring them home."

In a white robe that badly needed to be scrubbed and cleaned, Fra Filippo returned to his *bottega.* He wrapped his treasured works in an old curtain, and carefully stored the paintings and the newly sketched panel in a corner of the room, out of harm's way. Then the monk walked out toward the Piazza Mercatale.

Even if he took Lucrezia and the child away from Prato, they'd still need many things, and soon: a cradle and some linens; a cushion for Lucrezia's chair; a tiny piece of coral to hang around the baby's neck to ward off evil spirits. Hoping his silver would buy these few things, the monk hurried along the streets, joining the crowds that had arrived in the city for the coming *festa.*

At the door of Santo Stefano, he entered the dusty light of the building and stopped at the locked gates to the Chapel of the *Sacra Cintola.* There, he fell to his knees. The Blessed Mother had done what they'd asked.

"*Sancta Maria*, Mother of God. I pledge myself to you."

Feeling his vigor renewed, the monk prayed loudly and gestured exuberantly. When he was finished, he stood and brushed off the front of his robe. Glancing toward the *cappella maggiore*, where his assistants kept up their steady patter, he thought of the many days and long nights he had spent there in painful tribulation. The very space of the church now seemed transformed by his joy.

He felt himself pulled toward the frescoes, his attention riveted on the scene of Saint Stephen being switched at birth. His eyes moved over the green demon, to the *balia* in her orange robe, and came to rest on the *sacra cerva*, the holy deer that had suckled the infant saint and kept him alive, according to legend. The deer's legs, beautifully folded under her, were still shining with the last layer of color he'd instructed his assistants to add.

"*Grazie,*" the painter whispered to the *cerva*. "Thank you for watching over my son."

"Good maestro." The voice was soft, but right behind him, in his ear. Fra Filippo turned. It was Young Marco. The boy had paint smudged on his cheek, a streak of brown the color of the deer's fur. "Maestro, I've finished all that you asked, and hope you will look at what I've done, and tell me if it is good."

The painter stared down at the boy, his eyes soft as the doe.

"Young Marco." He spoke the *garzone's* diminutive name for the first time. For the rest of his days, whenever he smelled the oil soap used to scrub church floors, he would remember this moment. "*Si,* Young Marco, it is good. What you have done is good."

—⁓❦⁓—

At dawn the next morning, Provost Inghirami was on his knees in his private chamber. The streets outside were quiet, but they wouldn't be so for long. Pilgrims were arriving from as far south as Calabria and as far north as Piemonte, and a low buzz was filling the neighborhood around the church. Already it seemed the entire city had heard the rumors of the missing belt, and only his staunch denial, backed by the lies of the prior general who swore he'd seen it, had kept the priests of the church and the officials of the *Comune di Prato* at bay. Now, he'd run out of time. With the tolling of Terce tomorrow, the *Festa della Sacra Cintola* would begin, the streets would be swarming with horses, carriages, vendors, and traveling merchants, everyone praying and chanting and straining toward the Piazza della Pieve.

Provost Inghirami pictured the faces of the crowd turned up to the holy pulpit, waiting for him to appear with the Holy Belt. He cringed as he imagined their rising fury and jeers when he stood before them, the evidence of Satan's work in Prato revealed by his empty hands.

Since dispatching his faithful messenger with a bag of gold and a note for the *balia* in the small village outside of Bisenzia, Provost Inghirami had been on his knees for nearly a full day and still there was no sign from the Holy Mother. What more did she want from him? He'd tried to make reparation. He'd heard the Virgin's message and had the child returned to his mother's waiting arms. But perhaps the Virgin was not yet ready to forgive. Perhaps she was upset because he'd defiled the house of God by stealing into the bell tower for the taste of things he had no right to know. Inghirami's shoulders shook as he thought of the pleasure he'd found with the young painter.

"Dear Queen of Heaven," the provost prayed in final desperation. "Dear Mother, I beg for your kindness and mercy for me, and for Young Marco."

He bit his fist to keep from wailing. The name of Michael Dagomari was forever remembered in Prato as the man who'd brought the relic to their city for safekeeping, and now his own name, Gemignano Inghirami, would be remembered as the man whose sins had brought about this loss and disgrace.

At the first sound of the monks and archpriests in the sacristy stirring for Lauds, Provost Inghirami forced himself to his feet. In the event of the belt's miraculous return, Santo Stefano had to be ready for the *festa*, and this job could be entrusted to no one but himself.

Everything was silent as he made his way into the nave just before daylight. The keys on his belt jangled against his hip, his footsteps echoed on the cool stones, and he turned to the gates of the Chapel of the Holy Belt. Just enough light streamed in from the small window for him to see the narrow lock, into which he inserted the key.

Please, Holy Mother, forgive my sins. The provost held his breath as he approached the golden coffer and gently lifted the lid.

It was still empty.

In vain, Inghirami reached into the box and ran his fingers around the velvet lining. When he still found nothing he shut and latched the box, closed the gate, and locked it again. The dimness of the church gave way as the provost moved through the transept toward the apse, where light was penetrating the darkness through a pair of arched windows. Two floating shafts of illumination crisscrossed in a corner of the church, and he squinted through the scrim of dawn to the statue of the Madonna. His gaze moved from her face, down her smoothly carved limbs, to the place where the light spilled below her waist.

Circling the hips of the Madonna was a green belt, its gold trim shimmering as if on fire.

Holding his breath, the provost hurried to the base of the statue. A spark went through him as he touched the belt, and he knew it was real. He was forgiven. The *Sacra Cintola* had been returned.

Chapter Thirty

The Feast of the Sacred Belt, the Year of Our Lord 1457

It was an especially warm day and Sister Pureza was sweltering under her robes. Her eyes were wide open, her chin high, as she watched the slow figure of the prior general leading the line of chanting nuns toward the Piazza della Pieve. Nothing in his expression belied his humbling, but she was certain he'd had many dark hours of doubt, perhaps even remorse, and this gave her some satisfaction.

"What did you say to the prior general when he came to the convent?" Prioress Bartolommea asked as they reached the piazza. "I've wanted to ask you for some days."

The old nun turned to the prioress. Her friend looked very tired, and the smell of urine seemed to surround her always.

"I asked him to send for your sister, Jacoba," Sister Pureza said, letting her gray eyes meet the prioress's milky gaze. "I think you're tired, and perhaps your judgment isn't as clear as it once was."

The prioress opened her mouth, but her response was drowned out by the sound of cheering. The hundreds of spectators and worshippers who packed the piazza outside the church looked up as a flash of red robes appeared on the Pulpit of the Holy Belt. The cheers mounted into a deafening roar, and shouts of joy filled the air as Provost Inghirami hoisted the Holy Belt of the Virgin Mary into the air.

"Holy Mother of God, Gate of Heaven, Blessed Virgin," Inghirami shouted as the crowd thronged ever closer to the church. The assembled sisters of the Convent Santa Margherita broke into wide smiles of relief, and began to push their way to the portal of Santo Stefano to pray for a year of good fortune, wisdom, and blessings.

As the crowd swelled, Sister Pureza felt a gentle tugging at her shoulder, and was delighted to see the crooked-tooth smile of Fra Piero.

"So it's done," he said softly.

In the warm sunlight, the terror he'd felt as he'd crept into the church under the cover of darkness and groped behind the doorway that led to the campanile seemed far away. Then, Fra Piero's heart had hammered in his head like the anvil that had hammered nails through the limbs of the Savior. But when he'd seen the provost's belt and keys hanging on the same spike where he'd seen them twice before, Fra Piero had known that the Virgin was with him, and all would go as he'd planned.

"Thanks to you," Sister Pureza said softly.

"And to the Holy Mother," said the procurator. He remembered the jangle of the keys on the provost's belt as he'd stepped out of the bell tower staircase, and how the night wind had risen as if the voice of the Holy Spirit were covering the rush of his footsteps across the transept floor. The heavy key had turned easily, the gates of the Chapel of the Sacred Belt had opened as quietly as the rising of dawn.

"Mother and child are well," Sister Pureza said. She'd already said her good-byes to Lucrezia, promising to send word through Paolo as often as possible, and to visit when she was able. "They're waiting at the convent."

"The monk is on his way now," the procurator said.

"Praise be the Virgin Mother of the *Sacra Cintola*." Provost Inghirami's voice rang out above the throngs, and the two conspirators turned their eyes to the pulpit.

"*Si*, praise be the *Sacra Madonna*," Sister Pureza whispered. As she closed her eyes, she said a silent good-bye to the daughter who'd left her long ago and gone to heaven on angels' wings. "Praise be the Lord, who is good and just."

⁂

*A*rriving at the convent, Fra Filippo didn't ring the bell at the front gate, but stopped by the pear tree, picked the firmest fruit he could find, and lofted it skyward so that it fell beside the door of the infirmary with a soft plop. He waited, and in a moment the pear came back over the wall again. He heard the distant voice of Sister Spinetta, and when he listened closely, he heard the cries of his child. His son.

As Spinetta came around the corner of the convent wall, he reached into the pocket of his robe and fingered the small piece of coral strung onto a delicate leather cord. He'd bought it in the market, and had Fra Piero bless it with holy water. The amulet would keep Filippino safe. But it was he, Fra Filippo Lippi, who would keep him fed, and protected, and see that the child was learned in all the ways of the world.

Lucrezia was sitting on the edge of the cot, holding her baby, when she looked up and saw her sister leading what appeared to be Fra Piero, under a dark hood, into the infirmary. She looked behind him for the white robes of Fra Filippo, but there were none. Quietly, her sister turned and left, pulling the infirmary door shut without even a backward glance. Lucrezia held the boy tightly against her body, and said not a word. The monk lowered his hood. And there was her beloved Filippo.

"Oh." Both breathed a single sigh; there was no need for anything else to be said.

"Come, Lucrezia, let's not wait another minute," Fra Fililppo said. He took the child from her arms, and held Filippino in the crook of his elbow. The baby was dressed in a gown Lucrezia had made from worn, soft cloth. "Signor Ottavio was kind enough to send us his errand cart. He would have sent the carriage, but it's being used for the *festa*."

Lucrezia smiled and stood, straightening the plain brown dress that hung below her full bosom and billowed to the floor. Her legs were sturdy, her body was healing. But even more important, her spirit and her soul were strong and sure.

"I came here in a rough cart pulled by a donkey," Lucrezia said, remembering the stars that had followed them on that night. "I don't care how I get home. As long as my home is with you, and as long as it's safe."

Fra Filippo drew the corded piece of coral from his pocket. It was shaped like the bone of a chicken's wing, and colored the deep yellow of a wheat field ready for harvest.

"For the baby," he said. He handed it to her, and held the child out. "You can put it on him. It will keep him from harm."

Lucrezia's eyes filled. She reached the cord over the child's head, his face a blur through her tears, and whispered the words she'd heard Sister Pureza say on the night that he was born.

"Ego te baptizo in nomine Patris, et Filii, et Spiritus Sancti."

Teresa de' Valenti greeted the provost and the prior general on the balcony of her palazzo with a gracious sweep of her hand.

"Welcome," she said, smiling broadly.

The signora looked every inch the strong, vibrant matron of Prato.

Her silk gown was elegant, the *bredoni* sleeves edged in lace, the bosom scalloped to enhance her décolleté.

Her son, Ascanio, was with his nursemaid in the children's quarters, in final preparation for the presentation that would mark the first anniversary of his birth.

"Please have some wine and food," she said. She linked her arm through Prior General Saviano's, and led him toward the grand buffet of goose and roasted pig surrounded by artichokes, olives, and a silver platter of sardines that had been broiled under the open flame in her kitchen.

"You're lovely today, Signora," the prelate said. His eyes roamed the feast table greedily.

"The Lord has been good to me, as He has been good to all of Prato." She acknowledged his compliment with a modest nod as she handed him a goblet and waved for a servant to fill it. She let him drink, but held fast to his arm.

"I have a special request of you, Prior General," she said, beaming warmly.

"Of course I will do my best to please you," he said. The good wine made him quite agreeable.

Signora Teresa didn't stop smiling. She knew her smile was one of her many great assets.

"You can grant Lucrezia Buti the protection of the Order for as long as she may need it, and under any life circumstance the Virgin may prescribe to her," she said.

The prior general choked back a bray of indignation. Across the room, he saw Ottavio acting the benevolent host in his fine velvet robes. The merchant's eyes wavered on his face and the prior general raised his eyebrows, his expression a question mark. The merchant answered with a barely discernible nod of his chin and a flicker of his gaze in the direction of his handsome wife. Then Ottavio smiled at another guest, and turned away.

"Of course she has her child, but the title of *suora* is one that offers a woman protection in the name of the Lord. I believe the Virgin herself wishes the woman and her child to be protected by the hands of the Lord's servants on earth."

Signora Teresa was perhaps the only woman outside the convent who believed she knew and understood the link between the child Filippino's return and the return of the Holy Belt. Of course there had been no official confirmation that the belt had disappeared, but she did not underestimate the powers of Lucrezia and Sister Pureza—neither on earth, nor with the saints in heaven. If the prior general and the provost had shown up at the convent in a foaming fury, as rumor had it, there must be at least a shred of truth to it. She would ask Sister Pureza, someday, although she doubted the old woman would reveal anything.

"Perhaps you have reason to agree," she added, demurely, to Prior General Saviano. "Lucrezia and the painter seem to have the Virgin's blessing."

Teresa de' Valenti held his arm firmly as she led the prior general into the private quarters of her home, chattering as if she hadn't just made an egregious request.

"What they've done is against Church law," the prior general said, keeping an even burn in his voice. "A monk. And a nun."

"A painter. And a young woman. In love."

Teresa de' Valenti's smile wasn't only on her lips, but in her eyes, as well. She had every reason to be happy on this day, and good reason to know the power that rested with her as the wife of Ottavio.

"I'm sure their transgression cannot be irreparable," she said. She came to a stop, and with a slight incline of her head, gestured toward the painting on the wall before them. "My servants call this our *Miraculous Madonna*. It's not for me to say on whom or what the Virgin confers her favor. But I'm certain the girl has the blessing of the Holy Mother. And what heavenly intervention doesn't allow for on earth, my husband is prepared to pay for in the dispensation of indulgences."

The prior general looked at the painting. The novitiate's lips were plump and soft. Her eyes sparkled. Her forehead was high and wise.

"The price for such an indulgence could be very dear," Saviano said stubbornly. "And if Rome denies us, I cannot override the decision of the Curia."

Teresa de' Valenti nodded.

"Understood," she said.

The prior general remembered the girl's gasp under his body, the shock of her blood.

"I'm sure there is a fair price," he conceded, perhaps with less reluctance than his words indicated.

"And the mother and child will live in peace?"

"As much peace as there is in my power to grant," the prior general said. And as he spoke the words that would bind their agreement, the cleric was grateful to Saint Augustine who, in his wisdom, had found a suitable penance for Saviano's own sin of debauchery. "I give you my word."

Lucrezia's heart was light as the donkey finally pulled the cart to the corner of the Piazza della Pieve. Fra Filippo held the reins beside her, his back straight and proud, his eyes squinting in the bright sun. The child was in her arms, covered by a blanket to keep the sun from his face. All around her was the celebrating and chaos of the *festa*, but the joy inside her was even stronger than the revelry of a thousand voices.

"Look, Filippo," she cried as the *bottega* came into view and she saw a large basket of fruit, bread, and cheeses on the doorstep.

Bringing the cart to a stop, Fra Filippo tethered the donkey and reached up to take the baby from Lucrezia. He held the child in his weighty arm, and put out his hand to steady Lucrezia as her boots once again stepped onto the city's dusty ground.

"We have friends," she said, happily surveying the gift of nuts, cheeses, meats, and a pile of small gowns for the child, made of the softest linen and cotton.

For our Miraculous Madonna, the note in the basket read. *From the Honorable Ottavio and Teresa de' Valenti*.

"Sorella?"

Lucrezia turned at the sound of Paolo's voice behind her.

"Paolo?" She hadn't seen him since that Lenten day when he'd refused to come up the path to her home.

Beaming, Paolo thrust a small package into her hands.

"*Mia madre*," he said, and lowered his eyes. "She sends this for the child."

Lucrezia took the gift and slowly unwound the piece of cloth to reveal a small carved cross, ornamented with tiny purple flowers, each petal made with a single drop of paint.

"It's beautiful," she exclaimed, looking into his happy face. "Did you make it yourself?"

"*Si*." He nodded. "And my mother painted it."

Fra Filippo put out a hand, and ran a finger across the purple flower petals.

"Violets," the painter said. "The Virgin's flower."

The baby waved his hands in the air. The three turned toward him as he opened his mouth and let out a gusty wail.

"You're home," Lucrezia said, taking her child from Fra Filippo's arms. "We're home now."

They opened the door to the *bottega*. And there was Ser Francesco Cantansanti, his fine costume rumpled from the long day of festivities.

Chapter Thirty-one

"Home," the emissary drawled. He stood, his voice drunken, but still commanding. "You've been gone, Fra Filippo. And I've been looking for you."

"Not gone," the monk said, stiffening. "I've been working at Fra Piero's house in the hills, sketching the altarpiece for the convent where no one could disturb me."

The baby let out a cry, and Lucrezia rushed past the men, into the bedroom.

"I've been waiting for an hour. I see what you've done." Cantansanti gestured toward the altarpiece, which Fra Filippo had stored carefully in the corner. It was arranged under the window, where the light played over the lovely face of the Virgin, and the empty face of the Christ child.

"I've heard again from Florence," Ser Francesco said. "I've come to tell you what they say."

In his mind, the emissary ran over the letter he'd dispatched to Florence after the monk had slipped from his sight.

I watched him all week, and remained by his side to assure his diligence, Cantansanti had written. *He worked, God he worked, and then last night he took off, I know not where.*

"I know I've missed the promised date." Fra Filippo refused to hang his head. "But you can see the work is good."

Ser Francesco shifted in his heavy boots and picked up the correspondence he'd received that morning.

"Look." Cantansanti thrust a rumpled parchment toward Fra Filippo. "Look at it."

Fra Filippo heard Lucrezia soothing the child. He steeled himself and took the paper, blinking in confusion.

"What is this?" he asked at last.

"The Medici have approved your sketch for the frame. It will take many months, but it is to be executed as you described. In great detail, and at great expense. This is an order for the woodwork."

"You said no more money," Fra Filippo managed to say.

"There is none," the emissary said sharply. "The money will go through Ser Bartolomeo, who will place the order according to your specifications. The sketch for the frame is impressive, Filippo, I commend you. And the altarpiece." The emissary brushed a hand through the air, to move the painter to one side. "The altarpiece is magnificent. Each part of the work is as good as anything you've ever done. Better."

He'd written to Cosimo's son, in whose charge the work had come to be:

Good Giovanni,
The man is surely mad and forever finding trouble, and yet his work is brilliant, unsurpassed in splendor. He will finish it, if I have to beat him to do it, or else you can send your agent Bartolomeo, who may have more patience with the painter than I.

"The light, the forest, the hands of God." The emissary leaned closer to the panel, studying the layers of colors in the scene of the *Adoring Madonna.* "The colors are so brilliant, it's as if you'd held a mirror to the window and captured what God put into the reflection."

Ser Francesco shook his head. He'd been living too long in the painter's world.

"But the Christ child," he said, pointing at the blank oval. "Where is the infant's face?"

He looked at the monk, whose hands, for once, appeared to be scrubbed clean.

"But of course," Cantansanti said wryly. "These things take time."

In the bedroom, Lucrezia nursed the baby. She put a finger into his lips to break the suction and move him from one breast to the other. Filippino let out a gasp, and then a robust cry.

The men heard it, and looked at each other.

"I can see the face now," Fra Filippo said with a smile. "Yes, Ser Francesco, now I can finish the piece."

"Then get to work, Brother," the emissary said, picking up his cloak and turning to the door. "I'll be watching you. Remember, the eye of the Medici is on you, always."

The Brancacci Chapel of Santa Maria del Carmine
Florence, Italy
Thursday of the Twenty-first Week of Advent, the Year of Our Lord 1481

Light filters through the stained-glass window of the small chapel in Santa Maria del Carmine, and falls on the artist. The man on the scaffolding is large, with shoulder-length brown hair and a well-defined mouth. Chewing his bottom lip, he takes measure of the flesh tones he's been laboring over this afternoon, slowly layering ochre onto the green undertones in the face of Saint Peter on the throne.

The artist sighs. It is painstaking work, repairing this fresco created by the great Masaccio.

As he dips his brush into the ochre paint, the young man shakes his head at the ruin: more than forty faces in the scene depicting Saint Peter raising the son of Theophilus from the dead, and at least ten of them damaged beyond recognition. It's difficult for him to understand why the Medici, of all people, would have allowed this great work to be destroyed in their honor, in *damnatio memoriae*. Yet the faces of the Brancacci family and friends—the Medici's enemies—were scratched out in a fury of vengeance in 1434, and have remained destroyed for nearly fifty years.

It's a warm day. Below the scaffolding, the monks and a cadre of priests carry on in a hum of activity, getting ready for evening Mass. The painter's assistants are cleaning their brushes and storing their supplies as they prepare to go home. Daylight is fading, but the artist isn't ready to stop working. Having accepted the weighty job of restoring the frescoes to their original splendor, he's been in the chapel every day studying the shapes of the men depicted, the careful arrangement of figures, their expressive faces filled with suspicion, awe, anger, and hope.

These are not just the faces of anonymous men: many are painted to honor the friars of Santa Maria del Carmine. There is a self-portrait of Masaccio himself, and one of the figures has been painted to resemble the great Leon Battista Alberti.

Leaning closer, the artist uses his fingernail to remove a flake of chipped paint from a nobleman's chin. The way the work has been damaged only accentuates the power of the hand that created it: the weighty robes of the figures, the solid architecture of the building in Antioch where the miracle took place. As he studies the work, the artist closes his eyes and remembers the first time he stood beside his father, on a similar scaffolding in the church of Spoleto. His father's hands, caked in paint, had been strong and sure beside his own young, tentative fingers.

"Hold your hand steady, and wait. Inspiration will come when you're ready."

His father has been dead twelve years, but the young man remembers his words clearly, and thinks of them each morning as he prepares to work.

"To paint is to pray. To pray is to paint. Remember this, and God will be with you each time you take up your brush."

The words ring in the son's memory, and he sees his father touching his shoulder, tracing the perspectival lines, turning his face into the light, showing him how to draw the curve of a woman's shoulder or to portray a man's anger in strong, sure strokes.

"Wait until you're certain. Then, be bold."

Filippino Lippi opens his eyes and surveys the fresco. All the figures surrounding young Theophilus's tomb are men. For once, there is no Madonna.

All his life, it seems, Filippino Lippi has been looking at blond and lovely Madonnas—each one resembling his mother with her pale skin, her warm blue eyes, the *cinabrese* lips. He's lived apart from her for most of his life, yet his mother's beloved face is indelible in his mind. The paintings his father and his followers created with her likeness are everywhere, looking over him, waiting for him.

"God's perfect rendering of heaven on earth," his father would say, showing the boy his Madonnas.

Although his parents made their homes in different cities for the last years of his father's life, and Fra Filippo never lost his charm with women, Filippino is sure that his father remained devoted to his mother and that he loved her above all others, in his own way.

Filippino thinks of his mother, who lives now in close proximity to his sister, Alessandra, and her family, in Florence. Lucrezia's life hasn't been easy, but she doesn't complain.

"There's always blood and struggle," she says, whenever trouble looms. "But from blood come strength and beauty."

The first time she spoke those words to him he was young, having wrenched his shoulder and skinned his knee falling from a tree outside the *bottega*. She'd helped him up, stroked his cheek, and cleaned his wound with a cool cloth. Her spine was straight, her eyes blue, her smile sad and wise.

"From blood comes strength, and beauty. Remember this, my Filippino."

Later that same day, she'd given him a small silver medallion of Saint John the Baptist.

"A gift from my own mother, which I pass to you," she'd said, her breath warm on his cheek.

Filippino Lippi, a man as large as his father and as beautiful as his mother, fingers the medallion he has sewn into the hem of his tunic. Then he steps back, picks up a brush heavy with *terra verde*, and moves toward the fresco once again. He squints, and purses his lips. The lips are his mother's, full and sensuous. But the hands, the eyes, the sharp gaze: these are from his father. He waits. And when the *intuizione* moves through him, he begins again.

Authors' Note

With the eye of the Medici upon him, Fra Filippo finished the altarpiece for King Alfonso and sent it to Naples in May 1458. Cosimo de' Medici was not in attendance when the gift was presented at the palace, but a letter in the Medici archives confirms that the altarpiece was received favorably in the court, and that it pleased Alfonso the Magnanimous.

After a long illness, Pope Callistus III died in August 1458. In a surprising vote by the College of Cardinals, Enea Silvio Piccolomini was named Pope Pius II. The new pope had deep ties with the Medici; he also had two illegitimate children. Under Pope Pius II, Father Carlo de' Medici, illegitimate son of Cosimo de' Medici, became the provost of the Cathedral of Santo Stefano following the death of Gemignano Inghirami in 1460.

Undoubtedly encouraged by the Medici, Pope Pius II took an interest in the plight of Fra Filippo and his lover, Lucrezia Buti. Vatican records indicate that he granted dispensation for Fra Filippo and Lucrezia to marry in 1461.

However, Fra Filippo Lippi remained an ordained Carmelite monk for the rest of his life, while in 1459 Lucrezia Buti took her full vows as an Augustinian nun in the Convent Santa Margherita, in the presence of the vicar of Prato, the Bishop of Pistoia, and Prioress Jacoba de' Bovacchiesi, who'd taken over for her sister, Bartolommea, as prioress of the convent. Several sources indicate that by 1461 Lucrezia was once again living at the home of Fra Filippo. If the two did become man and wife, there is no record of this union. Their second child, a daughter, Alessandra, was born in 1465.

Fra Filippo Lippi completed the frescoes in Prato in 1465 and went to Spoleto in 1467, where he lived with his son, Filippino, training him as an artist as they worked on the final fresco series of the painter's life. When the painter died in Spoleto in 1469, guardianship of his son passed to his longtime assistant, Fra Diamante.

Filippino Lippi became a celebrated painter whose name and works are perhaps even more renowned than those of his father. In 1481, Filippino Lippi restored sections of the famed Masaccio frescoes in the Brancacci Chapel of Santa Maria del Carmine. The figures and faces of Brancacci friends and family—enemies of the Medici—had been destroyed in a *damnatio memoriae* when the exiled Medici returned to Florence in 1434. In an example of life's beautiful symmetry, the son restored the very frescoes that had first inspired his father to become a painter when he was a young monk in the monastery of Santa Maria del Carmine.

It is undisputed that Fra Filippo Lippi was an ordained monk in the Carmelite Order. However, in historical accounts and legend, Lucrezia Buti is variably referred to as a novitiate, a nun, or simply as a young woman living in the Convent Santa Margherita at the time of her meeting with the painter. Similarly, historians are not in agreement concerning the date of her father's death, nor the circumstances or even the year of her confinement to the convent with her sister Spinetta. The Convent Santa Margherita closed its doors in the late eighteenth century.

While Prioress Bartolommea de' Bovacchiesi, Spinetta Buti, Fra Piero d' Antonio di ser Vannozi, and Ser Francesco Cantansanti are true names of record along with those historical figures named above, the character of Prior General Ludovico Pietro di Saviano is a complete invention, as is Sister Pureza. If one imagines what could have compelled the artist and his young lover to live in defiance of Church law and the strict codes of conduct operative in fifteenth-century Italy, it seems undeniable that they were swayed and subjected to forces outside of their control, including the needs of powerful political figures and their own intense romantic longing.

The Feast of the Sacred Belt on September 8, 1456, is purportedly the day that Fra Filippo Lippi "kidnapped" Lucrezia Buti and took her to live at his *bottega*. The Sacred Belt, believed to be a miraculous relic of the Virgin Mary, has been housed in the locked chapel in the Cathedral of Santo Stefano in Prato, Italy, since the thirteenth century. It is presented to the public several times a year, most notably on the annual Feast of the Nativity of the Blessed Virgin Mary, which commemorates the birth of Mary on September 8. The *Sacra Cintola* has been recognized by the Church as a sacred relic for centuries, and was venerated by Pope John Paul II in 1986.

At the time of his meeting with Lucrezia Buti, Fra Filippo Lippi was a successful artist with many outstanding commitments and a record of legal problems. He'd been at work on the fresco series in the Church of Santo Stefano for six years, and dragging his feet on the Medici's King Alfonso altarpiece for many months. The frescoes, which were finally completed in 1465, are a high point in the painter's remarkable career. His cycle of frescoes was fully restored in the beginning of the twenty-first century under the auspices of the Italian Ministry of Cultural Heritage. The newly refurbished cycle, featuring the painter's famed dancing Salome and the remarkable scene of the infant Saint Stephen being switched at birth, was reopened to the public in 2007.

The central panel of Fra Lippi's *Adoring Madonna*, gifted to King Alfonso by the Medici, was destroyed or lost sometime after the sixteenth century. The side wings of the altarpiece depicting Saints Anthony Abbot and Saint Michael are now in the Cleveland Museum of Art in Ohio. *The Madonna Giving the Sacra Cintola to Saint Thomas, with Saints Margaret, Gregory, Augustine, Raphael, and Tobias,* in which both Lucrezia and Prioress Bartolommea appear, survives in the Palazzo Pretario of Prato as a testament to the incredible love between a cloistered woman and the extraordinary painter-monk who left behind some of the most beautiful artwork of all time.

Acknowledgments

Our agent, Marly Rusoff, provided unwavering enthusiasm and insights that were crucial to the completion of this novel, as was the support of Michael Radulescu. We were fortunate to work with an editor as smart and enthusiastic as Jennifer Brehl, who made the book better than it was before. We are especially grateful for Mary Schuck's stunning jacket design, and for the support of Lisa Gallagher, Ben Bruton, and Sharyn Rosenblum at William Morrow. In Prato, we had the gracious help of Claudio Cerretelli, Simona Biagianti, Odette Pagliai, and Paolo Saccoman. Daniel G. Van Slyke, associate professor of church history at Kenrick-Glennon Seminary, patiently answered our many questions.

The opportunity for us to write this novel together was nothing short of miraculous. These pages spring from a friendship that goes beyond words, to shared bonds that stretch from the mystical to the mundane. We are each blessed by the love of a kindred spirit who made this collaboration an enriching, life-affirming journey.

Professor Michael Mallory of Brooklyn College first introduced me to the art of Fra Filippo Lippi, and my professors at the Institute of Fine Arts instilled in me my knowledge of art history and my faith in myself as a writer on art. My husband, Eric Schechter, gave me endless support, and, despite being of Eastern European Jewish descent, is the finest Italian cook I have ever met. My daughters Isabelle,

Olivia, and Anais sweeten the pot, always. I thank all of the following for their support and their friendship, which in ways large and small also helped to make this novel possible: Alison Smith, Monica Taylor, Pilar Lopez, Katica Urbanc, Neil and Kerry Metzger, Laura Berman, Mark Fortgang, Lisa Rafanelli, Françoise Lucbert, Barbara Larson, Robert Steinmuller, and Marilyn Morowitz.

—*Laura Morowitz*

My life is peopled with friends and relatives whose words, wisdom, vision, and creativity are daily nourishment. Writers (and readers) Emily Rosenblum, Toni Martin, and Anne Mernin gave me ongoing support and encouragement, and Nadine Billard never turned away my phone calls, no matter how dithering. My children, John and Melissa, have become expert at blocking all communications to my third-floor office when I am working, and I'm forever grateful for their love and respect. The grace that my dear friends Kathleen Tully and Matt Stolwyk each brought to their careful readings of the manuscript is a testament to their generous spirits. Thanks also to the many publishing people and teachers who have helped me along the way, especially Larry Ashmead, Jennifer Sheridan, Tavia Kowalchuk, Lisa Amoroso, Margo Sage-El and the staff at Watchung Booksellers, Jed Rosen, and Jagadisha, whose yoga studio is the most pleasant 105-degree room I have ever visited. My sisters and extended family, especially Donna, Linda, John, Paula, Andrea, and my mother-in-law, Rosemarie Helm, are ballast for my creative flights. And Frank, my husband, is a true gentleman who makes all things possible for me.

—*Laurie Lico Albanese*

Bibliographical Notes

This is a work of fiction inspired by historical and biographical events, and we referred to many published materials for information about quattrocento Italian society and culture, and the life and work of Fra Filippo Lippi. Although we relied heavily on the following sources, any mistakes or inaccuracies are our own, and are the product of artistic liberties taken for the harmony and integrity of the novel.

For detailed information on Fra Filippo Lippi, we returned many times to the works of two American art historians: Jeffrey Ruda, *Fra Filippo Lippi: Life and Work* (London: Phaidon, 1993) and Megan Holmes, *Fra Filippo Lippi the Carmelite Painter* (New Haven/London: Yale University Press, 1999). Two Italian texts dedicated to the fresco series in Prato were of great use to us: Mario Salmi, *Gli affreschi nel Duomo del Prato* (Bergamo: Istituto italiano d'arti grafiche, 1944) and *I Lippi a Prato* (Prato: Museo Civico, 1994).

Excellent introductions to the context and style of fifteenth-century Italian art are found in Frederick Hartt, *History of Italian Renaissance Art* (Englewood Cliffs: Prentice Hall, 1976) and Evelyn Welch, *Art in Renaissance Italy 1350–1500* (London: Oxford History of Art, 2001). Michael Baxandall's *Painting and Experience in Fifteenth Century Italy: A Primer in the Social History of Pictorial Style* (Oxford: Clarendon Press, 1972) remains the fundamental text on the way in which works functioned in Lippi's day.

Colorful primary sources such as Giorgio Vasari's *Lives of the Most Emminent Painters, Sculptors, and Architects*, trans. Gaston du C. de Vère

(New York: AMS Press, 1976; first published in Rome, 1550) and Iris Origo, *The Merchant of Prato: Francesco di Marco Datini 1335–1410* (Boston: David R. Godine Publisher, 1986) helped bring the world of Renaissance Prato and Florence to life. The texture and details of many scenes in our novel benefited from the excellent information available in works on the daily life of Renaissance Italy including Elisabeth S. Cohen and Thomas V. Cohen, *Daily Life in Renaissance Italy* (London/ Westport: Greenport Press, 2001); Christiane Klapish-Zuber, *Women, Family, and Ritual in Renaissance Italy* (Chicago: University of Chicago Press, 1985); and Jacqueline Marie Musacchio, *The Art and Ritual of Childbirth in Renaissance Italy* (New Haven/London: Yale University Press, 1999). Information on herbs and herbal remedies was drawn primarily from the Internet source www.botanical.com.

WORKS BY FRA FILIPPO LIPPI MENTIONED IN
The Miracles of Prato

Portrait of a Woman with a Man at a Casement
> About 1435–1436
> Panel, 122.6 x 62.8 cm.
> Metropolitan Museum of Art, New York

The Barbadori Altarpiece
> Begun 1437; finished c. 1439
> Panel, 208 x 244 cm.
> Musée du Louvre, Paris

The Coronation of the Virgin (the Maringhi Coronation)
> 1439–1447
> Panel, 200 x 287 cm.
> Uffizi, Florence

The Annunciation
> Late 1430s–1440
> Panel, 175 x 183 cm.
> San Lorenzo, Florence

The Madonna del Ceppo (Madonna and Child with Saint Stephen, Saint John the Baptist, Francesco di Marco Datini, and Four Buonomini of the Hospital of the Ceppo of Prato)
> 1453
> Panel, 187 x 120 cm.
> Galleria Communale di Palazzo Pretario, Prato

Saint Anthony Abbot and Saint Michael, side wings of the now lost
Adoration triptych for King Alfonso of Naples

    1456–1458

    Masonite (transferred from panel), each 81.3 x 29.8 cm.

    Cleveland Museum of Art, Cleveland

The Death of Saint Jerome

    Early to mid 1450s

    Panel, 268 x 165 cm.

    Cathedral of Santo Stefano, Prato

*The Madonna della Cintola with Saints Margaret, Gregory, Augustine, and
Raphael with Tobias*

    Late 1455 to mid 1460s

    Panel, 191 x 187 cm.

    Galleria Communale di Palazzo Pretario, Prato

Lives of Saints Stephen and John

    1452–1465

    Frescoes

    Main chapel, Cathedral of Santo Stefano, Prato

All other works in the novel are the invention of the authors.

About the Text

This book was set in Centaur, an old style serif typeface originally drawn as titling capitals by Bruce Rogers in 1914 for the Metropolitan Museum of Art. The typeface is based upon several Renaissance models. Rogers's primary influence for the Roman was Nicholas Jenson's 1475 Laertis, considered the model for the modern Roman alphabet. Centaur also shows the influence of types cut by Francesco Griffo in 1495 for a small book titled *De Aetna* written by Pietro Bembo. The 1929 typeface Bembo is based primarily upon that specimen. Rogers later added the Roman lowercase, and the italic, based upon Ludovico Arrighi's 1520 chancery face. It was drawn by Frederic Warde, and is the typeface released for general use in 1929 by the Monotype Corporation Ltd.

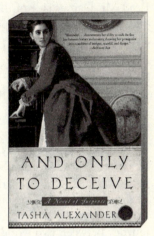

AND ONLY TO DECEIVE:
A Novel of Suspense
by Tasha Alexander
978-0-06-114844-6 (paperback)
Discover the dangerous secrets kept by the strait-laced English of the Victorian era.

ANNETTE VALLON:
A Novel of the French Revolution
by James Tipton
978-0-06-082222-4 (paperback)
For fans of Tracy Chevalier and Sarah Dunant comes this vibrant, alluring debut novel of a compelling, independent woman who would inspire one of the world's greatest poets and survive a nation's bloody transformation.

BOUND: A Novel
by Sally Gunning
978-0-06-124026-3 (paperback)
An indentured servant finds herself bound by law, society, and her own heart in colonial Cape Cod.

CASSANDRA & JANE: A Jane Austen Novel
by Jill Pitkeathley
978-0-06-144639-9 (paperback)
The relationship between Jane Austen and her sister—explored through the letters that might have been.

CROSSED: A Tale of the Fourth Crusade
by Nicole Galland
978-0-06-084180-5 (paperback)
Under the banner of the Crusades, a pious knight and a British vagabond attempt a daring rescue.

A CROWNING MERCY: A Novel
by Bernard Cornwell and Susannah Kells
978-0-06-172438-1 (paperback)
A rebellious young Puritan woman embarks on a daring journey to win love and a secret fortune.

DARCY'S STORY
by Janet Aylmer
978-0-06-114870-5 (paperback)
Read Mr. Darcy's side of the story—*Pride and Prejudice* from a new perspective.

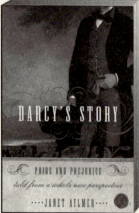

DEAREST COUSIN JANE:
A Jane Austen Novel
by Jill Pitkeathley
978-0-06-187598-4 (paperback)
An inventive reimagining of the intriguing and scandalous life of Jane Austen's cousin.

THE FALLEN ANGELS: A Novel
by Bernard Cornwell and Susannah Kells
978-0-06-172545-6 (paperback)
In the sequel to *A Crowning Mercy*, Lady Campion Lazender's courage, faith, and family loyalty are tested when she must complete a perilous journey between two worlds.

A FATAL WALTZ: A Novel of Suspense
by Tasha Alexander
978-0-06-117423-0 (paperback)
Caught in a murder mystery, Emily must do the unthinkable to save her fiancé: bargain with her ultimate nemesis, the Countess von Lange.

FIGURES IN SILK: A Novel
by Vanora Bennett
978-0-06-168985-7 (paperback)
The art of silk making, political intrigue, and a sweeping love story all interwoven in the fate of two sisters.

THE FIREMASTER'S MISTRESS: A Novel
by Christie Dickason
978-0-06-156826-8 (paperback)
Estranged lovers Francis and Kate rekindle their romance in the midst of Guy Fawkes's plot to blow up Parliament.

JULIA AND THE MASTER OF MORANCOURT: A Novel
by Janet Aylmer
978-0-06-167295-8 (paperback)
Amidst family tragedy, Julia travels all over England, desperate to marry the man she loves instead of the arranged suitor preferred by her mother.

KEPT: A Novel
by D. J. Tayler
978-0-06-114609-1 (paperback)
A gorgeously intricate, dazzling reinvention of Victorian life and passions that is also a riveting investigation into some of the darkest, most secret chambers of the human heart.

THE MIRACLES OF PRATO: A Novel
by Laurie Albanese and Laura Morowitz
978-0-06-155835-1 (paperback)
The unforgettable story of a nearly impossible romance between a painter-monk (the renowned artist Fra Filippo Lippi) and the young nun who becomes his muse, his lover, and the mother of his children.

PILATE'S WIFE: A Novel of the Roman Empire
by Antoinette May
978-0-06-112866-0 (paperback)
Claudia foresaw the Romans' persecution of Christians, but even she could not stop the crucifixion.

A POISONED SEASON:
A Novel of Suspense
by Tasha Alexander
978-0-06-117421-6 (paperback)
As a cat-burglar torments Victorian London, a mysterious gentleman fascinates high society.

PORTRAIT OF AN UNKNOWN WOMAN: A Novel
by Vanora Bennett
978-0-06-125256-3 (paperback)
Meg, adopted daughter of Sir Thomas More, narrates the tale of a famous Holbein painting and the secrets it holds.

THE QUEEN'S SORROW: A Novel of Mary Tudor
by Suzannah Dunn
978-0-06-170427-7 (paperback)
Queen of England Mary Tudor's reign is brought low by abused power and a forbidden love.

REBECCA: The Classic Tale of Romantic Suspense
by Daphne Du Maurier
978-0-380-73040-7 (paperback)
Follow the second Mrs. Maxim de Winter down the lonely drive to Manderley, where Rebecca once ruled.

REBECCA'S TALE: A Novel
by Sally Beauman
978-0-06-117467-4 (paperback)
Unlock the dark secrets and old worlds of Rebecca de Winter's life with investigator Colonel Julyan.

THE SIXTH WIFE: A Novel of Katherine Parr
by Suzannah Dunn
978-0-06-143156-2 (paperback)
Kate Parr survived four years of marriage to King Henry VIII, but a new love may undo a lifetime of caution.

VIVALDI'S VIRGINS: A Novel
by Barbara Quick
978-0-06-089053-7 (paperback)
Abandoned as an infant, fourteen-year-old Anna Maria dal Violin is one of the elite musicians living in the foundling home where the "Red Priest," Antonio Vivaldi, is maestro and composer.

WATERMARK: A Novel of the Middle Ages
by Vanitha Sankaran
978-0-06-184927-5 (paperback)
A compelling debut about the search for identiy, the power of self-expression, and value of the written word.

THE WIDOW'S WAR: A Novel
by Sally Gunning
978-0-06-079158-2 (paperback)
Tread the shores of colonial Cape Cod with a lonely whaler's widow as she tries to build a new life.